An Intrigue of Pharaohs
First printing; August 2023

ISBN 978-1-951506-39-1 print book

Cover art: Deranged Doctor Designs
Print interior formatted by The Killion Group

AN INTRIGUE OF PHARAOHS

THE ADVENTURES OF SMITH AND JONES

3

OTHER BOOKS BY MARIE ANDREAS

The Lost Ancients

Book One: The Glass Gargoyle

Book Two: The Obsidian Chimera

Book Three: The Emerald Dragon

Book Four: The Sapphire Manticore

Book Five: The Golden Basilisk

Book Six: The Diamond Sphinx

The Lost Ancients: Dragon's Blood

Book One: The Seeker's Chest

Book Two: The Finder's Crown

Book Three: The Hunter's Chalice

The Asarlaí Wars Trilogy

Book One: Warrior Wench

Book Two: Victorious Dead

Book Three: Defiant Ruin

The Code of the Keeper

Book One: Traitor's Folly

Book Two: Destroyer's Curse

The Adventures of Smith and Jones

A Curious Invasion

The Mayhem of Mermaids

An Intrigue of Pharaohs

Broken Veil Trilogy

Book One: The Girl with the Iron Wing

Book Two: An Uncommon Truth of Dying

Book Three: Through a Veil Darkly

Books of the Cuari Trilogy

Book One: Essence of Chaos

Book Two: Division of Chaos

Book Three: Destruction of Chaos

Magic and Sorcery Chronicles Trilogy

A Touch of Magic

A Slice of Sorcery

A Dash of Devilry

ACKNOWLEDGEMENTS

THANK YOU TO ALL OF you who have enjoyed my worlds, especially this one of Nettie and her friends. It has been wonderful to share their adventures with you!

I'd like to thank my editors-beta readers: Lisa Andreas, Patti Huber, and Lynne Mayfield—excellent work! Any errors or mistakes that remain are completely mine.

Thank you to Deranged Doctor Designs for the amazing cover. And to The Killion Group for formatting the print interior.

CHAPTER ONE

NETTIE SCOWLED AS SHE NARROWED her eyes and held up the two options for her apparel for Rebecca's wedding. Both garments were more than suitable. In fact, they were quite lovely. Sadly, her disposition couldn't be said to be similar.

It had nothing to do with the impending wedding. Rebecca and Damon fell in love almost upon first sight. Damon had been a butler here in the Society of the Exploration of the Unexplainables' London headquarters. Rebecca worked with Nettie in the coroner's office; until Rebecca's burgeoning clairvoyant skills brought her into the Society. Nettie was sincerely happy for her best friend and hoped for nothing but happiness for her and Damon.

She put the dresses down on the bed and looked out the window to the gloomy London sky. They'd left Wales a little over three weeks ago, their collective assignment finished.

Wales wasn't less gloomy weather-wise than London, but there was a wild beauty there that she found she missed. She thought that coming back to Gaston's manor with the other agents from the Society would make her happy. Mostly growing up in London, being tossed like an unwanted Christmas pudding among various extremely distant family members, gave her a fondness for it. Or it did.

There were far more agents living here than when she'd first moved in, so that was nice. Rebecca and Damon would be moving out to their own flat after they came back from their honeymoon. But both would be here regularly for work unless they were out on assignment.

Although Damon didn't begin as an agent, he'd started agent training in Wales and was now ready to take his place in fighting criminals and peculiar beings not of the known world.

Looking out the window wasn't helping her disposition.

Until a certain sandy-haired, brown-eyed American walked out on the grass, talking with Homer. Caden. He might be a contributing force to her current disposition. He was now her fiancé, a change in circumstance that she first welcomed. He was funny, obstinate, wickedly intelligent, over-confident, and quite attractive. She'd fallen in love with him in Wales. Possibly before that, but she wasn't going to admit it.

But the excitement over his proposal, and spending her life with him, waned as she wasn't sure how to proceed. Mostly, watching all the excitement, parties, random events, and whatnot that whirled around Rebecca's wedding greatly disturbed her.

She loved Caden. She wanted to marry him. But the events attached to a wedding were frankly too much. She'd never even attended a wedding before this, let alone been swept up in the rigamarole involved. It was completely overwhelming.

That was it then. The source of her annoyance was found. As much as she cared for Caden, a marriage simply wouldn't work. She took a deep sigh. She would miss him, and they could still work together, but that was that. She glanced down at her engagement ring. It was a lovely ring. Not large and ostentatious, it fit her personality well. So did he.

"Drat the man."

The knock came at the same time as the door opened. Rebecca stuck her head in. "Drat who?" She bustled over and looked out the window. "What has Caden done now? That level of annoyance wouldn't have come from Homer."

Homer was a former air pirate—or so he claimed—as well as a part-time secret agent. He was a solid man who appeared that he'd be more at home waving a sword on the deck of a ship. His hair was thick and white, as was his beard. Caden was a few inches over six feet, but Homer was taller. And bigger. He had a ready laugh and a good heart.

"No, not Homer. Not really Caden either, aside from him making me fall in love with him as he did. Quite rude when you think about it. I'm just annoyed that we can't marry." A loud sigh escaped her as she observed Caden laugh at something Homer said. Even that was terribly endearing.

Rebecca had been drifting away from the window but came back with a start. "What? Since when? You love him, your eyes get all misty when you watch him in the meetings." She folded her arms.

"I do not get misty. I do, however, love him, that is true. But all these parties and events around your wedding. And how many people are coming? Three hundred?" Nettie shuddered. "I simply can't go through that." Nettie didn't mind people if she was in her normal position as an agent or scientist. Casual socializing was never her strong point.

Rebecca laughed. "You do realize that you don't have to do any of this, right? Homer is able to officiate at weddings. I wanted to have him do ours, but my parents wanted someone else. They also are the force behind many of these events. Damon has little family and is going along with whatever is presented. Caden's family are all in America, as are most of his friends outside of the Society I'd guess." She leaned forward and took Nettie's arms. "You can make your wedding as small and intimate as you want. As long as you don't fail to recall that I will be your matron of honor."

Nettie tilted her head. "I didn't know there were options." Admitting she didn't know something was hard for her—less so when it fell in the realm of social obligations. "So, just a few of us, say here at the mansion, with Homer making it official, would be okay?" She glanced down to where Caden and Homer were heading toward Homer's airship and smiled.

"Yes, you goose. It's your day. Well, yours and Caden's. But on the whole, men don't seem to care about the details much. Is that why you've been off the past few days?"

Nettie turned from the window. She felt a bit foolish now. "Yes, although I hadn't realized it at the time. I am very glad you sorted me out."

"Now, I believe the best thing to do would be to celebrate with some tea, biscuits, and sandwiches. I'm the bride and you're my maid of honor and I say we need sustenance to finish these plans."

Nettie laughed and headed for the door. "Agreed." She felt better than she had since they left Wales.

They went down the hall arm and arm, nodding to the few lady agents who were about. It was late morning and many were already out on assignments. Gaston made sure the wedding party was off-rotation for a few days.

The parlor was a lovely room for a casual tea, or something stronger, and with most agents out and about, should be empty.

"There you two are." The speaker was a tiny woman of indiscernible age with short silvery hair and a mischievous grin. She didn't get up but motioned to the two high-backed chairs at her table and tea set. "I hoped you both would pop down. I've taken the liberty of requesting that Chef send out sandwiches and biscuits. I already have tea."

Nettie laughed as she and Rebecca took their seats. "Have you been poking about our heads, Lisselle?" She didn't really think Lisselle would do such a thing, but she did have uncanny intuition. And magic. As a witch, she did have certain abilities. She was an older agent, like Homer, and she also came and went as she pleased. Mostly the two went out on only the highest-level assignments but mainly assisted Gaston in running this branch of the Society for the Exploration of the Unexplainable. There were branches all over the world, but this one was the first.

"I didn't need to. You have been moping about and I had hopes we could work through whatever was troubling you. But it appears to have been resolved." She grinned at both of them. "Tea?"

At their nods, she filled their cups. Within a few moments, the newest kitchen attendant, Kilia, came out with the full tea tray. Chef complained that he needed far more help now with so many agents actually living here. When Gaston was the only regular resident, taking care of him was easy. Thirty or so regular residents were making Chef even crankier than normal. Kilia was of middle age, had been sworn to secrecy as was true of everyone who worked in the mansion, and was extremely efficient. Her slight bow when they all expressed their thanks was automatic and professional, but not too familiar. She vanished down the hall immediately.

"She is extremely effective." Nettie helped herself to a delicate egg salad sandwich.

Lisselle's gaze was still on the hall, then she turned back. "She is almost too much so." Her gray eyes darkened for a moment, then lit up as she smiled. "Now, tell me all of the newest plans."

That was all Rebecca needed to set off.

Nettie almost expected Lisselle to question her concerning her noted mopiness, a term Nettie completely disagreed with. However, most likely Lisselle would wait until they were alone and then drag it out of her. Going through her negative reaction to being married and Rebecca's quick resolution wasn't something she looked forward to.

Gaston showed up toward the end of Rebecca's long discussion. It was a good thing that Nettie had been told that she didn't have to do the same as her best friend. There were far more things going on for this wedding than she'd known or imagined existed.

He helped himself to some tea but waved off any biscuits or sandwiches. Then he took his favorite seat, a massive monster of a chair adjacent to the fireplace that appeared to be older than the actual mansion.

Rebecca finished her list and started tucking into her food.

"There is a lot to plan for these things, isn't there? Nettie? What of you and Caden? Have you set a date? Should we expect another full onslaught?" Gaston grinned over his cup. He wasn't a large man, which was made more apparent by his large chair, but he had a presence.

"We don't have a date as of yet. But I believe one extravagant event per year is sufficient." Nettie smiled. Again, grateful that the issue was resolved before being asked such a question and having to face Gaston and Lisselle.

"Sensible. Always sensible." He nodded. Gaston was short and on the roundish side. He had deep almost black eyes and his dark hair was losing the fight to stay on his head. When he nodded like that he looked a bit like a gnome. Then he turned to Rebecca with a smile. "Not to say your wedding isn't sensible, Rebecca, it just doesn't fit our Nettie."

A loud pounding at the front door cut off any responses. The parlor was the room closest to the door and thusly, Gaston often kept the shades drawn. The neighbors thought he ran a boarding house for eccentric creatives, but there were other people—the ones the Society was formed to fight against—who might know otherwise.

Damon, no longer the butler, but still acting as such until the new one could be deemed acceptable, ran to the door with his shadow, Niles, the butler trainee, right on his heels. Niles looked like a bruiser but was extremely well-spoken and ecstatic at joining the Society in any position.

Damon opened the door with Niles standing behind it, ready to attack if needed.

Whoever was on the other side was either silent or speaking too low to hear. Nettie could hear Damon politely ask what the visit pertained to, but nothing else.

Lisselle frowned at something she did hear, or sensed, and got to her feet.

Which of course made Nettie, Rebecca, and Gaston do the same.

"I see. I will have to ask that you excuse me while I speak to the Master." Damon shut the door immediately. This time Nettie didn't think the other person even had a chance to respond.

Lisselle moved into the hall, so the rest followed.

"Who was it?" Gaston didn't greet people unless they were expected. But he looked as concerned as Lisselle did as she crept closer to the shut door.

Niles stayed behind the door when it was open and moved out of her way as she held a hand out and moved close to the surface of the door.

"*It* would like us to believe that it is an old washer woman, begging for cast-off scraps." Damon frowned.

"But if so, then it is an exceptionally well-armed washer woman. There is an outline of a long dagger on her hip and possibly another one at her back, based on her movement."

"If it even is a she." Lisselle stepped back from the door. "Not that my gender can't be up to nefarious activities, but the feeling out there is not female."The space between her brows furrowed. "Well, not completely." She waved her hand before Gaston's question came out. "Don't ask. I can't tell you how or what, but whatever is out there isn't a human female. I feel like I can almost sense what they are…but not quite."

"Shouldn't we find out what they are? What if they intend to hurt us?" Rebecca quickly switched from bride to agent and looked far too eager to engage in the mayhem.

"Now, easy there. There could be any number of nonhuman things out there. I think we just wait." Gaston returned to the parlor and resumed his seat and tea.

Nettie narrowed her eyes. That was an exceedingly non-Gaston thing to say and do. "Who are you and what have you done with Gaston?" She didn't really think it wasn't him, nor that he'd been taken over. But he was behaving oddly.

"I installed a bell near my chair yesterday. It rang to the back and Homer and Caden would have heard the summons. Right now, they are most likely apprehending our guest." He looked far too smug as he sipped his tea. "Damon, you and Niles can go back about your business. We'll take care of this situation."

Damon nodded and Niles bowed and they silently went down the hall to continue Niles' training. A butler of the Society needed to be able to do so much more than butler.

Lisselle stayed standing but moved away from the door. Her annoyed glare as she folded her arms took Gaston's smugness down a step or two. "And you thought to tell the rest of us about your toy, when?"

"I haven't had the opportunity. Once we take care of our issue out front, I'll show you all my creations. It's very *inventif*, inventive." Gaston's French accent came and went, and usually, if he slipped into actual French it was a planned distraction. Considering that Lisselle had been working with Gaston longer than Nettie had been alive, trying to distract her was pointless.

Before anyone else could contribute anything else, a mild explosion rocked the room.

Explosions by definition are usually not mild, but this one was. The tea service didn't even jiggle. Damon and Niles came racing back and even Gaston went to the door.

"Grab it!" That was Caden, not far from the front door.

"There are two, three! They're getting away!" Homer sounded like he was running.

At Gaston's nod, Damon opened the door. The front porch was covered in streaky green smoke and Caden and Homer were almost out of sight down the street as they chased after several short, rag-covered people.

"Should we follow?" Damon was tapping into his new agent training, but Nettie wondered the same thing.

"Non. Whatever that was, those two are completely prepared to handle it. I would say we were not dealing with a human, however." He shared a look with Lisselle.

"I can sense them stronger now…covelins, I believe." She stepped toward the smokey wall and held one hand out over it with her eyes closed. "Yes. I hate those." She shuddered and wiped her hand on her trousers even though she hadn't touched anything. "I will explain when we're back inside, but it bodes ill if they are coming out during the day. They shouldn't even be on this island. We're far too cold for them."

Everyone went back inside once Gaston waved off

Niles' attempt to clean the walls in the front stoop. "Don't worry about that now, it can wait."

They returned to the parlor where Damon and Niles joined them.

"Are you certain Caden and Homer are all right? And do these things often explode?" Nettie prided herself on the gathering of knowledge pertaining to creatures found by the Society. That she had never heard of these things was almost as disturbing as the explosion.

"Covelins are underbelly creatures, almost like rats. They come from a long line of misguided magical genetic experiments that began back in the days of the early Egyptian empire." Lisselle took a long sip of her tea and Nettie noticed that her hands were shaking ever so slightly.

"Are they that dangerous? They didn't look much larger than children," Rebecca said as she too resumed her seat.

"They're more of a nuisance than an actual danger. Now, that wee explosion could have been painful if someone were directly next to it, but it's more defensive than offensive." Gaston shook his head. "However, their being here indicates that what we feared has happened." He looked around the room, but when no one, including Lisselle, looked like they had they slightest idea what he was talking about, he waved a hand.

"I am sorry. This was a topic that was to be brought up this evening to the entire company. That is one of the problems with so many agents living here. I forget who has been made aware of what. Three weeks ago, the head office in Edinburgh lost contact with the headquarters near Cairo, Egypt. They still haven't regained it and as of last night, no recon team has been sent. We were just notified of this yesterday."

"That's not good. They are one of the largest non-European offices in the world." Lisselle shook her head.

"They can't all be missing. And why hasn't Edinburgh sent assistance?"

"One hundred and twenty-five men and women to be specific. None of them are responding to any of the three Mudgers that are stationed there." He focused on his teacup. "And yes, Edinburgh did try the witches. However, they are refusing to send anyone to investigate at this time. And they are being silent as to the reasons." The grimace on his face reflected Nettie's opinion. Edinburgh was the center of all of the Society for the Exploration of the Unexplainable agents. That they refrained from telling anyone of this problem for three weeks was disturbing. Almost worse than them refusing to act.

Lisselle scowled and looked around at the other four. "The Egyptian branch is unique in that they have more monsters and nonhuman creatures than anywhere else. Things that used to roam the world at large but started there. In the past thirty years, they'd managed to get most of them back within their borders."

Niles looked around with a confused look on his face. "No offense intended, and maybe I'm missing something, but why not just kill them if they're dangerous?"

Gaston looked at Damon and nodded.

"Because most of them aren't dangerous, just nuisances," Damon said calmly and clearly. He was new to being an agent, but he'd been working in the mansion for over five years. "And getting them to go back into a controlled environment is easier if they don't fear being hunted. Plus, both Egypt and India don't have the narrow-mindedness that the West does, common people are more likely to accept strange things in both countries."

That was sometimes a difficult issue. Nettie and the rest of the agents were well aware of other creatures, including aliens, vampires, and mer-people. Nettie herself was a half-vampire, and possibly a partial mermaid. The scientists were still processing her blood, but she hadn't turned mermaid since they'd left Wales.

There was also an unknown Egyptian element to her blood that no one had been able to completely sort out.

But while the agents, and their close employees all knew, it had been determined long ago that the common British people would be devastated to find these things out.

Not to mention that even before her brief time as a vampire, Queen Victoria forbade the Society from letting the truth be known.

"Tres bon, Damon. Yes. We in the Society for the Exploration of the Unexplainable will kill if needed, but that's not the first option. Unfortunately, there are far more dangerous things than covelins there. If there's no one watching them in their native land of Egypt, we could have a serious problem."

"Not to mention that someone would have had to help get the covelins here." Lisselle ran her fingers through her spiky gray hair. "I hope Homer and Caden can bring something useful back. I need to run some magic over those things to see what connections I can find."

"And we might be able to find more information on them in one of the dungeons," Nettie added although neither room was actually dungeons. There were two large labs in the basement of the mansion. One was technically Gaston's and the second was given to Nettie. Primarily to keep her out of Gaston's lab.

"True." Rebecca chewed the nail on her thumb as she looked around. "I hate to be a problem, and I know the Society comes first, but this won't interfere with our wedding, will it?"

Damon reached over and took her other hand.

"A wedding is important too. Never fear, we will see you two married." Gaston was almost a little too hearty, which always made Nettie wary. But she agreed this time.

The look of impending doom on her best friend's face needed to be assuaged.

A low conversation came from the front door and it was unlocked before either Damon or Niles could get to their feet. An extremely smoky-looking Caden and Homer came into the parlor.

Homer immediately went to the liquor cabinet and filled two glasses with whisky. He handed one to Caden, both shot the drink down, then turned to Gaston.

"They were covelins for certain. They had explosive devices strapped around them, and they got away." Homer poured another glass for himself and then slammed that one down as well.

Caden came to Nettie but didn't sit, even though there was plenty of room on the sofa. He was filthy, so it was understandable. "They got away, but I did get this off the one we grabbed before he bit Homer and fled." He held out an evidence bag. There were multiple pieces of fabric in it.

Caden easily had the ability to run an analysis on this, but his giving it to her first was a true sign of devotion. Not to mention that he'd carried the evidence bag with him and used it. Proper gathering of data was crucial. She took the bag with a smile, then gasped. In her focus on Caden's behavior, she'd missed what he said.

"Homer was bit?"

CHAPTER TWO

NETTIE JUMPED TO HER FEET and stepped to Homer. Granted, it had been used primarily in her former job as a coroner but she did go to medical school. "Where? You really should sit down. Bites can be horrible, even from other humans."

Lisselle was on her feet as well. "You should have led with that. You know the protocol, injuries first." Her annoyance was spread equally between Homer and Caden.

Homer was reaching for the whisky bottle again when Lisselle grabbed his hand. "*Now.*" She increased her glare at Caden too. "Next time, if he doesn't tell us up front, you do. Or there will be hell to pay." She looked Caden up and down. "Were you injured?"

"No, ma'am." Caden's American accent had been fading in the past few months, with focused help from him of course. But he was pure embarrassed American in those two words.

Lisselle pulled Homer after her as she led the way to the medical wing. Caden, under orders, followed. Nettie joined, as she might be able to help. Gaston and Rebecca did just because.

Damon and Niles stayed back. "We'll continue our training," Damon said as they left.

Homer outweighed Lisselle by at least three times, and

he was quite a bit taller. But no one would argue that right at this moment, Lisselle was in charge.

"It's not a deep bite, I'm fine." Homer wisely didn't try to pull away from Lisselle's grasp.

Lisselle didn't slow down, but if looks could kill, Homer would currently be a very late airship pirate. Actually, as a witch, Lisselle might have spells that could kill with a look. "If you ever pull this kind of a novice stunt again, I will kill you myself. Slowly."

He shut his mouth as they went into the smaller medical wing. The larger one was mostly used as storage, but it was designed for major catastrophes. Lisselle took Homer to the first open bed in the smaller suite and shoved him into it.

"Well? Show Nettie and me where you were bitten."

Gaston and Rebecca made themselves busy gathering medical supplies. Caden stayed near the door in case he needed to bolt.

Homer pushed his shirt sleeve up. "It got me through the fabric."

Gaston turned around quickly, and a look of concern ran across Lisselle's face. But neither said anything.

Nettie almost started swearing when she saw the injury. "You are not fine." She got her admonishment out before Lisselle did. The mark was almost perfectly round and glaringly red. There wasn't much blood, the red was from an infection.

Lisselle pushed Homer on his back. "Help me get the shirt off." She looked up pointedly. "Caden, help me get the shirt off. *Now*."

Caden didn't argue but looked dubious. However, the fact that Homer didn't say anything or try to assist either Lisselle or Caden was a bad sign.

Nettie looked into Homer's eyes. He appeared aware, but his eyes were unfocused and his pupils were huge. "What's wrong with him?" His symptoms weren't matching any known injuries, but to be fair they hadn't taught any nonhuman physiology in medical school. There was no way to know what had been in the creature's mouth when it bit him.

"The bite. Those weren't regular covelins and I think they wanted to be caught by one or more of us." Lisselle started wiping down the injury with antiseptic. "They left a gift inside there and if we don't get it out, it will take over Homer." Her voice was calm but the fear on her face was apparent.

Rebecca and Gaston brought their supplies over.

"We'll need the straps; it's going to get bad." Lisselle didn't look up as she spoke, just continued to focus on cleaning the injury.

Gaston put the assorted supplies on the table next to the bed and pulled out a collection of bands. Extremely sturdy leather bands were brought out and secured around Homer's arms, legs, and across his forehead.

As if on cue, Homer started thrashing.

"Can we sedate him?" Nettie wanted to help but wasn't sure how.

"No. It will only make the poison, and the possession, go faster. But I think we're going to need Damon and Niles to help hold him steady. Nettie, I'd like you to operate. I'll talk you through it, but..." she held up her hands to show both were shaking.

Lisselle and Homer had been married, and divorced, long ago and were still extremely close. Nettie looked to Caden holding down Homer's legs—she didn't know if she would be able to operate if it were him on the table. She nodded and washed up, then donned surgical gloves. The majority of her prior patients were already dead when she worked on them. But the bodies were all the same.

Damon and Niles came in and Gaston had them hold Homer's legs as still as possible. Fortunately, Niles was big and strong—Homer was a powerful adversary even when he was unaware of what he was doing.

The operation involved digging into the wound and finding and removing a small bug-shaped item. Lisselle was too worried to give much description but clearly anything that didn't look like human tissue needed to come out.

A flash of something small and dark blue glinted through the blood. Homer fought harder, and all the men holding him doubled their efforts. Nettie switched instruments, whatever that thing in there was, it appeared to be about half an inch long. She needed a larger set of forceps.

It took three tries, but she grabbed it.

Homer screamed as if his soul was being ripped from his body.

And the lights flickered and went out.

Emergency lights flashed on and Kilia and Chef came running into the room. They both held huge cleavers and appeared ready to use them.

"What's happened? Are we under attack?" Chef usually spent most of his energy getting mad at agents. Clearly, he was able to focus it elsewhere. Kilia stoically looked on but hadn't lowered the cleaver she held.

"Not directly. But I'll warrant that the lights going out was because of that thing." Lisselle pointed to Nettie, just as the dark blue bug freed itself from the forceps, and tried to return to Homer.

It scuttled on the floor until it was impaled by a large cleaver. The tip of the cleaver embedded itself, through the bug and into the specialized floor Gaston installed in the medical rooms.

Chef beamed. "Good job my girl, I told you the training would work." He looked around with a shrug. "This is a dangerous household; I want everyone to be trained to defend themselves. However, if we are no longer needed,

I will set about restoring the rest of the lights." Just as Chef finished his sentence, the lights flickered, came back on, and the emergency lights turned off. "That works as well." He shrugged.

Gaston patted him on the arm and bowed to Kilia. "Excellent work. Those scarabs are deadly." He bent down to view the bug pinned by the cleaver as Chef and Kilia left. "Do we have acid in here? It's still kicking."

That the bug survived almost being chopped in half, and pinned to the floor while wiggling its legs, was almost as disturbing as the fact it had been *in* Homer. Nettie spun back to her patient. "There couldn't be more in there, could there be?"

"Easy there. Only one can be put in a body to control it. They have been noted to travel in massive packs, but not when they are being used to control another." Lisselle brushed Homer's forehead but still didn't remove the straps.

Rebecca brought over a specialized container with the word 'acid' on it. Gaston called Caden over and together they got the scarab into the container and sealed it.

"Can I close the wound now?" Nettie didn't want to interrupt Lisselle's gazing down at Homer in a very non-Lisselle, almost dreamy, manner, but if there were no more bugs to come out, it should be closed.

Lisselle blinked and shook her head. "Yes, please do. I can place a spell on his mind to help him relax, but we might also need to use laudanum in a bit. He needs to rest."

Nettie gently sewed the bite closed, trying without success to wipe the memory of that scarab from her mind. She didn't normally drink much alcohol, but today might be an exception. Her unique metabolism meant she couldn't get truly drunk, but she could numb things. Once she'd closed the injury, and Rebecca wrapped it in gauze, Lisselle came back with the laudanum for Homer.

"On second thought, I'm not certain I trust my magic in this case." She dosed him.

Once the bug was removed, Homer's thrashing about settled. But the laudanum relaxed him even more.

"Can we take the straps off?" Damon asked. No one was holding Homer down at this point, but Damon and Niles hadn't left yet either.

Lisselle blinked again. "What? Possibly. Although," she looked to Gaston, "we might want to leave a guard down here. I've only heard of this kind of possession attempt, never actually seen it. Leave the straps on his arms and legs for now. Plus, a guard." She released the strap from Homer's forehead. "I have no real idea of any lasting issues that might arise."

"I agree." Gaston looked down at his old friend and patted his shoulder. "Recover quickly, I fear we'll need your skills sooner rather than later."

"If you don't need us for other duties, Niles and I will stand guard." Damon tilted his head. "Just in case."

Both were trained fighters, but if something lingered in Homer, his strength and skills could beat either one alone.

Gaston agreed and the rest went upstairs.

Caden plucked at his filthy shirt. "I'm in need of a shower. I assume we're rejoining in the parlor?"

"Yes, I think we could all use some fortification after that." Gaston narrowed his eyes. "You're certain that you weren't bit?"

Caden smiled. "My pain tolerance isn't as high as Homer's. Trust me, I would have noticed and yelled." He split off down to the men's wing as the rest went to the parlor.

The remains of their interrupted tea were moved aside, and glasses of whisky were handed around. Even Rebecca took one, and she drank less often than Nettie.

"That bug looked alarmingly like the ancient scarabs

of old." Nettie took a sip and let the fiery liquid burn down her throat. "I've never heard them as being able to possess' people, however. I know most of what I've read of them were from mundane sources, but I would have noticed such a skill in my studies in Edinburgh." Another sip, slightly shorter this time, helped burn away the image of that horrible bug.

"Those are natural scarabs. That thing, which is hopefully now completely dissolved by that acid, wasn't natural." Lisselle frowned. "That's not completely correct. They were magically enhanced centuries ago. They are their own subspecies now, but were thought to be extinct."

"Mon deu, covelins, scarabs, all contact with Cairo lost. This is bad. I do need to notify Ramsey." Gaston mentioned the second-highest agent. Ramsey was stationed in Edinburgh and was best reached by the Society's secret communications device, the Mudger.

The Mudger screen was a bit of technological magic named after a prominent eighteenth-century member of the Society, Thomas Mudge. Whilst known as a famous horologist to the rest of the world, he was far more than a watchmaker to the Society. He didn't invent the Mudger, but his studies led to its creation after his death. With it, branches of the Society across the world could speak to and see each other over long distances, although the images were grainy and glitches were common.

But Gaston poured himself another drink before he got up. "I truly hoped for more downtime for all of us. I fear that's not to be the case." He finished his drink, got to his feet, and bowed. "If you ladies will excuse me, I will return once I've spoken to Edinburgh."

Caden came in moments after Gaston left. Now in clean clothes and with damp hair, he silently poured himself a drink, then sat next to Nettie. "Did I miss anything?"

"Gaston went to notify Edinburgh, but that's all." Nettie

shivered. "That creature was horrible. And I normally am fine with bugs."

"You have some gifts on the paranormal side of things. You could be picking up on the modified nature of the creature," Lisselle said as she sipped her whisky.

"Or the fact that it entered through a bite, and didn't die even when it was almost cut in half." Rebecca shuddered.

"I didn't even see any of those things. The creatures ran from us but then stopped to fight before we got to the river. They fled after they bit Homer. Which should have been a clue."

Nettie turned Caden's head to face her. "I'll repeat what was said before; if you ever fail to tell any of us immediately if you've been injured, I'll make any repercussions from Gaston and Lisselle seem like a holiday." There wasn't a clue as to whether them getting the bug out sooner would have helped, but many times injuries and illnesses needed to be acted on immediately. Taking that scarab out of Homer was going to haunt her for a long time.

"Yes, dear." He knew how to woo her and lowered his head while looking up at her with his soulful deep brown eyes.

Nettie shook her head and looked away. "Don't you 'yes dear' me. I mean it."

"Agreed. This isn't a game. Our conflicts with nonhumans, present company excepted, has been getting worse," Lisselle said. "We have to be aware of everything that goes on outside these walls."

Rebecca nodded too vigorously. "Hear, hear!"

"And no more for you my dear." Lisselle plucked the nearly empty glass from Rebecca's fingers.

"I promise that I will report the tiniest scratch the moment that it appears." Caden took Nettie's fingers. "Better?"

"Yes. Just keep in mind which one of us is stronger." Of course, Nettie's strength came from her vampiric, mermaid, and possibly the unknown nonhuman aspect in her blood. However, it remained that she was stronger.

"I'm fine with that." His cheeky grin appeared, then fell as he turned to Lisselle. "How much trouble should we expect from these covelin creatures? Up until that one bit Homer, they weren't much of a threat. Aside from the explosion, which wasn't that impressive actually."

Lisselle nodded. "That's what they want you to think. But appearances can be deceptive. Either their goal was simply to cause havoc—if they were allowed inside the mansion, that explosive could have caused far more damage. Or they were trying to get the scarabs into more of us. I'd guess that the other two contained them inside their bodies as well. Which raises the question why?"

"If we're going to be facing more nonhumans from Egypt, we're going to need information. I don't know about the rest of the agents in this house, but I feel woefully under-prepared." Nettie looked over toward Rebecca. Who was now listing to the side. She got up and poured some now cool, but strong tea for her and handed her the cup. "Drink all of it. This is no time to have your wits addled."

Rebecca opened her mouth to complain, then shut it and took the tea. She silently continued sipping until Nettie went back to her seat.

Nettie understood Rebecca's disturbance. Nettie had been involved with the Society longer than her. But Rebecca jumped in so quickly and with such vigor, that it was hard to remember that she'd only been a part of this nonhuman world for a short while.

However, losing oneself to drink wasn't the answer.

"Agreed. There are some resources here, in Gaston's back library, but we'll need to have more sent down from Edinburgh if we're to get a handle on this potential invasion." Lisselle looked like she was already creating battle plans.

Gaston's steps were fast and loud as he came down the hall. He wasn't a thin man, but those footsteps were of a man annoyed.

"Ramsey was too busy to speak to me. So, I reported our situation to a fourth-tier agent who was probably only out of his nappies five years ago. We have been told to stand down. Continue reporting any such incidents, but do not engage. They were also disappointed that we destroyed the scarab. We are out of the situation."

CHAPTER THREE

LISSELLE WAS ON HER FEET immediately. "What? They can't do that. We're the primary agent facility in England. Could you leave a message for Ramsey?"

"I tried. Whether it will get to him or not is doubtful." Gaston started for another shot of whisky but instead poured some of the lukewarm tea. "There is something larger taking place, and we are being shut out. The agent did offer to send Runners down to get Homer to have him receive treatment back in Scotland. I declined." His eyes softened as he looked at Lisselle. "Unless you want to send him. But none of us could go with him."

Runners were human-shaped alien beings garbed in solid black fabric from head to toe, who crashed to Earth long ago while looking for the Atlantian people. The Atlantians already moved to the oceans by then and were unable to help the stranded aliens. The Runners who survived remained hidden until Agent Zero of the Society found them. They worked for the Society, traveling great distances within a blink of an eye.

Lisselle weighed the idea for a moment then shook her head. "No. I don't trust all the secrets that take place in Edinburgh. They are almost more political than the palace. Aside from the Queen, I don't like people from the palace, either. But we need to find out what's causing this." She stomped in a small circle, muttering to herself, then stopped and snapped her fingers. "Torlian. I can see what that old wizard has to say."

Gaston almost spit out his tea at the name. Nettie never heard the man mentioned, so she wasn't sure what caused such a response.

He didn't look happy once he finished swallowing his tea. "That hooligan? Don't you know anyone that isn't a borderline criminal? Us excluded, of course."

"He was a good agent. And, although he left the Society, an idea I'm beginning to see the wisdom of, he was never convicted."

"What was he accused of?" Caden got the question out first, but Nettie was thinking about it. Technically, Homer was a criminal as a sometime airship pirate. But as he mostly worked on the side of the law for the Queen and country, he was excused.

"Murder. Robbery. Treason, no, the Queen expunged that one eventually. A few things." Gaston shook his head. "He was a hellion as a young agent and never outgrew it."

"Sounds like an interesting man." Caden shrugged and ignored Gaston's obvious annoyance. "He's a witch, too?"

"Wizard is the preferred term for male practitioners, but he was never a stickler, so usually referred to himself as a witch. Good man, though." Lisselle turned to Gaston and folded her arms. "This is your mansion, it is up to you whether I call him here, where we can all explore this situation together, or I go meet him in a seedy pub somewhere."

Gaston muttered a few unmentionable French swear words under his breath, then finally nodded. "But how will you reach him? Certainly, he doesn't have access to a Mudger."

"We have other ways." Lisselle looked appropriately mysterious, then wrote a brief note which she rolled up tightly, went to the window, and held out her hand until a large gray pigeon appeared. Lisselle spoke a few words, the bird took the rolled-up note, and flew away.

"That was amazing." Rebecca was sobering up quickly and stood to go to the window. "Can you teach me that, or do you have to be a witch?"

"Works better for a witch, but I'll see what we can work out when things have settled." Lisselle stayed by the window as everyone else sat.

"We *can* start planning without Torlian's immediate input, you know." Gaston didn't appear ruffled about the former agent anymore. It was most likely leftover annoyance from being excluded by Edinburgh.

"Oh, he'll respond quickly. Never fear." She smiled and stayed near the window.

"Fine. We need to find out what other sightings of Egyptian nonhumans have been made. Most of the agents are out today, but I'll set up a meeting after supper. I think—" His words were cut off as the pigeon, or one like it, clattered at the window.

Lisselle opened it, took the note, and sent the bird off. Then she laughed. "He says to open the front door."

Gaston didn't move, but Caden darted to the front door and opened it. Nettie ran over as well. Just as a man on a broom came zooming in. He shot past the parlor, then spun in the hallway and came back.

"Lisselle! My darling!" Torlian was tall and slender, with a goatee and an elaborate mustache. His eyes were covered by goggles used by some airship personnel. His hair was dark and slicked back but there was enough gray at his temples to make him look distinguished. He lifted his goggles and scooped up Lisselle as she ran to him.

"Always the classicist. A broom?" She laughed as he set her on her feet.

"The old ways are the best. You're the one who kept wearing those pointy Welsh witchy-looking hats."

"Years ago, not recently."

"How did you fly here so no one saw you?" Nettie believed that a man flying across town on a broom would probably be noticeable. Like all the nonhumans, or non-fully-humans, known about by the Society, witches and wizards kept themselves hidden from the general populace. What people didn't know about, they couldn't worry about.

"Ah, it's all about airspeed and the benefits of flying in a cloudy city." Torlian bowed. "I am Torlian, by the way."

Lisselle turned back to everyone. "I'm sorry, your unusual arrival threw me off. This is Nettie, Caden, and Rebecca—all relatively newer agents. Nettie has been with us for over two years and Caden came from the Americas. You already know the cranky Frenchman in the corner."

Gaston shook his head, but Torlian shook the hands of the other three.

"Gaston isn't cranky, he just hasn't forgiven me for abandoning my duty as an agent for the Society."

"You had a calling." Gaston scowled from his seat.

"One that no longer fit me." Torlian's jovial smile vanished. "You don't know how it is in Edinburgh. You mostly stay ensconced in your mansion doing what you want. I've heard things are getting worse up north, and they were bad years ago." He nodded when Lisselle held up the whisky bottle, then sat after she poured him a glass. "I still have connections, and the chains of command are getting muddled up in Scotland right now."

Nettie, Caden, and Rebecca all resumed their seats. Nettie leaned forward. "How long ago did you leave?" She loved being in the Society, and being as they knew what she was, might not ever have a choice of leaving it. Agents who failed their induction had their minds wiped of all time during their initial training—she assumed the same would be for any who left the Society. But Torlian seemed intact.

"Three years, five months, and ten days." He grinned. "Not that I'm counting, mind you. I used to know the hours, minutes, and seconds."

"What's it like being out? What do you do now?" Nettie looked around at the surprised faces around her. "I'm not thinking of leaving. I just wonder what it's like to leave such an exciting life." Granted, she'd only been an agent a short while, but being part of the Society meant almost as much to her as Caden did.

Lisselle laughed. "Oh, didn't you know? Torlian is a world-famous painter. He runs with all those wonderfully wicked artists."

Nettie, Caden, and Rebecca all said 'ah' with about the same tone and head nod. The artist community of London was quite healthy and often extremely scandalous.

"You look like an artist." Now that she knew what he was, Nettie understood his style. He looked far more like a painter than a witch. But apparently being both wasn't a problem.

"Thank you, Nettie. I do try to keep up appearances." He finished his whisky. "As wonderful it is to see you all, I don't believe that was why I was contacted."

Gaston started to explain, but Lisselle spoke first and quickly told him all that had transpired.

His smile vanished immediately and his frown went deeper the more she spoke. Finally, he shook his head. "Ramsey not being available for calls, low-tier agents telling you that you're being shut out. Who broke the rules?" He looked around at the small group.

"What? None of us broke anything. It's just a mix-up of some sort." Gaston tried to sound like he believed it, but it was clear that he didn't. He already come to the same conclusion, yet hadn't wanted to admit it.

"Are you certain no one broke code in Wales? Yes, I do still keep track of things. A lot was going on up there."

Such as Nettie becoming a mermaid. She still carried

the genetic markers for that in her blood. But the brief examination in Scotland before they came back to London indicated they were mostly dormant. Further tests were run before they came back to London, but as of yet, no results had been communicated.

"Nothing. We resolved the problem, brought a new group of friendlies into the fold, and that was it. The merpeople will be assets to the Society," Gaston said with more force than needed.

Torlian leaned forward and rested his elbows on his knees. "There must be something. Come on, Gaston, you've been an agent long enough to know when they're closing someone out. Lisselle too, or as much as she enjoys my company, she never would have contacted me to come here."

"They don't shut out an entire branch. Just individuals." Gaston narrowed his eyes, he wasn't giving in.

"A branch is made out of individuals," Lisselle said softly. "And if they felt we were all beyond saving?"

"Mon dieu." Gaston pulled out an envelope from his inner vest pocket. "I received this yesterday afternoon. But wanted to speak to Ramsey before I said anything to anyone about it." He handed it to Nettie.

"It's about me?" Edinburgh congratulated her on handling the mermaid situation so well. Why would they send a letter to Gaston about her? Conscious of all eyes upon her, Nettie unfolded the single page of paper from the envelope.

"A medical report?" Yes, they'd run tests on everyone who'd been involved in the mermaid incident. But they already knew she was half-vampire and now carried some mermaid elements. This paper was a full workup of her blood and not watered down for easy consumption of the information. Again, her medical degree came in handy.

"What is this mysterious element XCV?" She looked

up and tried to ignore the startled expressions from both Lisselle and Torlian.

"It's a component that the researchers have been trying to narrow down for decades, as long as the Society has been in place. It's traced through the Egyptian deities." Torlian didn't wait for Gaston to explain. And the sympathy in his eyes was hard to process.

"You mean from the Egyptian rulers? The queens and pharaohs?" She was proud that her voice didn't shake, the same couldn't be said for her hands as Caden gently took the letter from her. The issue came up briefly while they'd been in Llandudno, Wales, but to be honest, she'd forgotten about it.

"There is a lot of evidence that the line of pharaohs held powers. Some would say magical. And that they were still alive, but hiding," Lisselle said. "There was another focused study in Scotland about twenty-five years ago. Then nothing came from it, and all the Egyptian nonhumans were relegated to their home country. Agents were assigned there, but honestly, there wasn't much to do. The line of pharaohs was dead."

"And they think I'm part of it?" Nettie didn't rattle easily, but this was extremely disturbing. And the reactions from everyone aside from Rebecca and Caden were even more so.

"On your mother's side. We all know she is a vampire and no one in the Society has seen her for more than ten years. But there is an odd matrilineal chain that they found when they were testing you after Wales. It was never noticed before, so it could be that the mermaid influence brought it to the surface." Gaston looked like he wanted to hug her. Which was unusual enough that it increased her concern.

"So, because I might or might not be related to a vampire with ancient Egyptian blood, we're all being expunged?

This is outrageous." Nettie was too upset about the Society trying to get rid of them that she shoved aside the further implications of that letter. "Might I?" She didn't snatch it from Caden but only because he released it immediately.

She scanned it again and stabbed the paper with her index finger. "See? Here? They *theorize* that I might have a small portion of similar genetic make-up as the genetic bit they are looking for. Long dead. As in, how do the researchers know for certain? This is ridiculous. I will clarify this mix-up directly." She blinked rapidly as tears built up.

"They want to be careful. There was an uprising three hundred years ago. It shook the foundations of the world before it was stopped," Torlian said.

"Then why have we never heard of it?" Rebecca looked furious on Nettie's behalf.

Caden was silent but kept his arm around Nettie's shoulders.

"Because it served the Society, and all of the world's rulers at the time, to keep it secret." Gaston shook his head. "The line of pharaohs was ended."

"Unless a vampire was carrying their blood and passed it to her child," Lisselle said. "We know there was an Egyptian aspect to your blood up in Wales—it just seems that it is stronger and more specific than we thought."

Nettie looked down as everything swam around her. She was not a woman who swooned—ever. But the idea that she might be forced out of the Society, or worse, dragged back to Scotland as an experiment, terrified her. She almost felt swoony.

"They're not taking you." Lisselle came over and dropped in front of Nettie. "I promise that I will do everything in my power, all of my power, to keep them from locking you up. We will get you out of this."

Nettie was touched at her fierceness. Looking around

revealed Caden, Gaston, and Rebecca wearing the same look.

Even Torlian appeared ready to fight for her. "I know we just met, but I will do whatever I can to help. Both Lisselle and I lost someone we cared about to a hunt by the powers that be. I'd hoped that had changed."

Normally Nettie would want to hear what happened. But neither of them appeared ready to talk about it, and considering the news she just received, neither was she.

A ruckus came down the hall toward the parlor. Niles' voice, then Damon's, then…Homer's?

Lisselle caught it just as Nettie did and she jumped to her feet to head Homer off in the hall. "You need to go back to bed, right now." She tried pushing him back, but even with the help of the two men, he wasn't going to be moved. Unless she used magic. "I will spell you."

Homer still looked paler than usual, but otherwise upright and functioning. He did come to a stop at the entrance to the parlor with a sigh. "I'm fine. Once you got that wee thing out of me, my body healed." He held out his arms for examination. "See for yourself." He glanced into the parlor. "Torlian! Good to see you! Lisselle dragged you into this? Now these looks can't be about those covelins and the bug. What's happened?"

Lisselle made him shut up as she listened to his heart, lifted his eyelids, and checked his pulse. Finally, she stepped back. "You can stay. For now. But if I feel you're overtaxing yourself, you will go back to your room immediately. Agreed?" She came up to the lower part of his chest, but he nodded like an errant schoolboy. Then took a seat.

"Edinburgh is cutting us off and there's a letter that might have something to do with it." Caden took the letter and handed it to Homer when Nettie didn't move. "I still don't know that's what's caused them to ignore us though. They knew about her blood before we came back to London. Look at the small date written next to the initial results. We've been in contact with Ramsey and the rest in the three weeks that we've been back here. No indication that there were problems with any of us."

"You received this yesterday? And the covelins showed up today? It seems to be interesting timing." Torlian stroked his goatee.

Nettie felt that he probably did that a lot; it was a very artist thing to do. Seeing everyone working through the issue made her feel better. Even having been an agent for a few years, she was still used to defaulting to being on her own when a crisis arose. She'd never had a real family growing up and it still surprised her that she did now.

"I agree with Caden." Homer rubbed his arm where the scarab got in, but stopped when he saw Lisselle watching him closely. "There's something going on here, but I don't think Nettie's blood is the cause of it. I wish we could talk to Ramsey. There are some politically focused people up there, but he was always a good egg."

Niles looked out of place. Yes, he was going to be a butler for a large group of agents and went through basic agent training, but this was beyond that.

Damon noticed and turned to Gaston. "We're going to go continue our training. We'll also see if we can't find the source of the lights dropping. Since we no longer must watch someone sleep." He shook his head at Homer.

"I'm fine. Seriously." Homer kept up his protestations as Damon and Niles left the parlor. "No one believes me."

Damon might have held off from glaring at Homer, but Rebecca didn't. "You shouldn't even be conscious, let alone marching about. I saw the amount of laudanum Lisselle gave you." The look in her eyes made it appear that she wished she had some with her to dose him again.

Nettie gave a small sigh of relief at the focus moving away from her. But Rebecca did have a good point. That laudanum should have kept him out until tomorrow at the least.

Homer laughed, took some cooled tea, then set the cup down. "I have been working on building up my tolerance to laudanum and a few other well-known substances." He shrugged when a new round of frowns came his way.

Gaston rang the bell, since more tea was clearly needed, but swore at Homer. "Shouldn't you have shared that with me?" He glanced at Lisselle's annoyed face as she split her stare between Homer and Gaston. "With *us*? That needs to be in your file."

Kilia appeared as if she'd been waiting down the hall with a fresh tea tray, swapped them out then, with a bow, she left the parlor.

Caden leaned into Nettie. "Are we certain she's not related to the Runners? She looks human, but?" The Runners were advanced alien robots, and didn't in the least look human. At least they never had before. There were things going on in Scotland, that weren't being shared with the rest of the agents. Maybe far more than they currently knew.

Nettie vowed to keep a close eye on Kilia.

Caden kept his voice low, but Homer still chuckled. "Might be. Now what are we going to do about this insult to our team?"

Gaston poured tea and handed it around. He rarely did that unless there were important guests, but he appeared to be out of sorts at the moment. "I need more information on several things before we move to act. I still believe we need to investigate the breakdown of the guarding agents in Egypt, as well as track down those covelins. Then look up references to the line of the pharaohs. Lisselle, can you and Nettie work on duplicating what was supposedly found by that study?" He waved at the paper that Homer still held. "We also need a way to stop future attacks by those scarabs. Aside from avoiding being bit."

"The covelins can also spit the scarabs at their victims." Torlian helped himself to a nice collection of tea sandwiches and returned to his seat. "Nasty business. They go in through your mouth."

"That's disgusting," Rebecca said around a mouthful of egg salad sandwich. Chef's egg salad sandwiches were mystically amazing, so she wasn't disgusted enough to not finish eating them.

"How do we prevent that from happening? Either way, actually," Caden asked.

Torlian was mid-bite, but swallowed it, took some tea, then nodded. "We're going to need magic. In the old days, heavy armor and helmets helped, but those would be a bit noticeable on the streets of London today. Not to mention unwieldy."

Lisselle leaned forward to see Torlian better. She'd moved her seat to be next to Homer; she wasn't kidding about sending him back if she felt he was faking his recovery. "I can't imagine a spell that could hold either attack off."

Torlian nodded. "True, not a traditional one. But one thing about being within the artist community, I've learned to look far beyond the obvious. There are two parts. But we need a covelin and their blood to make them work."

"We have to capture one of those things, without it biting us or spitting in our mouth, so we can find a way to stop them?" Homer was clearly not happy about that idea.

A sentiment that Nettie agreed with. As part vampire, she was faster than an average human, but even she didn't know if she could move quickly enough to avoid something being spat at her. "I agree, that seems to be a bit problematic," she said.

"What if we did a flash stun? I agree that those things were hard to catch, but what about using one of those stun grenades you have on your airship? Stun one long enough to tie it up and put a steel-lined bag over its head." Caden looked too pleased with himself. Nettie held no doubt who was going to volunteer to do the task.

Lisselle shook her head. "Those grenades don't have the ability to make sure they hit the right target. A spell can be more specific."

Torlian smiled. "You're thinking of the awe spell, aren't you? If we hit one of them with it, they definitely wouldn't be able to fight back. The spell doesn't last long, but we should be able to get it secured with time to spare." He turned to Gaston. "You do still have secure chambers in this boarding house, correct?"

Gaston's left eye twitched at his beloved mansion being called a boarding house but simply nodded in response. "Precisely where they were the last time you were here." There was little inflection in Gaston's voice so there was no way to tell if Torlian were there as a guest or as a prisoner.

By the smirk on Torlian's face, it had been the latter and hadn't ended well for Gaston.

The discussion broke down into a concentrated plan of attack. Not a single person pointed out that Edinburgh ordered them to stand down. It was agreed that if this wasn't the start of a full Egyptian invasion, then they needed to catch a covelin before they escaped, as they might not be planning on staying in England since their first attempt went awry.

The final decision left Rebecca and Gaston guarding the mansion along with Damon and Niles and three agents who were home and who would be read into the situation once the others left. Gaston originally wanted to keep Nettie at home as well—he was still concerned about the letter from Edinburgh.

With backup from Lisselle, Nettie finally convinced

him that the odds of Edinburgh sending down a team to grab her off the street were slim. And that she would take precautions. And that her speed and strength could help restrain the covelin should the spell not work as hoped.

Gaston gave in eventually, but he still wasn't happy.

Torlian and Lisselle led the way, much to the annoyance of Caden and Homer. The two consoled themselves by each grabbing one of Homer's flash stun grenades from his airship along with two gear guns.

They'd gotten a block away from the mansion when a covelin, not even trying to hide, ran in front of them half a block away. Then another.

"Anyone get the idea that they want us to follow?" Caden adjusted his gun holster and the stun grenade.

"A third and forth." Lisselle shook her head. "What are they doing?"

"Trying to distract you. And it worked." The voice was low and exotically accented. "None of you turn around, nor reach for any weapons or spells. We want one of you, but the rest can either be let go or killed. It depends on the next few moments."

With their magic users at the front, and possibly blocked in any attack they might make by their friends, Nettie knew it was up to her. She might not have magic, but she had her own unique abilities because of her nature.

The man behind them took two steps forward. Nettie saw his hand reaching for Homer's arm out of the corner of her eye. She spun with vampiric speed and jumped for the tall stranger.

CHAPTER FOUR

NETTIE SHOVED HIM AWAY FROM her friends and held both of his arms up and out of the way. His left hand held an odd tube that crackled as she pushed him. She squeezed the arm holding the object until he released it, then kicked it away. It didn't look like a gun, but there was no way to tell what it was at this point.

He'd been wearing a hooded cloak which came loose as she threw him to the ground.

She almost froze as his face flashed into an image of a jackal—like the Egyptian god of the dead, Anubis. But the image was gone before she could convince herself that she hadn't imagined it. When the image vanished, a handsome, dark-skinned Egyptian man was before her.

Her friends recovered quickly and Caden stood with his gun less than two feet above the man's head. "Trust me, I wouldn't even twitch right now."

The man sneered, but his body relaxed. "I'm not a danger to those fighting on the side of light."

Homer peered down at him. "And you're working with those wee buggers who attacked us? I'd say you're on the wrong side, my friend." He also was armed but didn't pull out his gun. He did stand close enough to the man's head that if he moved, Homer might simply stomp on him.

"The covelin are tools, nothing more." He kept his body still, but his eyes looked around the group.

"We're awfully noticeable out here." Torlian wasn't facing their prisoner but was keeping watch around them. Londoners were usually good at ignoring, or pretending to ignore, odd activities in their city. But Nettie agreed that this might be a bit too much.

Lisselle dropped down near the man and kept her voice low. "I sense something dark about you. Odd since you follow the light. As you saw, we are stronger, faster, and have more magic than you." She held a spell over his face but didn't release it. Whatever he was, Lisselle clearly felt he already knew of magic. "We wanted to take one of your covelins back, but you will be much better. Just know that if you fight, call attention to us, or do anything to slow us down, we will destroy you."

If the man clenched his teeth any tighter, Nettie felt his jaw would snap. She saw a brief flash of light gold in his dark eyes, then like the image of Anubis, the gold vanished. "We should use the bag we brought. Cover his eyes and restrain his arms. There's more to him than appears." She now felt more confident that she'd seen the head of Anubis, the Egyptian god of the dead when his hood first fell off. She just wasn't sure what it meant. Nor did she trust him.

"I mean you no harm," he stopped talking when he was surrounded by more hardened looks. "I will go willingly with you."

"That's lovely, mate." Homer took the bag they'd brought for the covelins. "Unfortunately, we've learned to be suspicious of people who threaten to kill us."

Torlian bent down to pick up the odd tube the man had been carrying. "And who are you to be carrying a spelled stun weapon? I haven't seen one of these in decades." He nodded to Homer. "I'd get that bag over his head immediately."

The man didn't fight as the bag was slipped over his head, and his hands tied together by Caden. They got him to his feet with little struggle. He was even taller than Homer, but quite thin. Even with his head covered and hands bound, he moved smoothly and confidently. Nettie thought there were no other words that fit the way he moved as they surrounded him and made their way back to the mansion. It almost wasn't human. As if he were the one taking them prisoner.

One or two Londoners did notice their odd progression, but Caden smiled comfortingly. "It's all fine. This is a dangerous criminal, but we have him well in control." In each case, the passerby nodded and hurried on their way.

Gaston answered the door with Damon and Niles directly behind him. Both looked put out at his actions. "So soon?" He stepped back as Homer and Caden walked their prisoner inside. "That is not a covelin."

"No, but it's someone we need to put in a magic-proof cell." Lisselle's fingers were twitching and both she and Torlian looked ready to send their worst spells if the man in question breathed wrong.

Rebecca stayed in the doorway of the parlor as they passed, but followed them as they went below to the cells.

Damon and Niles remained at the locked and bolted front door in case someone, or something, wanted to free their prisoner.

Nettie wasn't familiar with the cells. She knew they were there, and they'd been part of her tour when she started as an agent. However, she'd never seen them used.

They were unlike what she would have expected: dark, dripping stones, creaking gates, and flickering torches. These cells looked more like a dormitory in a college, aside from the heavy metal bars and locked doors. There was no one else down here, which was reassuring. She didn't think that prisoners might have been kept here without her knowing. Of course, the only time she'd held a prisoner, had been in the coroners' lab she'd worked in and the Runners were dispatched to bring him to Bath. With the recent actions from Scotland, she doubted they would be called this time.

The man was uncuffed, then he shrugged and walked inside the cell.

Homer leaned forward. "We'll remove the bag, but keep your eyes closed until we lock you in. We could leave you here bound and bagged instead if you prefer to cause trouble."

There was a brief nod and Homer removed the bag. That Lisselle and Torlian both stood to each side with spells raised was comforting.

But the man kept his eyes closed until the door was shut and locked.

"You can't keep me here. I have to return to Egypt." He looked through the bars, then sat down on the thin cot. "If I don't go back to Egypt, things will happen. Horrific things."

"You did threaten to kill us." Lisselle kept her spell hand raised. "And you admitted bringing the covelins here—one of whom bit a good friend of mine." She didn't look toward Homer.

"I am greatly sorry for that. You don't have to believe me, but my purpose for bringing the covelins was only to distract and gather information. I didn't know they were already working on someone else's agenda. They carried in the scarabs without my knowledge." His lip went up in a snarl that made it appear he was telling the truth.

Nettie knew appearances could be deceiving. "Who were you after? You said you only wanted one of us, who was it?" She had a feeling it was her. They'd been worried about Edinburgh sending someone to grab her, but others could have heard about this mysterious blood she had. The results were weeks old, after all. If there were troubles in Scotland, they could also have leaks.

"The Lady Lisselle." He gave a slight nod toward her. "Although my sources failed to tell me she was a fully functioning witch. The implication was of a spell dabbler."

"What? Why me? And who told you anything of magic?" The spell she was holding came to life.

"I'll be blunt. All the witches, wizards, and other magic users in my land are losing their abilities. It happened slowly, and no one could find the reasons behind any of it. Then they simply fell silent and vanished. Much like your missing agents."

Gaston stomped forward. "What agents?"

"Come now. In case you haven't guessed, I'm not a human. All of us know of the Society for the Exploration of the Unexplainable. There was no idea you had a day-walking vampire with you." He glanced at Nettie but then turned back to Lisselle.

"It is believed that your magic is strong enough, and different enough, to help us stop this...plague." He winced. "That's not a term we use lightly in my country, believe me. But that's what this is. Someone is slowly removing agents and magic users from reality. There are forces at work that haven't been seen in thousands of years."

Nettie was intrigued by his choice of term, but she turned to Lisselle. Her friend was powerful but didn't use her magic that often, or at least not around her. However, Nettie always believed she was just another witch. Aside from the fact that there wasn't surprise on Lisselle's, Torlian's, Homer's, or Gaston's faces.

"I need more details, and lots of them." Gaston scowled. "No one in this house will help you, nor will we let you go, until I am certain that you speak the truth."

"Can you control those covelins?" Caden stayed at the back of the group. "They're running around free to spit those scarabs on people."

"If this cell wasn't magic-proof I could. There are six of

them left, but you're right, they can't be left to run free. I am called Zarius, by the way. I know of all of you except the wizard." He sat a bit higher as he spoke his name.

Nettie had a feeling Zarius might not be his full name. Nor even close. Being called something didn't guarantee that was a given name.

"Tell me how to stop them." Lisselle nodded to Torlian. "My friend and I can use whatever spell you were going to." Neither she nor Torlian mentioned Torlian's name.

The glint in his eyes indicated that Zarius noticed that as well. But he nodded. "You'll need a trap for them. They mostly follow commands, but clearly, whoever gave them the scarabs has orders that override my own. I can find something that should work." He then started speaking fast and deep in what sounded like Latin. However, Nettie knew it wasn't, as she understood that. Lisselle and Torlian both moved closer and Gaston motioned for the rest to leave.

Everyone else headed for the stairs except Homer. He came halfway but turned and shook his head. "I'll stay down here if you don't mind. Maybe right at the base of these stairs." He did pull out his gun but kept it pointed down as he faced Zarius' cell.

Gaston watched the three magic users discuss whatever Zarius thought would work against the covelins, then nodded. "Excellent idea." He smiled and held his arm out to Rebecca. "I believe we have a wedding to work on?"

Rebecca hadn't said much since they come back, but the relief was clear on her face as they went down the hall. She wasn't self-centered enough to want to focus on her wedding when there was danger around, but if Gaston suggested it, she would gladly agree.

Caden and Nettie followed the pair, and he leaned closer. "Not really a great time, but have you thought of our wedding?"

Nettie pulled back to get a better look at him but didn't

release his arm. He hadn't brought it up except once since he'd proposed in Llandudno. She wasn't concerned as men seemed to be less worried about these things.

As they walked, she briefly told him of her plan; a small wedding on Homer's airship. The idea of being on the airship itself just came to her, but she found that she rather liked it. It also would force a much smaller ceremony.

He visibly relaxed at her words. "That sounds wonderful. To be honest, Damon nattering on about everything he and Rebecca planned was making me nervous."

Nettie laughed. "Me too." That was a relief and one thing less to worry about. "Now if solving this Egyptian emergency would be as easy. Or whatever is going on with Scotland." She was not going to address the issue of her blood. It might be something better to ignore until they obtained more information and increased resources.

Caden had no answers and vanished as soon as he realized that Gaston hadn't been simply trying to reassure Rebecca about wedding planning; he was in full final preparation mode as they got to the parlor.

Caden offered to replace Damon so he could join in and then went patrolling the mansion with Niles.

Nettie felt torn. Rebecca was like a sister to her, and Nettie would do whatever she needed to make her wedding as wonderful as possible. She just didn't want to sit in a long discussion on place settings.

Although she thought she had schooled her face well enough, she clearly failed as mid-conversation Rebecca looked over with a smile.

"I know this isn't what you enjoy. And I fear you have too many things on your mind to make a worthwhile contribution." Rebecca leaned forward with a grin. "I have these two to get me through this. Maybe you could go duplicate the study of your blood?"

Nettie bounced to her feet. Then stopped. "Only if you're certain?"

Rebecca waved her hand and turned back to the book they were looking over.

"Go," Gaston added. "You can even use my lab; it has better blood-separating machines than yours." The book he opened literally contained nothing beyond drawings of different types of table settings. And he looked happy about it.

"I think I shall!" She didn't run from the room, but it was a brisk walk.

"So much excitement for one day, yes?" Kilia hadn't been in the hall one moment, then she was. As always, her posture was perfect. Just on the verge of strongly disapproving of something, but still polite.

"Very. But that's how things are here. How are you enjoying working in the mansion?" Nettie really wanted to go to Gaston's lab and get some work in, but this was the most Kilia said to her beyond asking what she'd like to eat for breakfast.

"It is very interesting. Would you be willing to follow me down the hall? There is a question I need to ask about an agent. They haven't come out of their room since last night."

Nettie started to turn back to the parlor. This was a Gaston situation. Then she thought of how happy Rebecca was to work on her impending wedding. "Which agent?"

"Lady Geyer came back yesterday evening complaining of not feeling well, but she is not opening the door. I don't feel right unlocking an agent's room."

Nettie wasn't sure about it either, but Geyer was a newer agent and had been having troubles with her health since she came to London. If she was in distress, they needed to check. "Let's go see her, she might have simply overslept." Ignoring the fact that it was now late afternoon. Some people simply kept to different times.

Nettie led the way to Geyer's room and Kilia handed

her the key. The door stuck a little, but when she pushed, it opened.

But it was partially blocked by a body on the floor.

CHAPTER FIVE

NETTIE HAD EXCEPTIONAL SPEED, BUT Kilia was even faster and shoved her into the dark room, then jumped in afterward, and slammed the door shut. Trapping them inside.

Nettie tried to get one of the lights to turn on. Gaston had spared no expense to have the most modern electric lights installed in all the rooms, but the switch wouldn't work.

Kilia was not only fast, she was strong. The only advantage that Nettie held was that she didn't fight fair. Once she'd recovered from the initial attack, and shifted around to shove Kilia's arm up. At that angle, Kilia's arm should have been broken.

Instead, Kilia rose on her toes, unnaturally twisted her torso, and broke free.

Nettie had only seen one type of being move like that—a Runner. There was a chance that there was an advancement in their appearance, they'd always appeared as a black fabric-covered form, with no human features. However, this attack seemed a bit aggressive if this was a modified Runner from Scotland.

As she stepped back, Nettie flung open the curtains to let the late afternoon light in to enable her to see better. The room was in shambles and the body on the ground looked suspiciously like Agent Geyer.

Kilia's face was immobile but Nettie thought she saw a brief flash of anger in her eyes before she charged.

Nettie stayed near the window but held her ground as Kilia rushed her. At the last moment, Nettie grabbed Kilia's arm and flung her through the window.

Kilia didn't even scream as she flew out and crashed onto the lawn with enough force to dig holes in the dirt. It took her only a moment to get to her feet, snap her neck back into place, look directly up at Nettie, and then run away.

By the time Gaston, Caden, Niles, Rebecca, and Damon came running into the room, Kilia was long gone from sight.

"What happened?" Gaston was the slowest of the assembled group, but the first to speak as he took in the state of the room, the body, and the shattered window.

Caden and Rebecca came running over to Nettie.

"Are you hurt?" Came out from both at the same time.

"A little jostled. Kilia killed Agent Geyer, then tried to do the same to me. Or something else, but it wasn't going to be nice whatever it was." The more Nettie thought about it, the more she realized that Kilia was trying to restrain her more than kill her. She wanted her alive for some nefarious purpose.

Rebecca gasped and ran back to the body, gingerly turning Geyer over and crouching over her. "I think she is still alive. Barely."

Niles immediately went to pick the injured agent up, but Gaston stopped him. "Get a gurney first, we've no idea what happened to her."

Niles and Damon ran to the medical wing.

Gaston joined Nettie and Caden at the broken window. "I take it she jumped out to get away when you overpowered her?"

Nettie shook her head and told him everything that

happened. "I think she was a Runner in disguise or some variation of one of them. Had I not been able to send her through the window, I don't know who would have won." That was a difficult thing for her to admit. Yes, there were vampires and mer-people who'd ended up matching or bettering her in a scuffle. But it was rare.

"This is bad, very bad. If Kilia was something connected to the Runners and Scotland, they have all the information she gathered over the past three weeks."

"And that was the date on the blood work processing, as well as when we came back to London." Caden looked out the window. "Do you know anyone who might have access to Edinburgh that we could find some answers from?"

"I'm working on that. I'm still hoping that whatever is going on, Ramsey will shake it off and get in touch. Even if it's not a direct route." Gaston turned as Niles and Damon returned and, with Rebecca and Nettie's assistance, carefully placed Agent Geyer on the gurney.

"I will examine her, but we might need Lisselle as well," Nettie said as she and Rebecca prepared to follow the gurney out.

"I'll get her and tell the others what happened." Caden jogged out in front of them.

Gaston stayed lost in thought as he surveyed the ransacked room, but he waved them on.

Nettie was glad that Agent Geyer was still alive, but she didn't like her countenance. Her face was extremely pale and her eyes were moving rapidly under her eyelids. Her jaw was clenched as if she were awake and fighting not to scream in terror. Not to mention that it was impossible to see any other injuries on her aside from a few bruises that could have occurred when Nettie forced open the door.

Had attacking Agent Geyer simply been a ruse to grab Nettie? If so, why? There were plenty of times that

Kilia could have absconded with Nettie in the past three weeks. Why now?

"You have that look, the one where you're ripping through scenarios," Rebecca said as they took the ramp down to the medical rooms. There was a lift, but it had been acting up as of late.

"Just wondering why Kilia, or whoever that was, waited so long to attack? And wouldn't simply waiting for me to be alone have worked just as well, if not better, than this setup? There's something that we're missing." She hated the feeling of a clue being right in front of her that was somehow overlooked.

Niles and Damon directed the floating gurney into the smaller medical room and moved the agent onto the bed. "If you don't need us, I think we'll go check security around the mansion."

Nettie was already focusing on her patient but looked up. "Could you check the lawn where Kilia landed? Especially the hole where she hit? There could be clues she left behind." It didn't look like anything fell off, and she'd fled quickly, but there might be something.

Damon nodded and they left.

"What's wrong with her?" Rebecca asked as she prepared a tray of medical supplies. She and Nettie also put on full medical smocks.

"I don't know, which is going to make it extremely difficult to revive her. I'm hoping that Lisselle can tell more when she arrives. But let's make her comfortable until then."

Agent Geyer was stiff, far more so than an unconscious and injured person should be. And more than she'd been when Nettie helped get her onto the gurney just minutes ago. As Nettie watched, the agent's limbs all started to tighten. As if she were awake and curling into a ball.

"I've never seen that." Rebecca was coming closer with her tray, but suddenly stopped and blinked her eyes.

She also froze.

Rebecca had shown clairvoyant abilities in the past. Which was the primary reason that she'd been recruited to the Society. Not every agent was a nonhuman or one with supernatural skills, but many were.

Nettie was about to shake her friend out of her stupor when Rebecca dropped her tray and started pushing Nettie out of the room. The first time that Rebecca had a seeing around Nettie, she'd actually created an image of the potential future that both she and Nettie had lived through before snapping back. It wasn't pretty—they'd both died and felt every part of it.

They'd gotten that under control, so that now, unless she wanted it to happen, Rebecca's images stayed in her head.

From the look on her face, these weren't good images.

"Out! Out now, bolt the door. Are there other ways in or out?" Rebecca's bright blue eyes were huge as she frantically looked around for things to shove against the door to make sure nothing was getting out. There was a glass window set in the door, but it was made of extremely thick glass and was even designed to be bulletproof. Something Nettie kept meaning to ask Gaston about.

"Only this one that I know of." That was one problem of living in a secret agent mansion, there were secrets everywhere.

Rebecca was hauling over a heavy bench to put against the door when Lisselle, Homer, Caden, and Torlian came running up.

"Is Agent Geyer inside there?" Lisselle didn't question why they were barricading the medical room, but Homer helped Rebecca with putting the bench across the door.

"She is. Or what's left of her is." Nettie watched her friend, but she was too focused on whatever terror she'd seen in her head. "Rebecca had a vision, then shoved me out of the room. Are there any other doors?"

Lisselle shook her head, but Homer nodded.

"A small emergency door that leads out down the hall. Caden, come with me, we need to block it." Homer took off before waiting for a response. Caden was on his heels.

Rebecca shook herself and blinked as everything that could be in front of the door, was. "Oh dear." She climbed over the bench to get to the small window. "It's happening."

"What's happening, child?" Lisselle helped Rebecca get down and then climbed up to see for herself. "Oh no."

Nettie was proud of holding her patience, but it was about gone now. "What is happening?"

What sounded like an explosion inside the medical room caused Lisselle to pull back. "Agent Geyer was dead, or close to it. She had dozens of scarabs inside her." Lisselle stepped down from the window and Nettie could see the bugs slamming against the glass. They were smashing themselves so hard, many were being destroyed in their attempt to shatter the glass.

Another explosive sound came from down the hall and Nettie ran after Homer and Caden.

From the way both were braced against the shorter door, they'd gotten there just in time. What sounded like an explosion was the scarabs slamming against the door with even more force than the ones at the main door.

Nettie looked around and grabbed a stone bench and dragged it over. Caden darted out of the way as she shoved it against the door.

"That has to weigh a few hundred pounds!" Homer yelled as he continued to brace the door. "Can you get another one?"

Adrenaline was increasing her natural strength, but that was heavy even for her. Still, she nodded and darted around the corner. This part of the medical wing wasn't used for much beyond storage. A massive armoire, filled with heavy machines no longer in use, was her next target. Caden joined her and together they pushed it up as Homer darted out of the way.

Even though they couldn't get out, the scarabs continued to keep throwing themselves against the door.

Nettie found her arms shaking. Good to know she had limits, but not good to have them tested in such a manner.

They walked back to the front entrance to find Torlian and Gaston talking a few feet from the door, and Lisselle trying to comfort Rebecca.

"I saw…I saw…all of us destroyed by those things. They weren't trying to take us over; they were trying to kill us. Then they went out into London." Rebecca grabbed her stomach. "Is there a bucket around?"

Gaston broke off his talk with Torlian and brought over an empty planter. "Here, child. You saved everyone, possibly most of the city as well."

Rebecca got ill, then Lisselle walked her down the hall a bit.

"Then Kilia is working for whoever brought in the covelins? She's not a Runner? And I thought the scarabs tried to take victims over, not kill them." Nettie was standing closest to the door. The thumps were growing weaker.

"I don't know that we can presume anything at this point." Gaston frowned at the door. "I think we'll need to show Kilia's likeness to our Egyptian friend and see if he recognizes her."

Homer ran his fingers through his hair. "And as for her not being a Runner, Scotland did lose track of a few of them during the alien invasion in Bath. It was believed the parts found before the hive was blown up were the missing ones, but if they weren't? I wouldn't guess that anyone outside of Agent Zero and the rest of Edinburgh could recreate a Runner. But maybe someone could."

"Or there are people in Edinburgh working around the Society rules." Gaston watched the barricaded door as if it could give him answers. "We need to find out more about Kilia. Take apart her quarters, ask Chef for anything she was often around. If he knew any place she went on her days off." He tilted his head as he listened to scarabs still bashing themselves against the door. "And we need to get Damon to flood the med room with voliane gas. Those things are killing themselves, but too slowly for my liking. None of them can be allowed to survive."

After some discussion, everyone went to take care of their assignments. Homer stayed near the medical room while Caden went to get Niles and Damon. Both to see if they'd found anything from when Kilia crashed into the lawn, as well as have Damon fumigate the medical room. Even though Damon had only been an actual agent for a short while, he'd shown exceptional skill with chemicals.

Gaston and Lisselle were going to talk to their prisoner again. Nettie escorted Rebecca to her room to rest; visions took a lot out of her. Then, once they'd confirmed that Rebecca's room was clear, and Rebecca locked the door, Nettie went to the servants' wing to see Kilia's room.

The servants' wing didn't look very different from the rest of the mansion. People who worked here needed to be specially trained for skills beyond their jobs, but they were paid extremely well and were given room and board equal to the rest of the agents.

Nettie asked two of the housekeepers heading toward their rooms, which one was Kilia's.

It was set away from the rest, which was interesting as the wing wasn't that long. It only took Nettie a few moments to pick open the lock—a skill Caden had been helping her with.

The room was exceedingly small and dark compared to the other servant's quarters. The electric light flickered a bit before staying on.

There was only one light and the bed was upended against the far wall. This room looked more like a closet than a room. But the room, closet or not, didn't start with all the journal pages and images tacked against the wall once the bed was moved. Complete itineraries for at least most of the agents who lived in the mansion. Layouts of their rooms. And at least ten sketches of Nettie. None of them were public observations, and all had a red ink slash through them.

CHAPTER SIX

NETTIE WASN'T EASILY DISTURBED. IT was more a part of her upbringing than her becoming an agent. However, these images were disturbing. The artist was extremely accurate, even if there were no emotions in the sketches.

There was a lot of feeling in the red slashes, however.

Runners were free from emotions for the most part, even though Nettie tried to teach them manners and general polite behavior. A Runner could have done the drawings themselves. But the slashes were different.

Nettie wanted to take them down to go over them more carefully. She wasn't a strong student of psychology, but there was something wrong and unbalanced about these drawings as well as some of the other pieces. A closer look showed they were of Rebecca. But there were only three and while there were red circles around her image, there weren't any slashes.

However, it would be best to leave them all where they were in case there were subtle clues that she missed.

The closet was also filled with lists and sketches, but no further ones of agents. A quick walk around the room a few more times revealed little else aside from some oddly heavy marks in the middle of the floor. Something large had scuffed the wooden flooring, but was gone now.

She went to the narrow window. The curtains were

far too large, but bunching them up made it pitch black in the room if the light was off. She pushed them aside. The view was of the front drive. An odd angle but an excellent viewing point if someone was standing here, hidden in the shadows of the heavy drapes.

The light flickered again, and Nettie made a mental note of it. Once the power was restored after the first scarab attack, no other occurrences happened. Neither had the source of the problem been found. What if Kilia modified the lighting through her room? Normal people couldn't do such a thing, but a modified Runner could.

There wasn't even a chair to stand on, but stretching on her toes, Nettie could tell that the area around the light looked to have been hastily repaired. Gaston could bring in a team to determine what was done.

She dusted off her hands as she slowly turned around the room. Something was missing. If she were a spy within a mansion of spies, she would have a secret place to hide things. Possibly more than one. Nothing was remotely visible, so Nettie slowly made her way around the room, tapping the walls as she went. She'd go after the floor next.

The wall to the right of the closet gave back a suspiciously hollow sound. And she tapped around it to determine the size and perhaps how to open it. Minutes later she figured out the shape, but no way of opening it.

Using a marker left behind the bed, she drew the outline of where a hollow would be. Then continued around the room and finished approximately twenty minutes later. She'd found four hidden areas in the walls, and one in the floor near the window.

None of which could be opened without tools.

"Find anything?" Caden opened the door as he knocked, which defeated the purpose of knocking. Nettie gave up pointing that out to him when they were still in Wales.

"Yes, some are far more disturbing than others. Shut

the door, I don't think we want everyone knowing until Gaston has had his meeting."

Nettie gave Caden the tour, there was a lot of information tacked to the walls for such a tiny room. Caden tried to open the spots she'd marked, but like her, he couldn't get anything to budge without tools.

"The most upsetting are those sketches of you. The ones of Rebecca are upsetting as well, but none have that red slash. Didn't you say she was strong like a Runner? Do we now have a Runner with a grudge against you?"

"I have no idea. I have never been anything but polite to them. Not to mention a Runner capable of anger to that level is a disturbing thought." Nettie paced in a circle. "And when she grabbed me, Kilia was angry, but she was trying to restrain me, not injure or kill. Those slashes appear far more violent than simply wanting to kidnap someone."

"I agree. Shall we get the others? The scarabs in the medical room have been killed and their bodies destroyed. Our Egyptian friend is extremely upset about Kilia, Geyer, and the planted scarabs. He claims that no human would be able to do what was done. He is unaware of the Runners, or so Gaston believes."

Nettie agreed with Caden's unspoken opinion. Zarius was a spy; spies knew things about others even if they weren't direct enemies. He probably was extremely aware of the Runners but wasn't going to let that knowledge, nor how he knew it, go easily.

Nettie went to move the curtains back into place, but paused at movement on the sidewalk below them. "Is Torlian leaving? I figured he would at least stay until tomorrow." Yes, they had a better understanding of the events in Egypt now, but he was still helpful.

Caden scowled out the window. It was twilight now, but still light enough to see the wizard leaving. On foot.

"He told Lisselle he would take one of the guest rooms here in the mansion."

"And why doesn't he have his broom? It's a rather ostentatious way of travel, but he seemed quite taken with it." Nettie watched as he darted across the street and casually walked down the road. If his leaving was due to something bad, he didn't seem to be concerned.

"We need to get Gaston," Caden and Nettie both said at the same time as they ran. Nettie spun back and locked the room. It wouldn't do to have someone accidentally wander in and muddle things about.

Caden waited and they ran down the stairs together.

Gaston's voice echoed from the parlor as they ran down the hallway and then burst through the doorway. He was talking to Lisselle and Torlian. And Torlian was sitting and didn't look as if he'd just rushed back in.

Nettie froze and waved her hand toward Torlian. "We just saw you leave." She knew he was a friend of Lisselle's but her trust in unknown people was growing thin.

"Easy there. He's been right here for the last half-hour." Gaston glanced between Caden and Nettie but didn't move.

Torlian started to rise, but Caden shook his head. "I wouldn't. Unless you want to see how fast Nettie can move." He was closer to Torlian than Nettie but was correct in his assessment. Wizard or not, she knew she could hit Torlian before a spell left his lips. She felt her fangs start to drop into place, but kept them under control. Unlike true vampires, Nettie didn't feed with her fangs, but they could be a deadly weapon if she were pushed too far.

Lisselle stood near the beverage cart. "I can vouch as well; he was right here. What did you see and when?"

Nettie and Caden stayed at the doorway to the parlor, both watching Torlian, as they told them what they saw.

"You were in Kilia's room?" Gaston got up and looked

out the window. "Don't look at him right now, but what was the Torlian you saw outside wearing?"

Nettie and Caden both looked away from the wizard, and Nettie responded. "He wore the same dark suit as when he came in."

She looked back and if she were a swearing person, she would have engaged in some choice words. He was wearing a neatly pressed beige linen suit. That was extremely unusual that she didn't notice the change when she came in.

"I needed to change clothing after getting rid of the scarabs. They were extremely messy."

"How did we not notice that when we came here?" Nettie shook her head before anyone could answer. "Never mind, we were distracted and it's easier to see what is expected when stressed."

Caden continued to scowl at Torlian. "Then who did we see leaving? And why? They actually didn't leave from here or all of you would have noticed."

A brief discussion was held as to the contents of Kilia's room and what was observed out the window.

"This must be seen. But I agree that we need to find out what walked away from here."

Torlian rubbed his chin. "How advanced are the Runners now? When I left there was a small group working on changing them."

That brought everyone's attention. Even Gaston hadn't been aware of that.

"Should you be talking about it?" Gaston looked like he didn't really care but his response was habit. He strongly supported the Society and all it stood for.

"That's why I'm not part of them anymore." Torlian nodded toward the agents around him. "And the fact that the powers-that-be were working on such a thing years ago, and yet three longtime agents were unaware that it was in the works? That supports my decision to leave."

Nettie had a bad feeling that those disassembled Runners that she'd found in that downed spaceship in Bath, weren't destroyed as everyone believed. The question was, who rescued them, and who had the ability to repair and modify them. Their technology was far beyond even what the Society could create.

"Then we're thinking that it was Kilia, disguised as Torlian…why?" Caden shrugged.

Nettie was as perplexed as him. At first. Then she started for the stairs. "What if Kilia kept a security system in her room and I triggered it? Seeing Torlian walking away did make both Caden and I come down here."

She kicked into her vamp speed and hit the door to Kilia's room just as it was shutting.

The person inside tried to grab the light switch, but she rushed them toward the window. Her friends came barreling in after her. Caden jumped on the back of the person she was fighting and slowed them down. Already some of the sketches and lists had been torn off the walls and thrown into a pile.

Nettie was expecting to see Kilia, but as Caden was thrown off and the person barreled for the door, another far more familiar face showed. Damon.

Torlian, Lisselle, and Homer blocked him from leaving, while Caden jumped onto the pile to make sure he stayed down.

"Damon? Another Runner?" Nettie's first thought was for Rebecca. How long ago had he been replaced? The wedding was in a few days.

The sound of running people coming their way caused Caden and Homer to draw their pistols and keep them on the open doorway—while still managing to keep Damon pinned.

Niles and Damon came racing up.

Neither Caden nor Homer lowered their guns.

"Now see here, we can't stay at a standoff." Lisselle

nodded to Nettie. "If you could take my place here, I can see who we're dealing with." She flashed a look toward Niles and the second Damon. "I'd advise you two to stay particularly still. Both men are exceptionally good shots."

Nettie scrambled to sit on the pinned Damon, even punching him when he tried to free a hand.

Lisselle stood before Niles and Damon, but in such a way that she wasn't blocking either Homer's or Caden's line of sight.

"Now hold still." Staring into Damon's eyes, Lisselle softly spoke some spell words, then snapped her fingers. There was no change. Just to be certain, she repeated the spell and snap with Niles. He appeared concerned but barely breathed as she tested him.

"That does indicate that *you're* not who we thought," Lisselle said as she dropped down to where the fake Damon was immobilized at the bottom of the pile of agents. "You can change on your own, and we promise to treat you humanely, or make this difficult and end up taken apart and sold as rubbish."

Nettie watched the Damon copy carefully and his face twitched at Lisselle's words. If it was a Runner, they were going further in their emotional training. That reaction was extremely human.

Lisselle started to go through her spell, but the false Damon at the bottom of the pile cut her off. "No, I'll show you." The voice wasn't that of Damon, so it was a good thing they hadn't tried to pass as him. Obviously, the appearance was meant to simply distract them.

Damon's face changed, leaving Kilia's.

"And?" Gaston scowled down at the thing. "We all know this isn't your face."

The face transformed again. Each time the images softened and then whirled gently around the surface of the face before disappearing.

And ended up being a bland, robot-appearing Runner.

"I was sent here on a mission." The Runner was no longer fighting the three men sitting on it. "You are in danger."

Gaston squatted to get closer to the Runner. "You killed one of my agents and somehow injected her with creatures that could have destroyed half of the city of London. *You are* the danger."

"That was not me. I knew something was wrong with that agent. I was told to watch for her. I didn't kill her."

"Why did you draw my face with red slashes?" Nettie knew there were far more questions, but this one annoyed her.

"I didn't. I collected those from Geyer's room. There is a danger here, she was working with another. I was sent to save you." The way the Runner looked over to Nettie sent a chill down her back. There was something wrong with the story and with the Runner.

"Could it be our friend down below?" Gaston asked softly, but Runners have excellent hearing.

"Zarius? He is the one I was watching for. He and Agent Geyer. Yes."

Gaston turned away with a slight nod. He hadn't forgotten the Runner's hearing; he was counting on the Runner's response.

"Who sent you? Head Agent Lickenten?"

"Yes, Head Agent Lickenten sent me. Assigned to protect you all."

Lisselle and Gaston shared a knowing look. Nettie was sure that Homer would have as well, if he wasn't sitting awkwardly on top of the Runner.

Nettie didn't recognize that name. The Runner shouldn't have either since it was most likely fictitious.

"Can we?" Torlian asked.

"Yes, shut it down until we can talk to Head Agent Lickenten."

Torlian rolled off the pile and reached around to the back of Runner's head. "They changed it." With a sigh, he got down closer and started fussing with the casing on the back of its head.

"I told you, I need to save you all. You are in grave danger. You arrrrre...iiinnnn..." Then it froze.

"Whoever modified this one really changed things around. Most of the wiring's in a weird place." Torlian dusted himself off and stepped back.

Homer and Caden also got off.

"Do we believe that about Zarius? It seemed like a confused Runner, if that's possible." Caden looked down at the form. The entire face and body changed to the black fabric and metal of the Runners. "Or about Agent Geyer? I only met her a few times, but I don't think she was the double agent stalker type."

"But for a Runner to have those kinds of emotions?" Lisselle walked around it to the drawings on the floor. "These aren't normal."

"No, they're not. I think we need to immobilize this Runner. Then I am going to attempt to reach Agent Ramsey once more, and we are going to sort this out." Gaston looked up to Niles. "Please ask Chef what time for dinner, and then make sure that all agents who are in this evening come to our meeting. And anyone who comes in, stays in tonight. We have been caught unaware, and I don't want that to happen again."

Homer and Caden began removing wires from the Runner with direction from Torlian.

Damon nodded to Niles, and the butler-in-training left the room.

"Why did it take my place? I'm a newer agent, but well known in the mansion." As usual, Damon was calm.

"Probably to confuse anyone who saw it. It must have walked out appearing as Torlian, then come back here to destroy the evidence," Gaston said.

"But why? The things I found, the sketches and the lists, would be incriminating if we didn't already know that Kilia was bad. But since we already knew?" Nettie shrugged and handed over two of the random and, apparently nonsense, lists. Then she looked down at the Runner. She, like the rest of them, wanted more answers. Ones they most likely would not be getting from this thing.

"Something in here, either what you found or something else, was worth the risk of coming back." Gaston scowled at the pages. "Nettie was a target, but so was Rebecca. That could be an additional reason for the Runner changing to appear as you." He looked at Damon.

"Is Rebecca in danger? Where is she?" Damon was mostly unflappable, but young love changed that somewhat. His dark eyes went wide.

"She's resting in her room. I did a full check of it before I left her, then she locked herself inside. But it would make sense that she would open the door to you." Nettie now had a frantic urge to check on her friend. When she'd first moved into the mansion to live, she relished the massive size of it. Now it seemed far too large. There would be no way to search the entire thing if there were more dangerous Runners or spies inside. She paused. "Do you think that adapted Runner can travel the way the real ones can?" Runners appeared where they were called. Traveling through everything in their path. Distance, walls, people. They left one place and a short time later appeared on the other side of the country. Or the world.

Torlian looked down. "There's no way to tell."

"Torlian and Homer stay here—keep that thing disconnected and watch the room. The rest of us should check on Rebecca." Gaston barely finished his words when Damon took off running.

Caden and Nettie ran after him, with Gaston bringing up the rear.

Rebecca's door looked just as she'd left it, but that simply meant no one tried to break in. Yes, they'd stopped the Damon duplicate, but what if there was a second? He wouldn't have needed to break in.

Nettie shook her head, there was no reason to start creating scenarios. Rebecca was fine.

Rebecca's scream made Damon start slamming himself against the locked door. Nettie was right behind him.

Chapter Seven

NETTIE GENTLY MOVED HIM ASIDE when he ran back for another run at the door. "I can open it faster," she said gently. The look of terror on Damon's face was clear.

He nodded and stood back. Nettie knocked on the door, then broke the handle and opened the door.

Rebecca spun around, clutching her dressing gown closed. "All of you, for a mouse?"

"A mouse?" Nettie covered her mouth to hide her laughter. She wasn't afraid of rodents, but she didn't want her happiness at the scream only being mouse-centric to make Rebecca think she was mocking her.

Rebecca gave her a narrow-eyed glare even though Nettie kept her hand over her mouth. "I was resting, and a tiny furry thing ran across my dresser. Yes, it was a mouse, not a scarab, or anything else." She looked around. "How did you all get here so quickly?"

"There have been interesting things happening while you were napping." Nettie and Damon came further into the room as Caden and Gaston stayed back toward the door.

Damon hugged Rebecca. "I'm so glad you're okay. You should rest." He looked ready to pick her up and tuck her in by force if necessary.

Rebecca pushed him back with nothing more than a

look. "I'm fine now and I do believe that I need to know what has happened. The full accounting."

Nettie turned to the men now making their slow escape toward the door. Even Damon appeared ready to leave since Rebecca was safe. And annoyed. "Men. She is covered, you know. However, I will update Rebecca on our situation. I take it you will be ripping apart Kilia's room to find what else was there?"

Rebecca's eyes went wide at Nettie's statement, but she didn't say anything.

"That was my plan." Gaston coughed, then left with Caden and Damon walking quickly after him.

Nettie shut the door. "You missed quite a lot."

"I want to hear it all, however, let me change first." Rebecca vanished behind her changing screen, then popped out a few minutes later. All agents wore clothing that was far easier to get in or out of than societal norms. It looked normal, but functioned much better. It wouldn't do to have an agent hurt or killed due to being stuck changing clothing. "I would have done that when they came in if they hadn't acted so odd. It's not like I'd stepped out of a bath after all."

Nettie nodded in agreement and the two sat at the small tea table. Rebecca stayed still for most of the tale but paled at the part where the drawings of both she and Nettie were brought up.

"Why would Kilia, or this Runner, want to spy on the two of us? And such hostility about it. Aren't the Runners fairly…stoic?"

"Emotionless, yes, but they do react to things. But this one isn't normal. We believe that the damaged Runners which were thought to be destroyed in Bath months ago, were rescued and repaired. By someone with nefarious purposes."

"But how?" Rebecca reached for the kitchen bell and

then caught herself. "Oh dear, can't call Kilia. And I'm sure Chef and his other assistants are far too busy to bring tea. But I could do with a cup."

"Let me tell you the rest, then we can go hunt some down. Gaston wants all the agents who are not on away assignments to stay inside this evening. We'll be having a full meeting after dinner."

Nettie quickly filled Rebecca in on the rest, including Damon throwing himself against the door.

"Oh! He's so gallant!" Rebecca swooned a bit. Which was fair, as she would be marrying him quite soon.

There may be an invasion of scarabs, spies, and rogue Runners, but that would not stop this wedding. Just as a crisis of the kitchen staff would not stop tea.

Once Rebecca was suitably caught up, they went downstairs toward the kitchen. It had only been about fifteen minutes, yet there were far more people in the halls than previously.

"I've never seen it so full." Rebecca kept her voice down as they walked arm and arm down the hall. "Gaston is truly bringing everyone in on this. Oh! It just dawned on me that you probably never did get to run the tests on your blood."

"No, sadly. But I'm sure Lisselle will help me with it after dinner and our meeting. It will be interesting to see if anyone noticed anything odd about Kilia." They nodded to the agents coming back from their tasks as they went downstairs and the bulk of agents went upstairs.

"Or if some will now say they knew all along." Rebecca rolled her eyes.

It was a valid point. To be a successful secret agent, one did have to maintain a certain level of gumption. Some agents pushed that a bit too far in Nettie's opinion.

Chef ran a tight kitchen, but it was a large kitchen. Nettie often found herself peckish at odd times and so found a way to go into the lesser used part, gather tea and biscuits, maybe even a few sandwiches, then sneak back out without being caught.

She took Rebecca along a little used corridor that led to storerooms and the back of the kitchen. There were two doors to the outside, both designed to help with bringing in supplies. There was also a smaller door, one that appeared to belong to nothing more than a short closet, in the wall between the corridor and the kitchen.

Nettie glanced down the ends of the hall, then carefully pushed open the door. She waved Rebecca in, then shut the door.

"This is a linen closet. An empty one." Rebecca whispered.

"Ah, that's what you're supposed to think." Nettie pressed on the middle of what should be the back of the closet. "This has most likely been here since the mansion was built, but I don't think anyone knows of it beyond me and possibly Gaston. And now you."

The door creaked a bit, so Nettie opened it slowly. This part of the kitchen was often darker than the rest, as it was only used for grand events. But it appeared dimmer than normal this time. Nettle felt an odd skin-crawling feeling and pulled Rebecca down behind a counter. "Do you sense anything?" Sadly, Rebecca's clairvoyant abilities didn't work on command—not yet anyway. Rebecca shook her head. Even though she wasn't getting a sending, the concerned frown on her face indicated that she also felt something was off.

The hair on the back of Nettie's neck rose and her fangs partially dropped into place. She forced them back where they belonged, not a good idea to scare the kitchen staff, but paid attention to their warning.

She'd discovered that she did have a bit of her own extrasensory perception. Nothing tangible really, but in times of danger—even if it was a danger that she didn't notice yet—her fangs would drop into place.

There were people speaking in the other part of the kitchen, but too softly to understand the words. There was also a flickering to the nearest electrical lights.

"Stay behind me." She would have preferred to send Rebecca back to her room. Getting her injured before her wedding would be bad form and probably not in keeping with being a maid of honor. However, Rebecca was a modern agent and was now used to the risks. She would have fought being sent away.

They crept forward, staying low, as Nettie led them toward the primary portion of the kitchen. The voices were a little louder, but they were still keeping their words too low for her to understand. She motioned to Rebecca to stay down and remain here, then Nettie crept forward and peered around the higher counter.

The lights were swaying and arcs of electricity bounced between the fixtures. Chef and five of his staff were tied up on the floor. With their backs to her, she couldn't discern if any of them were conscious, but none moved. He might not be an agent, but she knew there was no way that Chef would have held still for an invasion of his kitchen. Not if he were able to fight back.

Seven black hooded and cloaked attackers stood in the center of the room, waiting on something. The lights flickered more and the arcs of electricity moved faster. Then the tallest of the cloaked beings threw back his cloak. Nettie exhaled her breath when she saw him move, whatever was causing the skin-crawling feeling she was experiencing was tied to that person.

But she heard a slight gasp from Rebecca as the form turned.

He was even taller than originally assessed and had the head of a falcon. The body of a man dressed extremely unseasonably for London, with a lot of tan skin showing, but the head was definitely a large falcon. She first thought it was a giant mask, but the mouth moved as it spoke.

Since she was closer now, she could hear the words, but it wasn't as helpful as she'd hoped. The language was Egyptian, but not the modern one she'd learned, there were many archaic words and terms that threw her off. Not to mention, he spoke exceedingly fast.

Rebecca gasped again and Nettie turned to see her struggling with one of the black cloaked individuals. The face wasn't visible, but the knife held at Rebecca's throat was.

The falcon-man shouted a command and the remaining cloaked attackers ran for her.

She'd fight them, this time she didn't control her fangs when they dropped down, but first, she needed to free Rebecca.

Nettie spun and jumped onto the counter, landing closer to the person holding Rebecca. At the same time, Rebecca stomped back on the person's feet, then kicked back against their leg as she dropped out from under their arm, spun, and punched them in the face.

The attacker lunged for Rebecca again, temporarily lifting her off her feet by the throat and shaking her.

Nettie jumped toward them but the attacker moved out of range. Rebecca fought and kicked, but while the creature wailed each time she hit it, it didn't release her. Nettie jumped over another counter, grabbing a massive skillet as she did so. She smacked the thing in the head. Rebecca jumped free, rubbing her throat as the person in the black cloak collapsed. Nettie and Rebecca nodded to each other as the rest of the attackers charged them.

Nettie took on the bulk of them, but who she wanted was the falcon-headed one. He looked alarmingly like the Egyptian god Horus, but she doubted that if an actual god wanted to take over the mansion, or London for that matter, they would have needed assistance.

"Grab their cloaks!" Nettie called as she noticed that all the fighters worked hard to keep their hoods down over their faces. Horus, or whoever he was, didn't appear to be having difficulty no longer being hooded, but the kitchen was still dim.

Rebecca jumped on the back of an attacker and slid off, taking his entire cloak and hood with her.

Nettie almost got grabbed by another one as the creature who had been under the cloak Rebecca tore off became visible. The man before her looked nothing less than a mer-person who'd been left to die in the air. And lived in a cave his entire life prior to that. The creature had giant white eyes and the mouth was almost completely round. It gave a high-pitched scream, and when it couldn't get their cloak back from Rebecca, it dove under a table.

Nettie looked at the lights, there must be a way to stop the flickering and dimming, but she wasn't sure how. Obviously, it was connected to these creatures and full light would hurt them. She didn't have time to find what was wrong with the lights, however.

The main kitchen door burst open, shattering off the doorframe as Caden, Homer, Lisselle, Torlian, and five more agents ran in waving sticks and clubs.

Nettie agreed with their choices of weapons; guns in such close fighting wouldn't be a good idea. She did wonder how they knew to come here so quickly as the door was clearly barricaded from the inside so no one outside of the kitchen would have known what was happening.

The being who appeared as Horus yelled to the remaining cloaked attackers—there were only three still standing—and with a screech like a giant bird of prey, the Egyptian god, and his people, conscious and unconscious, vanished. The lights flicked once more, then returned to normal.

Caden looked around frantically, then ran to Nettie. "Are you hurt? What was that thing? It wore a mask?"

Torlian, Lisselle, and Homer stalked around looking to see if any of the attackers remained, but it appeared they'd all vanished when Horus did.

Two agents remained near the door, and the other three untied Chef and the kitchen staff.

"It wasn't a mask, it somehow appeared to be the Egyptian god Horus." Nettie nodded as Lisselle went to help with Chef and his staff. They all appeared to be groggy, but aside from a few scrapes, were mostly uninjured.

Gaston came over to Nettie. "That wasn't a mask?"

"If it was, then it was a type unlike any I've seen. The beak moved and it looked like a functioning mouth on the inside." Nettie paused. "From what I could see. Perhaps there is an easier understanding of what happened than a god suddenly appearing in our kitchen." It was always best to start with a basic answer, before moving on to the absurd.

"Horus? I didn't see them well before they vanished, but you're certain it was Horus?" Lisselle looked up from treating a shallow cut on Chef's forehead.

"Human body? Huge falcon head?" Rebecca asked as she and Damon stepped forward. "That's what I saw."

Nettie looked over to where two agents were interviewing the kitchen staff. "What did they see?"

Gaston shook his head. "Nothing. From what we could gather, the lights flickered a few times, made a popping sound, then the next thing that any of them knew, they were being woken up by us."

"But they have injuries." Rebecca pointed out. "Wouldn't that mean they fought back?"

Gaston shook his head as he surveyed the battle zone kitchen "Looking closely it appears that they were not treated gently as they were tied up and dragged out of the way. Once that is taken into consideration, their injuries are better explained."

"Horus or not, why would any potentially magic being want to invade this kitchen? Poison everyone? Were they going to serve us in their cloaks?" Nettie was vexed. This attack made no sense and she didn't like things that failed to assume a logical formation.

"That's a good question, but I was coming to Gaston with some information from Zarius when we came down here. He decided to be a bit chattier. This information involves the followers of the god Horus." Lisselle lowered her voice.

Nettie agreed that keeping the fact that it was an ancient Egyptian deity who presumably attacked their kitchen a secret, for now, might be a good idea.

"You'll get whoever was behind this, right?" Chef was up and putting on a new apron. From the look on Lisselle's face, she might like him to go to their secondary medical wing. From the way he pulled down pans and started making dinner, that wasn't happening.

"We will stop them, never fear." Gaston was already heading toward the door. If his agents cleared the kitchen staff, that was enough for him.

Caden and Damon were studying the lights. "These were fine before the attack?"

"Aye. Even when the rest of the mansion went out, these stayed. Then they acted up and that was it. We will be making dinner now." That was as close to an apologetic statement as Nettie had ever heard from Chef. It was also a not-so-subtle hint to get out of his kitchen.

Gaston led his agents out but left two near the door. "I won't fight with him right now, since the lights appear fine at this point, but we need to have all the wiring and connections checked. There could be a short."

"Or something worse," Homer added then shrugged.

"We were all thinking it, I just said it. There's no way to know what's been done at this point."

"Should we be looking into it?" Nettie twisted back toward the kitchen. A small army of agents was rebuilding the door. "If it's a danger?"

"*We*, as an agency, are, but we're going to access the kitchen lighting through the storage corridor." Gaston nodded as three agents armed with tool cases crossed in front of them and down the direction that Nettie and Rebecca went before.

"I guess keeping agents in tonight was a better idea than we thought." Homer nodded to a few older agents as they joined the group heading down the hall.

"I do not like invasions inside my home. And yet, today, there have been multiple ones." Gaston bristled with anger as he led them to his office. A large, well-appointed place that was rarely used, as he preferred the parlor. However, it was the most secure location in the mansion outside of the two dungeon labs. There were about fifteen other agents gathered by the time they went in.

Two dangerous-looking agents, bristling with weapons, one male and one female, appeared out of nowhere when Gaston got the group into his office. "Do not leave this door. If something untoward happens, one of you goes to help, and the other gets us, understood? You don't leave together." Both agents gave a nod and he swung the door shut.

Gaston faced them all with a grim expression. "I hate to say it, but I believe that was the god Horus or the being that once went by that name." He nodded to Lisselle. "It appears the Egyptian deities are alive and coming back to claim their world."

CHAPTER EIGHT

NETTIE LOOKED AROUND THE ROOM, but everyone around her looked as confused as she felt. "Are you certain? I will admit that's what it appeared to be, but it's a bit of a long shot—even for what we normally examine." She frowned. "Although, I do believe I saw the image of Anubis flash on Zarius' face when we were bringing him in."

Lisselle nodded. "He's not Anubis, but his attendant. He warned us that there were people against us with powers. He called them stolen powers but wouldn't say from where. For someone who wants to help us, he's not as helpful as we might like."

"So, Zarius doesn't look like what we see?" Nettie wasn't certain if that made her feel better about him or not. "Those cloaked people who were helping Horus, we saw one without the cloak. It appeared to look like a pale, white, fish out of water. And they couldn't stand the light."

Lisselle and Gaston shared a look, and she spoke. "No, Zarius is as he appears. However, none of the guards or attendants serving the Egyptian deities should look as you described. Those were something else."

"Which means that might not have been Horus," Gaston added.

"With that kind of power?" Rebecca was holding

Damon's hand but still looked ready to fight something. "We saw that falcon-headed man take himself and his people out through thin air. They just vanished. That sounds pretty godlike to me." She had a slight mark on her throat but stated she was fine and wasn't going anywhere until this was resolved. Both Lisselle and Damon continued to glance her way repeatedly.

"I think she's right," Homer said. "I didn't want to, but if Zarius believes there are Egyptian gods capable of roaming around London, then that's what we saw. But we all need to be brought up to speed with all of Lisselle's and Torlian's information gathered from Zarius."

Lisselle glanced at Torlian and when he nodded, she began. "First, as Gaston implied, none of this can go out of this room. Everyone here has been specially selected to be part of this. But I have a feeling the rest of the agents assigned here will need to learn of it sooner rather than later. Zarius is the attendant of Anubis, as we said. He is also a few thousand years old and like his god, was recently awakened. The Egyptian deities never died; they went into stasis deep underneath the Great Pyramids with their closest attendants and guards when their influence began to wane. Their chambers were designed when the pharaohs were building their pyramids, but then the workers were all made to forget they dug them." She paused.

"The reign of the gods was ending and some of them weren't happy about peacefully stepping aside. Horus was one of the good ones, but it is feared that while they were in stasis, some body switching occurred." She looked to Torlian with a frown. "That was a part I didn't understand, but it was something to do with some of the pharaohs and the deities who didn't want to leave. The issues in Egypt are far worse than have been let on, and Zarius believes that the missing Society agents could all be dead at this point. No one has been able to find them and as an attendant, Zarius has access to abilities normal humans do not."

"And Nettie is connected to them." Caden held on to Nettie's hand and spoke softly, but it didn't change the words.

"I still haven't duplicated the bloodwork that Edinburgh reported; they could be wrong," Even as Nettie said it, she felt a lump in her stomach. The odds of Edinburgh being wrong on this were microscopic. Her only hope was if someone in Edinburgh was not what they seemed and had planted false results to discredit her.

Caden squeezed her hand. And everyone else gave her sympathetic looks. Even the agents she didn't know well. Since they were in this small meeting, they'd been read in on everything.

"We'll run a full spectrum blood analysis after this meeting." Gaston looked like he wanted to pat Nettie like a small child who fell and cut her knee. "Never fear, we'll get to the truth of it."

There was some more discussion, mostly of what already occurred with the scarabs, Kilia, and Agent Geyer. Nettie and Rebecca filled everyone in on the full detail of their battle in the kitchen.

Most of the agents took notes and nodded thoughtfully at each new item. One, Agent Folth, held up his hand. "Agent Jones, would you say the creature under the cloak looked male or female?"

Nettie almost said male, in her mind it held a more male stance. But thinking about it, and sharing a look with Rebecca, she shrugged. "I would say both? Maybe neither would suit better. It's odd, but looking back, it had genderless features. Neither male nor female."

Rebecca nodded as well. "I agree. Strong, genderless beings. One was able to hold me up with a single hand."

"They could be thilia," Torlian said. The term was unknown to Nettie but judging by the reactions of

Lisselle, Homer, and Gaston, it was known to some. The other agents appeared to be unfamiliar with the word as well.

"Those were myths. There were no findings to support that they were anything more than a tale to scare young children to keep them from going into the water." Homer's words said he doubted what they were, but his face said otherwise.

"Not necessarily. I think we need to talk to Zarius, again. Now." Gaston didn't wait but ran for the door. The two guards jumped when he flung it open. "Follow us." He led everyone down to the dungeon.

Zarius was lying on the floor of his cell, his neck twisted unnaturally and his eyes wide and staring.

Lisselle reached his cell first and unlocked the door before Gaston could stop her. Her scream brought the rest running.

Zarius sat up, snapped his neck back into place, and grimaced. "That was most uncomfortable."

Lisselle was clearly torn between wanting to run a thorough examination and the fact that he'd appeared dead a moment before. "You...you were dead. I touched your neck, there was no pulse. Are you a vampire?" She rose and moved back toward the open cell door.

Nettie stepped closer. An ancient Egyptian vampire might be a bit much for her to take on, but she was the best suited in this group to deal with one.

"No. But the one with you is ready to rip out my throat if she feels otherwise." Zarius laughed and turned toward Nettie. "Easy, young one, aside from our awkward beginning, I mean none of you harm." He remained sitting on the floor, appearing as comfortable as if he was on a silk carpet, until Lisselle backed completely out of the cell and locked the door.

"This was locked when we got here, who tried to kill

you?" She rattled the lock to confirm it was solid and so was the cell door.

"That is an excellent question." Zarius got off the floor and sat on the bunk. "Whoever it was, they *did* kill me. I just don't remain dead. I stopped counting the times I've been killed eons ago. Alas, I had my back to the door when they came in. And I was dead when they left so I can't confirm whether they unlocked and relocked it, or simply went through it." He stretched his neck a few times. "I hate dying that way. At any rate, since you have brought down a massive entourage, I assume that something of importance has occurred?"

Gaston nodded and told him about the attack, Horus, the beings with him, and the electricity connection. He finally wrapped it up. "We have no idea how they got in, left, or what they were planning to do."

"You believe those things were thilia. The mythical creatures of the Nile who came ashore to feast on humans, but lived in the bottom of the great river." Zarius looked around. "I see it on more than a few faces."

"They aren't real." Homer had no force left in his words, but he was hanging on to his belief.

"Oh, but they were. They were the souls of the damned, changed and released on an unsuspecting population long ago. The ones who created them were destroyed and their creations who survived were put to sleep. I'd say something woke them up."

"But they can be killed, right? I believe that when the one disguised as Horus took them and left, a few were dead." Nettie believed Zarius in that these thilia were real. She didn't like the idea that while their creators were destroyed, they were not.

"They can be killed, but it would take far more than anyone here could accomplish. They don't do well on land or in the light. I'd guess that Horus was trying to destroy the electrical lights completely." He gave a small smile. "He would be woefully ill-prepared for what the lights were and was unable to accomplish his task. I'd say that his goal here might have been to come after me, as I am far weaker here than on Egyptian soil. I believe he was the one who killed me. Before the attack in your kitchen."

Rebecca frowned. "Wouldn't he realize you don't stay dead? If he knows you enough to want you dead, after all."

Zarius smiled. "He should. But as this might not be the true spirit of Horus, or at least the one from a millennia ago. He might have believed that I would be weak enough on this lifeless soil to stay dead."

"England is not lifeless," Damon said defensively. "We are far more fertile than your homeland."

"As it is now, yes. But as it was in my time?" Zarius gave a sad smile. "The beauty would have astounded you. However, the term lifeless in this case refers to far more than plants. There is a force in my homeland that is not found anywhere else. It is what gave rise to our gods and our pharaohs and the greatest kingdom this world has ever seen."

Damon looked ready to again defend Mother England, but Gaston shook him off.

"How do we guard against this Horus person?" Gaston still wanted answers but clearly wasn't certain what help Zarius would be.

Nettie agreed. So far Zarius hadn't done much beyond confirming that the thilia were real, and that a being who might, or might not, truly be the god Horus could go through walls. What they needed was a way to defend against him. Whether that was the original Horus, or something else, it was far too powerful for anyone in this mansion to deal with directly.

"You don't." Zarius shrugged. "The people of this world can't defend against the gods and goddesses of old.

Our pharaohs held some control over them, in the sense of knowing how to avoid being destroyed by wrathful deities. The deities themselves are too powerful. Even the amazing weapons you have created can't fight against beings who can vanish with a thought."

Lisselle frowned inside the cell. "And yet you came here to get help from us? Why bother if the world is doomed?"

"And if they were that powerful, why did the deities' slumber when their followers waned? They can't have gained new ones after being gone for thousands of years." Caden joined in on the glaring. "How could they come back now?"

"Not the entire world is doomed. And being here in England will wear out all of the deities, thilia, and attendants. I'm surprised that the thilias survived here at all—far too cold for them." He looked to Nettie. "And even this country will be safe if the pharaoh's daughter is removed. I came here looking for Lisselle to help the magic users of my land. I did not expect to find the pharaoh's daughter here." He gave a bow in Nettie's general direction.

Nettie turned to look around to see who he was talking about. But the way Lisselle and Gaston watched her confirmed her fears—he was talking about her.

"I'm not a pharaoh's anything, thank you very much. And just where would I go if I were?" She folded her arms tightly and gave him her harshest glower.

He failed to notice. "Back to Egypt. To the land of your distant kin." He tilted his head as he seemed to look through her. "Some of your kin, at any rate, you are a unique child."

A horrific thought came to Nettie. "My mermaid aspects aren't related to those thilia things, are they?" As far as she knew her attributes were strictly the result of being bitten by a sea person while in Wales.

His smile was possibly the first real one she'd seen on him; it changed his appearance from exotic to quite handsome. "Not directly and not in the way you're thinking. The merpeople are not directly related to the thilia. However, it was the merpeople who the gods were trying to recreate when they created the thilia."

"I don't want to move to Egypt. My supposed ancestry aside, I don't like the weather. Or the bugs. Or the asps." Nettie continued to keep her glare on him in the hopes he'd feel a little of her annoyance. Not to mention, she didn't want to look at her friends or fellow agents right now. She wasn't the one who caused these things to attack, but if they were after her then she did have to take some responsibility.

"You wouldn't have to stay forever. Just until we can send everyone back to where they belong. The time of the deities and the pharaohs is long gone. Unfortunately, some don't believe that and have managed to wake up. This world isn't suited for our kind."

"You would go back to sleep as well? Wouldn't you rather live another life?" Caden's tone was more than a little adversarial.

"I would go back to my dreams. I lived hundreds of lifetimes. I don't need more. Anubis feels the same. But unlike Horus, he can't risk leaving Egypt to resolve this." He stretched out on his bunk. "I'm not sure how long I can stay here. But, if you are determined to keep me prisoner, I will wait here until I fade away."

Lisselle watched him, then turned to Gaston. "I believe he tells the truth and might be better able help to us out of that cell, than in it."

Gaston watched Zarius for a few moments, then sighed. "As long as you don't take anyone from this country to Egypt, and promise to help us resolve what is happening, we will let you out."

Zarius didn't move and Nettie wondered if this was a

good idea. He came back from the dead, repeatedly, if he was to be believed. That cell could be their only way of controlling him.

Zarius turned to Nettie and finally nodded. "I agree. I can't stay in this land much longer, but I will take no one against their will." That wasn't exactly what Gaston requested, but close enough for him and he waved to Lisselle to unlock the door again.

Zarius kept his movements slow as he walked through the doorway of the cell. Seeing fifteen pairs of eyes focused on him, he bowed, stepped back into the cell, then put his hand through the wall without problem. "If it makes any of you feel better, I could have left on my own."

Gaston stomped over to glower at him up close. That Gaston needed to tilt his head back to aim his look at the much taller man's face, clearly didn't improve his disposition. "Then why didn't you leave before?"

"Once I realized just who our lady vampire was, I understood the need for building trust between my people and yours. However, if my imprisonment lasted long enough to be a threat to me, I would have been gone before any of you noticed. This invasion by Horus raises the danger level for everyone."

"Before you leave, can you help us defend against Horus and his people?" Gaston asked.

"Why didn't Horus have regular guards in attendance?" Lisselle asked at almost the same time.

"Yes, I can. But you won't hold long with the pharaoh's daughter here. Her blood will call them to her, and I fear Horus is just the first. As for no guards, that is a quandary. And one that cannot be divined on this soil."

Gaston and Lisselle escorted Zarius up the stairs. The rest of the agents followed closely behind.

Nettie stayed with her friends toward the back of the group, as she wasn't certain she was happy with the glances the rest of the agents were shooting her way. She felt guilty about not volunteering to leave for Egypt immediately, but she still questioned the blood situation.

"It *will* be okay," Rebecca said from her left side.

Caden, on her right, took her hand and held it tightly.

Nettie smiled at Rebecca and squeezed Caden's hand. There was plenty she would like to talk about, but not in a crowd of agents.

Lisselle turned back briefly and waited at the top of the stairs for Nettie. "I want to go over a few things with Zarius and Gaston first but meet me in the secondary medical labs in a half-hour. I still intend to run your blood work." She patted Nettie's shoulder. "Don't worry, no one is dragging you to Egypt." Then she caught up with Gaston and Zarius in time to vanish into Gaston's office.

"I'm heading for the parlor before dinner. Care to join?" Homer and Torlian were behind them, and Homer was addressing them.

"I believe that I need to check on Niles. He is doing extremely well, but this has been an exceptionally odd day." Damon squeezed Rebecca's shoulders, then went down the hall toward the kitchen.

"I'm free." Rebecca took Nettie's other hand as they went down the hall. "And I believe Nettie is as well."

There were times that Nettie felt the need to be alone, some were good, some not as much. Rebecca seemed to sense when Nettie was ill-at-ease and endeavored to keep her focused on other things.

"I believe I could do with a bit of tea, then maybe some food once things have settled." Nettie smiled at her friends. She was certain she'd feel much better once Lisselle verified that her blood was not as Edinburgh reported. Ignoring Zarius' confirmation of it was fine in her book. For now, anyway.

They settled in the parlor with both tea and whisky being handed out. Sometimes both to one person. None of the other agents in Gaston's task force chose to join them.

"It's because of me, isn't it?" Nettie sipped her tea and shook her head. Prior to joining the Society, she never maintained many friendships. Being handed around to distant relatives, plus being a bit too bookish and odd, made it work out that way. She'd always been far stronger than others and until the confirmation of being part-vampire was established, she feared hurting people accidentally.

Now she knew what to control. But not having friends for most of her life meant she understood when she was being shut out.

"No, of course not." Caden's smile didn't reach his eyes. Caden was one of those people who made lifelong friends standing in line at the market.

Nettie did wonder sometimes how the two of them ended up together.

Rebecca sighed and shook her head at Caden. "They're simply reacting to what they don't know. Enough of them aren't fully human either, but they aren't as gifted as you. And this Egyptian thing has them rattled. Don't worry, once this settles down, everything will be back to normal."

"That is after you're married." Nettie squeezed her friend's hand. She knew Caden meant well, but in this case, Rebecca was right.

The discussion drifted to the wedding, but Nettie didn't mind talking about the details as much now that she knew Caden didn't want anything big and fancy. It would be in a few days, but Nettie doubted they would have resolved their current crisis by then. Hopefully, the world would be well-behaved enough that it would allow for a few hours of ceremony.

If keeping things from impacting Rebecca's wedding was within her reach, Nettie would make it so.

Caden was talking with Homer and Torlian when Niles came in with two large trunks.

"These were delivered, Ag- er, Torlian. Damon asked if you would come with me and select a room for your stay here." Niles caught himself, but it was odd to have a *former* agent.

"You're staying?" Homer clapped Torlian on the back.

Clearly, Torlian hadn't told anyone. Nettie did hope that Gaston knew.

"Just for a short time. I figured the more help with the Egyptian situation the better." He sighed. "And I realized that I might have seen covelins near my house. Didn't dawn on me at the time, but if someone is targeting the Agency, due to the Egyptian studies we've done in the past, they could include me." He twirled his mustache. "Safety in numbers and all." He rose to his feet and led Niles and the trunks out.

CHAPTER NINE

NETTIE WATCHED HIM GO. "IS he really what he seems? What was he like as an agent?" Torlian came across as not having a care in the world, and not very serious.

Neither description would be used for any agent that she'd met. Even a former one.

Homer took a sip of his whisky but nodded. "Aye. He's as genuinely Torlian as can be. Honestly, he was a bit more focused as an agent but would pull out his devil-may-care card when he felt it would annoy the higher-ups. The fact is, if he didn't care, he would have stayed with the agency. He's a good man and was a good agent." He looked ready to say more, then took another sip of whisky instead.

"I suppose I shall invite him to the wedding, it's only the polite thing to do. I am *not* inviting those dead fish things from the kitchen though." Rebecca folded her arms.

Lisselle laughed as she came into the parlor. "I don't think we'd be inviting them to anything." She turned to Nettie. "We finished early; shall we go see what's in your blood?"

Nettie found herself strangely nervous as she rose. She was willing to face whatever needed to be faced, but she was concerned.

"I'm sure your blood is fine." Caden stepped over to her. "Do you want me to go with you?"

That was the perfect thing for him to say, but not in the way he meant it. Nettie was fiercely independent and he of all people knew that. For him to even ask…she must be letting her concerns show and that was simply not acceptable. She stood taller but refrained from snapping. He meant well.

"Thank you, but I will be fine." She nodded to Homer and Rebecca, then followed Lisselle down to the dungeons. Normally a medical blood draw would be conducted in the medical wing, but Lisselle was leading her to the dungeon labs.

"I thought this might be better than the medical labs." The grin on her face pointed out that she'd picked up on Nettie's ill-ease as well. The dungeons were Nettie's favorite places.

"I'm fine." She took a seat. "We already knew there was something odd and Egyptian about my blood while we were still in Wales. That's all this might be."

"Of course, you're fine. But it can't hurt to be cautious. I know that's not what you were referring to, but it's still valid."

Lisselle turned to get the needle and the world blurred.

Rather, a small section of it blurred and a Runner appeared between Nettie and Lisselle. It looked like a normal, featureless Runner, but it lunged toward Nettie.

Nettie was quick, but not as fast as a Runner. It grabbed her arms as Lisselle turned and threw a spell at it.

Which deflected off of it and slammed into the doorway.

Nettie fought back but a moment later Lisselle and the dungeon were gone.

She still felt the Runner's hands on her arms, but she couldn't move as they seemed to be flying through a dark fog. If it wasn't that it took her completely against her will, and might be bringing her to be locked up, or worse, in Edinburgh, she might have enjoyed the trip. Or at the least been intrigued. Right now, she was simply furious.

Nettie had no idea how long this would take; information on other agents being conscious while traveling via Runner was unheard of. Or rather, she hadn't heard of it. She also was uncertain as to where she would end up. This appeared to be a non-modified Runner, which implied that Edinburgh did send it. However, after the issue with Kilia, the people behind her might have felt that making it look like a normal Runner would be a better idea. So, she could be being taken to the enemy's lair. One of their enemies.

The lights and sounds they burst into were horribly startling after the darkness of wherever the Runners traveled between. And being unceremoniously dropped onto a hard marble floor didn't make things better.

The Runner stepped away from her.

"Thank you for joining us, Nettie Jones. We would have sent an invitation, but we didn't believe you'd agree to come." The voice was unfamiliar.

It took Nettie a few rapid blinks to get her eyes to focus. Next time she traveled via Runner, she would keep them closed. There was nothing to see and the adjustment period once in the light was unacceptable.

The marble floor made her first think she was in Edinburgh, however, the lack of using the title of agent in her name indicated otherwise.

She stayed on the floor as she looked up. Along with her vision, her balance took a beating by that form of travel.

The person speaking to her wasn't anyone she recognized. Short, pale, and a bit round. The people standing in a semi-circle around him were tall, dark, and heavily armed, but they also weren't people she recognized. They all appeared to be in vaguely Egyptian clothing.

"Why have you brought me here?" Asking who they were and where this was would be important questions as well. She doubted they would tell her either.

"The pharaoh's daughter has an important position to take. We are making sure you are where you need to be for the time that is coming." The speaker was extremely English, even down to almost ginger hair and pale blue eyes. If he went into the open desert, he'd most likely burst into flame.

"I am not a daughter of Egypt. My parents were from England."

The speaker dropped down lower and shook his head. "Nettie, might I call you that? We know more about you than your precious agency does. We have looked for you since your mother was discovered long ago. Had she not been a full vampire, we would have used her to call forth the greatest empire. However, your half-vampire status will not cause an issue." He wrinkled his nose. "Nor that unfortunate mermaid contagion."

"First of all, no, you may not use my first name. I go by Agent Jones or even Dr. Jones. Secondly, why could you possibly think I would help you when you've done nothing but attack me?" She would refrain from asking more questions for now—mostly to keep him from sorting out what she did and didn't know. Although, if she asked the right ones, she might get him drawn out in a long monologue. Those were often useful for sorting out a situation. And they were alarmingly common among evil-doers.

"Because this is your destiny. We have waited for the one who would bring us back to our Egyptian glory." He held out his arms and two of his companions brought forth an elaborate beaded robe that should be in a museum somewhere.

Nettie thought about getting to her feet, but her head was still spinning. "You do realize that you are not of Egyptian blood, right?" She knew that as Britain still controlled the country, there were some odd English who determined that they were Egyptian. However, the robe he wore was easily a thousand or more years old. He was speaking of old Egypt.

"But I am. My people followed Seti the First. And we will be the ones to bring back Egyptian dominance to this weak world. After Seti left this plane of existence, we followed Merneptah. It was with the blood of my people that he defended our lands against the invaders."

Both of those were pharaohs, not gods, so that might be an easier issue to deal with. "What do you think I can do?"

"The blood of the pharaohs and their gods has become diluted even in the most devoted followers. With you at my side as my bride, we will take our place and rule this land."

Nettie ignored the bride part, that wouldn't happen. But… "You want to rule England?" She'd figured they were probably in the south; Cardiff or Bath as that was where the Runners were lost. But trying to take over England seemed a bit extreme even for an Egyptian pharaoh.

There were heavy white curtains in the circle of the wall behind her unnamed captor. At his nod, they were pulled back.

Revealing a view of a broad desert and three pyramids in the far distance. There were buildings clustered below them, but none appeared close.

They brought her to Egypt.

Nettie let out her breath slowly and was grateful that she didn't try to stand. Knowing how far and fast Runners could move was an academic endeavor. Going through it was something else entirely.

She'd been concerned about Zarius bringing her here against her will. Apparently, she was focusing on the wrong being.

"I shall be known as Seti. Simply Seti. You shall be my princess and want for nothing. The people will feel who you are and they will be joyous. We shall be immortal."

If she didn't already question the sanity of this man, she would have with the smile that followed his proclamation. Asking him just how he intended to do either of those things, take over Egypt and make them both immortal, wasn't something she wanted to go into.

She was a scientist and needed answers. But she was also an agent of the Society. The first rule when captured, was to get out. Answers would be useless if she remained trapped or was killed.

A slow look around the room, as if in admiration, showed her a dozen weapons on display. The collection of bronze-tipped spears and the curved khopesh, among various axes and smaller swords, was impressive looking, but also incredibly useful for someone trying to escape.

"I see the travel and this news has left you weak." He peered down at her. "I hoped someone with your lineage would have a stronger constitution. But you are still only a woman. We will give you a place to recover before we move forward."

Nettie forced a smile. But if he'd looked closely, he would have noticed that her teeth were clenched as well as her fists. This was an open room, far more so than wherever he was planning on locking her up. She waited until two robed men stepped forward to lift her up. The Runner who brought her in was nowhere in sight, but she knew it, and any others working for this madman, could reappear at any time.

She leaped to her feet, swearing at the idiocy of full skirts, then ran, rolled, and jumped past the attackers to the wall of weapons. They were better secured than she thought, but she was still able to break a khopesh free. Her fangs only partially dropped into place, an annoying situation. But that didn't hinder her faster-than-human speed.

Only to have the weapon torn from her grasp when two Runners appeared out of nowhere. They discarded the curved blade, then each took one of her arms. She struggled out of frustration, not because she felt she could get free. The Runners were made out of metal and it would take more than her wild kicks to make a dent.

"It is good to see there is some spirit." Her captor, she refused to call him Seti even in her head, smiled. "That is admirable, but we can't have you disturbing our plans." He clapped his hands together and human guards came into the room. "Take her to the chamber I prepared, and make certain she cannot get out. We have other concerns to deal with."

Nettie braced herself. If the Runners handed her over to the humans, she might have a chance. Instead, she was picked up and carried by the first Runner, with the second one leading the way. The five new human guards, who did look to be at least partially Egyptian, and were wearing ancient appearing clothing, marched behind them. They each wore unique headdresses and Nettie twisted to see them better.

Then it dawned on her—the pharaoh's bodyguards. Each pharaoh held their own legion to protect them, and this madman was adopting that behavior.

She didn't have time to sort out more when the Runner in front of them swung open a pair of ornate doors, then the one holding her tossed her toward the bed.

They were gone and the doors were shut and locked by the time she scrambled off the massive thing.

Once she adjusted her clothing, Nettie slowly and methodically went around the walls of her prison. This might be larger and more comfortable than the cells back in the mansion, but there was no doubt what it was. She pulled one out of the long pins in her hair and tried to open the door when she got to that wall. She wasn't on Caden's level of lock-picking, but she was fairly practiced.

Alas, the door lock was well prepared against such attacks.

She made it around to the far side without finding so much as a slightly loose board. There wasn't even a window to orient herself with the outside. This was most annoying.

She rubbed her arm where the agency's tracking device was embedded. It should, in theory, give Gaston and Caden a chance to find her. Aside from the fact that the devices grew weaker the further away from Edinburgh that they got. They might find her in a week or so.

Which meant she was left to her own devices at the moment. She stomped back to a chair along the wall, the only place with somewhere to sit that wasn't extremely overfilled, and froze mid-step.

In her investigation of the room, she'd stayed near the walls, looking for anything weak enough to get through. But the step she just took gave a slightly hollow sound. Extremely subtle, it took her four steps across the area to determine that there was something under the loose rug. Or rather, that something was missing from under the floorboards beneath the rug.

A weak section of the wall would have been preferable to a potential crawlspace under the floor, but she would take whatever this was. While not an ancient building, it was clear that a lot of work had been done to make it appear both older and newer than it was. The paint on the walls was thick enough that there might have been a passageway that she missed.

She pulled the rug free and studied the floor. There were elaborate tiles on the floor near the door, but nothing except wood here. Moving aside another rug pointed out the same, but that part of the floor sounded less hollow. Obviously, designing the place to look sumptuous only went so far.

She carefully slid a thin blade out from the folds of her skirt. She'd never needed to use it, or its mate on the other side, as a weapon, but it would come in handy for prying up the wood.

Sadly, it wasn't as quick as she would have liked and she needed to stop twice as she heard heavy feet marching outside her door. But finally, she was able to pry loose the wood.

There was an actual tunnel here. Dusty, and only about four feet wide, but far better than what she'd feared.

She quickly ran back to the bed, ruffled up the covers, put the bolsters in a position similar to a sleeping body, then blew out all of the candles and slipped into the tunnel. It might slow any inquiry of her.

It took a bit of maneuvering to get the wood flooring back in place from the outside and still be able to pull the rug back over it. Not easy, but she made do by creating a hook out of one of her hair pins and was able to pull the rug into place. Satisfied that it would at least slow them down in their attempts to find her, she crept down into a tunnel.

CHAPTER TEN

NETTIE'S EYES WERE BETTER IN the dark than a pure human's but there was still a lot of movement by touch as she moved forward as quickly as possible. She hoped that her ruse of a sleeping body plus the covering of this entrance would slow down any pursuit, but it was always better to be prepared for the worst.

She could stand fully here, but the way grew narrower and she began to wonder if this was a good idea. Not that she had options at the moment. Of course, once she got out, she was in a strange land, with no money, minimal weapons, and no way to contact her friends. Her best bet would be to find a safe place in the village she saw they were in and wait for the tracking device to lead her friends to her.

She paused as she came upon a split in the tunnel. The narrower continuation of the one she was currently in went up, in a hopeful direction. However, the new branch was wider, even if it did appear to tilt downward. She carefully sniffed both. She didn't bring it up often, but her vampire blood did appear to have more advanced abilities than simply strength and vision. There were a few agents of both genders that she needed to avoid as much as possible due to their obsessions with the newest colognes and perfumes. Her increased sense of smell meant the aromas made her eyes water and caused her head to swim.

After giving both tunnels at least three solid and deep sniffs, she chose the new one. It smelled better, but she couldn't define it further than that. After going a few feet into the continuation of the initial tunnel and then stepping backward in her footsteps to the transition junction, that was. Again, it might not stop them from finding her, but it should slow them down.

She also used the bottom of her skirts to wipe away her trail in the new tunnel for at least five minutes.

She pulled out the second slim blade from the folds in her skirt. The first one had taken a bit of a beating in her escape. They were not true knives, but more like wider stays. She froze and flattened against the wall as she heard loud noises crossing over her location. Dirt shifted down, but the ceiling held. A second one crossed over and she realized they must be carts or carriages. She was out of that madman's house and under a road. Lovely, if this led to a way out.

Otherwise, the ceiling didn't seem sturdy enough if more traffic crossed overhead. The downward slope slowly began to rise. That was both good and bad. Good in that she'd rather not be trapped in a deep underground ravine, but bad in that it would bring her closer to the road above. She mustered on but continued to pay close attention to the sounds of vehicles and horses overhead. With any luck, this tunnel only briefly crossed under the road but didn't run under it for long.

Her progress was slow as there was simply no light. If they'd kidnapped with her utility belt she would have had many more options. However, even if she'd started with it, the odds of that madman letting her keep it were slim. Her weapons consisted of the two thin weaponized stays, one now bent, and three more hairpins. Plus, her own vampiric strength.

The sounds of the horses and carriages grew fainter and the tunnel began to go up at a sharper incline. She wasn't sure what this tunnel was originally built as—getting people in or getting them out, but she was grateful to see diffused light up ahead.

Then she scowled at the mass of rocks and debris that blocked her from the exit. Someone either knew of this tunnel and wanted to keep it from being used, or found a nice hole to dump their discarded rocks in. Her scowl grew deeper as she got closer. There appeared to be discarded artifacts from the pyramids as well. Those really should be sifted through before being dumped and judging by the pieces that looked to possibly be important, that hadn't been done.

Wherever this tunnel entrance was, there didn't seem to be people nearby. She had excellent hearing and nothing but the soft calls of distant sheep could be heard. She could easily be back in England in a small village. It was thrilling to think that once she got out of this tunnel, she'd be in Egypt. She'd lied when she said she didn't want to go. While she was far fonder of England's notoriously cranky weather, she was intrigued by Egypt. However, she didn't like the idea of being forced to come here due to some issue with her mother's blood.

For good or bad, she was here now and her excitement level was rising.

Until she reassessed the pile of debris before her. Pulling the wrong items down too early could cause the entire pile to fill the room. She would probably be able to get out in time, but there was a lot of debris.

She couldn't circle to the back of the pile as it was stopped by the walls of the tunnel, but on this side, some far larger pieces appeared to be anchoring the rest from spilling out across the tunnel floor. She nodded to herself and started removing higher pieces while staying clear of the larger bottom ones. Time was important, but she didn't want to muddle things by going too fast and having them crash down. Not to mention that coming up in a field of sheep would be fine, as long as the shepherds weren't nearby. Her best bet would be to stay low, and not be seen until her friends could find her. That would be difficult if rumors spread of a strange Englishwoman climbing out of the ground in a sheep pasture.

A half-hour later, she had cleared enough to get out and the remaining pile should help her to scramble to the top. She waited a few more minutes, listening closely for any sounds of humans.

Even the sheep appeared to have moved on. The rock pile she made to stand on wasn't particularly steady, but it was sufficient to get her close enough to the opening to scramble out. It did take three attempts, as she kept pulling in dirt with her. She finally hoisted herself up and out of the tunnel. The sheep were in the distance and even better, there were no sounds of people.

"I'd stay right there if I were you."

Except for the decidedly Egyptian-accented male voice that came from behind her.

Nettie slowed her breathing and prepared to turn and fight whoever was behind her.

"I have nothing you would want. I fell down the hole." She kept her own London accent neutralized but continued facing forward.

"That hole was full just an hour ago. I don't want to hurt women, especially the English, but I will if I have to. Turn around slowly."

Nettie turned, but there was nothing slow in her movements. Flashing fangs didn't seem a good way to start her interaction with the true Egyptian people, so she forced them to stay retracted. But she tapped into her vampiric speed.

She tackled the man, knocking away the rusty pike he held, and sat on him. "I apologize, but you were pointing that at me and this has been a difficult day." Peering down at him she realized he was younger than she originally believed from his voice. He was taller than her but quite slender. His hands, one of which she'd pinned and the other he held still at her stern look, were scraped and bruised.

Not sheep farmer hands, but digger hands. She scowled at him as if she could sort him out simply by looking closely.

"I promise not to hurt you. But could you please get up?" His smile said he was too polite to say she was hurting him, but she was sitting on his chest and stomach.

"Just recall how quickly I took you to the ground. I do not like to make a habit of such behavior, but I shall if required." She got to her feet and kept an eye on him as she dusted the assorted bits of dirt and debris from her dress.

He got up slowly and gave her a short bow. "I am Darwish, a humble sheepherder."

Nettie folded her arms. He clearly was more than that. And while he was slender, there was corded muscle on him. Her assessment of a relic digger in the pyramids could be incorrect. Or, the damage to his hands might have come from military training.

Even if his clothes were those of a simple farmer.

"I am Nettie. I was with a Cook's group but became lost. Then fell down that hole."

"A tour group visiting this village?" Darwish gave a small smile. "We aren't that close to the pyramids; the tours don't come out this far. We're too small to be of interest."

Nettie gave an equally small smile. "I have become *extremely* lost." They were both aware that the other was lying, but this wasn't the time or place to resolve things. The more time she spent in the open, the better chance that the madman would find her. "I believe I will simply find my way back. Good day. You might wish to fill in that hole better. It's a menace."

She started to turn when he called out something softly. "What did you say?" She debated letting her fangs down to aid in getting away—and to deal with Darwish should he prove to be formally trained.

"The lily is gilded, but the bird is not." He didn't look away but watched her carefully as he repeated the soft words.

The Society created code phrases for those agents undercover. They changed regularly. This was one from almost four weeks ago—but it was a real one.

"The bird is behind the tree but fails to see the leaves. And is very behind on codes." Luckily, she memorized codes and the responses as part of her morning routine. And had an exceptionally good memory.

"Thank all." Darwish looked around nervously. "I've been waiting for reinforcements for weeks. Where are the rest of your agents?" He'd held his calm until he knew who she was with, but the fear was clear on his face now.

"That is an exceptionally good question." Nettie winced. Darwish would be upset to find out she was in need of rescue, not a rescuer. "Is there a safe place to speak? People are looking for me."

He looked at her clothing and frowned. "I know you English don't do things like the rest of us, but that doesn't seem to be a functional outfit for any type of work. Where is your gear?"

Nettie searched the area, she hadn't been outside where she was captured, but if the tunnel was mostly direct, it was one of those large white houses down the road. There was no hue and cry that she could hear, but she'd only been gone less than an hour by her reckoning, so they might not have noticed her escape. Something that wouldn't last long with the Runners at their disposal.

She moved closer to Darwish and dropped her voice.

"I was brought here against my will, by some Englishman who thinks he's a pharaoh. I escaped. He has Runners."

Darwish's dark face paled at the last bit. "I think I know who you mean, we thought he was simply a confused eccentric. But we didn't know Runners were working with him. Do you still have your tracking device?" He started walking back toward the tunnel entrance.

"Yes, I'm hoping my friends will find…" She'd been marching alongside him but stopped. "I blame whatever rattled my head coming here. Those Runners have the ability to track agents." Which made sense with how easily the Runner grabbed her. Also, how Kilia managed to not get caught during her time in the mansion. Those recovered and reassembled Runners from Bath had maintained that ability.

"Very possibly. We had no idea they were here, but it is probably how they've been capturing our agents." He pushed up his left sleeve and showed a thin scar on his bicep. "I removed mine because of the attack on our headquarters. We have to get yours out immediately." He started moving again but stopped at the tunnel. "Before I can take you to my safe house."

"You're going to remove it out here?" Nettie wasn't squeamish but this seemed a bit much. "With what?"

Darwish pulled out a short, curved knife. It was so well hidden; she didn't notice it. Then again, her brain had been rattled significantly as of late.

"It won't be pretty, but I've needed to do this more often in the past few weeks than I'd like to admit. We'll have to drop back down in the hole. There doesn't appear to be anyone watching, but we can't allow anyone to see me carving something out of your arm."

"You fear spies?" Nettie went to the edge of the tunnel.

He dropped down and then helped her descend. "No, gossiping old mothers and fathers."

Nettie thanked her modified wardrobe and her looser

than normal sleeves. A few buttons and her sleeve could be pushed up her arm completely. Darwish was quick and her arm was bandaged in a moment.

Nettie was going to tell him not to bother, the cut was small and her vampire side would quickly stop the blood flow. But, even though they were both agents of the Society, some things should stay on a need-to-know basis until she knew him better.

Darwish took her tracking device and smashed it between two large rocks. "That should do it."

They climbed out of the hole. "Thank you on both counts. How far is your hideout?"

He gave a bit of a wince but shrugged. "Not far and it's not really a hideout. Those of us still free are using the hide-in-plain-sight rule. But you'll be safe. I do want to get something to cover you. Burkas aren't common, but some of the older mothers wear them. Just stoop when we walk through the village."

Nettie nodded and followed him to a small shed. He grabbed a pack and handed her a large pile of black fabric. "It will be too big, but we need to get you inside without being seen. This village isn't a place English tourists visit. They rarely make it past the Great Pyramids."

She slipped it on, even pulling over a piece of thin fabric over her eyes. "Then we definitely don't want word getting out that an Englishwoman has been spotted roaming about." She scowled as her pale hands peeked out from the long sleeves. She folded each hand into the sleeve of the other. "Do I look okay?"

"It'll pass." He started walking a bit slower, assuming a contemplative pace. They turned down a dusty road and came upon rows of small shops and even smaller shacks. "Don't pay attention to anything you hear." He dropped his voice so low, that she barely heard him. Then he threw his shoulders back and spat out some guttural-sounding slang at two men hunched over a table outside a shop.

They retorted in the same tone and language, neither looking up.

Whatever was said was acceptable to Darwish as he picked up speed and ducked down an even narrower alley. He stopped in front of a sad-looking door attached to a battered small shack. He did an odd patting around the door frame, then unlocked the door and motioned for her to follow.

She started to speak, but he shook his head and stayed next to the door after he bolted it with three heavy locks. After a few tense moments—during which she was certain she'd heard footsteps and an odd sniffing outside, he nodded and turned back to her.

"I believe we were followed. However, if they were certain of who we were, they wouldn't have passed by." He lit some lamps and Nettie removed the burka.

"Who were those two you spoke two? Agents?"

"No, hashish dealers. They keep an eye on things and help me. Once they determined that I was not a dealer and wouldn't cut into their business, that is."

Nettie knew different lands held different vices, and hashish wasn't unknown in London, but to see the peddlers of such out in public waiting for customers was startling.

"Thank you for all of your help. I have no way to contact my people though, and your fellow agents are scattered. I need to get back to London quickly."

"I know. And I wish I could help, but if I had a way to reach London or Edinburgh, I would have done so a while ago. All of the Mudger devices were kept hidden and the ones who knew where they were stored have been taken. Out of over one hundred and fifty agents, I only know of ten who are free. I think the captured survivors are being held somewhere. But I'm not even sure who is behind it."

Nettie told him about what happened to her. At first, Darwish thought that perhaps the man who kidnapped her was behind the attack on the agents here. But the scowl on his face grew the more she explained.

"That doesn't sound like someone who would have the ability to take on the Society—adjusted Runners or not."

Nettie watched him for a bit, then took a chance. Either he truly was an agent or he could have already killed her. "Have you heard of the Egyptian deities and their attendants coming back from the dead?"

"Deities? Like who? Ra?" He laughed and went to the small kitchen to fix tea. "That's what the one who grabbed you believed?"

"No, he actually thinks he's the Pharaoh Seti the first. Although he's dropped the first part." She told him of the covelins, the scarabs, Zarius, and Horus. Darwish almost dropped the platter he carried out with tea and food when she mentioned Horus and the thilia.

"Are you certain? How…" he awkwardly sat the tray down and then dropped into his seat. His dark brown eyes were wide. "The thilia were myths, tales to scare children from getting too close to the Nile during flooding. But your description of them is accurate. As for the rest? That is terrifying if true." He held up one hand to stop her protest. "I'm not saying I don't believe what you think you saw, but I am not one to believe in supernatural beings."

"How are you part of the Society? It's what we do?"

"I know. And I am an agent. But most of the things we've dealt with here have been human."

"And no one has seen fit to fill you in on those cases that were not." Nettie shook her head. The Society higher-ups of Egypt might have made their own takeover much easier than it should have been. If they kept vital information about the more unexplained side of what they faced hidden, most of the agents wouldn't have been prepared.

"It's been fine so far." The furrow between his brows indicated he might have reached the same conclusion as she.

"Well, supernatural beings do exist. And I'd planned on holding this off, but here we go." It took a moment, but her fangs dropped into place.

CHAPTER ELEVEN

DARWISH DIDN'T YELL OR JUMP, so that was hopeful. He did, however, pull out his small curved knife and a larger dagger from the back of the couch he sat on. "What foul trickery is this?" His voice was low and dangerous; he might be young, and had been misled on a lot of things the Society came across, but he was prepared to fight.

If Nettie was not half-vampire, he would have been a formidable opponent. "I am half-vampire, on my mother's side. I could kill you even though you are armed and clearly well-trained." She shrugged. "I've also been impacted by a mermaid contagion, for want of a better word. But that is harder to demonstrate unless we want to go to the Nile." She settled back and retracted her fangs. "There is far more to this world, and what the Society takes care of, than they've shown you."

He watched her carefully for a few moments, even after she'd retracted her fangs. "I'd often felt that there was more. But I've only been an agent for a year, maybe they were still testing me before telling me of these things?"

"If so, that was possibly a fatal mistake on their part. And not how things are run in the United Kingdom. Do you now believe me?"

"I don't think that I have a choice. But if the deities and

their attendants are back? Is that who took our agents?" He put away his weapons.

"It's hard to say for certain, but I'd say there are two sides. Anubis and Zarius seem to be on the good side. Horus, or something pretending to be him, is not. Even Zarius wasn't certain what exactly was happening." Nettie took a sip of the tea. Far different from her normal English tea, but she found it enjoyable.

Darwish sipped his tea and shook his head. "But why? Why did this Zarius go to London? Horus? The thilia? None of them would survive well that far from Egypt." He shrugged. "If the old tales are to be believed."

"They were looking for something. I failed to tell you something else about my bloodline, rather, my supposed bloodline. Edinburgh believed my mother ingested the blood of an Egyptian pharaoh at some point in her long existence. And his blood stayed with her and was passed to me. We were unable to prove or deny this, however, as I was taken by the Runner before we could complete the test."

"The pharaoh's daughter?" He laughed. "Now *that* is a myth. I even have the tale in one of my books here."

"That's what they called me, daughter of pharaohs. But, even if I have that blood in my veins, it's not an accurate term." She was being pedantic, but to her it was important.

Darwish got up and looked through the books on a shelf. He turned with a slim volume and handed it to her. "You're welcome to keep this, providing we find a way to get you home and bring in reinforcements to get my people back."

Nettie glanced at the book; a collection of short stories based on ancient tales. She kept it on her lap. Along with more clothing, she would need a bag of some sort if she was to remain here for any length of time. "Now, about this Seti person who has the Runners. What do you know of him? He might or might not be involved with the attacks on the agents here. Honestly, even with the Runner's help, I doubt it. He's focused on the power and majesty of being a pharaoh. Not to mention, he didn't appear terribly bright." The question was if he wasn't the power behind this, but he was part of it, who was behind it?

"We call him King James, he first showed up saying that was who he was. A bit of a local joke, he came here a year ago and took over the house of a suspiciously missing wise man. The Seti affectation is new. He mostly stays inside his compound, although he has been known to march through the streets from time to time."

"A year ago?" Nettie sipped more tea. "That would be about when the group of Runners was destroyed in Bath. There were four of them; not only had they been torn apart, the place they were in was blown up. How were at least two of them saved, rebuilt, and turned to evil?" The Runners were the survivors of a crashed alien ship thousands of years ago. Humanity still hadn't advanced far enough for them to have the technology to get them home, but at least they could function within the Society. And unless the Society did have traitors, others outside of it figured out how to rebuild them. "There is no way that this James person had the skill or intelligence to do any of that. There is clearly someone using him." She refused to call him King James and Seti was also out.

"Those are excellent questions. I knew only a little about the Runners. But considering how much we were not told; I'm surprised that I was even told that small amount."

Nettie nibbled on a biscuit as her stomach growled. It didn't dawn on her until now that she'd been taken before dinner in London, yet it was early afternoon here. "What day is it?"

Darwish didn't pause. "The twenty-fifth."

"Interesting. Either the Runner's travel took longer than what they normally do, or I was actually unconscious when they brought me to Egypt and only thought I was awake when we arrived. I wouldn't recommend that mode of travel, by the way, it is most disturbing. I was taken on the evening of the twenty-third." Which meant that Rebecca and Damon should be getting married tomorrow. She closed her fists tightly.

"What's wrong?"

"I just realized an important non-Society related event that I will be missing." She wasn't going to explain it was a wedding of two agents, and therefore, sort of Society connected. It wasn't relevant to this current case. "I have much to pay back James for. And whoever is pulling his strings." Yes, compared to a life-or-death situation, which might be what these missing Egyptian agents were facing, something like a wedding would be of low importance. But Rebecca was like a sister to her, and Nettie was not happy about this disruption to what should be Rebecca's happiest day.

Nettie shook her head. Ruminating on the injustice of the situation wouldn't help anyone. "How do you contact your other agents?" With her tracking device removed, she had even less of a chance of rescue from the Society. They would simply have to complete it themselves.

"We have a drop spot for coded messages. I have only seen any of them from a distance."

Nettie looked around the small shack. The small, possibly compromised, shack. "Is there someplace that would be better to gather? You said yourself that we might have been followed." She looked down at her dress. "And I'm going to be in need of some other clothing." The burka kept her hidden, but she felt like it also called too much attention. If someone were looking in the area for a missing Englishwoman, seeing a tall woman wearing a full burka might trigger unwelcome interest.

"I can get some other clothes for you, and we can use a plant compound to darken your skin. As for a location? That is going to be more difficult. But I shall see what I can find. What is our plan, Agent Nettie?" He got to his feet and hid the couch dagger in his clothing.

"I'm afraid we will have to see what we can find about that as well." Nettie didn't doubt that between them they could come to a solution, but her mind still felt muddled from the travel. Not to mention that realizing how much time was lost was almost as distracting. She briefly thought of Caden. He wouldn't have dealt with this well. She needed to get back to London soon.

Darwish nodded, and had his hand on the door handle, when the door blew in.

Nettie leaped to her feet, fangs down, and ready to fight. Darwish was stunned and appeared to have a gash on the side of his head, but he was alive. The remains of the door, and a giant whirlwind on it, were keeping him pinned to the floor.

"Who are you?" Nettie yelled over the whirling wind. She'd seen real windstorms before, but they'd never shown the ability to keep a person pinned.

The winds slowed and turned her way. That was more than a little disturbing and she didn't know if her fangs or vampire strength and speed would help her in this case. Defending against sentient whirlwinds had not been in any of her Society courses.

"Nettie?" The voice was splintered as if it were many crammed into one. Then the whirlwind stopped.

Caden, Homer, Lisselle, and Torlian all dropped to the floor. Zarius remained standing on the door. And on Darwish.

"Dervish!" Darwish might not be as injured as she feared as he shoved the door upwards.

Or tried. Along with not remaining dead, Zarius was difficult to move when he didn't want to.

"That's not truly accurate." Zarius stepped off the door and bowed to Nettie. "I'm glad to have found you. Was this one holding you against your will?"

Caden and the others got to their feet but stayed between Nettie and Darwish.

"He helped save me. His name is Darwish and he is an agent of the Society." She retracted her fangs and shook out her arms to release the tension.

"You're okay?" Caden grabbed her and held her tightly. The worry and concern in his face was touching.

She almost pushed him back, but she understood. She might not be as emotional as some on the surface, but she was able to put herself in his place. She would have been terrified if he'd vanished as she did.

"I'm fine." She looked to Zarius. He might have stepped off the door, but he still held a hand over it and Darwish was still pinned. "Darwish is on our side. And he's injured."

Zarius released whatever he was doing to keep the door in place, then removed it. He also reached down to help Darwish up, but Darwish scrambled away from him. Zarius' mode of arrival unnerved him more than Nettie's fangs.

"That's a dervish. They work for the underworld." Darwish drew his dagger as he continued to back away from Zarius.

Zarius stepped away from him and shook his head. "That's a tale that's been twisted. First off, I am Zarius, attendant to Anubis. I am honored to meet one who saved my friend. Secondly, I was the original dervish, as you called me. And I assure you, I do not work for the underworld." His eyes flashed gold and Darwish took a few more steps back until he hit the wall.

"Come now." Lisselle stepped toward both men. "We're all friends here. We found Nettie and one of the missing

Egyptian agents. I think we all need to settle down. And replace the door." She made a good point. There was no one outside that Nettie could see, but that wouldn't last long. Particularly with the explosion of the door.

Zarius dropped the glowing eyes trick and held out his hand. "I do apologize for making an assumption." He flicked his other hand over his shoulder and a door appeared. Not the original one, as it was in bad shape.

Darwish took a deep breath, then with a nod to Nettie, stepped forward and shook Zarius' hand.

"See? All friends," Homer boomed. "I'm Homer, that silently lurking fellow is Torlian, the one with Nettie is her fiancé, Caden, and this is our lovely Lisselle."

Darwish let out a long breath after nodding to each person. "I have to admit, even though Nettie told me of these events, I was still skeptical in my heart. My superiors never let me know of most of the unexplained things. Are you truly a god?" He'd stepped back from Zarius again and was watching him carefully.

"I am no god. I follow Anubis and have abilities that humans do not. But I am no god." He looked around the shack. "Is this the best place for conversation?"

"We were in the process of finding another place, and the few remaining free agents, when you broke down the door." Nettie smiled at her friends. "Which I do appreciate as I know you were trying to rescue me, but I already escaped. How *did* you find me, however?"

Lisselle pointed to Zarius. "He's tricky at finding missing people."

"Only ones I know. I have a temple we can use, as long as no one minds being underground?" Zarius looked around the room.

Darwish frowned. "I don't know of any accessible hidden temples. I grew up here. And hunted for antiquities prior to joining the Society."

Zarius smiled. "I didn't say it was accessible. Fear not,

you will be able to breathe, but you will have to travel my way."

"In the whirlwind? But if there's no other way out..." Caden left the rest of his comment hanging there. No other way out and if something happened to Zarius they could all be trapped.

"Do not fear, I will create another way out once we are there in case something happens to me. Lisselle will have to hold it, as it contains magic."

Darwish's eyes grew wide and he moved away from Lisselle.

She laughed. "It's okay, I am a good witch. A user of heka but only against evil."

Darwish relaxed. "There is a lot to process right now. But, if it means we can save my fellow agents, I will adapt."

Nettie belatedly noticed that all of the others, aside from Zarius, wore a pack on their backs. "Did you happen to bring my bag?"

Both Caden and Lisselle smiled and pointed to the ones they carried.

"Rebecca helped us gather what you'd need. Lisselle and I are carrying them." Caden rubbed her arm. "The wedding is postponed, although Gaston refused to let Rebecca or Damon join us."

Nettie felt both bad and good about that. She didn't want to be the reason for the delay, but she was touched that Rebecca and Damon were willing to hold it off.

"Now, shall we?" Zarius moved closer to the new door. "I believe I hear a large number of feet coming this direction."

"Yes. Oh, wait." Nettie shook her head. "Darwish and I have removed our tracking devices as the Runners are using them to find agents."

Lisselle smiled. "We came to the same conclusion once we confirmed with Edinburgh that they hadn't sent Runners for you. Ours have all been neutralized."

Zarius motioned to all of them. "This will be easier if you're standing closer together. Quickly now."

Nettie and Caden moved close to Zarius—she heard the approaching feet as well. They weren't running, but keeping a good pace. That was a mob of some sort.

Once everyone was where he needed them, Zarius raised his arms and chanted something in a language that Nettie only caught the edge of. The room spun around them, then vanished.

She felt a brief moment of concern, as the dark void they went into was reminiscent of the trip she'd endured with the Runner.

Then they were in a large chamber of some sort. Torches flickered to life almost immediately, but there was no smoke from them. It was sort of like a temple, with massive columns along the walls, but not to any single deity. Every Egyptian god or goddess that she'd heard of was on the walls around them. All the same size, same style.

"I didn't think they all got along? Who built this?" Nettie moved closer to the reliefs, slowly examining each one.

"Many of us did, long ago. It is a chamber of protection, not really a standard temple. I am the only one who has returned who has access to it." Zarius' face fell. "I fear that whatever woke Anubis and I up, did not intend to do so."

"So other deities, ones who don't like humans, could be coming back, but leaving the rest of you in slumber?" Torlian scowled around the chamber. "You failed to mention that back in London."

"Because until I came back here, I wasn't certain. Anubis is currently blocked from me, and that is disturbing. I am safe here, but I fear that I'm too exposed on the surface now. I must stay down here."

Darwish walked around the reliefs, but at a further

distance than Nettie had been. "That's not good. You would be extremely helpful in getting my people back."

"I will try what I can without leaving here." Zarius nodded and a heavy stone table and chairs appeared in the center of the chamber. "I can create most things you will need."

Lisselle took a seat. "Thank you. I believe we need to hear from both Nettie and Darwish as to what has happened. Then go out and try to find the other agents and bring them here." She looked around the chamber. It was large, but adding ten more people, or even more, would make things cramped. "Can you address expanding the space in here?"

Zarius smiled and waved a hand. A hallway opened to his left. Also, with torches and lined with doors. "Yes. I just shouldn't leave."

The rest took their seats as Nettie told them of her trip, losing time, James, and her escape. It seemed far shorter than it felt at the time. "After we hear from Darwish, I would love to bathe and change. Then eat. I still feel dirt from the tunnel on me," Nettie said, once she concluded her tale.

Darwish nodded and quickly gave his story. He didn't have much information. The missing agents, including his superiors, simply vanished without a trace one day when he'd not been in the building. The headquarters for the Society in Egypt was emptied of agents when he came back. Access to the Mudgers was gone, since as a lower agent, he didn't know where they were kept.

Short of taking a boat to Scotland, there was no way for him to contact the Society.

"It was only through chance that I found the few other free agents. There could be more than the ten I know. We weren't hiding really, just not appearing in our usual places, such as our homes. More could be hiding."

Everyone was silent as they processed the information.

Finally, Lisselle turned to Nettie. "I made you a small pack of clothing and necessities, it's tucked inside my larger one. You might wish to go change, as I have a feeling we will be going back out soon."

Torlian nodded. "I agree. There are many threats out there, but we need to get those agents back. I don't like that this James person is fashioning himself as a pharaoh and has access to Runners."

CHAPTER TWELVE

NETTIE EXCUSED HERSELF AS THE rest drew up plans. She would be involved, but right now being ready to return to the fight outside was more important. She found the pack with her clothing and went down the hall.

Each door led to a small room, but they each contained a cot and bathtub. One that filled automatically when she approached. She wasn't going to argue with what was provided, so she quickly bathed and changed. The dress she'd been captured in wouldn't have been something she would wear on a mission, but fortunately, Rebecca picked out some of her more active clothing to put in her pack. The ones with hidden locations for more than just a pair of thin knives.

Her friends were still in full debate when she came back to the main room, but there was now food and tea on the table. Nettie's stomach growled again, but she wanted to take care of things first. "Is my gear in Caden's pack?" Mostly she wanted her utility belt and additional weapons.

Caden broke from the conversation, which appeared to be centered on a map that she hadn't seen before, and handed her a smaller pack. Nettie quickly removed her utility belt, then buckled it around her waist. She exclaimed when she pulled out a pair of goggles from the bag. They were not in her possessions back home, nor had she ever seen them. "These are wonderful." She slipped them on and adjusted the size. The goggles themselves contained various lenses that could be dropped into place. Her normally better-than-average night vision would be well increased by these. "Where did they come from?" Although they might stand out in London, they would be well suited for the dusty climate here.

She loaded a plate with sandwiches and took a cup of tea that Caden poured, then settled in.

"Gaston and I were working on them as a side project before all of this happened." Homer's grin indicated they might have been his idea. "They were to be rolled out next spring, especially for agents in desert areas. Or for those of us on the airships. But we have enough that we each get a pair. Plus, there are a few extra for Darwish and a few other agents once we find them."

Nettie continued to adjust the lenses; they were truly fascinating. "Thank you." She resumed her seat next to Caden and pushed the goggles up on her head. "Do we have a plan of attack?" Now that she had more backup, she wanted to return out there. But there was still a risk of being found by the Runners, even without their tracking devices. "And do we have a way to block being taken by the Runners? There were four missing from the explosion in Bath last year, and while Kilia is disabled, that leaves three possibly in James' hands."

"Ah! Forgot to include that." Homer got up and rummaged through his pack. He came back with a collection of bracelets. "Not as magical as our fair Lisselle, but Torlian, Gaston, and I created these right before Zarius said he'd found you. They scramble the Runners' systems. Now, be aware, they won't stop them from physically grabbing or hurting anyone if they find us on their own. Just that they won't be able to travel the way they normally do with any of us."

Lisselle took hers and snapped it over her wrist. "And, don't forget, that also means that the Edinburgh Runners can't rescue you. Right before we left, Edinburgh was still sorting out sending their Runners, or any agents, here. They wanted to interview Zarius first." She shrugged.

"You all disobeyed Edinburgh?" Nettie looked around the table.

Homer smiled. "Aye, lass. When Zarius said he knew where you were, there wasn't even a discussion."

Nettie was touched. Depending on how serious Edinburgh was about not sending anyone into this situation, her friends all endangered their careers. Aside from Torlian.

He saw her watching him and flashed a smile. "I needed to go along, just to be difficult for Edinburgh. Plus, while I have studied Egypt, I've never actually been here."

Darwish looked around the group. "I want to thank you all for coming here, I was afraid things were hopeless." He wore his bracelet but continued to adjust his goggles.

"I'm just sorry we weren't able to bring more agents." Lisselle shook her head. "It appears that there is a major incursion here, and yet, Edinburgh hasn't sent anyone. There is something bad afoot both here and there."

"But never fear, we will find your other agents. And free the ones who were taken." Homer smiled. "Your outpost didn't have any airships, did it?" Homer was fierce on land as well as the air—but given his choice, he'd take the air anytime. Even if it was in a borrowed airship.

Darwish finished playing with his goggles and looked up. "No. The weather here isn't conducive for them. The winds can be fierce. Not to mention that since our people haven't been using them, Society airships would be extremely noticeable."

"Sorry, my friend." Torlian clapped Homer on the back. "You're grounded like the rest of us."

Nettie studied the map, it appeared quite old, but

from what she could tell it was of this village and the areas immediately surrounding it. "Where did this come from?"

Darwish nodded. "It was mine, or rather, the Society's. I was able to get some of my things out from my former house before I fled."

There was a circle around a larger compound and Zarius tapped it. "This is where Darwish said the person who kidnapped you lives. Over here is where the Society's compound *was*." He pointed to another circle with a slash through it.

"Was?" Nettie looked at Darwish, but his face was still.

"I was able to reach out to the area. I can't go out, but can still do some observations." Zarius looked around. "There is nothing left of it. It is as if a vengeful deity smote it from the very ground it stood upon."

"And I went by there yesterday evening," Darwish said. "I check regularly in case any more agents appeared. The building was fine then."

Even though by his own admission, there was nothing left inside the Society building, the loss of the structure itself was clearly hard for him. Hopefully, no agents sought to hide there when it was destroyed.

"So, I assume that's the first place we'll be going?" Nettie looked around. "Or do we think it's a trap?"

"It could be." Zarius pointed to another section of six smaller scribbled outbuildings on the map. All were between James's compound and the Society building. "Somehow all of these places vanished last night as well."

"Direct line of sight for the one who kidnapped you." Caden kept his focus on the circle where James' compound was. Nettie knew if it were up to him, *that* would be the initial focus of their investigation. However, it would be more of a full attack than an investigation.

Caden was rash at times and didn't often favor patience. Nettie squeezed his shoulder. She appreciated his thought, but they needed to do this carefully. Especially since the consensus was that there were people behind James—powerful ones—that they needed to find. Stopping James would simply slow things down, not remove the problem.

"We will need to break up the group, you will be too noticeable sticking together." Zarius looked them over.

"We could say we're with a Cook's tour? I've heard of them." Torlian appeared to be focusing on committing the map to memory but looked up to give his suggestion.

"I already tried that." Nettie flashed Darwish a smile. "Apparently this village is too far from the pyramids to warrant the tours coming out here."

"I think we need to stay together," Lisselle said. "There are too many unknowns. Correct, some might question a group of English roaming the village. But we could be an academic group touring the outer areas, looking to find the true Egyptians. Darwish could be our guide. Providing he can look extremely put upon and frustrated with us, it might work. I would think most people here don't think highly of the British."

Darwish gave a small smile. "Not really. And you might have a good idea. I'll have to change my clothes. And I can hide the bracelet, but I'm afraid the goggles won't work."

Caden held out his hand. "I can carry them for you. Just make me look even more eccentric. That way, if you need them, they are nearby."

Darwish flashed him a grin and handed them over. Each pair was slightly different, and Caden's were flashier than the more stripped-down style of the pair Darwish had. Caden already wore his own on the top of his head but looped Darwish's pair on his pack.

Zarius surveyed the entire group, then walked around them. "I'd say Lisselle should be your leader; a professor of artifacts from Cambridge would lend a nice weight. Darwish can be your extremely educated tour guide."

"I don't look posh." Darwish almost looked insulted. Judging by his studied appearance, Nettie realized he probably was well off but tried to look otherwise.

"No, you don't, but you sound it. Anytime that you can avoid hiding your real self, is better overall for a solid disguise," Lisselle said.

Zarius nodded. "Agreed. Keep things as simple as you can." He tapped the map and a duplicate appeared. "You should take the copy with you, there are strange magics on the original. And this way I can track you." He waved over the original map and a mark appeared, along with a bunch of tiny ones.

Nettie moved toward the hall. The mark moved as well.

Lisselle gave a low whistle. "I don't suppose that those are tricks you can share?"

Zarius' laugh was rich. "I might be able to teach you a few. I can feel your gift following you. I would ask you to stay while they go out but I fear you be needed out there. I don't have the full pre-cog abilities of some of my cousins, but I have some and I feel that there is danger. But you need to face it." He nodded at something in his head. "I was wrong about you splitting up. This will take all of you."

"Darwish? We should start with your former place of employment." Lisselle pointed to the larger scribbled-out blob on the map. "What roads should we take?"

Darwish pointed out a winding route that wasn't direct. "Even before the warnings, I don't think that we should be on the larger roads. Besides, I am a thorough tour guide, and will show you all the best places." He changed his voice a bit and gave a florid bow.

"Okay, then how do we get back here?" Homer turned to Zarius.

"Ah, that is a very good question. I could possibly be able to pull you back if I pick up on danger, but I might not see everything." He unwound a long, beaded string that had been on the chair next to him, said a few words, and the beads separated. They all hung about five inches above the table. "Each of you take one and hold it in the palm of your hand." Once everyone held their bead, he nodded and raised his hand.

Nettie watched as the beads sunk into her hand and those of her friends. But she didn't feel anything.

"Similar to those tracking devices you had, but not based on technology. Good old-fashioned magic. Simply close your fist and say my name. You'll be transported to this temple. Or at the least, get my attention."

Once everyone nodded, Zarius waved his left hand. There was a flash of light, and then they were on a narrow street.

Homer took a few steps down the lane and then nodded. "Empty. Lead on?" He bowed to Lisselle and Darwish.

Darwish took the lead, with Lisselle next to him as he discussed various obscure areas as they went. Just because no one was in sight, didn't mean it was a good idea to drop their ruse.

They crossed a wider street, but there still weren't many people about. Then they continued down the side street.

Nettie and Caden walked behind Lisselle and Darwish and she listened to their fake conversation with half an ear. Maybe it was Zarius' concerns, but she felt like they were being watched.

"You're awfully jumpy for walking alongside your terribly attractive fiancé," Caden said with a low voice as he smiled.

"Walking with you is always a pleasure. But I almost feel like we're being hunted."

Caden's smile fell. "I don't feel anything, but you do have unique abilities." He raised his voice. "I say, when will we be seeing any artifacts?" As he moved forward, he whispered to Lisselle.

She looked back to Nettie and nodded.

If both she and Lisselle were noticing something, the odds were good that there was something to be noticed.

"I believe we have items of interest coming up. A bit of Roman architecture. The Roman remains were built into another building, but are still visible at the base."

Lisselle nodded and Darwish took them down a narrow alley, then crouched before the base of an extremely old building.

Nettie had seen buildings in England built atop Roman ruins, and these didn't look at all the same. From the way Darwish was focusing on the road behind them, they weren't.

Everyone crowded closer, but Torlian and Homer stayed near the back. Each one carefully watching the alley entrances.

Lisselle pointed to some spot on the wall, as if it were of interest, but kept her voice low. "Nettie and I both feel it, we're being followed by someone. Or something."

"I don't think it's the Runners." Nettie focused on the bricks and nodded as if they were important. "They might not be able to track us, but they could still pop over if they saw us."

"Do we wait? Keep going?" Caden kept his voice low and also managed to appear fascinated by the dusty wall. "I'd prefer to settle this before we go poking around the remains of the Society headquarters. It will be difficult to push that off as an academic exploration."

"Agreed. But I'm not sure what—" Darwish froze as he looked up.

"Are those falcons?" Homer swore as he watched the flying shapes disappear.

"You ran into a being acting as Horus, yes?" Darwish stayed calm, but stood up and carefully dusted his hands on his tunic. Close to where one of his daggers was hidden.

"Yes. It might or might not have been the god himself, but falcons following us is a little suspect." Nettie continued to watch the sky but without drawing attention. There were three bird shapes by the time they'd been noticed. However, none had returned.

"Now, the falcons did more than just represent Horus. They might be on our side?" Darwish's voice was falsely hopeful.

Nettie agreed. The odds weren't in their favor. "I think we should continue with our plans. We have too little information as to what and who is behind this. Just keep a closer eye on the sky than before." That would be more difficult for herself and Lisselle as both held parasols. It would be odd if two English ladies had them and didn't use them in the still bright afternoon sun.

The others looked ready to debate, but a nod from Lisselle stopped that and she turned to Darwish. "Thank you for showing us this. I believe we can continue."

Darwish smiled and the two made their way down the alley. Nettie and Caden stayed directly behind them, with Homer and Torlian drifting a bit behind. They would be the best to spot any airborne visitors. Or anything that might try to sneak up behind them.

The rest of their route, while twisted, and now staying under broad canopies that stretched between buildings wherever possible, was without incident. Nettie didn't want to break their current status by risking whispering to Lisselle, but she didn't have that skin-crawling-being-watched feeling anymore.

She also seriously doubted that normal falcons would have caused such a feeling.

They came out of yet another twisting alley across the street from the deep hole that had once been the Society for the Exploration of the Unexplainables' headquarters. Considering that it was in the middle of town, and extremely noticeable, it was surprising that the few locals walking in the area were studiously ignoring the crumbled building debris and large hole in the ground.

They were also staying as far from it as possible.

Darwish turned to Nettie and the rest and smiled but kept his voice low. "Superstitions are running high. But, as English, you won't be expected to know to stay away from this place. I will act suitably uncomfortable as you demand to see it."

Lisselle flashed him a smile, then turned to Homer. "Since there would be no academic interest here, I believe you boys should take the lead in our exploration."

Homer's grin was quick, but he raised his voice. "I say, what happened here? Looks like something exploded."

Torlian and Caden gave muttering agreements and all three moved forward. Darwish gave a half-hearted attempt to slow them down, then shrugged.

"I would be careful here." But he trailed behind with Lisselle and Nettie.

Nettie had never seen a building destroyed this cleanly. Nothing else around it was touched and there wasn't even much debris. Had it occurred years ago, she'd guess the locals took what they could. But it was doubtful that overnight they would have acted so quickly. Particularly since it appeared that no one wanted to come near it.

"It's as if someone just lifted the entire thing out of the ground." Lisselle frowned as she moved forward. "Someone with a lot of magic. This wasn't done by technology." She rubbed her arms and almost looked ready to be ill. She continued moving forward, but at a slower, and more determined, pace.

Nettie didn't feel ill, but she also wasn't a witch. Granted, her unique paranormal status did grant her some sensing abilities, but in this case, there was no indication of what happened.

Aside from someone being able to remove a rather

large building and the land under it without notice in a heavily populated part of town.

Looking in the direction where the map showed the other missing structures exposed a suspicious gap in the skyline. She knew they should be investigated as well, but going closer to that madman who thought he was a pharaoh wasn't going to be fun. Unless it was to lock him and his renegade Runners up.

"There is nothing left." Caden made his way back as Homer and Torlian continued across the hole. "I've never seen anyone able to do this. It wasn't blown up; it was stolen."

"With magic?" Nettie had been exposed to various forms of magic, but witches and wizards weren't that common even within the Society. The amount of power to do this was terrifying.

Lisselle nodded as she started putting distance between herself and the hole. "Yes. Technology leaves a specific feeling, there's none of that here. Or if there was, it was used in conjunction with magic. Someone has far too much power of any kind."

Darwish stayed close and avoided the hole itself. "I don't think that the one who grabbed Nettie, Seti, James, or whatever he wants to call himself, could do this. There were plenty of studies of him done before our people were taken. It was determined that James was a blowhard with delusions of grandeur, but no real power."

"Did your people know that he controlled some of the Runners?"

Darwish frowned. "No. But it could have happened after we were attacked. Or during it."

"There seemed to be a few layers to that building he is in, beyond what is noticeable from the outside." Nettie now regretted not exploring the areas, but she was focusing on getting out at the time. "Could they be holding the agents there?" She still didn't feel that he was the mastermind behind this, but hiding a hundred or so agents underneath a madman would be good cover.

"There's no way to tell without going inside. And I'd want far more people before we tried that," Homer said as he and Torlian came back. "I think we need to look at the rest of the buildings that were destroyed, find out what they were, and then sort out what it means. Before jumping in." Homer was known for being rash, but clearly, this current event was disturbing him enough to change that.

Darwish studied their surroundings as well as the air above them, but turned back. "Agreed. And I believe we want to do it before it becomes dark. I'm not a magic user nor paranormal, but there is something unfavorable in the air."

Homer nodded. "Aye, good training can enhance the senses. And you'd have an innate feel for what this place should feel like."

"Shall we go on?" Lisselle pitched her voice to be heard, although only a few locals were even within eyesight.

Darwish gave her a bow, then started toward the road that contained the next missing building.

All in all, including the Society building, there were six missing buildings. All were completely removed, none of them impacting their neighbors as they vanished.

And no one was willing to talk about it.

There were even people moving out of neighboring homes, quickly gathering their things, and fleeing to who knew where. They wouldn't talk either.

"That's the place I was held," Nettie said calmly from across the street of the large white compound. It was more like a fortress from this angle than it appeared when Darwish pointed it out to her after her escape.

"Was it always this well-fortified?" Homer stroked his beard in thought as he asked Darwish the question. He was already planning on the best way to break in.

"No. The outer walls and gates are new. The turrets on each corner as well. I wish my people had taken him more seriously."

"There was no way to know, lad. We all have to make calls—" Homer's comment was lost as the building they were standing near blew up.

CHAPTER THIRTEEN

THE BLAST OF SOUND WAS overwhelming and that alone almost flattened Nettie to the ground. Only her supernatural strength kept her partially upright. The rest of her companions weren't as lucky.

Homer helped Lisselle to her feet and the rest got up on their own. Lisselle looked armed with a spell to blast anyone who came near them.

The building that they'd been ten feet away from was completely gone. Like the others that had been taken, there was nothing but a crater where it once stood.

Darwish was pale as he backed away from the hole. "How…no one can do that."

Caden and Torlian ran to where the building had stood. The hole wasn't as deep as the others but it had also happened in the light of day—and right next to them.

Lisselle didn't move away but turned in a slow circle with Homer covering her. Nettie stayed near Darwish and fought to keep her fangs from dropping into place.

Then everything froze. Nettie could still move, but her friends, the locals, and even a stray dog froze completely.

A swirling mist appeared, pulled in tighter, and came to a halt in front of her. At first, she thought it might be Zarius, even though he'd said he needed to stay underground. Then the swirling stopped and an Egyptian goddess, easily seven feet tall, and with the head of a lion stood in front of her—Sekhmet.

"You should not be here. The pharaohs are not to return." The voice was hauntingly soft and not what Nettie would have expected for the goddess of war.

However, she was terrifying.

"I am not of the pharaohs." Nettie let her fangs drop and held out her hand. It took some effort without being in water, but she managed to get the mermaid webbing to appear between her fingers.

"You are of many things. Why have you come?"

"Anubis sent for us." Not a direct truth, but Zarius was with Anubis and he wanted them to help. A chill crawled over her.

"Anubis shouldn't be awake. I am not sure what madness and chaos is ruling this world, but it will be stopped. One way or another." She darted forward and put her ghostly hand through Nettie's head.

Nettie couldn't move. While it was disturbing to have this giant goddess standing there with her hand in her head, it actually didn't feel like anything.

Sekhmet nodded and pulled back her hand. "Tell the right hand of Anubis to resolve these issues. If he cannot do it, I shall." The ground trembled and Sekhmet was gone.

Nettie found her knees buckling as the world returned to normal around her.

Caden grabbed her and she leaned on him for a bit. The being who was pretending to be Horus wasn't terribly frightening. However, Sekhmet chilled Nettie to her bones. There was so much bottled power within her that it was terrifying.

"See here, what's happened?" Lisselle bustled over to them. "Was this from the building?"

"No. Something else happened. Something that only I

was party to." Nettie suddenly felt exposed. "I think we need to go back."

Caden rubbed her arm. "You're freezing."

"It will be dark soon, and I believe we don't want to be out here when night falls." Darwish watched Nettie carefully but didn't say anything about what she might have seen.

"Do we do it all at once?" Torlian held open his hand.

"I want Nettie to go first." Caden continued to support her.

She almost disagreed out of stubbornness, but the fact she still needed him to support her indicated that he was correct. She nodded and closed her palm and called to Zarius in her head. It took a few moments, then she was back in the temple.

Zarius caught her as she started to fall over.

Her friends all arrived quickly as Zarius took her to a divan.

"What happened to her?" He stepped back.

"That's what we'd like to find out," Homer said as he watched Nettie. "Another building vanished, with us right in front of it. Then Nettie went cold and started to collapse. We came back here immediately."

Nettie coughed to clear her throat. "Sekhmet. Right after the building disappeared, everyone around me froze. A whirlwind appeared and then turned into the goddess Sekhmet. At least that's who I believe she was." Nettie told them everything, including the part about the goddess recognizing Nettie as having pharaoh blood, and the bit with her hand in Nettie's head. Then she looked to Zarius. "She's not happy about what's going on and if you and Anubis can't stop whatever is happening, she will."

"That's not good." Darwish dropped into one of the chairs around the table. "She had a violent way of dealing with things."

"She wasn't even doing anything when she was there, but I was terrified." Nettie was starting to feel a bit better, but that was an extremely scary being. Goddess or something else, the terror she created was real.

"I need to speak to Anubis; this is most worrying. And she traveled in a whirlwind? Not common for her." He started to walk away, then turned. "Stay here. But if you must leave, Lisselle can get you out. Take care until my return." He spun, ran toward the wall, then turned to dust, and vanished.

"That's really disturbing. Almost more so than a goddess putting her hand in my head." Nettie took a few long breaths but didn't feel the need to get off the divan yet. That was almost more disturbing than meeting Sekhmet. Or her projection. Nettie had an odd feeling that the lion-headed goddess might not have actually been there.

"We need to know what's bringing them back." Torlian shook his head as he paced. "The idea that the Egyptian deities were real and simply went somewhere else has been hypothesized long before I even joined the Society. But they cut off all studies of it six years ago." He faced Homer. "It was Curchielf. She stopped those studies."

"Now, I know you two didn't get along, but she wasn't that bad."

"Yes, she was," Lisselle answered before Torlian could respond. "She and her group were one of the reasons I refused to stay based in the north. After Torlian quit, I threatened to do the same if they attempted to move me out of London."

"But she retired four years ago," Homer said.

Nettie didn't recognize the name, and judging by the look on Caden's face, neither did he. Of course, he would have been in America four years ago, and she would have been in medical school. But Lisselle's reaction to that woman was telling.

She and Torlian shared a look and Homer watched them both. "She didn't retire? They said she did."

"They created a separate category of agents. Agnes Curchielf was the leader. That was when I decided to leave." Torlian was trying to stay calm, but the twitch in his cheek gave him away.

"So, this person put an end to the deities' research six years ago?" Darwish looked almost as unhappy as Torlian. "I wasn't an agent yet, didn't even know such things existed. But I do recall an incident six years ago. A team of English and Egyptian archeologists were working in the subterranean chambers of the pyramid of Khafre. They vanished without a trace. No collapsing areas, no cave-ins, there was nothing to indicate what happened to them. Six people just gone."

"You think they could have all been agents? Isn't that a long shot?" Caden asked.

Darwish shrugged. "They were supposed to be theological researchers from the Flon Academy. That was the cover for the Society. Maybe it wasn't connected. But I have a feeling it was."

"They could have been. Theological researchers were the people that Edinburgh was reassigning," Torlian said. "I didn't think they were killing them, however."

"I think we need to see this pyramid," Lisselle said.

"It happened six years ago, will there be anything to see?" Darwish was relaxing a bit, but that Sekhmet made an appearance shook him badly.

Lisselle shook her head. "Something is going on in this world and I believe it might have begun here six or seven years ago. The pyramid of Khafre is the one with the unexplored secret lower levels, correct? The ones that are haunted?"

"No one has ever confirmed the hauntings." Darwish nodded slowly. "But yes, those are the ones. But they are completely closed off. No one can go down there now." He paused. "Since the incident with the vanished archeologists."

"This is starting to get weirder." Nettie didn't mind solving problems. That was what the Society did, after all. But that a current issue started six years ago without anyone noticing? That seemed extremely ineffective.

One thing the Society for the Exploration of the Unexplainable was, it was effective. This news was concerning and annoying, to say the least.

"We really should wait for Zarius." Homer looked around the stark main room. "I do hope he gets back soon. I could go for some more food; I only had a single sandwich before."

No sooner had the words left his mouth, than a feast appeared on the table behind them.

"Maybe some ale too?" Homer was already piling up food on a plate when he thought to ask about that. Pitchers of both water and ale, judging by the contents, appeared along with a large teapot with cups and saucers.

"Now that is impressive." Lisselle looked around. "Thank you, Zarius."

"You are welcome. Enjoy." His voice was wispy and faint.

"He sent us this food?" Darwish was the only one holding back.

"I'd say he's got enough magic to have it ready for us. That felt like a spelled response." Lisselle smiled as Homer rose and pulled out her chair. "That doesn't mean that this isn't real, or dangerous," she added as Darwish still appeared hesitant.

Finally, after everyone else began eating—and more importantly, had not died or been turned into something unnatural—Darwish joined them.

"Can Zarius hear us, do you think? Or did he preset the responses to go with this feast?" Homer slowed down on his food and half of his first glass of ale was still sitting there.

Nettie noted that while drinking was common with many agents, they held off when things were dangerous. Caden drank less of his than usual, and Torlian didn't even pour a glass.

"I'm fairly certain it was all automated." Lisselle sipped her cup of tea. "We shouldn't be out and about at night, and we'll need horses for the journey to Giza. But I fear that if Zarius isn't back here by morning, we may have to leave without him."

People pushed themselves away from the table as they finished. Darwish was trying to recall any connections between the missing buildings. But none of them, even the one that vanished right before them, seemed to have any connections to anything.

Eventually, the idea of calling a halt to sleep was made, and everyone went toward their bedrooms. The hallway with the monastic rooms split into a twin hallway, so there were more than enough chambers for everyone.

Caden was twitchy as they all got ready to sleep. "Shouldn't someone stay on guard?"

"Against what?" Lisselle's smile was genuine. "If anyone can find us in here, a guard would be of little purpose. I think right now we need to get enough rest to continue our investigation."

Caden still looked like he wanted to keep watch, but finally nodded and everyone left for their quarters.

Nettie bathed again and got into her nightclothes; she'd have to thank Lisselle once more for packing enough of her things to make her comfortable. She could make do without them, but as there was no way to determine how long they would be out here, it was nice to have some comforts while on this adventure.

The cot wasn't the most comfortable thing, but far better than sleeping on the floor. However, it wasn't the fault of the cot that she couldn't sleep. She felt as if there was something important about Sekhmet's visit that she'd forgotten. Perhaps, something she was made to forget. The amount of power the goddess, or whatever was appearing as her, had, was easily strong enough to hide what she really was after.

But Nettie felt like she'd been given a clue. If Sekhmet could completely obscure what she wanted, and yet Nettie still felt something was there—the logical assumption would be that Sekhmet was testing her.

That was a challenge. Nettie still doubted she was related to the ancient pharaohs, but as she knew little of her mother, aside from her name and that she was a vampire who abandoned her husband and young daughter, she couldn't discount it completely.

If enough evidence pointed toward an unwelcome conclusion, then it appeared it might be the valid one.

Unwelcome or not.

She poured through the events of the past few days, focusing particularly on what occurred since she'd been here. Just pondering things could sometimes stir up the mental connections and she continued hoping that something eventually would come forth. But sleep finally won without her reaching any significant conclusions.

She didn't recall her dreams but awoke to sounds of people yelling and heavy smoke filling her massive bed chamber.

The size of the sumptuous room pointed out that she was, indeed, dreaming. But it was extremely realistic.

Torches illuminated the painted walls and the fabrics on the bed were soft and clean.

"Pharaoh!! We're under attack! We must retreat." The voice came a few minutes before the door burst open and a group of men—pharaoh's bodyguards, if she must guess by their clothing and weapons—came in.

They stood at attention by the bed. "Is there no way

to stop them?" The voice was low and came from her… sort of. She looked down and saw a male torso, but also her own nightclothes. Two bodies sharing the same space. Extremely disturbing.

"They have broken the front gates; the temples have been destroyed. We must leave."

She/he got to their feet and quickly ran down the hallway. There were symbols that Nettie felt she should know, but they flashed by too quickly. Then they stopped at a wall, one with a massive image of the sun god, Aten. The pharaoh she was traveling with spoke a few magical-sounding words, and a secret door slide back.

"Nettie! Wake up!" Lisselle shook her from the side of her bed.

"What? Where am I?" The jump between her dream and waking was harsher than usual.

"In the temple that Zarius set up for us." Lisselle peered closely into her eyes. "Where were you?"

"I was in the body of a pharaoh, one in a lot of trouble. And might have been my ancestor." She frowned. Those words weren't good to say but felt true. Unfortunately. "I think it was Akhenaten."

The room started shaking.

CHAPTER FOURTEEN

LISSELLE GRABBED NETTIE AND TOGETHER they ran out of the chamber and into the main room. Their friends were there, all looking as confused and sleepy as Nettie felt.

"What's happening?" Caden yelled as he went to Nettie's other side.

"I don't know. I just had a nightmare and said Ak… the pharaoh who was in my dream." Akhenaten wasn't the most popular pharaoh after he'd passed…or vanished. There remained contested proof of a missing body in a few secret texts. But the people of Egypt fought against his monotheism after he was gone—to an extreme. It might be odd to think there was a connection between saying his name and an earthquake, but the tremors were fading now. She didn't want to chance bringing them back.

"That wasn't good." Darwish looked around. "I'm not sure we should stay here."

"It could have to do with a name Nettie said." Lisselle patted Nettie's arm. "Or perhaps her dream. I believe we are safer here than out there."

Surprisingly for the amount of shaking, there seemed to be no damage to the chamber.

"I think I'd like to go change before anything else

happens." Nettie looked around. "Has Zarius not come back?"

"Not yet." Homer nodded to all of their sleep clothes. "Changing and getting ready would be good for all of us. We can address what might have occurred when we're above ground again."

Nods all around and everyone went to their rooms. But Darwish held back and followed Nettie. "The name you said, it was of the heretic pharaoh?"

"I believe he has been referred to as that in some texts, yes." She waited for another earthquake, but nothing happened.

"Be careful speaking of him, even in this modern time." Darwish gave a nod, then jogged down to his room.

Nettie changed into traveling clothes; a skirt with pockets and far less bulky than her prior one. There were a pair of trousers in her pack but something nudged at her to put them aside, even though she frowned as she did so. Intuition would be far more helpful if there were logical reasons for it.

She tried to think of what she knew of Akhenaten, but it wasn't much. Nefertiti was one of his wives, and his son, Tutankhamun was far more famous than he. And he introduced monotheism ahead of his time.

The gods and goddesses who appeared to be awakening might not have liked that.

If he were her extreme ancestor, she'd have to be careful. She shook off the ill feelings of that strange nightmare. She was going to see a pyramid. While not as much of a follower of Egyptian artifacts as a large portion of London society, she was intrigued by them. Mostly, the manner in which the pyramids were made. The realization that they would be going to the three pyramids of Giza, and inside one, pushed aside her concern about who might or might not have been her ancestor.

She was only the second one back into the main room, with Lisselle having beat her there.

"I did mean to ask; how did you know to come wake me up? Had I been screaming?"

Lisselle shook her head. "I'm not sure. You didn't scream, but I felt an overwhelming wrongness—focused on you. I wouldn't be so certain that person is your ancestor. There was a feeling of duplicity in the sending I received. I think someone could be trying to trick you." She looked around the room and raised her voice. "It would be nice to have some tea and breakfast, please. And if Zarius can hear this, we need to be leaving soon."

It took slightly longer than dinner had, but tea, water, and a very large array of breakfast items—all British in style and content—appeared on the table.

Nettie and Lisselle helped themselves.

"I have to say, this isn't a bad lifestyle." Nettie buttered a piece of toast. "Granted, we have food prepared for us at the mansion, but we don't have to deal with Chef hovering over us." Chef was an excellent cook, but his disposition left something to be desired.

Caden appeared first, coming to give Nettie a quick kiss on the cheek before gathering food and tea. Then the rest trickled out, dropping their packs near a wall before coming to the table.

"Still no Zarius? It would be handy to know he was at least here waiting for us while we head out." The pile on Homer's plate was double the size of everyone else's.

"I know it's a risk, but I'd be happier if he could come with us." Darwish didn't have the same hesitation about the food he'd shown at dinner, but still looked mildly concerned.

"True, but it would be safer if he can protect us from here. If something is threatening him, he needs to remain hidden." Torlian looked around the room. "Eh, was hoping calling him out might bring him forth."

"Why do you wake me?" Zarius' voice came into the room first, followed by him in a slightly whirlwind status. He stopped and solidified.

"Good to see you're back, we were worried about you." Lisselle smiled.

His brow wrinkled and he rubbed the side of his head. "Had I gone somewhere?"

Lisselle was on her feet immediately and went to him. "You were going to speak to Anubis. About Sekhmet, among other things."

He pulled back. "Sekhmet was here? She shouldn't be awake."

Lisselle glanced over to Nettie and Nettie joined her. She quickly explained what happened.

"And I left. I recall sending you all out. I knew you come back...but nothing after that. I woke up in my room just now."

"Why don't you sit down, you might feel better." Nettie led him to a chair.

"My food system is working, I see. That's nice. But why can't I remember leaving? Or about Sekhmet?"

"Maybe you ran into her?" Nettie shrugged. "That trick she did to me with sticking her invisible hand through my head, could she have done that to you? I don't think she changed anything to me, but she might have."

Sekhmet demanded that Zarius and Anubis solve the current crisis, but from what she'd read, the Egyptian deities could be quite capricious.

Zarius frowned. "She could have done that. She ran by her own codes. Unless Ra told her to do something. I hope *he* hasn't woken up." He went to the divan and sat. "I am going to try to reach Anubis, but only in my mind. Less chance of interference that way."

Lisselle came over. "I will keep an eye on you as well. Please don't smite me if I try to wake you out of your communication."

He nodded and closed his eyes.

Which wasn't very exciting, so everyone else returned to the food, tea, and speculation as to what happened.

"There is too much going on in areas that we can't access. What if Sekhmet, or someone else, took Zarius' memories? What if someone planted that dream in my head? There has to be a way in which to level the playing field, as it were." Nettie realized she was working on her fourth cup of tea, but didn't regret it. Dangerous times called for proper fortification.

Torlian frowned, but then reached for his pack. "There might be. My magic works differently than Lisselle's. But between us, we might be able to protect all of us, including Zarius, from this type of intrusion. My studies of the Egyptian pantheon showed me how difficult they could be. And their pharaohs weren't much better. We need to protect ourselves. I think I can build something..." He faded off as he began to pull wires and other parts out of his bag.

Darwish watched Lisselle and Zarius with concern, and now included Torlian. "You're a wizard? And an agent?"

Torlian looked up from his rummaging. "*Former* agent. But yes, on the wizard portion."

Darwish's eyes got wider. "I didn't know there were former agents. Alive ones, anyway."

Homer shook his head. "I think once this mess is all cleaned up, we need to have Edinburgh look over what the Society leaders here were doing—or not doing."

Zarius yelped, then opened his eyes.

Lisselle raised one hand and was whispering a spell, but he shook her off. "I'm fine. Just a bit startled. Anubis said I did come to see him. And he was now able to replace my lost memories. He couldn't tell for certain who took them, but he is certain it was another deity."

"What game is Sekhmet playing?" Homer paced around the room. That was usually Gaston's standard routine, but as he wasn't here, Homer picked up the behavior. "She visits Nettie to tell her to get Zarius and Anubis to solve the current problem. Then wipes out Zarius' memory when he goes to get help? I assume Anubis isn't happy?"

"Not at all." Zarius did look better now that his missing memories were back—but he was also furious.

"Maybe she was trying to find Anubis." Caden finished his breakfast but looked thoughtful as he pushed away from the table. "Think about it. She couldn't reach Zarius down here, but she got ahold of Nettie. She waited until Zarius was coming back from Anubis then ambushed him." He shrugged. "If you can't get your primary target, you work around people they know."

"And neither Anubis nor I would know, because those would have been memories Anubis couldn't replace." Zarius closed his eyes, nodded a few times, then opened them again. "He agrees and has set the appropriate protections." He turned to Nettie. "He believes that if Sekhmet reappears, she should be treated as an enemy. Until proven otherwise."

Darwish shook his head. "We need more people on our side." He nodded to Zarius. "Ones who aren't forced to hide. The trip to Giza isn't long, but it is in the open desert. Not to mention getting the camels."

Torlian returned to digging through his pack but looked up sharply at Darwish's words. "Camels? I thought we'd get horses."

"They are more noticeable as usually only the well-off of this village ride them. Finding ones to borrow would be difficult. Donkeys would be less so, but they have their own issues. Camels are safe and sturdy. Just don't make them mad."

Torlian muttered under his breath.

"Oh, no. That story was real?" Homer's laugh almost shook the walls. "I thought someone you'd annoyed made it up."

"It was real, and we don't need to talk of it." Torlian dropped a slim rod that he'd been clutching tightly onto the table.

Homer turned to the others. "It involved a traveling circus outside of London, one with a very cranky camel."

"Not. Talking." Torlian folded his arms and looked away.

Lisselle patted his shoulder. "It's not a point we need to hear about. However, I do agree that camels would be better than donkeys. Can you secure them, Darwish?"

Darwish leaned forward, he clearly wanted to hear Torlian's story but got to his feet. "I can get camels for us. Perhaps Homer could join me? Although he is English, his size is intimidating."

Homer's grin cracked through his beard. "I'll stay as silent and looming as possible."

Zarius came closer to the two men. "I will put you near the location of this temple. Above it, actually. We are near the way out toward Giza, and it will be easier to get everyone on their camels there. I assume you will be dealing with Ahmed the Lesser?"

Darwish nodded. "He's the least untrustworthy of them. But if you have been asleep for thousands of years, and hiding, how do you know of him?"

Zarius sighed. "I've been awake for a few weeks, and until recently, didn't have to hide." He pulled out an old-looking gold coin and handed it to Darwish. "Give that old man this, tell him a friend sent you, but don't mention me by name. He'll know. He'll not only be less likely to cheat you, he will stay quiet about the transaction." He shrugged. "For a while at least. But the fewer people who know where you are going at this point, the better."

Darwish nodded and pocketed the coin. Homer stood next to him, and Zarius nodded and sent them both out.

"Was there any information besides watching out for Sekhmet that Anubis gave you?" Lisselle poured herself some more tea.

"Not much. As far as we know, Anubis was woken by accident and none of his allies are awake."

"But what is their plan?" Caden asked first, but Nettie, and it looked like Lisselle and Torlian, all had the same question. Although Torlian went back to the growing mountain of gadgets on the table in front of him.

"I fear as limited as he and I are, we can't see the larger picture. But there are many elements, and that they have now gone beyond Egypt doesn't bode well."

"Did they come to London simply for me?" Nettie doubted that—especially seeing as there were possibly multiple aggressors in this. Horus and his people, Kilia and whoever was controlling her, and whoever sent the scarab-loaded covelins.

"That is an excellent question," Zarius said. "When I first arrived in London, I would have said no. However, there have been many revelations that counter that. Unfortunately, I can't risk exposing myself and possibly Anubis to return there."

Nettie nodded. "I believe when we return from Giza, we should look at that Seti/James person. I feel he had something to do with the missing agents." She didn't relish returning to that compound, even with her friends. But the more she thought about it, the more she believed he was involved. Not the mastermind behind things, but a willing minion. One with re-programmed Runners at his command.

She'd been having a number of hunches as of late. Something the scientist part of her didn't like but felt oddly comforting.

Lisselle gave a small smile and nodded. "I was feeling that same thing. There are many elements at play here, and the missing agents were the first move. That we're aware of."

"And finding more agents would help with everything

else." Torlian shook his head. "We need to be cautious, and we need more people."

Zarius stayed quiet but kept glancing contemplatively between Caden and Nettie. Lisselle and Torlian were sinking into their own debate of getting more people to help with recovering the missing Egyptian agents, while he started putting together something.

Nettie nudged Caden when Zarius finally motioned for them to come over to him.

"Is there a problem, Zarius?" Nettie studied Caden as they walked over, but he appeared fine to her.

"I was going to ask you two that. You are in love, yes?"

Nettie felt her face go red, even though it wasn't by any means a secret. Well, it wasn't common knowledge to most agents, but not really a secret. "Yes, we are engaged." She took Caden's arm in case there was any sort of question. She knew she wasn't the most demonstrative person in the world, and traveling with a large group made that even more apparent. But she did love him.

Caden didn't appear uncomfortable and he patted Nettie's arm. "She has agreed to be my wife, and she can't go back on that now. Bad form and all."

Zarius nodded. "I thought as much, but there is a subtle, yet potentially dangerous tension between you two. It wasn't present when we were in London, or if so, I didn't feel it. But I feel something…hesitant…between you. I'm not asking to pry, but we are facing what could be a battle involving Egyptian gods and goddesses. Anything you have read about their fierceness and capriciousness is still not telling you the truth. None of you can afford a distraction. An unresolved matter of the heart would be a major distraction and could give our enemies power over one or both of you." He gave a pointed look where their arms overlapped.

Nettie didn't release Caden, but she did pull herself up taller. "I will give my life for the Society and what it stands for, but I am not giving up my love. Not to mention, it's not unresolved, we are to be married." Her words were more forceful than she'd intended, but the very implication was horrific.

Zarius' grin was wide and genuine. "That was the opposite of what I was suggesting. I believe the tension radiating between you is in part due to your in love yet still unmarried status. It is a distraction and one you two cannot afford. I watched Caden try to figure out how to swim to Egypt if needed when you were taken from London. A marriage won't absolve that. But it will strengthen your connection. Make you both stronger. That's not the case for all married persons, but it would be for you two."

Caden gave a sharp laugh. "I don't think we have time to go back to London, get married, then come back here and fight assorted Egyptian deities and pharaohs."

"I was thinking that we could have a brief ceremony here. I know you will want to share one with your friends back in London, but I feel that recognizing the love you two have officially will help our cause. I have the power to wed, and have officiated at many ceremonies in the past."

"Ceremonies?" Lisselle came over. "If you two get married without Homer proceeding, he will be crushed. I do think it's a good idea, however. Strengthen bonds, etc."

"By all means, I will stand by and offer my silent blessings to the couple, however. If that would be acceptable." Zarius bowed to them both.

"Ha! I did it!" Torlian shouted from his collection of things on the table. "So sorry, didn't mean to interrupt. But I believe I can block our fair Nettie from beings like Sekhmet, as well as any Runners who might happen to actually see her." He frowned. "Ideally, we all should have them, but I don't know that I have enough gear for more than one or two." He waved his contraption her way. "You do seem to be the focus of many unfavorables."

"It looks like a mismatched pair of…gauntlets?" Nettie wandered closer just out of curiosity. One of the items looked almost like an archer's brace of old, aside from the wires and gizmos attached to it. It was connected with wires to a series of bracelets. "That doesn't look convenient to wear. And what is it supposed to do again?"

"Oh, once I show you how to wear it, it will be easy. In brief, it will block supernatural activity coming at you, but increase any you already have. You should be stronger, faster, do whatever mermaids do better." He paused before adding more. Such as "whatever this pharaoh's daughter did." But it was in his awkward smile. "Now, what is it you were all talking about?"

Before they could fill him in, Nettie still wasn't sure this was the best recourse, but she did love Caden and fully intended to marry him, the timing was just awkward, Homer reappeared.

"We have the camels. Darwish is waiting with them for us up top," Homer said as he opened his hand releasing the spell to bring him below. "The stablemaster was happy for the coin and treated us like kings." He looked around at everyone. "I think I've missed a bit?"

Nettie, Caden, and Lisselle told him about the planned wedding. Torlian grinned at the news that he'd missed, then held up his toy.

"We were only gone a brief time." Homer scowled at the complicated contraption. "Right?"

"Yes, but we have things to do." Lisselle nodded to him. "Are you willing to officiate without your airship? Zarius can do it if not."

"Of course, I can. Nothing against you, Zarius. But I've been waiting for this for a while." He patted his vest pockets until he brought out a well-worn bit of paper.

"I take it we'll do a second ceremony for the London people? Gaston planned on giving the bride away."

Nettie would have said there was no need to give her away like a bit of crockery, but she knew it would mean much to Gaston. "Of course." She looked down at her attire. It was better for climbing through pyramids than being wed. "Will this do?"

Caden spun her toward him. "You look lovely. You have only grown in beauty since that day you tried to kill me." He laughed at her shocked expression and snuck in a kiss. "Shall we?"

Nettie laughed. "Technically, I thought I was defending *you* from a murderer. It wasn't my fault that the interloper looked more like you than you did. But thank you."

Homer held up his paper, then made sure everyone was standing where he wanted them, Zarius stood just behind Homer, with Caden and Nettie in front. Lisselle silently stood next to Nettie, with Torlian standing in support of Caden.

Despite the length of the paper, the service was short. Homer reminded them of the times they'd saved each other's lives and said now they would be forever unified. Then he got to the rings.

"Oh no, we don't have them." Nettie glanced over to the wires behind them, but a ring of wire didn't seem right.

Zarius smiled. "*That* I can help with. Take these with the blessings of my people. There are no spells, magic, or curses attached to them." He put one hand over the other, then removed the top one. Two shimmering golden rings sat there. One larger and heavier, the other thin. Both were wrapped in delicate designs.

Caden smiled and took them both, and handed Nettie the man's ring.

With the exchanging of rings—both fit perfectly—they said their vows and shared a kiss.

Homer beamed like it had been all his doing, and they loaded up their packs and put on their goggles.

Torlian walked over to Nettie with his odd invention. "I think putting it on before we go out would be a good idea."

Nettie took the gauntlet and gave Torlian a questioning eyebrow raise. The Society did like gizmos, but on the whole, Nettie had never seen the need for them outside of the lab.

However, if this odd thing could keep more bad things from happening to her, she was all for it.

"Here, let me show you." Torlian buckled the gauntlet on her left arm, then adjusted a few wheels, ran the wire across her back, and attached the bracelets to her right arm. "There you go!"

Nettie looked down. "How do I know it's working?"

"There is a slight hum…or there will be once I turn it on." Torlian flushed and flicked a tiny switch on the gauntlet.

Nettie heard it immediately. But it was so low that she doubted anyone else could. "It's humming." She turned to Zarius. "I believe that we're ready? Thank you for the rings."

He smiled and a moment later they were surrounded by camels.

CHAPTER FIFTEEN

NETTIE HAD NEVER SEEN A camel in person. Nor, more importantly, smelled one. Even worse, was a group of them and having the increased olfactory senses of a partial vampire.

She was seriously contemplating if walking wouldn't be a better idea.

Homer grinned and walked over to her as she slowly backed away from the large animals. "Don't worry, they're not going to bite."

"But they do smell." She wanted to see the pyramids, both for furthering their investigation as well as for her own knowledge, but the smell was already making her eyes water.

Lisselle pulled out some leaves from her pocket and gave her one. "Rub the oil from it under your nose. With your sensitivity, you'll probably need to repeat it every few hours, but it should help."

The leaf was long and oily and not one that she'd seen before. But she needed to try something and quickly rubbed it under her nose. Then sighed in relief. "Thank you. What is it?"

"Eucalyptus. I have them imported from Australia. They have many medical applications, but when spelled, they can also block odors. Quite handy when dealing with some of the more noxious spell components."

Lisselle handed out the long thin leaves to everyone. Darwish first started to shake her off, then shrugged and took one.

She smiled. "Just hang onto them everyone, they last a while."

There were stepstools to help get on the camels and soon everyone and their packs were ready. All of the camels were dromedary; they only had a single hump, and weren't *that* uncomfortable to sit on. Nettie did wonder how long she would be able to believe that however.

Darwish nodded and headed out.

Riding a camel was far different from riding a horse, and Nettie realized that it was a good thing she wasn't prone to seasickness. Caden looked to be turning a little green but was fighting it down.

"Go with the motion. Relax into it, you'll do much better." Darwish called back. "Torlian, are you all right?"

Nettie glanced back. Torlian's legs were sticking straight out and his facial grimace appeared to be etched in stone.

"No. Is there something stronger than eucalyptus? Preferably with alcohol in it?"

Nettie dearly wanted to know what happened to him with a camel long ago, but wasn't going to push it. Lisselle took pity and rode back to travel alongside him. She handed him a small round stone, most likely spelled.

Caden began to relax as they rode side by side and his stomach became used to the swaying motion. "How are you liking this form of travel, Mrs. Smith?" His grin was broad.

Nettie never thought about taking his last name. Jones was not particularly any more memorable than Smith, but she'd gotten quite used to it over the years. When they were alone, she would point out to him, that professionally, she would still be Dr. Jones. But now wasn't the time.

"It is an adventure. At least I can't say you don't provide entertainment to your bride."

Darwish twisted back and smiled. "You two got married? Very lovely. Congratulations."

"It was complicated, but yes." She smiled. The ring on her finger that joined her engagement ring looked appropriate there. And she supposed that she felt married. Even though she didn't want a big fancy wedding, this was a little underwhelming. However, she hadn't realized that she needed the bond between them supported like this, but she did. It was an odd feeling, but a welcome one. She felt much stronger now.

"Don't worry, we'll have a small, proper, and on an airship, wedding once we get back." Caden's smile calmed her concerns.

Darwish was playing tour guide, primarily to keep up appearances for anyone who did see them, and Nettie began to listen in to him. This part of the village honestly wasn't that impressive, but she could see the open desert not far ahead of them.

She was just about to ask Darwish about a small stature off to the right when the statue moved. And the gizmos that Torlian made for her on her arms began whirling and whistling. However, the high-pitched sound that was getting louder wasn't coming from them.

"Scatter!" She didn't know what or who the statue was, but it was running toward them. And so were coconuts. Rather, weaponized coconuts if the steam pouring from them was any indication, as they flew through the air.

There weren't many locals around, but they all screamed and ran for cover. Nettie and her friends scattered but remained on their camels.

Caden stayed by Nettie's side as she steered her camel out of the line of fire. For beasts with such a bad reputation, all of the camels moved out of the way quickly. They might be cranky, but they were intelligent.

The air chilled and Nettie knew what was about to happen moments before everyone around her, including the camel and Caden, came to a halt. They were frozen in place. Again.

She put her hand on the gauntlet. It was rumbling louder so hopefully that meant it was doing its job.

The statue was of a baboon. A very aggressive one, if the face and teeth were any indication. Unlike everyone else around her, it kept coming.

"I can protect you." The whispered voice came before the image did, but she didn't arrive in a dust storm this time. "There are many forces after you, let me protect you." Sekhmet appeared and reached forward to touch Nettie. Then pulled back as the gauntlet and bracelets decided they didn't like the feline-headed goddess and shot out sparks that struck her. "What have you done?"

"I'd release my friends and take your pet with you." The former baboon statue stopped his charge forward and started to look less alive and more tarnished.

Sekhmet glanced over her shoulder. "That isn't mine. Lazy magic. Look, it's going back." She shook her head as the baboon froze completely. "You couldn't do this before. Take off whatever is allowing this to happen." She folded her arms and waited for Nettie to obey her.

"Why would I do that?" Nettie smiled. "If I can withstand your invasion of my mind, the implication would be that I won't be obeying you either. And once you free my friends, you might want to hide. They know what you did."

Sekhmet tried to hold her glare, then turned and vanished into a scatter of sand. The world started moving normally again.

"How'd you stop that thing?" Homer looked first at the baboon statue and then up to the sky. "No more bombs?"

"Coconuts. Sadly, I didn't stop either. But we had

the first test of Torlian's toys." Nettie raised both wrists. "Sekhmet couldn't fight against them but did claim the baboon wasn't hers. I didn't ask her about the coconuts." As the coconuts dropped to the ground, and were no longer whistling through the air, they *did* look like they'd simply fallen from a tree. But they didn't look that way when they were coming directly at them.

Darwish was watching the street as the locals started coming back out. "We probably want to get away from here. Now."

"I agree." Homer got his camel to move.

"One moment." Lisselle nudged her camel over to the baboon statue and muttered a few words.

Nettie didn't see anything change, but Lisselle nodded after a few moments. "We can go now. Oh, and I'll need a heavy bag." She reached out and the coconut nearest to them hovered in the air. "Hurry, this isn't as easy as it looks."

Homer held open a dark bag and closed it tightly when the coconut was inside.

"Very good. Now we can leave."

Darwish looked around to make sure there would be no other commands, then continued toward the open desert.

"What was the baboon?" Nettie kept her voice down as she rode alongside Lisselle.

"I'm not sure. However, it gave a psychic imprint from the one who created it." She frowned. "It might take a while to sort out the identity, but deities don't leave imprints, which indicates it was someone other than a god or goddess. At least according to the studies." She sighed. "I do wish I could see her once."

"Sekhmet is impressive looking, but also terrifying. I don't like how easily she froze all of you. You didn't notice at all?" Nettie had abilities that others didn't, but magic was foreign to her. She'd been counting on Lisselle more than she'd realized. It was upsetting that neither magic user was able to avoid being frozen. Twice.

"Nothing." Lisselle looked back to Torlian who shook his head. "As far as I could tell the coconuts started heading for us, the baboon statue came alive and charged us. Then they stopped and you were standing there appearing quite concerned."

Nettie raised her arms and jiggled the gauntlet and bracelets. "If Torlian can make more of these, would others be able to see Sekhmet?" She wasn't concerned about Sekhmet getting into her head now, that had been validated. However, she wasn't certain if the blocking would allow others to see the goddess.

"I'd say no." Torlian stiffly jogged his camel closer to them as they hit the open desert. "They should stop her, or any other deity, from getting inside one's head. But this taking people out of time, is more complicated."

Lisselle nodded and Nettie watched both of them closely as her mind processed his words.

"Taking out of time? I thought she just froze everyone else?" Granted, as far as she could tell, everyone in the village was also frozen both times. But still, *time*? This was not expected, nor welcome.

"I'd agree with Torlian. We weren't frozen those two times; you were moved out of normal time. I didn't think of it before when it happened, but I'd agree with it now. There's a quickly fading time disruption around you. One I failed to notice the first time."

"Then why was the baboon able to follow? It kept moving after everyone else froze. Sekhmet insisted that he was lazy magic and not of her doing. So how did it follow her and me out of time?" Finding answers would help shove the fear about being taken out of time into the back of her mind. For the moment, anyway.

"Whoever sent the baboon had access to someone who could also move time. And might have been tracking Sekhmet." Torlian was relaxing as he was given something else to focus on rather than his camel. "The psychic imprint on the statue indicates not a deity, but pushing through time indicates there was one. Someone is working extremely closely with a god or goddess. So closely, they are sharing powers."

Nettie was not pleased. She was extremely aware that the world was not as it appeared, but time shouldn't be allowed to be disturbed. By anyone.

"And the coconuts? They stopped moving when all of you froze. Or rather, it appeared that whatever accelerated them, stopped." Which might be inconclusive either way.

"I want to look at the one we have when we've set camp for the night." Lisselle glanced around and motioned to the land they rode through. "Maybe for now we should enjoy the beauty here. We would never see this anywhere in England. And I fear nothing can be resolved at this time."

Nettie didn't like open ends, but it was true. Riding on camelback didn't give one a chance for scientific exploration. "It is lovely." The sand spread out before them, flat and unending. Or so it looked. Even before Zarius praised the vivid green of the Egypt of long ago, Nettie knew the land was very different thousands of years ago.

But this was what she'd seen in the drawings and sketches in books. And there was still an intense beauty to it.

"Not like home, is it?" Caden's smile was broad.

"I've read that the Americas have wide swaths of deserts."

"They do. I've only been through one once. But, that's not my home anymore."

Nettie hadn't thought about that either. For the most part, she forgot that Caden was an American. He'd fit in so nicely into the English lifestyle. "I never did ask about that—do you want to go back?" Not that she was averse to seeing more of the world, including the United States, but she hadn't given a thought to the issue if Caden wanted to return home permanently.

"Nope. Not that I wouldn't mind showing you some places there sometime. But England, and you, are my home now."

"If you focus your goggles, you can just see the three pyramids of Giza." Darwish lowered his goggles over his eyes and adjusted them as he pointed to the horizon.

Nettie and Caden quickly modified their own. Sure enough, the massive pyramids appeared clearly on the horizon.

Torlian grunted. "Are they as far as they appear? I'm ready to get off this ride now."

Nettie tried not to smile as she turned back to him. She'd only known him a short time but he'd come across as a bit of a dandy. That was certainly not the case now. He was dusty, clearly uncomfortable, and annoyed. His mustache even drooped.

"Can't you just magic something up to make you feel better?" Homer appeared to be thoroughly enjoying his camel ride and also poking at his old friend.

"Play nice and don't give him ideas." Lisselle appeared to be lost in her thoughts but glanced up at Homer's comment. "No. Torlian, do not try to magic anything here. There is an eddy of something across the desert floor. It's tugging at my magic and if you weren't so focused on your seat, you'd notice it too."

Torlian flushed. "You're right. I didn't notice. It is terribly faint. Malicious?"

"I'm not certain. I noticed it a few moments after we came clear of the village. I think just keeping an eye on it should be enough. And no spells."

"How are we going to enter the pyramid if it's been

shut to all?" Nettie motioned around to the group. "We are fairly noticeable."

"We are. But I have a plan." Homer gave a wink.

Lisselle and Homer were the de facto leaders of this exploration—based on their seniority in the Society. But Lisselle shot Homer an odd look and shook her head as they continued to ride.

She didn't, however, say anything.

Darwish continued his tour guide ruse, even though it didn't appear that there were any other people nearby.

Just as Nettie thought that, however, a cloud of dust rose over the horizon. It was coming from the right side, aiming for the trail they were on, not coming from the pyramids. And it was moving quickly.

"Be prepared." Homer frowned at the dust. "Aside from it probably not being a deity, as they seem to just appear, we could be facing anything."

Caden pulled out his gun, something he rarely did. Homer and Torlian held pistols as well.

Lisselle sighed and shook her head. "You know, whoever they are, they might *become* hostile with all of those weapons. Darwish, please bring us to a halt and continue your ruse of being our guide."

Nettie didn't have weapons, aside from her teeth, speed, and strength. But she forced a slight, fang-free, smile as the riders came to them.

There were eight of them on horses. Six Englishmen, judging by their attire and extremely red faces, and two Egyptian guides.

"I say! Are you heading to Giza?" The closest Englishman, about as tall as Gaston, but twice as wide, rode forward. Then he saw Nettie and Lisselle. "I do apologize." He removed his hat and gave a bow from his horse. "I wasn't expecting the fairer ones to be out here. It's a dangerous place." He frowned sharply at the men in their group.

"I assure you, the decision to come out here was made by all of us." Lisselle rode forward. "I am Professor Lisselle Hope, of Cambridge. My esteemed colleagues and I are conducting studies of the Giza pyramids."

Nettie kept her face neutral. That wasn't Lisselle's last name. She could actually be a Cambridge professor though. Many older agents in the Society joined with varied backgrounds. But if not, she certainly had enough knowledge to play the part.

Providing the men before them weren't from Cambridge themselves.

"Ah, I see. I am Sir Fredrick Clowel of Birmingham. A man of commerce." He schooled his face to appear humble, but the Sir portion removed that. He might be a businessman but he didn't get his hands dirty.

The other five Englishmen were similarly introduced, and obviously from the same social tier.

Homer introduced himself as Professor Tarl also from Cambridge, Darwish as their guide, and none of the rest.

Nettie noted that the other guides had not been introduced.

Sir Clowel waited for the rest of the introductions to follow, then gave a forced smile when Homer closed his mouth. "It is lovely to meet all of you. We got slightly misdirected on our way to Giza, might we all ride together?"

Nettie watched the two unnamed guides as he spoke. Both frowned and looked away. It could be an embarrassment at getting lost—or something else.

There was no way to avoid riding with them once they asked. Unless Homer and Lisselle decided to go back to the village.

The pause was heavy, but then Lisselle broke it with a tight smile and a nod. "I believe that would be acceptable, what say the rest of you?" She turned away from the newcomers and gave a small nod.

Nettie, Caden, and Torlian murmured in agreement.

"As long as you understand that we will keep mostly to ourselves. The world of academic spies is fierce and we are investigating new theories." Homer's smile was less friendly than before and he still hadn't put away his pistol.

CHAPTER SIXTEEN

"GUNS ARE REQUIRED FOR ACADEMIC endeavors? Yet you bring women to a hostile land? You are interesting people indeed." If Clowel was offended at the sight of guns, or of the subtle implication that he and his companions were little more than academic spies, he gave no indication.

"We have our calling," Lisselle said. "Now, if your guides would like to take the lead, we shall travel with you." She wasn't as hostile as Homer, but she clearly wasn't pleased.

She did however come across as a professor no one would want to mess with.

Clowel shrugged and shouted at their two guides to lead the way.

Nettie continued to watch them closely. There was something odd about the entire group and odd was showing to be dangerous as of late.

The horses moved quickly but Darwish kept his camel's pace the same as before. Horses would win a race against camels—at least a shorter one and not in the open desert. However, even Nettie knew that if they kept that pace for too long, the horses ahead of them would be in trouble.

"Now what?" Homer kept his voice low as the others pulled ahead. "My plans for a distraction to let us slip inside the Khafre pyramid won't work if we have a collection of watchers."

"They aren't what they are pretending to be either." Torlian relaxed further on his camel and like the other two, finally put away his weapon. But he was watching the horse riders with narrowed eyes. At least they appeared narrowed, like the rest, he was still wearing his goggles.

"There is something wrong with those guides too." Darwish kept close by. "I won't know more until they speak, but they have the look of people far to the south and east. If you are hiring local people to lead you, they should be actually local."

"And I don't think they like the ones they're guiding. Or at least not the leader." Nettie shook her head as the horse riders increased their distance. "They weren't happy about joining us either."

"How do we get away from them? We need to get into Khafre, right?" Caden asked.

"I'm afraid that for the moment, we can't. I think we should keep all of our apparent interest on the Great Pyramid of Giza, nothing about Khafre," Lisselle said. "And we should probably at least augment our speed a bit."

Darwish nodded and they increased pace. Not enough to catch up to the horses, unless their riders realized their mistake and slowed down, but enough to make it look like they weren't avoiding them.

"Times like this, I miss having Gaston along. He would have put that man in his place." Homer shook his head. "I wish he and the others were here."

Torlian laughed. "The great Homer backing down? You held your own."

"I just meant that I'm not comfortable with the upper tiers of society." The emphasis he put on the words, "upper tiers" indicated he felt they were anything but.

Lisselle gave Homer an understanding smile. "You did fine. And I'm sure there will be something to beat up or smash quite soon."

He gave a deep sigh. "I do hope so."

Their arrival at the pyramids and the Sphinx was both more impressive and less so than Nettie had expected. Sketches and drawings of them didn't do them justice and even though they were now battered. In her mind, she could imagine what they looked like when new.

She scowled at the horsemen ahead of them. They'd faced deities, Runners, and threats from beyond, yet this group of six wealthy Englishmen was more of an annoyance than any of those.

"They are majestic." She forced herself to look away from the men and take in the majesty around them.

Sir Clowel and his group turned toward the Great Pyramid. Much to the concern of a group of dusty archeologists who were heading that way themselves.

The latter came from a simplistic camp made of a few ragged pieces of fabric stretched to form a crude cover from the sun and most likely had recently broken for lunch. No expensive clothing here, rolled up shirtsleeves and open collars were standard.

A discussion started between the two groups that quickly turned into a yelling match.

Homer brought their group to a halt and grinned. "This might work." He looked around but the Egyptian diggers were all watching the show—and not them. "We need to leave our camels near the third pyramid, then sneak back. Darwish has a map that shows a secret entrance to Khafre. If any of those people see our camels they'll believe we snuck into Menkaure."

Nettie found herself watching the Sphinx with a wistful look. "Maybe we could go over after we searched what we can." The Sphinx wasn't far, but still, they needed to stay on focus. What happened to those missing agents six years ago could give them a starting point to unravel what was going on now and what happened to the current missing agents. Her curiosity would have to wait. Being this close was vexing, however.

"Come this way." Homer got off his camel and led the animal away from the escalating altercation. Darwish, Torlian, and Caden did the same. Lisselle and Nettie stayed on their camels for now. It was easier than getting off quickly. Not to mention it might cause more attention to have the two women disembarking.

Caden and Homer quickly helped Nettie and Lisselle off their camels once there were out of sight from the other two groups.

"They're going to figure it out when they can't find us in this pyramid." Lisselle pointed to the pyramid that they were securing their camels near.

"They might not." Darwish blushed a bit. "I told Homer, but meant to tell you all, I heard gossip that the Americans who was working on this one left on a steamer two days ago. It was sudden and no one else has taken the contract."

Lisselle laughed at Homer's expression. "You and your secrets. Don't worry, Darwish. Homer could have told us also. One of you lead on please." She loaded a small pack on her back while Nettie checked that all of her items were secure on her utility belt.

People might have given her some laughter when she first put this utility belt together. But as her experiences over the past year had shown, being prepared was essential. She studiously ignored the slight jingling sounds she made as she walked.

Darwish took the lead with Homer close behind. They all moved quickly as the shouting on the other side of the pyramid began quieting down.

Nettie didn't blame the archeologists at all for not wanting Sir Clowel and his people inside their pyramid. She certainly wouldn't. She'd heard of people like them. They ransacked ruins to find treasures, leaving broken relics and shattered art in their wake. She might only currently be pretending to be an academic, but she agreed with them that no relic was valueless simply because it wasn't made of gold.

The entrance Darwish and Homer led them to was little more than a crack in the massive stones. A longish one, but still far too thin for even a slip of paper to get in.

Until Homer tapped in the center three times and once in the upper right corner.

The stone slowly slid away about a foot, revealing a dark passage.

"How did that…how did you…" Lisselle gave up and shook her head. Then she turned on one of the powered lights created by the Society. "Well, lead on. Unless you want others to see your secret entrance?"

The lights were solid tubes with a pair of batteries that gave forth a decent light. They were calling them flashlights, although Nettie wasn't certain that was the best description. She did agree that they were handy.

Nettie shared a look with Caden and put her hand over her mouth to cover her mirth. That was as close to actually being peeved as she'd heard from Lisselle in a while. Directed at Homer, no less.

He had the decency to hang his head a bit, but then quickly entered the passage.

Darwish stayed at the end and closed the entrance behind them.

"How are we going to get out?" Caden wasn't the fondest of closed-in places but Nettie agreed with him that some concern was justified here.

"It will respond to the knock from inside as well. Three sharp raps in the middle, and one in the left. From this side. Right from outside." Homer also lit his flashlight as he nodded to Lisselle, while still avoiding her glare. "Yes, I understand that we'll be talking about all of this another time."

Torlian barked out a laugh, but a sharp look from Lisselle made him swallow the rest.

Homer continued.

Nettie's eyes took a moment to adjust to the light thrown by the flashlights, but once they did, her superior vision let her see the detail in this tunnel. It might be a secret passageway of sorts, but someone had taken the time to leave markings along the way. Not real hieroglyphics, but old enough to have come from the same period.

There wasn't time now, but Nettie hoped to have a chance to come back and study them.

They traveled for at least half an hour, although it was difficult to judge time down here. But all they saw was more tunnel. It seemed solid enough, but she knew Caden was not enjoying this. Just as she was about to suggest that he go back to guard their camels, the passage opened up into a massive chamber.

Everyone raised their lights as high as possible, but the ceiling remained lost in darkness.

"Bother." Lisselle held her free hand out, palm down. "I don't feel the odd magic that was across the sands on the way here—but I'm wary to try any magic here. Zarius said the magic of the land was being stolen or drained and this doesn't feel like the area to test it in."

Torlian did the same holding of his hand out and finally shook his head. "I didn't notice the disturbance outside until you mentioned it. But I don't feel anything inside here." He moved closer to Lisselle. "I can stand guard, and if something weird happens, I'll cut off your magic."

She nodded and said a soft spell. Bright lights, no larger than a small rock, appeared before her and zipped above everyone.

The effect was dramatic. They were in an elaborate chamber of some kind. One that extended up at least a hundred feet and was covered in detailed markings.

Caden whistled. "We might be the first people to see this in thousands of years."

"Or not." Darwish went to the closest wall and bent to pick up something. He held it up. A pair of rusted glasses with their lenses cracked. "I believe our missing people came this way six years ago."

CHAPTER SEVENTEEN

TORLIAN GOT TO HIM FIRST and gently took the glasses when Darwish handed them over. "These are definitely English-made. And easily look to be about the right age."

Caden walked along the wall. "Do we leave or go on?" Judging by the way he kept walking slowly but didn't drop down to pick up anything, he wasn't finding much.

"If they were kept here, I would believe that there would be more debris. Even after six years." Since the pyramid was locked up not long after the agents vanished, any evidence should still be around. Nettie also moved to the wall, walking in the opposite direction as Caden as she looked for the slightest clue. "Unless of course, this was just a throughway to wherever they were held."

"I hate to speculate since there is no current way to prove or disprove it, but it appears that there might be blood on the frame of the glasses." Torlian called up a small magic light and focused it on the metal.

"We suspected they were dead. Unless they were taken somewhere else and held prisoner for the past six years. I just didn't believe we'd find evidence so quickly." Lisselle shook her head as she looked around the room.

Caden finished his walk and returned to where Darwish found the broken glasses. "Nettie, do you have a collapsible shovel on your belt? I left mine on my camel."

Nettie nodded and removed the small folding spade from her utility belt. It wouldn't do much for a serious dig but in a situation requiring finesse and light digging, it worked.

She handed it to him, then kneeled next to where he was digging. "You think there's more here than just that poor soul's eyewear?"

His handsome face was grim. "I think so. Can't explain why, but I have a hunch." He began digging. Most of the immediate area around them was loose dirt, another support for his theory. The majority of the rest of the floor was packed solid.

Nettie trusted Caden's hunches, as he called them. He might not be a nonhuman with *other* abilities, but he had been around enough to pick up weirdness when it made itself known.

She sucked in her breath as he was proven right again as he lifted something from the dirt. The thing was brownish, more from the dirt than age, but it was a finger bone.

"There appear to be a few more, but then the ground is solid again."

"They cut off his fingers?" Darwish's eyes went wide.

"That would be my guess." Nettie looked into the hole and gently removed a second piece of bone. This one didn't end in a joint but was sliced through.

"They tortured them. Someone, or something, knew they were agents and felt they knew information they wanted." Homer peered down at the hole but didn't come closer. "If those agents were taken simply to keep them quiet, torture wouldn't have been used."

"Agreed." Caden dropped the bone back into the hole and held out his hand for the one Nettie held. Her first instinct would have been to keep it for examination. But Caden was right. They didn't know where the rest of him was, but part of him should be allowed to rest in peace. She handed him the bone, and he covered it back up.

Torlian kept the glasses, however, and carefully wrapped them in a handkerchief and secured them inside his vest.

Lisselle called back most of her witchlights and dimmed them, then motioned for the remaining ones to follow her. "I'd say we should go further in. We need to see if anything more can be found."

With a grim nod, Darwish crossed the room and took the left tunnel. "Agreed, even if they are all dead, we should find out what became of them."

Not much was known about the attack on the agents six years ago. The official story Darwish heard, when he'd continued to ask, was that the six agents became lost while on exploration in the tunnels and were simply never found. There were many tunnel collapses at the time and that was what was blamed for the deaths. It wasn't reported to Edinburgh, or if so, it was kept quiet.

None of the older English agents were aware of it before.

Nettie felt an odd sensation as they descended the tunnel. This one was larger than the one they'd come in on but felt more constrictive. Caden moved closer to her and she heard his heart rate increase.

That was not a good thing. Rather, two not good things. Caden becoming more stressed about being underground was bad. And she could normally only hear heartbeats like this when she was in her vampire mode.

Her fangs hadn't dropped, and no red film was across her eyes. But she felt off. A master vampire had once taken her over, forcing her to change against her will. He'd also tried to get her to kill Caden as her first sign of loyalty.

She hadn't, obviously, and managed to fight free of the master vampire's powers.

However, she would never forget how being completely

under another person's control felt. This wasn't exactly the same, but close enough to warrant questioning. And preparation in case an attack of that sort came.

The groaning sound echoing in the dim recesses of the tunnel distracted her from those concerns.

"What's that?" Darwish was in the lead, but not by much as he'd slowed down the further they got into the tunnel.

"Maybe breakfast didn't agree with one of us?" Torlian shrugged.

Lisselle elevated her witchlights higher and raised her voice as well. "It sounds as if someone is trying to do a bad ghost impersonation. I have heard ghosts before, whoever you are. And they do not sound a thing like that. Stop mucking about and show yourselves."

Caden, Torlian, and Homer all unholstered their guns. Using such things while attempting to sneak around an off-limits pyramid wasn't the brightest thing, but Nettie agreed that they might be needed in this case.

Unlike Lisselle, Nettie had never heard a ghost that she knew of. And the odds were great that whoever was making that noise were flesh and blood.

The ghost-like wails stopped, then started up again. They were ahead of them. As there were only two options, forward or back, Darwish nodded and continued going. Unlike the Englishmen, he didn't carry a gun, but his dagger was out and raised as they went.

The ghosts apparently didn't like that whatever warning they were giving was being ignored and the wails changed to words. Ancient Egyptian words, if what Nettie was hearing was correct. They would have been more impressive if they hadn't sounded hesitant and unsure.

"If one is going to be haunting others, one really should take more care with their presentation." Nettie also raised her voice. "Are you reading from a printed script? I do believe your pronunciation is wrong."

The words responded by getting louder, but not better.

"I think you already said that." Caden joined in.

Darwish motioned to keep walking and everyone nodded.

Nettie was disappointed in a way; a real Egyptian ghost might have been intriguing. And considering their current situation, they could be imminently helpful if they weren't evil. Zarius didn't count as a ghost, as he was alive in his own way.

The fumbling and chanted words finally stopped as they came to another chamber. Unlike the prior one, this one appeared to be full of debris. Both from the crumbling of the room itself as well as things left behind by tomb robbers far long in their own graves.

"A sarcophagus? Just left in shambles like last week's rubbish?" Torlian darted to the side where a large shape sat. Even before Lisselle's light drifted down to it, it was clear that the wood had been lacquered well. Before it had been hacked apart.

"Why do they tear it apart? Once they got it open, and did whatever they wanted with the mummy, they could have simply left it intact." Caden walked over. He was far more interested in the here and now, but it was difficult not to be intrigued with a few thousand-year-old sarcophagus in front of them.

"There were sometimes jewels or other small items of value hidden in the sarcophagi. So, the robbers would take them apart." Torlian continued to delicately lift pieces of wood up and examine them.

"And they might have been vexed when nothing of value was there." Homer hadn't gone closer but he knew thieves.

Torlian sighed. "Too bad those thieves probably did this a thousand years ago. There are a lot of collectors in

England who would pay extremely well for an intact and highly ornate sarcophagus. Maybe when this is over, I can start making and selling replicas."

Homer laughed. "And will you tell them they aren't the real thing?"

Torlian folded his arms and looked insulted. "As if I would admit any such thing to agents of the Society."

Further discussion was cut off as the ground gave a sharp jolt.

Nettie and Homer maintained their balance the best—she due to her uncommon nature and he due to years spent on not-always-trustworthy airships. The rest recovered immediately, however.

"There have been a few of those. Can they be following us?" Caden walked away from the sarcophagus and watched the tunnel they'd just come down. He also moved closer to the wall. The problem with being in a large room like this was determining which might be deadlier if more shakes came—being in the center if the roof collapsed or being along the wall if it fell.

Normally, Nettie wouldn't have given it a second thought. Earthquakes didn't follow people. However, stranger things had happened. And the jolts had all felt extremely focused. She joined Caden along the wall.

"I don't think we can leave anything to chance." Lisselle remained near the center but bent down and put her hand flat on the ground. "Torlian? Tell me what you sense?"

He didn't question her, just dropped into the same position as her. "There's something underneath us. Something with power, but not…" He tilted his head. "Not conscious? They're magical or a stronger magic user. But they feel distant. Like they're asleep."

Lisselle stood and dusted off her hands. "They do. And it feels like the magic that was flowing over the desert floor on the way here."

"You magic users need to decide." Homer continued to watch the ceiling, but like the rest, he'd also moved closer to the walls. "Do we keep going and try to find evidence of what happened six years ago, or go back?"

Lisselle and Torlian shared a meaningful glance. Then both shrugged. "There's no way to tell. Whatever is causing the shakes, and apparently pulling magic across the desert, could wake up in the next minute. Or a hundred years from now. And without local magic users being able to tell us how long the drain has been happening, we don't have much of a clue about anything."

"Continue forward?" Caden stepped away from the wall. "We might not have another chance. There were a lot of people out there."

"And dealing with Clowel will be extremely annoying," Homer added as Lisselle paused. They may be sharing leadership, but as soon as magic became involved, Homer deferred to her.

"True. I think we should go forward."

Darwish took out his dagger, he'd wisely sheathed it while the ground had been moving about but now appeared prepared to do battle if needed.

They returned to their tunnel—there were no options this time—and continued downward. The slope was subtle, but they were definitely descending.

The air felt like it was getting colder, something that Nettie didn't think should be happening down here. She didn't have the same reaction to extreme temperature changes as others, but she noticed the others reacting by rubbing their arms.

"What could make it so cold down here? We aren't that far below the desert." Nettie knew that while the outside wasn't nearly as hot as it would become in the peak of summer, it was still significantly colder—and getting more so—down here.

"There could be a number of things," Homer said. "I'm

not sure what they are, but I'm sure there are reasons for it."

"I'd guess an underground ice cavern of some kind?" Caden shrugged.

"Or ghosts." Darwish brought it up, but when he turned to the group it was clear he didn't believe it. Of course, his time in the Society had been filled with fewer oddities.

Nettie would like to know why the administrators for the Egypt branch kept their agents so closed off from what was really going on. And if that had led to the endangerment of them all. Beginning with the mysterious missing six.

"I have a feeling we will find out soon enough." Lisselle walked ahead of Darwish with Torlian right behind her.

Homer had now taken the end of the line, with Caden and Nettie ahead of him. The passage grew narrower as they went and Caden paused, unsure whether to be in front or behind Nettie.

"You do recall that I am stronger and faster than you. Whichever position you assume will be fine." She gave him a warm smile to take some of the sting out, but he didn't seem to be stung.

"Oh, I'm well aware of how powerful my wife is." He returned the grin. "I will remain with Homer."

Nettie nodded. That word, wife, still thrilled and terrified her.

She shoved that thought aside as she followed the others, trying to see if any of her vampiric abilities would help her sense what was going on.

Or, if Zarius was correct, her blood of pharaohs. One would think that being inside a pyramid would assist whatever odd blood she might have to help her. As of yet, she hadn't noticed a difference.

A chill blast of air slammed into all of them and Torlian grabbed Lisselle to keep her from being blown over.

Lisselle straightened her clothing and marched forward. Torlian shrugged and followed her.

They didn't get far. A chamber with an exceedingly small entrance was around the corner. Lisselle, Torlian, and Darwish entered but stopped almost immediately.

Nettie, Caden, and Homer had to walk around them as they entered. Then they too stopped.

The entire cavern was a winter wonderland. If it were somewhere aboveground back in England, she'd say it was a lovely winter scene.

Oddly, even buried under a pyramid, that was completely what it looked like.

"Are we still below the pyramid?" There were underground passageways beneath most of the pyramids. And from what Zarius had said, there were far more than the experts thought, as the deities and their people took shelter far from prying eyes.

"We could be?" Darwish stood transfixed at the sight before him. "We did come down quite a way and we entered at ground level. Is this snow?"

"Not sure, but it's certainly icy. And where is that odd light coming from?" Homer also hadn't gone further in than the rest, but he was looking around with suspicion, not awe.

There was a faint bluish light emanating from the walls themselves. It said much that until Homer had mentioned it, Nettie hadn't even noticed. The entire cavern was simply overwhelming.

"The light does appear to be coming from behind the ice." Caden studied the entire cavern and looked increasingly upset. "This shouldn't be here. Nor would I recommend that any of us try to cross it."

"I thought you were from New Orleans?" Homer asked.

"That's where I was last stationed in the States before coming to England. Long before that, I spent six months in Montana. During the winter. I've never seen a glow like that, but the ground is coated in ice. Anyone who tries to cross it will fall hard."

"There's no way to go further unless we cross that." Torlian frowned at the ice and the continuation of the passageway on the far side of the cavern. "Unless you think maybe the missing agents are buried under the ice?"

Caden continued watching the scene carefully. "No, I don't think they are. But this might not have been in place six years ago. Look closely, it's freezing in here, but the ice on the walls is melting."

"And something is coming through." Darwish's look of awe changed to one of concern as a dark shadow appeared from behind the ice on the furthest wall. One about fifteen feet high and with massively long arms.

CHAPTER EIGHTEEN

THE ADDITION OF THE GROUND shaking didn't make anyone happy. Nettie stepped forward. "I will slow down whatever it is, but for the safety of all, please don't use your firearms. The ice above us is precarious."

"I can't let you face that thing alone." Caden was using his hero voice. Nettie had heard it a few times, and she hoped that getting married wasn't going to cause him to use it more often.

They might need to discuss it once the current crisis was over.

"You can't fight something that big. You're skilled, of that there is no doubt. But you are best with firearms and physical fighting. Neither of which can be done here." She wasn't one for extreme public displays of affection, but this was a crisis. Not to mention, they were, after all, married. She gave him a kiss. Not just any kiss, but one that meant business. "I can't be worried about you." She tilted her head forward and whispered the words after the kiss.

"I understand. But I will be here, right outside the door. There's no way whatever that is can fit through there." He kissed her forehead and turned. Nettie watched him go with a smile. She was exceptionally lucky to have fallen in love with a man who didn't care if he wasn't the savior most of the time.

Darwish and Homer followed, but Torlian and Lisselle didn't look ready to go.

"We're staying." Lisselle held up her hands. "Neither of us have guns and as strong as you are, you may need help. And I'm the leader of this expedition." She smiled and turned toward the dark, bipedal shape.

Nettie knew arguing with Lisselle, and by extension, since the argument would be the same, Torlian, would be useless. And since she had no idea what that thing was, they might be right.

"Then what's your plan?" She let her fangs slide down. They might or might not prove helpful, but they probably wouldn't hurt.

"I thought we'd wait until we see what it is first."

Torlian took a step forward, but stayed clear of the thick ice. "It looks like one of those snow beasts they found in Antarctica."

"I wasn't in on that case," Lisselle said as passionlessly they were discussing an ancient book. "Dead or alive?"

"Dead. Extremely dead. Something this fellow doesn't seem to be even though it is moving slowly. I would think it could just smash through the ice with those arms." He folded his own and scowled at the beast. "Anytime now."

Nettie was about to tell him not to challenge whatever was on the other side. But everything happened at once. The creature raised both arms and crashed through the eerie blue glowing ice that encased it. It was a snow beast, or that was what Nettie would have assumed it was. Dirty white fur, arms almost to the ground, and an extremely vile attitude. It shouted in ancient Egyptian, Nettie's eyes went red, and she collapsed.

"Nettie? Are you there, dear?" Lisselle's concerned face was the first one she saw. Either she'd lost all feeling in her back, or she was not on the icy floor. Caden was directly past Lisselle and looked pale.

Not a good sign.

"I'm here…what happened? And where's the beast?" She started to sit up, realized she didn't have the energy, and went back down.

"He's still inside the ice chamber." Lisselle checked Nettie's eyes and pulse. "Luckily, he moves extremely slowly. If I had to guess I'd say he had been frozen for an extremely long period of time and just awoke. Breaking through that ice on the walls brought him to a halt."

"And I just collapsed? What did that beast say? Was it a spell?"

Caden leaned closer. "You yelled first. In a language that Darwish said sounded like ancient Egyptian. The same language that the frozen monster used. You don't recall what you said?"

"I don't know ancient Egyptian. I know a little modern Egyptian, but that's all." Annoyance fueled her getting into an upright seated position. "This is unacceptable."

"Maybe the pharaoh's blood in you recognized the beast?" Darwish was standing near the entrance of the ice cavern, but watching both rooms.

"Is there a history of ice monsters in Egypt? I know the temperature was different a few thousand years ago, but I believe something like that creature would have been recorded." She was still out of sorts, but Caden quickly helped her get to her feet.

"I understood part of what it yelled." Torlian was on the other side of the passage from Darwish and was also watching both spaces. "It said it was returning to its ruler. Then something I didn't catch. Then 'die unbelievers'."

"Did you understand what I said?" That she didn't even recall saying anything, let alone shouting it in an unknown language was vexing her.

"Sorry, no. But it was just a few words."

Caden continued to keep his arm around her. "And you sounded furious."

Nettie leaned into him. Whatever had happened, it took much out of her. Another unacceptable item.

"Let me see if I react when I see the beast again." She listened to the protestations fly around her, then held up one hand. "I will stay on this side of the passageway and Caden can support me. In the name of science, we need to replicate the occurrence."

Lisselle and Homer shared a look and finally shrugged.

"Fine. But Caden, do not release her," Lisselle said.

Homer moved closer to the passageway but didn't block it.

Nettie felt like an old lady as she and Caden shuffled toward the passageway. Something had caused this, and she knew there was a chance that if it happened again so quickly, she might not wake up.

But at her core, Nettie was a scientist. And the scientific method required the repetition of actions and results. Still, she hung on to Caden a little tighter as they reached the opening.

The snow beast was only a few feet from the ice wall it broke out from and currently appeared to be more carnival statue than a living being. She held her breath, waiting to see if she would tap into some mystical source and start speaking ancient Egyptian. Hopefully, if she did, she'd understand what she said.

"Anything?" Caden rubbed her shoulder.

"Nothing. Odd beast though. He is moving, just so slow we almost can't see it." Since her vision was better than the others, she might have been the only one to notice it. But his right arm was slowly rising, and his left foot was minimally lifting for a step. "It did come out at normal speed, right? I seem to recall that."

"Yes." Torlian stepped into the ice chamber. "It was after you shouted that it froze." He put on his goggles, fussed with them a bit, and smiled. "You have excellent eyesight, Nettie. And you are correct—it is moving. At that rate, it might get to this opening in a few weeks."

"Could whatever I said have slowed it down?" It was annoying to have said something, possibly a spell of some sort, and have no recollection. Not to mention, she wasn't a witch—and she wasn't sure how she felt about this pharaoh's blood running spells through her.

If that was, indeed, what was happening.

"It might be? Without knowing what you said, or what was behind it, there's no way to know." Torlian focused on the opening across the chamber. "But do we risk trying to figure a way to the other side and continue our hunt? Or go back?"

"Go back." Caden's choice was quick.

"Not because of me." Nettie patted his hand. They might need to have that talk sooner rather than later. "As long as that thing doesn't move faster, I believe we're safe from it. But how are we going to cross that ice?"

"I believe between spelled gravel from the ground out here, and careful movements, we can cross." Lisselle didn't look pleased though. "I know we want to find out what happened to those missing agents, particularly since their deaths could indicate the start of what has been happening in this land. But I'm not sure that the risk is worth it."

"We might not get another chance." Homer stooped to gather bits of stone and rubble. "Not only are there more people looking into these pyramids than expected, there's no way to know what will happen to this chamber. Not only the beast, but the walls in that room are continuing to melt."

There were now small puddles of water along all of the ice walls.

"And we have no way of knowing that there aren't more of those ice beasts behind that ice." Nettie wasn't happy about it, but deep inside her intuition said those missing six agents were the key. "I agree with Homer."

The discussion lasted only a few minutes, and it was decided to continue on. Lisselle and Torlian spelled as much rubble and stone as could be found, and they slowly made their way across the chamber floor.

"I hope we can make it back." Lisselle shrugged. "I agree this needs to be done, but I still have hesitations."

Caden hadn't said much but continued to support Nettie as they crossed. The tension on his face pointed out that he wasn't happy, however.

Nettie needed to focus on the ground in front of her. Even with the spelled rubble helping them not slide, the way was treacherous. When they got to the end, she turned to look at the snow beast. Its right arm was now completely up and its left foot had almost completed the step. It was increasing speed.

Still trying to recall anything that she might have yelled, Nettie stood at the opening and watched the beast. But she still didn't recall yelling at it.

"Let's go. The sooner we find answers, the sooner we can leave." Darwish hadn't said much, but he didn't appear happy about the beast or their current situation. He also didn't look like he was giving up. Some of the recent agents taken might have been his friends. At the least, they were coworkers. He'd been trying to find answers and them since before Nettie and her friends came here. He wasn't giving up now.

The new way was far more open than the previous tunnels. The sides weren't etched but did appear to have been carved out a long time ago.

And something about it seemed familiar to Nettie.

She stopped and put her hands on her hips, her fatigue after her collapse was gone. She was also angry and searched inside herself for the source. "*Look, if there is something inside of me, something, or someone, who shouldn't be there, but might have some information about what is happening, you'd better speak up now. Or stay out of my head."*

Caden and the others waited for her but didn't say anything.

Nettie gave the weird thing in her head or blood a few minutes to respond or react. Nothing. She turned to her friends. "Some part of me recognized this place and wasn't happy about it. However, it won't be any clearer than that."

Lisselle nodded and she and Darwish continued.

Nettie turned to Caden as he walked alongside her. "You're still glad that you married me even with some sort of Egyptian presence in me?" She wasn't happy about admitting it, but the evidence of something odd was becoming overwhelming. Her mother might have given her more than vampiric abilities.

"Vampire, mermaid, now pharaoh's daughter? I love you no matter what." His smile was genuine.

"There's a coffin up ahead." Darwish's voice echoed down the way.

"A sarcophagus?"

"No, a standard-looking wooden coffin." He stepped back as they came forward. "Looks relatively new as well."

Nettie knew that not all ancient Egyptians were buried in fancy sarcophagi, but she agreed—this looked modern and far too new. Not to mention it looked like it had been placed in the middle of the passageway deliberately, not as if it had been dug up and abandoned.

"Why is it here? How is it here? Someone dragged a coffin through that ice chamber?" Homer narrowed his eyes as he stalked around it.

"Do we open it?" Torlian wasn't as interested as he'd been about the sarcophagus, but he looked curious. "Although, I'd think someone brought it way down here for a reason."

"I would say no, let whoever is in there rest in peace.

But I don't think we can ignore what could be a clue in this situation." Nettie felt an odd tug as she stepped closer to it. The lid wasn't completely closed, but there was no indication that anything had fallen on it to knock it askew. Almost against her will, Nettie gently pushed back the lid.

There was a body, one cloaked in an old-fashioned dark red gown with its arms crossed. The almost skeletal female face still had some beauty to it.

It also had long fangs and a familiar pendant.

CHAPTER NINETEEN

NETTIE STUMBLED BACKWARD AS SHE recognized the last time she'd seen that pendant—it was in a portrait of her mother. One her father had, that vanished when he died. The pendant was about the size of a florin coin with a stylized tree on it. Not what one would expect to see on a vampire.

"I believe that is my mother." The words sounded odd, but Nettie felt the truth of them as she spoke. She'd often wondered what happened to her, but she knew deep in her soul, that was her.

Caden swore and pulled the lid back over the body, but Nettie recovered and stopped him.

"No, it's okay. We might gain valuable insight into what's happening here. I don't recall anything about her beyond a few fleeting images, and that might have been wishful thinking rather than reality. She left us when I was very young."

"What is that pendant?" Torlian leaned forward once it was determined that Nettie was okay with the situation.

"My father never told me. I don't know if he didn't know, or if he didn't want me to know." Nettie moved closer to the coffin. "I think she wants me to have it." That was an extremely disturbing feeling. But she felt her mother's presence and it wanted her to take the necklace. She pulled herself away.

"I'd rather not haunt all of you." The ghostly words flowed around them. But unlike the moans of the prior haunting attempt, these were in accented English. "I'm glad you found me, Nettie. I am sorry I left you, but please take the necklace so I can move on."

Caden moved closer to Nettie. Not that it would help, as the voice was all around them. "Is that her?" He kept his voice low.

"I have no idea. I never knew her." Nettie crossed her arms and glared at the coffin since there was no way to focus a proper glare at the invisible voice swirling around them.

"That is my fault. I am sorry. I never intended to fall in love with your father or have a child. But you are a powerful being, and I am proud of who are. My enemies left my body here so I could never be free."

Something about the voice became familiar, and Nettie leaned in closer to the coffin. She'd been so young when her mother abandoned her—how could she possibly recognize her disembodied voice now?

"You have a lot of explaining to do. And if taking that necklace of yours is what lets you move on to whatever afterlife vampires go to, I'm not taking it. I might consider, if you start explaining about this pharaoh's daughter issue." There were many personal things she would have wanted to demand, but not here. And not right now.

"You have my spirit, good. And you've picked up a mermaid contagion. Interesting. I'm afraid my being a vampire might have made you more susceptible to other nonhuman influences in the world. I hadn't thought of that."

"Pharaoh?" Nettie didn't budge but folded her arms tighter.

"Fine. The stubbornness is from your father, by the way. I am sorry that he left you far too soon. I was over four thousand years old when I was killed. That's long even for one of my kind. I lived in Egypt for a few hundred of those years, both long ago when I was first made, and before I died. I was made a vampire when only in my twenties while in another land, but came here not long after. I did feed on some pharaohs, but never to death. Most of them were pure human, however, at least one wasn't. He was trying to pretend to be human, a mere pharaoh in service to his god. But when I tasted his blood, I realized he wasn't only human."

"He was a god?"

"No. But he was odd, only followed one deity. He might have been the offspring of a deity and a pharaoh. Something that should be impossible, or his oddness might have come from something else completely. I didn't sense how different he was until the week after I'd taken his blood. It was most disturbing and left me almost drunk for that entire week."

"Who was it?" Torlian leaned toward the coffin, although the voice was still drifting around the area.

"I honestly don't know his name." A tinge of embarrassment flowed through the voice. "I was newly made and a bit of a wild child. But I know the two main gods he followed at the time—Aten and Horus."

Nettie shared a look with her friends at the second name—it was doubtful that it was a coincidence. But they didn't have enough information to determine how much it was. "What is this daughter of pharaohs thing then? And when were you killed?" She knew that the second question had little bearing on their current situation, but it came out on its own. The lonely child she'd been growing up seemed to have shoved it forward.

"The myth of the daughter of pharaohs has been around since when I first lived here and the pharaohs, gods, and goddesses still walked the land. It was a tale of a woman, human and other, who would save Egypt from the worst calamity. Then the deities vanished and the pharaohs lost power. No daughter appeared to save them. The land turned to desert and the magic of Egypt vanished." She paused and a slight whirlwind of sand rose between Lisselle and Torlian. "I sense you are both powerful witches. If you lived here before the vanishing, you would have been like deities yourselves." The pause this time was heavy.

"I was killed ten years ago. Had I realized that your father had died as early as he did, I would have found a way to come back to you."

That was an odd way to put it. "You were alive, or whatever true vampires are, but you couldn't come to England? Where were you?" Anger helped Nettie shove back the feelings of loss she'd faced as a child.

"I was here. I was captured by something here in Egypt not long after I left you both. They kept me alive, but I never saw them. Then ten years ago, I was poisoned. It's difficult to kill one of my kind that way, but as you can see, it is possible. But my pendant kept me here."

Nettie tried to hear any lie in the voice, but disembodied dead vampires were hard to sense. "Do you know about the gods and goddesses coming back?"

"They have done what?" The swirling stopped and for a brief moment a ghostly, beautiful dark-haired woman appeared before them. "I was asleep, or mostly. Some people came through here a few years after I died. I tried to get one of them to remove my necklace and set me free. They wouldn't be able to keep it, only you can. But I would be released. They ignored me. How did the gods and goddesses come back?" Her image vanished again.

Nettie glanced at Lisselle and Homer, and when they both gave small nods she gave a brief explanation of Horus, Anubis, and Sekhmet.

"That doesn't sound like Horus, not if he had thilia with him. The Horus I knew would never have dealt with their kind. That sounds like Sekhmet, however.

You have to stop them. Good or bad, this isn't their time anymore. They need to rest. Has Zarius appeared? He was Anubis' attendant."

"Yes, he's the one who first contacted us. He also believes they shouldn't be out."

"You must take the necklace. Not just to let me go, I'll never be completely gone, you are my daughter. But also, to find the power to push them back to where they belong. If they are rising now, they aren't only after Egypt—but the world. As they gain followers, they will become unstoppable."

"That's what we're trying to do." Caden remained stayed silent, but stepped forward as he spoke.

Nettie took his hand. "Mother, this is Caden Smith, my husband. Caden, meet my mother." It had to have been the most awkward meeting of a parent in the world, but Nettie believed it was important. Particularly if she were going to release her mother's spirit.

"Hello," Caden paused and looked to Nettie for the name.

"Fila. At least that was the name of my mother on my birth certificate." Nettie had far too many emotions traveling around her head right now.

"I am pleased to meet the one who is in love with my daughter. Treat her well."

Nettie felt the wind hover over her and Caden's hands, then pull back over the coffin.

"You all have much to do. The survival of the world as you know it is upon all of your shoulders. Yes, all of you. Please Nettie, take my necklace and wear it. Time is speeding up and much will be lost."

Again, Nettie looked to Lisselle. She valued her opinion as a confidant, leader, and witch. Lisselle gave a nod and Nettie reached into the coffin and gently pulled on the pendant. The necklace easily came off in her hands.

"Thank you." The voice swirled around them again, and Nettie felt a hug from the air before it vanished.

And the tunnel began to shake again.

"This shaking is becoming tiresome. I bet no one on top is feeling this." Homer nodded to Darwish to lead them to the next cavern.

Nettie asked Caden to put the necklace on her. Yes, she could simply carry it but there was a weight of truth in her mother's words. Once on, the necklace could be a powerful ally. She hoped. Whispering a farewell to her mother, she and Caden followed the rest as they started running when the shaking grew worse.

The chambers here might be larger, but most of the passageways were quite small.

That wasn't the case for the one they were now running to.

All of them could have run through side by side and still have more than enough room. The shaking stopped once Nettie and Caden, the final two, made it through. This chamber was even larger than the last one and had statues lining the walls. Huge ones.

Now that the world wasn't shaking things apart, Nettie allowed herself to walk closer to the figures. They were stylized in a Greco-Roman manner which indicated they were from a more recent period. There were three sizes—massive ones that almost reached the vast darkness of the ceiling, medium—only about six feet taller than Homer, and average—only about a foot taller than Homer. As the tallest of their group, he was a good gauge for height.

Nettie moved closer. The largest were easy to identify—gods and goddesses of the Egyptian pantheon. The next level contained assorted pharaohs, at least judging from the headwear and their staves. But the smallest… "Why would they have made statues of ordinary men and women?"

Most everyone else was still working their way through

the deity statues, so it took a moment for Caden and Darwish to head back to her.

"They wouldn't have made..." Darwish walked closer to the nearest one. Then moved to the next. "These seem like modern Egyptians. Their clothing isn't, but there's something about their features."

Nettie continued down the row. "This one appears to be English. Down to the eyeglasses and mustache." It was disturbing to see someone so out of place. The clothing was of a simple Egyptian citizen of a few thousand years ago. Although all of the statues were clearly carved out of the stone walls that surrounded them, the fabric was done with such care it looked as if one could reach out and adjust the fold.

But the facial features were of a rather round, middle-aged, Englishman.

"Maybe they are something else?" Torlian stood behind her and Caden, but he sounded as confused as she felt.

Lisselle shook her head as she studied the statue. "No. The design is Egyptian or at the least Egyptian-Roman. But *that* is an Englishman and a modern one at that."

Torlian started muttering under his breath and patting his pockets. He quickly withdrew the cloth-wrapped bundle and held up the glasses they'd found. "That's not good. I'd say that one, and possibly five of the others, were created six years ago." The glasses in his hand were the exact likeness of the pair carved on the statue's face.

CHAPTER TWENTY

DARWISH TOOK A FEW STEPS back and studied the smaller statues. "There are more than six. Did some of the most recent agents who vanished end up here? How can someone do this? Was it magic? Turning them into statues?" He was beginning to panic and spun to Lisselle and Torlian. "Undo the spell, free them!"

Homer went to Darwish and put his hands on the smaller man's shoulders. "Easy, lad. These aren't actually people. They're too large, for one thing. Even if someone spelled them to stone, they'd be our size. Not to mention, how would that man's glasses be both on his face and in Torlian's hands?"

Darwish looked around, his eyes still appeared wild, but he was slowly calming. Homer kept his hands on the man's shoulders.

Probably a good idea.

"Then what are they? Why are they here?"

"These might have been done to control the actual people." Lisselle stepped closer to the one with the glasses. "Likenesses can sometimes direct a victim. If the spell caster has a lot of power."

Darwish also walked closer to one of the statues, but it wasn't the one with the glasses—he stopped in front of a woman. "I recognize her, Lydia Swithwite. Egyptian born, but of English and Egyptian parents. She was one of the six." He walked to the next statue. "Her as well. There was a painting done of them before they vanished. They were the best agents we had."

"I'd say closing this pyramid had more to do with *why* they were taken, than the fact they *were* taken." Caden went to the next one down the line, a stern-looking gentleman. "Look, this one is holding something."

He stepped closer to the statue and Nettie felt her necklace go hot. "Caden! Get away!"

Time seemed to freeze as an electrical arc snapped out of the statue Caden was moving toward, aimed at his heart. Nettie grabbed ahold of her mother's pendant, raced forward—moving faster than the arc, and slammed Caden out of the way.

The arc continued its reach, slicing into Nettie's right shoulder as she tackled Caden, then it vanished.

Caden pulled himself out from under Nettie. "What did you do that for? I wasn't going to touch it."

The entire event happened so fast he hadn't seen the deadly arc aiming for him. Nettie sat up, released the pendant, and shook out her hand. It felt like she'd picked up a hot poker, but luckily the discomfort was quickly fading.

"I saw it—only a flash though. You weren't going to touch it, but it was going to touch you." Lisselle looked toward the statue but there was no sign that anything was wrong.

Aside from the fact that it just tried to kill Caden.

"Are you okay?" Caden looked Nettie over, stopping at her shoulder. "You're bleeding."

Lisselle came over and motioned for Nettie to remain seated. "Hold still."

"It's just a scratch." The truth was, Nettie didn't feel anything where it struck her, but her sleeve was torn and blood was welling up. "It's numb."

"That's probably not good." Lisselle turned to the

others. "And you three, stay back from the statues, if you please. That shot was trying to kill Caden." Once she felt the others retreated enough, she turned back to Nettie.

"I'm going to have to rip part of your sleeve." She removed the small medical kit she carried in her pack. "It appears to be a thin slice, and nothing more. But better to be safe."

Nettie watched as Lisselle cut away the fabric, cleaned the wound with something from her kit, then held her hand over it and closed her eyes. Then she opened them and looked annoyed. "It's healed."

"Thank you." As a half-vampire, Nettie was a quick healer, but even she couldn't heal that fast.

Lisselle's eyes narrowed as she continued to scowl at the patch of pristine skin that had been injured. "I didn't do it. If I knew it was going to clear up that quickly, I would have examined the injury further."

"But she's okay now, right?" Caden stayed next to her.

"I have no idea." Lisselle put her medical kit away but continued to shoot concerned glances at Nettie's arm. "How did you know to push Caden out of the way? Also, while I know your vampiric ancestry increases your speed, I didn't see you move. You were standing near me, there was a flash from the statue, then you and Caden were over here on the floor."

"My necklace." Nettie touched it but it was cold now. "It flared with heat as Caden moved closer to the statue. I saw an arc of electricity come toward him. The world seemed to freeze except for me."

Homer stayed back from the statues but nodded to the one in question. "Darwish, do you recognize this one? Was he one of the six?"

Darwish was watching Nettie and Caden but then looked toward the statue. He started to step forward until Lisselle's cough stopped him.

"Thanks. They almost seem to make you want to come

closer. That one doesn't look like one of the six. But he does look familiar. Not an agent, I don't think. But someone I'd seen before." He shook his head. "I can't pin him down. Maybe a vendor in the market? Someone I saw but didn't see, if you know what I mean?"

Homer nodded. "Aye, that I do. We can assume that some people from the missing buildings are also represented here. But again, why?"

Torlian took a single step closer, but no further, as he cast a spell and walked down the line of statues. "There is a significant amount of psychic energy coming from these."

"What have you people done?" The voice behind them was both faint and booming. Then Zarius cleared his throat. "Sorry, rather, what has been done here?" His voice sounded normal now, but he looked partially transparent.

"How are you here?" Caden got to his feet, but didn't move closer to the hovering form.

"I shouldn't leave the underground temple, the trouble outside are getting worse. I fear to even contact Anubis right now. But I can project. Not easily, I've been trying since you left hours ago. The energy in this cavern is… wrong. Extremely wrong."

"These appear to be statues made from the essence of living people." Torlian frowned. "Or they were living. I'm not sure if they continue to do so. Also, pharaohs, gods, and goddesses. One of them just tried to kill Caden."

"Now we don't know what it would have done." Caden got to his feet and helped Nettie and Lisselle up.

"It had an electrically charged arc of something like lightning and it was aimed at your heart. I'd say it was trying to kill you." Nettie fussed with her torn sleeve to distract herself from almost becoming a widow on the same day she was wed. There was no help for the fabric, it continued to flop open.

It was annoying though. And a good distraction. She'd have a longer reaction to what almost happened when they were back somewhere safe.

Zarius drifting above the sand to come over to her was disturbing. Seeing through people was also more than a little disconcerting in her opinion.

"Something has changed with you." Zarius scowled as he floated around Nettie.

"I was just struck by some odd statue. That could do it."

He glanced at her torn sleeve and the untouched skin there. "But it's gone. On the outside. It might have done damage inside. Be wary."

"I also met my dead vampire mother and she gifted me this necklace. Might that be what you're sensing?" Nettie wasn't ignoring the possibility that the strike from the statue left something behind. But she felt she would at least know if something was wrong inside her body.

The necklace was an unknown element. One, that like her feelings concerning her mother, would most likely have to wait until the current crisis was over to be dealt with.

"Hmmm, it could be. One problem with being in this form is a limitation of my abilities." He floated to the statues. "Those are recognizable deities and pharaohs. But did you notice who was missing?"

Everyone followed Zarius as he drifted to the end of the row. There was a large pile of rubble that Nettie assumed was the leftover refuse from carving these. Looking closer, it appeared to contain pieces of statues.

"Anubis for one. Also, Sekhmet, Horus, and Ammit. There could be more, we have a lot of deities. However, I fear these remains are of the ones who were released. That Ammit is free is not a good thing. She could be vengeful," Zarius said.

"These were built, whenever and however they were built, and somehow destroying the statue frees the one depicted?" Caden didn't go closer to the rubble but didn't look happy. "Could we destroy the smaller ones and free those people?"

Zarius drifted back to the almost normal-sized statues and shook his head. "They are gone. Whoever freed the deities, used the ka of those poor people to do so. The people behind these smaller statues are truly dead."

Darwish dropped his head for a moment, then raised it and clenched his fists. "We have to stop them. We *will* stop them."

"Has anyone checked the next room? I hate to say it, but we've found what happened to the six, now we need to find everyone else they took." Caden turned to Nettie. "That man with the Runners who took you, could he have done this?"

Nettie shook her head. "King James, or Seti, or whatever he's calling himself? I seriously doubt it. I think he is acting on another's behalf—whether he chooses to believe it or not. I thought that maybe he was holding some of the missing agents, with the modified Runners' help of course. But I don't see him being able to do this." She nodded toward the statues.

Darwish didn't look ready to move into the next room, so Nettie and Caden took the lead.

The next chamber wasn't as large as the prior one but didn't contain any smaller statues. And only six or so of the larger ones.

Zarius waited until everyone went through, including Darwish, and then he floated in. "These stones have no life."

"The others were alive?" Homer looked at the statues but stayed a healthy distance away.

Zarius shook his head. "Not as you would see it. But the energy running through all of the nonhuman statues is close to life. These are dead."

Torlian was keeping a respectable distance away but

peered at the statues carefully. "These are older than the ones in the prior room. Significantly older." He turned to Lisselle. "Look at the style of carving."

Lisselle came closer, with the rest trailing behind.

Nettie hadn't studied Egyptian art, but it did appear even to her, that the technique was different. There were also far more worn.

"Who are they?"

"Some of the old ones." Torlian nodded as he walked down the line. "Ra, Atum, Geb, Nut, Tefnut, Shu."

"I know I saw at least Ra out in the other room." Caden peered closer at the others.

"Whoever built the conduits in the other room, might have come up with the idea from this chamber, but they weren't the same. The ones in the other room are who they are trying to bring back."

"I thought Anubis wasn't supposed to be free?"

Zarius smiled. "He wasn't. Me either. Since his appearance is distinctive, I don't believe we were awoken by accident. There might be someone working with our enemies trying to slow down or stop whatever mayhem the rest are planning. There could be someone on our side."

Homer kept his hands behind his back as he paced the length of the chamber. "Since we have no idea what we're up against, nor can we think that the Society will be sending help, that is exceedingly good news. We can't stop the rising of a bunch of Egyptian deities by ourselves." He grinned. "No matter how good we are."

Lisselle laughed. "Even with an airship or two?"

"Even with a fleet." He paused. "Officially, the Society won't let airships or zeppelins over here—but I do have many less conflicted pilots with airships in my world. If we can reach even just one, we can get them to come lend air support."

Zarius was the first to nod. "I have heard of these vessels;

I believe they would help balance the sides. I think we do need more though."

"We're back to finding where the rest of the more recently kidnapped agents are," Nettie said. "If they aren't in that room, they could still be alive."

That was generally agreed upon, and Darwish was most anxious to find a way into the compound where Nettie had been held. Like Nettie, he believed that at least some of the missing agents could be hidden there.

"I do think we need to see what else is down here before we leave." Lisselle nodded in the direction of the passageway on the far end of this chamber. "We might not get another opportunity."

"Yes, those people up top." Homer folded his arms. "I believe they are harmless but I could see where they could be a problem." He held out his arm toward Lisselle. "Shall we?"

She pulled back her witchlight stones and sent them ahead of them. Then flicked on her flashlight, took his arm, and they marched through the chamber.

Zarius drifted down on the other side of Nettie as she and Caden followed. "This image you saw, it was of your mother? You are certain? Some entities can disguise who and what they are."

"I saw her body in a coffin back down the passageway. There was an image, but only for a short while. Mostly she was just an invisible voice." Nettie had no proof, but sometimes it was important to go on feelings. "I felt that it was her. This necklace was in the only painted portrait I've ever seen of my mother."

Zarius nodded. "Just be wary. There are ways to get inside the minds of humans—even nonhumans." He drifted back to Darwish and Torlian and the three spoke softly as they followed into the next chamber.

Nettie hoped he was giving calming advice to Darwish. She knew this was far more emotional for him since the missing people were his friends and coworkers. But it wouldn't be good if he went into hysterics if they got into a fight.

The next chamber was smaller, and Lisselle's witchlights didn't have to go far to hit the ceiling. Everyone with flashlights turned them off. They were limited and good for the passageways as Lisselle's lights were also limited. By using both of them alternatingly, it was hoped they would both continue to work the entire time they were down here.

This room had carvings along the walls. But they didn't appear to be hieroglyphs or ancient Egyptian writing.

"Is that the snow beast that we saw?" Nettie frowned. She'd completely forgotten about it not long after they'd gone through the ice chamber. Yes, the statues were important, but she'd never had difficulty recalling multiple items or events in her life. Had it not been for the crude drawing of one of them before her, she might not have recalled it until they needed to pass through that room again.

"The what?" Caden was looking at something else, then turned to her. "The snow…oh my." He clutched the side of his head, shook it, then looked up with watering eyes. "Something didn't want me to think of that beast."

"But you remember it now?" At his nod, she called the rest over to her and pointed to the drawing. "Familiar?" Torlian and Lisselle had almost no reaction, aside from annoyance at being made to forget the creature. Homer and Darwish both ended up looking like Caden.

Zarius just frowned as he drifted over to the wall. "What's that?"

"A snow beast that broke out of an ice wall a few chambers back. Which, I believe we all forgot." Nettie gave the image a good scowl—just in case it had more things to remind her.

"A forgetting spell down here? That's almost worse than

the monster." Zarius leaned forward. "Was the goddess Khione in that first chamber? I know I looked but there are a lot of deities, even for me."

Darwish shook his head. "No, I didn't see her unless her statue was in the pile of rubble."

"A goddess of snow?" Nettie hadn't heard of that one.

"Not directly, but we also didn't have snow beasts when I was originally alive. The forgetting spell could have come from any number of beings. But Khione was closest to snow and ice and if she's been awakened could have been involved with bringing that creature in."

"Could she have done a spell of forgetting? Those are not easy for us mere mortals." Torlian continued to study the section of wall with the snow beast.

"They are easier for the gods and goddesses but aren't stable. However, if it were tied to the chamber itself, it might be possible."

"If people managed to escape the beast the first time, they'd forget when they went back and probably not make it out to report what they found."

CHAPTER TWENTY-ONE

THE GROUP WENT SILENT. NOW that they all remembered the snow beast, it was clear that getting out past it—particularly if it regained normal speed—was going to be an issue.

"There's more to this wall than simply the beast."Torlian waved toward some of the images. "Some of the words and drawings are fairly recent. But others are probably as old as the statues in the prior room. It's going to take time to sort it out, but I believe this wall, or at least this section of it was dealing with the return of the pharaohs."

"Not the gods and goddesses?" Nettie looked where Torlian indicated, but if it was going to take a while for him to sort it out, it would take longer for her.

"No, and considering that the pharaohs gained and held their power at the whim of their deities—that's odd."

Darwish suddenly turned and marched toward the next portal. He didn't respond to anyone's questions, which made Homer jog after him. And move in front of him. Finally, Homer held him in place, but Darwish continued to step as if he were walking.

"Some help here? He's moving but he's not aware of me."

Nettie ran forward with the rest. Darwish's jaw was slack and his eyes were glazed over.

Lisselle and Torlian held out their hands, looking like

they were searching for a spell. Both stepped back at the same time.

"Whatever is doing this, it's not inside him." Lisselle pointed toward the room he was trying to walk toward. "It's coming from there. We need to get out of here immediately. Darwish might have been struck first due to his being local." She stared at the room. "And a local agent. Zarius, can you project into there and tell us what you see or sense?"

Zarius vanished, but Darwish continued to try to walk through Homer. He didn't even appear to notice that he wasn't moving forward.

Zarius reappeared shortly. "It's not good. What I assume are agents of the Society are asleep in small cages. No one else is around, but they are being drained of their ka. And new statues are being formed."

"They have magic to do that without being there?" Caden had his gun out and looked ready to charge in.

"Yes. Or they are out of sight." Zarius drifted closer to Caden. "I believe you all need to leave."

"Are they still alive?" Homer also held his gun ready, but continued to keep one hand on Darwish to hold him in place.

"Yes, but—"

"We can't leave them behind." Nettie cut Zarius off. "Not to mention if they are being drained it is to bring forth more enemies. More enemies of Anubis and yourself as well as us."

"I can't help you. Not in here with this, or when you leave and go through that ice cave. I'm growing weaker and will have to return to the temple soon."

"We understand," Lisselle called up a spell and nodded to the others. "We need to keep Darwish in place. Hopefully breaking whatever is happening inside there will release him. If not, Homer, you'll need to carry him out."

"Agreed." Homer put back his gun, then tied Darwish's hands and feet. Gently laying him down so he didn't fall.

Darwish continued to focus on the room beyond them but couldn't get very far.

With him secure, the rest ran into the room.

Nettie felt a spell curl around her, but it didn't stick. Everyone slowed down but continued to the cages.

Fifteen people were in cages that were barely larger than they were. Lying on thin blankets on the ground they initially appeared to be sleeping. Aside from the odd, glowing balls sitting above their heads.

"What happens when we break the connection?" Lisselle asked Zarius as she used magic to pop open five of the cells. Torlian hit another five with his spell, and Homer broke two by hand.

"It should be fine. They will be weak, but pliable until the spell wears off. If you can get them out, and away from that magic, they will follow you." His words sounded more confident than his tone, but most likely he'd never seen anything like this either.

Nettie and Caden broke open the final three locks, they were flimsy and didn't require a lot of force.

"Now what?" Nettie stood in front of the poor woman on the floor in the cage she'd broken into. The glowing ball was getting brighter as the woman appeared to be fading. Or dying.

"Torlian and I need to break all of them free of the spell at the same time. If not, then as we release them, the spell on those remaining linked will grow stronger. I need a focus." She turned to Nettie. "That necklace is magical; can you use its power?"

Nettie didn't think so but she tried. "I don't feel anything specific, but could you send a spell through me? I'm not a witch, but my blood might be other enough to act as a conduit with whatever this necklace can do?"

Lisselle and Torlian looked at each other, then shrugged.

"Let's try." Lisselle reached out to Nettie and Torlian, said a few spell words…and nothing. The balls kept glowing.

"Try again." Zarius drifted between them and reached out.

"I thought you couldn't do much in this form?"

"I can't, and this will most likely send me back to my body rather abruptly. But it's worth a try." He might have encouraged them to leave these poor souls behind initially, but clearly, he felt he should help if he could.

This time the spell worked. The glowing balls exploded, the people all sat up with the same glazed look Darwish had, and Zarius vanished.

Nettie was guiding the woman she was with to her feet when the walls exploded.

Nettie dove to cover the woman as the walls across from them sent debris. Fortunately, all of the cages were along the non-exploded wall, but there were still enough chunks of rock and packed dirt to be a danger.

"Is everyone okay?" Lisselle's witchlights flashed off, but then most of them came back on. "Turn on your flashlights—I don't know how long my witchlights will hold."

Caden led the man in the cage he was in out, then ran to other cages to get more.

Once motivated, the former prisoners would get up, move outside the cage, then stand there staring.

"We have them out, how to keep them moving? And hopefully not wandering off?" Homer had a group behind him, but like the rest, they wouldn't move until nudged.

"What caused the explosion?" Nettie pulled the woman and the others that she rescued along with her, but there were no signs of explosives along the wall. "Was it related to our breaking them free?" She would have thought that if that were the case, the wall where the cages were would have been a better target. Then she saw a spark in the newly exposed rock. "There's something—"

"Nettie!" Caden yelled as the spark jumped forward and smacked Nettie.

Caden ran to her, but Nettie felt fine. At first. Then her fangs dropped and her vision became the acute version she got when she changed into a vampire.

"I'm fine, but I can't change back." She felt an odd itching on her hands and looked down to see the mermaid webbing and light scales appear. "What's happening?" There was an uncommon tone of panic in her voice and one she felt was justified. Not being able to change back from being vampiric, was annoying—but turning into a mermaid in the middle of the desert would be fatal.

"You're changing." Caden looked her up and down and shook his head. "No tail yet, I take it?" He was upset but was staying calmer than her. Something she welcomed as fear began to take her over.

Lisselle ran over and looked at the wall, the dying spark, and Nettie. "It looks like the force behind those glowing balls came from here and managed to trigger Nettie's unstable physiology. We need to get Nettie to the ice room immediately."

"But ice isn't water." Nettie shook her head as Caden started helping her out of the room. "Hopefully whatever was causing the melting hasn't stopped." Along with forgetting about the snow beast, she'd forgotten the chamber had been melting when they left. She hoped they got her there before she completely changed. Merpeople could be out of the water in their mer form, but not for long and it wasn't comfortable.

"Keep going, lad. We'll get everyone else and follow you." Homer gave Nettie a reassuring smile, patted Caden on the back, and went to help the others.

Darwish was still where he left them, and looked the same as he had. The spell must have worked its way into him so well that even the destruction of what was controlling him didn't break it.

"I'm sorry, Darwish, but they won't leave you behind." Nettie stepped around him quickly. The tightness of her skin told her the mermaid transformation was moving quickly whether she was near water at the moment or not.

She leaned heavily into Caden as he helped her. "Might see if we can move faster." She tried to keep her voice calm but the panic in Caden's eyes as he turned to her indicated it hadn't been a complete success.

"Do you need me to carry you?"

"Not yet. But you might need to. I must look awful." Nettie rarely considered her appearance, but a vampiric mermaid couldn't be terribly attractive.

"You always look lovely to me." He grinned then picked up his pace.

They were almost to the ice chamber when Nettie collapsed as her legs turned into a tail. "I can't..."

"I have you." He picked her up and jogged through the passageway to the ice room. The good news was that the ice was still melting and there was a deep-looking pool of water on the other side of the room.

The bad news was there were two snow beasts between them and the pool. And they were moving at normal speed.

CHAPTER TWENTY-TWO

"SET ME DOWN ON THAT mound of ice." Nettie had been feeling oddly weak as they ran here, as if the transformations were taking things from her. But that feeling vanished once they got to the ice.

Caden managed to get them both to the pile of ice without falling and gently put her down.

Nettie glared at the approaching snow beasts as she waited for whatever strange words she'd shouted at them the first time to come back. Sadly, wherever they came from previously, they weren't going to help out this time.

"Now see here." She pulled herself up as haughtily as she could as the snow beasts slowed down, but continued moving toward them. "You will stop this immediately. Obey your pharaoh." Out of the corner of her eye, she noticed Caden giving her a sharp look at her words, but she held her focus on the snow beasts. She also clasped her mother's pendant. The tree image was common in many societies, it might have come from her time in Egypt. Holding it didn't seem to do anything, but she figured it probably couldn't hurt. "Why do you question me?" She raised her voice and felt like it shook the walls. There were a lot of things going on inside her—vampire, mermaid, and now, pharaoh? One with far more powers than a normal human should have.

Which might have been the secret of the pharaohs' power.

"Obey." She released the pendant and crossed her arms high over her chest even though she lacked the crook and flail held by pharaohs. None of her actions felt completely like they were coming from her, but at least the snow beasts came to a slightly confused halt.

"Kneel." Her voice was louder and deeper than she'd heard it before. She saw the concern grow in Caden's eyes, but he stayed next to her.

"Who called you?" Control seemed to be coming back to her and she allowed her mermaid tail to curl and uncurl under her skirt to show her displeasure. She tried to tap into the way of speaking she'd heard during her odd dream—whether he'd been her ancestor or not, he'd felt real in her mind.

"The gods." The words were rough. Not surprisingly, as large fangs were taking up a good portion of the beast's mouth.

"Which gods?" Nettie lifted her head higher, as if she would smite those gods down.

"Anubis."

Still hard to hear, but that name was clear. Had they been wrong about who was truly behind this? They'd all believed Zarius was on their side and Anubis as well. If they'd been wrong, things were about to get excessively worse.

"Describe him." These things were both looking well over her head and their tiny eyes were made even more so by needing to squint. Their vision might not be what it could be.

"Tall, head of bird. Said An-u-bis."

Nettie gave a slight glance to Caden and mouthed the word, *Horus*. Obviously, Horus was aware of these monsters' limitations.

"Excellent. Why were you called here?" She was a little

happy that her bottom half was completely mermaid. The packed snow she was sitting on would have frozen her human behind.

"To stop."

She gave the creature a few moments to finish its sentence, but she could hear her friends coming through the final chamber before this one. They were quiet, but vampires had good hearing. This needed to be resolved before more potential victims came into the chamber.

"To stop what? Answer your pharaoh," Caden growled out.

Nettie kept her grin to herself and continued gazing at the two snow beasts.

"Stop people leaving." The beast was having more difficulty with his words and the second one was twitching more. This wasn't going along with what they were told to do, obviously.

"Very good. You have completed your task. Go back to rest." Her friends were getting closer and with sixteen walking, but unaware, people with them they would be hard-pressed if they needed to fight their way out.

Not to mention her skin was starting to feel exceptionally dry. That pool of water behind the snow beasts was taunting her. She needed to get in there soon.

"Rest? Gods say no. Eat man flesh. Hunt."

That was not what she wanted to hear, nor was she certain it came from Horus or Anubis. But the monsters obviously needed to be stopped.

The one closest to them took a step. Then another.

"You will halt!" Nettie yelled.

"No." The creature seemed to be fighting some power that had been holding him back but was now failing.

Nettie wasn't sure if it was her pharaoh's blood or not that caused them to stay back, but she couldn't fight them like this. Vampire fangs and strength would be offset by the tail situation.

Caden took out his gun. Using it in a chamber of ice could be extremely bad, but so could all of them being eaten by these two creatures.

The first one took two more steps and grinned. "No pharaoh."

The second one started moving as well.

Whatever element in her blood that affected them was gone now.

"Nettie! Caden! Duck!" Torlian yelled from behind them.

Caden dropped and Nettie flattened herself as best she could. Two bright streaks of magic flew over their heads and slammed into the snow beasts. Both monsters froze in place.

"Are you two okay?" Lisselle ran forward but kept one hand raised toward the frozen beasts. "Those spells won't hold them long; we have to get out of here."

Nettie sat up and lifted her skirts to show her tail. "I can't make it; I'm already feeling dried out."

"I was afraid of that." Lisselle turned behind them and Nettie saw Homer leading a line of slow-moving, rescued agents. The first was Darwish. He might not have been drained as the rest were, but whatever caused them to be complacent had gotten its hooks into him well. But he, like the rest, was following calmly. Tying them all together was probably a good idea. "Get them out. Take Torlian as well in case of any magic issues. Get a cart, steal it if you have to. Ride back toward the village."

Nettie truly didn't believe that the snow beasts were actually directed by Anubis, but she quickly told them what the beasts' said.

"We can't trust Zarius? Where are we going to take these agents?" Torlian wasn't happy as he continued watching the frozen beasts.

"I have a feeling it wasn't Anubis, but there's no way to prove it. And I don't know that anywhere is safe." Nettie's skin was starting to burn. "But I need to get to the water."

Caden scooped her up and with Lisselle spelling the ice in front of them, he carried her to the water.

Nettie closed her eyes in bliss as she slid into the icy blue water. The water was cold, extremely so, but her body could handle it for a while and right now being covered in any water felt amazingly wonderful.

"The rest of you, go. Caden and I will protect Nettie and get her out of here. Those agents can't defend themselves, rescue them." Lisselle put a lot of emphasis on the last words.

Homer nodded then he and Torlian started running. The agents followed at the same pace.

Nettie hoped they could find a cart to take them all once they got out. Who was she kidding, Homer would most likely *borrow* one from the groups clustered around the Great Pyramid.

Whether the original owner got it back was another issue.

"How are we going to get me out of here? I have a feeling that the transmogrification properties of that final chamber are what triggered my changes, but they don't appear to have receded as we got away from the room." She ignored the sharp pang of terror that struck her. What if that thing, whatever it was, permanently changed her? A nasty image of living in a specialized tank in the basement of Gaston's mansion struck her. Or worse. There couldn't be much use for a vampire-mermaid in the Society.

"I'll carry you." Caden was trying to be supportive, and he was strong. But Nettie was only a few inches shorter than he. A short distance was one thing—all the way back to the exit of this pyramid was another.

"I believe I can figure out a magical solution. But Caden will have to lead us both out." Lisselle scowled but Nettie recognized her look—it was one she usually wore when she was wrestling with a difficult problem in her head.

Nettie looked down at her dress. There didn't seem to be salt in this water, so hopefully once it dried it would be fine. Not that there was much of a choice. When they were in Wales, she'd found swimsuits for those times she went fishy, as Rebecca liked to call it. Alas, they hadn't been in her emergency pack from London. She was grateful for the intuition that suggested wearing a dress instead of her trousers earlier.

A sharp pain flared on the underside of her right forearm. She flinched and rolled back the sleeve, fearing that there were some sort of tiny monsters in the water.

Instead, a mark was rising to the surface of her skin. It didn't hurt now, but it was itching like mad.

She held it up to look at it closer.

"What's wrong with your arm?" Caden split his watch between the snow beasts and her but now looked ready to jump into the water if she needed saving.

"I don't know. This mark just started to appear." She rubbed at the location, but her skin felt smooth. The image finally solidified. A two-inch-high ankh sat not more than two inches from her wrist. "I appear to have a tattoo?" She'd only seen them on sailors and airship pirates. Homer had a few smaller ones on his arms.

This was probably not a good sign.

"A what?" Caden dropped down next to her and held up her arm. "How? And what is it?"

"An ankh. I believe it symbolizes immortality. As for how it appeared here, I have no idea. It came from within my skin." She scowled at her arm as if she could browbeat it into giving her answers.

Lisselle was worrying her own thoughts by the look on her face, but shook her head and focused on Nettie when she caught her words. "An ankh tattoo? What is this?"

Caden moved out of her way as she took his place and held her hand over the mark on Nettie's arm.

"This is interesting. Not a tattoo per se. But I don't believe it will vanish, either." Lisselle looked up. "It's not truly black, although it appears that way. It is created by your blood."

"My blood? As in the pharaoh's daughter's blood? What is it going to do?" The itching, like the initial pain, was vanishing, but she didn't like some strange mark just appearing on her skin without so much as a by-your-leave. Who knew what shenanigans it would cause. At the least, how would she enjoy wearing summer clothing?

"That would be my guess. However, as none of us heard that phrase until recently, I think we'll have to wait until we get back to Zarius for answers." Lisselle rose to her feet.

"And hope he's really on our side," Caden said. "We'd better go, those beasts are starting to twitch."

"I knew the spells wouldn't hold for long. Help Nettie out of the water. I can create a way of keeping her off the ground which should help us move her. With luck the farther we get from the device that triggered her, the quicker she'll recover."

Nettie sighed as Caden helped get her out of the water. Truth be told she was starting to get a bit chilled, but it was preferable to having her skin burn. The heavy dress she wore would help keep her wet for a while.

Caden held her in his arms and turned to Lisselle. "And?"

"And this." Lisselle waved her hands dramatically, then frowned at the empty space before her. "Or this." She waved her hands more dramatically and an almost clear sheet of something sled-like appeared about three feet off the ground.

"That's going to hold me?" It looked to be about six

feet long and three feet wide. And as thin as a slip of newsprint.

"Yes." Lisselle's smile wasn't very reassuring, but the snow beasts were slowly turning toward them. "I believe we are out of options." She nodded to Caden and he gently placed Nettie on the sled—but didn't release her completely.

"I think it will hold." Nettie patted Caden's hands and took a deep breath. There was a slight bouncing, but it soon felt solid.

"Good. It will follow Caden, so take the lead. Oh, and use your flashlights, my magic can't bring up the witchlights right now. I'm not certain how long the spell on that sled will last either, I have overtaxed my magic this trip, so go quickly."

Caden started out walking slowly, then picked up speed as Nettie's sled followed a few feet behind him. Nettie hung on to the side with one hand, but it was surprisingly stable even at the increased speed. Lisselle stayed a bit behind and magically pulled down some rocks over the entrance to the ice cave.

"That was the last of my magic for a bit. Keep going." She waved at Caden as he'd slowed a bit when she pulled the rocks down.

With a nod to both she and Nettie, he ran through the passageway they'd just come through.

Nettie held her flashlight ahead of them, covering the areas that Caden's bouncing light missed. There seemed to be thin cracks in the walls around them that she hadn't noticed on the way in. Or they were new.

She was about to say something when everything shook and the cracks grew larger.

"Keep running!" Lisselle caught up to them as Caden slowed again. Nothing had fallen—yet.

Caden nodded and picked up speed, Nettie was

impressed that the magical sled was keeping up with him. Another chamber and more cracks.

They needed to get out before the walls gave completely and crushed them. Whether the quakes were a reaction to Lisselle pulling down the passageway to the ice chamber, the blowing up of the machines stealing those agents' kas in the final chamber, or something else completely—they needed to get out before the entire place collapsed.

Nettie doubted that even in her altered condition she could survive the weight of the pyramid itself crushing them.

Caden went even faster when they entered the final chamber—or the first chamber, as when they came in. Nettie hated the thought of the unique carvings in here being destroyed, but they weren't even sure they could get out, let alone make copies of the walls.

"Halt! I have a gun!" The voice ahead of them was male and low. He wasn't well-lit, but the glint of a firearm was reflected when their flashlights entered the room.

CHAPTER TWENTY-THREE

"EASY FRIEND, THIS PLACE IS collapsing. We don't want any trouble; we just need to leave." Caden still held his flashlight as he raised his arms. But he hadn't taken out his gun yet.

"Caden?" The tone of the voice changed into Darwish. An extremely confused Darwish. "How did I not know who you were? And where did I get this gun?"

Caden walked toward him and held out his hand for the gun. "It looks like Homer's. What happened to him?"

The ground shook again, stopping the rest of his questions.

"Run, now!" Lisselle stayed next to Nettie and kept her flashlight focused on Darwish. "This place is collapsing. Go, we'll sort out what happened when we're free of here."

Nettie had a flash of worry when Caden said that was Homer's gun. But Lisselle didn't appear to share that concern, so hopefully, everything was fine. Even with her magic depleted, Lisselle maintained senses that others didn't.

Darwish stayed up near Caden, which was good, as explaining Nettie's current appearance was going to be awkward.

Nettie let loose a sigh of relief as light from the outside appeared down the long chamber. Unfortunately, the magic sled she was on started dropping. Slowly, but she was drifting toward the ground.

"Caden!" Lisselle shouted before Nettie could.

Caden spun around, motioned for Darwish to keep going, and came back to grab Nettie before she hit the ground. "Still fishy, I take it?"

"Yes, but I feel odd." Her body felt tingly and the scales on her hands seemed to be fading. Extremely slowly, however. She would still take that as a good sign.

"Go!" Lisselle took off after Darwish with Caden and Nettie following.

They were just leaving the pyramid, along with a disturbingly increasing number of shakes, when Nettie stiffened as a shock tore through her entire body.

"What was that?" Caden ran out of the tunnel just as Nettie started transforming back into herself.

Unfortunately, the change threw Caden off and he stumbled, tumbling them both forward.

Which kept them out of range of the bullet that went above their heads.

The gun was held by the shaking hand of Sir Clowel. He appeared even more surprised than Nettie and Caden when it fired and looked ready to be sick. Lisselle and Darwish stood still as another one of Sir Clowel's cronies held a smaller pistol on them.

"What are you doing?" Caden rolled to his feet and kicked the gun out of Sir Clowel's hand. Then punched him. Hard.

Darwish also kicked the gun of his assailant free. But held off punching the man.

"It's difficult to question someone when you've knocked them unconscious." Nettie smiled as she felt her skin change, her legs come back, and her fangs retract.

"I was in the moment. And he really annoyed me." Caden looked up where the others who had been with Sir Clowel were trying to make a slow escape. "Not so fast—I have two extra guns now. Where are our people?"

The group shuffled to the right, not as if they were going to run away, but to show him something. The fifteen rescued agents, all looking better than they had inside, but still not reacting to anything, sat in an open cart connected to a pair of horses. Homer and Torlian were collapsed next to it.

Lisselle was previously calm, but she wasn't now. She was a highly trained agent and was deadly with or without her magic. As she demonstrated by running right through the group of Clowel's men and knocked them all down without slowing.

She turned Homer over gently and checked his pulse. "Only unconscious." There was a lot of emotion in her voice. She and Homer might have divorced, but they'd never stopped loving each other.

Darwish ran to Torlian. "Same here. Unconscious but breathing normally."

Nettie got to her feet but didn't move. Her shoes and stockings had been forced off when she changed into her tail and with all everything happening, she'd forgotten to get them.

"I believe I will have to be careful how I move." She lifted her still soggy skirt to show her bare feet.

Darwish gave her a questioning look as he stood up from kneeling next to Torlian. "How did you lose your shoes?" He shook his head. "I recall running into the pyramid, but little beyond that. But we found some of the agents and Nettie lost her shoes. Memories are trickling back in, but slowly."

"Long story, but we need to know what happened here." Caden stood over the six men who Lisselle kicked or punched when she ran to Homer. "Someone speak first. I do still have two guns. Three, actually."

The man closest to Caden raised his hand. "It was Sir Clowel. He believed that you were a group of relic thieves and he wanted to claim glory by stopping you. Then that couple came along…" The man drifted off until Caden kicked his foot. "Sorry. They were witchy folks of some kind. With some sort of masks and tricks. Knocked out your two friends after they stole that cart and brought it over here. They told Sir Clowel they would make sure he received fame and glory and he just needed to listen to them. Then something spooked them and they abandoned us."

Nettie and Lisselle shared a look.

"Can you describe them?" Nettie had a bad feeling about witchy people in masks roaming around causing trouble. And someone powerful had spelled Darwish to come down and shoot them. Or at least trap them there until walls collapsed and they were crushed.

The man frowned and shook his head. "It's odd, but I'm already forgetting what they looked like." He turned to his friends, but they all shrugged.

Nettie noted that all of them wisely stayed on the ground where Lisselle had dropped them.

The one who had been speaking screwed up his face as if fighting something. "She was lion-like, he was bird-like. Not that they looked like lions and birds, that would be silly. Of course."

Sekhmet and Horus.

Nettie would like to know what chased them off. Unless it was that they knew they were going to get caught? That hadn't stopped either of them before. And Sekhmet, at the least, was powerful enough to have held her own against Nettie and her friends.

What was different this time? Nettie's ankh felt warmer. If it scared them off, she'd have to rethink its value.

"Can we go now? Please? I can see that you folks aren't relic thieves. You were rescuing those poor people. No one even knew about them being in there. The archeologists said no one is allowed in that pyramid, that's not good they were in there, is it?" His voice picked up speed until he was babbling incoherently, then he and the other men with him passed out.

Torlian sat up, rubbing his head. "I'd hoped there might be some more information from him, but he's useless. So, I knocked them out and slipped a forget spell over all of them. We can move them to the entrance of the tunnel, then I'll magically call for those archeologists to come investigate once we're well on our way." He winced. "No idea what hit me, but it had a serious punch."

"My guess would be Sekhmet or Horus." Nettie shifted her feet. "Might I have my camel? Standing here is most uncomfortable."

Caden sat down Homer's gun next to him, pocketed the extra one, and brought Nettie her animal. "My lady." He bowed, then helped get her on the camel. The animal wasn't sure how it felt about a soggy woman climbing on it, but it settled after a few pats on its neck.

While her wet clothing had kept her protected while moving around in her mermaid form, it was becoming extremely uncomfortable at the moment. She wasn't looking forward to the ride back to the village.

Torlian got up and looked at her feet. "I'll wait for the full explanation, as staying here too long will ruin my plan, but riding barefoot isn't going to be comfortable either." He said a few words and a pair of dull, but fully serviceable shoes appeared in his hand. "Here you go. Won't last long, but should get us back to the village."

"Always showing off." Homer's voice was rusty sounding, but he sat up without assistance. "I heard your plan though and I agree."

Lisselle rose and Homer got to his feet.

They quickly relocated the unconscious nobles to the entrance of the passageway into the pyramid. Torlian even went so far as to strategically place shattered stones and dirt around them to make it appear they'd been attempting to break in but had an accident. He didn't say anything about Lisselle's magic, or lack thereof, but he clearly understood that she was tapped out at the moment.

The agents continued to sit placidly in the cart. Their eyes were open, and there was less white film than before, but there was no response from them.

Nettie feared they might have been too late in their rescue. It was more crucial than before that they find the rest of the agents and other kidnapped villagers.

Darwish tied his camel to the back of the cart—they'd taken one that already had a pair of horses pulling it—then climbed onto the driver's bench and led them out.

They did want to make good time but they were limited by how fast the cart could safely go. Any of the agents could fall out if they went too quickly.

"How are you feeling?" Caden asked as they followed the cart. Homer and Lisselle were behind them, and Torlian was a bit farther behind as he made final tweaks to the spell he was going to nudge over to the archeologists at the Great Pyramid. It couldn't be too strong, or too weak. If it took too long to work, Sir Clowel and his cronies would recover and get away.

"A bit soggy, but feeling more like myself. Unfortunately, while I did change back, my newest addition did not leave." She pushed back her sleeve to show the ankh. In the sunlight, it did look a bit deeper red than black. Or it could only be because she knew what it was made up of.

"Nettie got a tattoo?" Homer rode close enough that he'd seen it when she held her arm out to Caden.

"Long story, you missed a few things after you left," Lisselle said.

"Aye, that I did. So, we think it was those two deities who got us? I'd like to pay them back for that. My head is still ringing."

"That's what it certainly sounded like." Nettie pulled

her soggy sleeve back down. She should button it but those tiny buttons were difficult enough without the fabric being wet. "But what chased them off?"

"That is a good question," Lisselle said. "And another point we need to wait to get back to a secure location to discuss. Sorry, Torlian."

"I wasn't saying anything."

"You were thinking it as you rode up. I could almost hear you."

A muffled explosion came from behind them and everyone aside from Torlian turned around.

He grinned. "Just a bit of flash, but it will bring everyone over from the Great Pyramid and should lead them to our friends." He frowned. "I did have to be careful about the placement. Someone had weakened the entrance to the tunnel, after we went in. It was hidden, but noticeable enough that I would have seen it initially."

Nettie watched the plume of smoke rise up the side of the pyramid. "Considering that Sekhmet appears to be able to freeze people in their place—it could have been done when you were all out there. I do wish we had an idea of what they're doing."

"Aside from trying to bring back more of their cronies in order to take over Egypt? I'd say that's enough." Caden turned to watch ahead of them. He'd gone a bit to the right of Darwish's cart to see ahead but as of now, there was nothing in front of them but sand.

"They're probably after the entire world." Nettie wasn't trying to be extremist, but the evidence pointed toward something larger than only Egypt. "We need more beings on our side."

"I note that you didn't say people." Lisselle finally turned away from the pyramid.

"Those too. I think getting the agents back will help us. But, there must be more deities who don't like what Horus and Sekhmet are doing. And how are they doing it? Zarius said the gods and goddesses left as their powers waned due to people no longer following them. That's even more so in modern times—how did they start coming back? I realize that spells using the poor people who were captured are contributing to it. And we now realize that it began six years ago with those first six agents...but what started that? And why did it wait six years to increase so exponentially? A few agents missing is tragic, but the entirety of agents in Egypt? Or almost all. And their building? That is extremely noticeable."

Caden nodded but continued looking ahead. "That kind of growth and lack of concern at being exposed implies that they have enough power now to not be stopped. They don't fear anything that could be brought against them."

"The entire Society? If Edinburgh focused on this issue, instead of ignoring it, they could put up a fight." Homer swore. "Which means that Edinburgh is most likely compromised, as we feared. They might be actively supporting the attack from Horus, Sekhmet, and the others with them, or are being led astray as to what to focus on."

"Neither is a good option, but I do agree. The Society could have stopped this, but they barely reacted to the original missing agents, and have shut off any help to Egypt even though they lost contact with their entire group of agents here. I'd say at least some of the higher-ranking agents are compromised. We can't look to them for help." Lisselle adjusted her seat on her camel. "Darwish, do you know of any hidden bunkers that your arm of the Society might have had? I didn't think of it until now, but many of the outpost agencies have an emergency backup. One is almost always with at least one Mudger. We need to contact Gaston."

Darwish looked over his shoulder. "I tried to find such a thing when the others went missing. I and the other agents left behind were too new and had no information where such a safe house might be." He nodded to the agent nearest to him in the cart. "However, this man is the second in command of the entire Egyptian organization. If we can get him back to his right mind, he should be able to take us to it."

From what Nettie could see, none of the agents in the cart ahead of them were responsive at all. She wasn't going to mention it, as it was probably on everyone's minds: there was a strong chance that there was no one left inside those bodies to recover.

CHAPTER TWENTY-FOUR

THAT WAS A SOBERING THOUGHT, and while Darwish gave a positive smile to all of them as he turned back to guiding the cart, Nettie saw the same looks of concern on the rest of her companions' faces.

"Never fear, we shall find this place. Once we get back to the temple. And hope Zarius and Anubis are truly on the side of good." Torlian stayed behind the rest even though his initial reason for doing so was growing more distant behind them.

With such cheerful thoughts, everyone drifted into silence as they rode.

The way back to the village felt faster this time, but Nettie knew that was mostly due to knowing where they were going. She'd like to think it was also due to urgency for the injured agents. They'd shown some recovery once outside the pyramid, but they had seemed to be fading now, not falling out of their seats, but slouching forward, as they rode closer to the village.

It was a good thing they were all seated low in the cart and that the sides were high enough to keep them in. As they crossed into the village itself, a few completely collapsed. They didn't fall to the floor because there were so many of them.

"How are we going to get Zarius? He was pretty exhausted when he left us." Darwish turned the cart down a smaller side road, probably a good idea. A cart full of unconscious people would cause notice and require explanations.

"I'm not sure. I'll try to call for him." Nettie closed her fingers over her palm where he'd put the bead and mentally said Zarius' name as Darwish continued down the dusty road. He was slowing down but seemed to know where he was going. Nettie knew that Zarius had taken all of them to the underground temple from almost halfway across the village, but if he was still weak, they might need to be closer to the temple for him to relocate them. Not to mention they had fifteen extra people. Plus, a stolen cart to get rid of.

"*I am here, child. The turmoil of your thoughts awakens me.*" It was Zarius, but faint.

Nettie outlined their situation, asking him to take the Egyptian agents first.

"*Have Darwish come to the stable, it is closer.*" Then his voice was gone.

Nettie repeated that to Darwish and he visibly relaxed. "I can do that." He turned down a slightly wider road. "But we need to hide this cart as soon as possible."

Homer laughed. "That we can take care of. Once it's empty, Caden and I will find a suitable spot to dump it."

Nettie smiled. Most likely Homer had a long list of experience in the regards of hiding stolen or borrowed goods. "You're turning my husband into a troublemaker, like you." It was odd saying the word husband and given the situation and whatnot, she still hadn't processed the entire marriage issue. But it felt right.

"He already was, lass. You just chose not to see it."

Caden turned back to Homer with a faked shocked look. "I was never! Okay, maybe."

Darwish guided them to what had to be the spot, as the stable was only a few feet away. There didn't appear to be anyone around, but that wouldn't last long.

"*Zarius*?" Nettie curled her fingers again and called out in her mind. "*We're here and extremely exposed.*" She held her breath as the sounds of crowds milling about came closer.

"Hopefully that's him." Darwish jumped out of the cart as the semiconscious agents began vanishing in groups of two or three.

"*Not Homer or Caden.*" Nettie wanted to stay up here as well, but the more of them in sight, the greater the risk. "*They need to hide the cart.*"

Still no response from Zarius in her head, but then Torlian and Lisselle vanished.

Based on the increasing sound, the crowds were getting closer. While it was odd to have an area in this village completely empty, Nettie hadn't noticed earlier that the locals moved about in packs.

Or mobs.

The hair on the back of her neck rose and she got off her camel. Fortunately, Torlian's magic-created shoes were still there as she had a bad feeling that they might have to run if Zarius didn't pick up the rest of them quickly. Racing camels through a crowded village market wasn't a safe option.

The people were now barely a street away, judging by their volume. And now a low-level chanting could be heard.

"We might have a problem." Nettie's fangs dropped into place before she could call for them. Her ankh also started itching. A glance revealed that no changes with the tattoo had taken place, but it was up to something. At least there wasn't a sign or feeling of scales this time.

"I believe you are correct." Homer looked over to Darwish. "I take it this isn't normal behavior in this village?"

Darwish took out his short, curved blade. "Not at all. And whatever they're chanting, it's not modern Egyptian."

"Zarius? Now would be a good time to take all of us." Nettie shouted out loud and in her head.

No response.

Aside from her ankh becoming more agitated. But she doubted that was related to calling for Zarius. An odd warmth filled her arm, then traveled up to her shoulder. Thoughts of the scarabs' way of traveling inside Homer's body made her fear the worst as she pushed up her sleeve again.

No sign of any lumps, but the ankh was softly glowing. The warmth appeared to be coming from it.

"What's wrong?" Caden had been focusing on the sounds coming near them but looked down in shock at her arm.

"Not sure, but it feels like it's building up for something. And Zarius isn't responding at all."

She pulled down her sleeve as the four of them moved closer with their backs to each other. Chanting, slow-moving mobs were most definitely not a good thing.

The mobs were coming from the three streets that all fed into this one and they came into sight at the same time.

Nettie had been expecting to see the white-glazed-over eyes like the ones of the agents they'd rescued, but these peoples' eyes looked normal. If unblinking and unfocused were normal. Most of them didn't have weapons, but a few had sticks.

Caden and Homer had their guns out and ready, but clearly didn't want to shoot innocents. Darwish looked grim as he held his sword.

Then the mob stopped.

Even though most weren't armed, Nettie had expected some sort of attack. But the chanting vanished and their movement stopped. They simply stood there looking at nothing.

"I'm not the only one who believes this is odd, right?" Caden kept his gun pointed down but didn't move.

"All I wanted was for Nettie to come with us." The voice came first, Sekhmet. Then the goddess herself. But this time Nettie's friends weren't frozen and they turned to her.

"I'm never joining you." Nettie wasn't completely certain what she could do against a full goddess, but she wasn't going down easily.

"Nice to see you, cat-lady, I think I owe you for a few things." Homer was on Nettie's left and had a good view. "But yeah, you're not getting her."

"How are they still moving?" Sekhmet's voice rose and she glowered at the three men next to Nettie. "How are you doing this?" The word ended in a hiss and her eyes narrowed.

"You don't know who you are dealing with, what you have released, to fight you." Nettie shoved back her sleeve and smiled. She heard it now, the ankh mark on her arm didn't like Sekhmet and was doing some ancient chanting of its own.

The goddess took a few steps back and actual fear crossed her feline face, making it look more human than before. "You…you cannot be." She turned and focused on the mobs, but none of them moved. "Aberration!" With that yell, she vanished and the people around them all collapsed.

"That was odd. Not that I'm complaining, but definitely on the weirder side of things." Caden put away his gun and went to the first line of unconscious people. After checking a few pulses, he nodded. "They just seem to be asleep. I don't think we should wake them. Nor should we be here when they awake."

"We need to move. If Zarius still can't bring us down, then we need to find another place to hide." Nettie was grateful that the villagers were sleeping things off—and hopefully would have no memory of what they had been doing or who they saw. But she agreed that they didn't want to be caught here.

"What about the cart?" Darwish started to walk to it, but Nettie put her hand out to stop him.

"Leave it, we need to be away from here. Immediately." She shivered, but couldn't tell what was causing it,

"Sekhmet?" Caden came next to her and rubbed her arms. "You're shaking."

"Not her, and not sure why I'm reacting like this. But my ankh isn't happy here." She retracted her fangs. She'd forgotten that they were down. That would have been a fine thing for those poor villagers to see when they woke up.

Darwish moved the horses and cart off to the side, near the stables, but not in them. The camels stayed near the stable as well, appearing extremely disinterested.

Then he motioned for the other three to follow him.

Nettie tried to mentally reach out to Zarius one more time, but there was still no response. She and Caden followed Homer as Darwish led them down even more twisted and thinner, paths.

"Do you think we're being followed?" Nettie kept her voice down but the hairs on the back of her neck were up and the slightly ill feeling she had when they were being surrounded by the mob was coming back.

"Yes. I don't think it's more of the mindless ones, however. It is someone more aware. And possibly more than one." Darwish quickly looked around, then took off at a jog between some open stalls.

If the feelings she had didn't tell her that there was still something wrong, the lack of vendors selling their wares would have. Sekhmet might be gone, and the spell sending the mobs after them had dispersed—but there was still something dangerous happening here.

Caden took her hand as they ran. "You can't say I

haven't made sure we had an interesting wedding day." He grinned.

It had been such a long day that Nettie had almost forgotten they were wed that very morning. "You definitely have done that, Mr. Smith."

Darwish went around a sharp corner faster than even Homer. Then he yelped and collapsed as a small rock hit him in the head.

Caden and Nettie were right behind Homer as he turned the corner and saw a wary woman before them, holding a long dagger with extreme confidence. Her clothes were dusty and torn, but they were of an English style and her skin was paler than Darwish's.

"Stay back. I will protect him and cast off whatever spell you've placed on him." She crouched down, ready to challenge all three of them to protect Darwish.

"If Darwish is your friend, then why did you knock him out?" Nettie stepped past Caden and Homer—sometimes woman to woman conversations worked better.

The woman growled at her and feinted with her dagger. "I had to; you had some spell controlling him. You were going to steal him like the other agents." Her eyes went wide as her brain caught up to her mouth. Agents could mean many things, but the agents for The Society for the Exploration of the Unexplainable tried extremely hard to keep themselves hidden from the general population.

This woman was clearly an agent. And, just as clearly, had obviously been hiding since the other agents had been taken.

Nettie gave a small smile and extended her hand. "I'm Agent Nettie Jones-Smith, of the London office." She'd said Jones automatically, but didn't want to upset Caden so added his last name as well.

They would sort things out when the crisis was over.

"Dr. Nettie Jones? You work with Gaston?" The

woman's deep brown eyes went wider at Nettie's nod. "I'm Agent Farida Wright. I worked with Darwish and believed he had been taken with the rest of our agency. I feared you were his captors." She stepped back as Darwish groaned and sat up.

"How did I…Farida? What are you doing here?"

"I escaped as they started taking everyone…" She stopped and looked up. Dark, swirling clouds were forming over the entire marketplace. Possibly the entire village. "I don't think we want to be outside right now. Follow me." Without waiting for agreement, Farida turned and darted back down the narrow lane.

Nettie didn't blame her for being cautious. Darwish had hidden in plain sight and found other agents to talk to from time to time. It appeared that Farida had been on her own. And that, unlike Darwish, she'd been in the headquarters when the rest of the agents were taken.

Darwish stumbled to his feet, but they quickly followed Farida. Until she was suddenly no longer in front of them.

CHAPTER TWENTY-FIVE

NETTIE WAS STARTING TO TURN around, perhaps she'd missed Farida's change in direction somewhere when Farida peeked out from behind a row of tapestries.

"This way, quickly." She held open the fabric just enough for all of them to duck through. Farida still looked worried as she dropped the fabric behind them. "We need to get under a roof." Again, without waiting, she darted through the back of the fabric stall. A narrow door was covered by dusty tapestry pieces and she had it quickly unlocked and ran inside.

Nettie hesitated, but Darwish didn't, so she followed. Soon they were inside a small storeroom. Better than nothing, but it was empty and not worthy of being locked. At least in Nettie's opinion.

"What are we—" Nettie cut herself off as Farida tilted her head and then held a finger up to her lips.

Farida was listening for something, but it wasn't clear what. Until the sound of thunder filled the small room.

"What was that? There weren't even clouds until a few moments ago." Darwish lowered his voice as he watched Farida.

"I don't know if any of you have…abilities?" Farida also kept her voice low.

Nettie recalled Farida threatening to spell them when

they first encountered each other. "We have two witches in our party, but both are elsewhere right now. I take it you have witchcraft as well?"

Farida froze at the question but then gave a slight sigh and nodded. "But none of you do?"

Nettie dropped her fangs. "I have these, I'm half-vampire." She pulled them back up. No reason to mention the mermaid situation. Or, at this point, the ankh and whatever it truly meant.

Farida smiled. "I wasn't certain if that was a rumor or not. Thank you for sharing with me." Her smile dropped. "That's a witch storm. They've run through here before, specifically after the attack on our headquarters. They are dangerous and unpredictable."

"They're most likely looking for us. We've managed to annoy a few deities." Homer held out his hand. "I'm Homer, by the way, that's Caden, newly wed to Nettie. We and our other friends are all from the London office."

"I see we have much to discuss. But not here. Wait until we get a loud..." Another crashing rumble hit the area and Farida dropped her words. Then pushed against what appeared to be the back wall of the storage room. It moved upwards but with an exceedingly loud groan. They all ran under as Farida held it, then she followed, and shut it behind them. She also slid three bolts in to keep it in place.

"Better, but let's go further inside." She jogged down a narrow hallway.

Darwish looked at the bolted door as the went after Farida and the continuing thunder. But the sound was muted in here. "What is this place?"

"Ha, fancy, isn't it? I've been on my own since the initial attack." A tapestry hung in front of an entrance of some sort, and Farida pushed it aside. "Welcome to my home, such as it is."

The room was small, but cozy, with a mishmash of

fabrics and furniture that pointed out they'd been gathered from various sources. But there were plenty of places to sit.

"Let me get some tea and we can talk. It's a good thing your witch friends weren't out there. The witch storms are dangerous for any, but particularly those with a magical leaning." Farida went to the corner of the room where a serviceable kitchen was set up. "They can completely disorient a witch, stunning them to be retrieved by other sources."

"Forgive me for being nosey, but how did you get these larger pieces in here? Magic?" Homer sighed as he sank into the overstuffed couch.

"Many of them were already here. None of these storage areas had been used for a long time, but I believe in years past they'd been used by smugglers." Farida winked. "The magic helped as well."

Caden and Nettie sat with Homer, but Darwish followed Farida to the small kitchen.

"I am sorry that I didn't know you were out here. I would have tried harder to find you." From the look in his dark eyes, especially when Farida looked away, Darwish had a bit of an attraction for his coworker.

"Pish, I didn't know anyone else was out. I escaped just as the spell to freeze everyone was released. I managed to hide in the building until I fully recovered from the partial freeze effects that I received and by then, everyone was gone. I had no idea which agents hadn't been inside when the attack came and was terrified that those behind it would be coming back for me."

"Did you happen to see who came to get the agents? Who cast the spell?" Nettie didn't like to eavesdrop, but it was impossible not to in this small room. Not to mention there was no personal conversation going on. As much as Darwish clearly might like there to be.

"I saw one of them, well three, but two of them were

mechanicals." Farida turned to Darwish. "It was that odd King James, or whatever he calls himself. He had two Runners with him, but there were others I couldn't see well. I hid the moment his back was turned."

"King James? The one with the white compound?" Nettie waited for a confirming nod before continuing. "He didn't seem to have any magical or other powers. He was the one who kidnapped me from London. Or rather, had his modified Runners do so. Honestly, he seemed more buffoon than a threat."

"That's the one. None of us believed he could be a real danger. But he was using magic, or someone was running it through him." She shuddered. "I felt it. How did you get away?"

Nettie gave a quick recital of her arrival, escape, and meeting Darwish as they sipped tea. "We found some of the missing agents under Khafre, they are recovering with the rest of our people."

"Did you happen to see anyone who looked like Sekhmet or Horus?" Darwish kept his voice steady, but Farida still gave him an odd look.

"As in the ancient goddess and god? I know some people take their religion seriously, but are people disguising themselves as deities? I thought King James claiming to be a pharaoh was bad enough."

Nettie set down her teacup and leaned forward. "It is hard to process, and it will only get worse. But Homer wasn't joking when he said we upset some deities. It appears that some of the ancient Egyptian gods and goddesses are back."

It took a while to get the entire story out, as it had been quite complicated in the happening. Plus, Farida kept asking questions.

"So, Horus went to London, with some thilia. Scarabs and covelins were there also. And someone named Zarius, an immortal attendant to Anubis, was also there, and is now here." They'd finished the entire pot of tea and she went to make more. "There has certainly been a lot going on."

"We believe that this started six years ago when those first agents were taken." Nettie decided that they might as well tell her everything—they desperately needed more people on their side.

Farida frowned. "I always thought that event was ignored too quickly. I'd only been an agent for a few months when it happened, but I knew some of those agents—our best people. They searched for a few days, then just said they were lost in a collapsed part of the pyramid and sent funds anonymously to their families."

"We believe they were all killed and their ka used to help liberate some of the gods and goddesses." Darwish didn't take Farida's hand, but he looked ready to do so.

"What?" She set down her tea and rubbed her temples. Then after a few moments, she nodded. "Then it is believed that someone from the Society was aware of things? They covered it up hastily and wouldn't call for assistance." Her face paled. "Is that what happened to the agents who were taken recently?"

"We believe so," Darwish said gently. "The ones we rescued were found under Khafre and appeared to be undergoing the procedure to remove their ka."

"Are they…dead?"

Nettie did reach forward and took her hand. "We don't know. Zarius was able to bring them to his hiding place, along with our friends. Then something went wrong and we lost contact with him." It could have been due to the impending witch storm, or something else completely.

Farida picked up her teacup and stared into it for a few moments. Finally, she nodded. "What do you need me to do?"

Homer had let the others tell the tale, but spoke up now. "You've been in the Society longer than Darwish has, do you know where the emergency locations are? In particular, one with a Mudger? I might be able to reach some people to help us."

"There are, or were, three of them. I know where two are and made it a habit to walk by regularly after the agents were taken, just in case any of the higher-ranking agents were free." She pointed to a pile of clothing. "In various disguises of course."

"But you can't get inside?" Caden asked.

"No. They lock them against any but the upper-level agents. I take it that England is not the same?"

"No. However, I'm pretty certain that I can get in if you show me the door." Homer grinned. "With or without the proper code."

"I can show you, but will agents from London come out here? I thought we'd been abandoned?"

"I'm going to be going outside of the normal channels. As your agency appears to have been compromised before the attack, and we fear Edinburgh might be as well. We are here without approval. I've had some experience with airships and I know some people who might be willing to help us."

Her eyes went wide. "Again, a lot of information to process. I would be interested in seeing these airships."

Nettie glanced over to the pile of clothing. "Do you think you could disguise us? It might not block certain deities from seeing us, although they can no longer track us. But too many people have seen us in the town, and we are noticeable."

"I believe I can. I even have some men's clothing." She turned to Homer. "Although, I'm afraid a robe over your current clothing and a head scarf is about the best I can do for you."

It took a few tries, but eventually, all of them looked far less English. Nettie hoped they were able to get into this secret location and use a Mudger. Not only for the airships, but she wanted to check on Gaston, Rebecca, and Damon. Granted, they had a mansion full of agents with them—but as previously shown, that might not be enough. Not to mention that by deactivating their tracking devices, there was no way for anyone in London to know if they were alive or not.

Darwish mentioned the tracking device, but Farida nodded.

"I already removed mine. I saw two agents get picked up in the doorway of a house where no one should have known who they were." She pushed up her sleeve to show a small mark. "We can all get new ones when this is over."

There hadn't been any additional loud crashes coming from outside, although they were harder to hear in here, so Farida led them back down the corridor.

"Doesn't the tapestry merchant think it's odd that you keep going through their stall?" Darwish adjusted his clothing as they walked. His original clothing had fit in well already, but like the rest of them, he'd been seen.

"I own the stall. Well, another version of me does. I bought it a year ago as a place to watch the common people. We're cut off in the Society and it has bothered me for a while. We're in place to protect people, yet we never look to see how it impacts the ones we are protecting. I have a cousin who runs the stall for me. She knows I'm living in there, but nothing else."

She silently pulled back the bolts, then spoke a few words under her breath, and pushed up the back wall. She motioned for them to go into the small storeroom.

"Magic?" Nettie noticed that the loud noise from the wall when they'd gone in was absent this time.

"Yes, but it takes more out of me each time I use it. So, I figure using the noise around us, when it's there, is a better way when I can." She grinned and led them out into the fabric stall.

The sky was now cloudlessly blue and there was no sign of any storm having gone through. Nettie rubbed her arms as a chill went through her. She might not have magic, but she had a feeling that storm had been hunting for them and some part of it still lingered in the air.

No one appeared to be paying them much attention as Farida and Darwish took them down winding paths in the marketplace, slowly heading to the edge of town.

Nettie tried mentally reaching Zarius again. She didn't want him to bring them back until they had the Mudger, but she wanted to let him know they were okay. And to make sure he and the others were as well. Sekhmet had managed to trace Zarius to Anubis. There was a chance, even with the protection they'd created, that she'd found Zarius' temple hiding spot.

Unfortunately, there was still no response.

Farida ducked down an alley and then pushed herself flat against the side of the building. The rest followed, but Nettie didn't see what caused her sudden change in movement.

Then a loud ruckus came down the road. Four large men were carrying a litter, with five more armed men following—all wearing ancient Egyptian garb following the style of pharaoh's bodyguards. Nettie's stomach sank as the litter passed them—it was King James, or Seti as he was calling himself.

He waved his hands to invisible watchers as if in a parade. But aside from trying to avoid him, his carriers, and guards, no one paid any attention to him.

"That's him, isn't it?" Caden looked ready to run out and tackle him as the group and litter slowly continued down the road.

"Yes, and no, your honor was not besmirched by him kidnapping me." She folded her arms and watched Caden closely until he shook it off.

"Sorry, I've never been a husband before. Wasn't sure how protective I should be."

Nettie grinned and gave him a peck on the lips. "You are perfect as you are."

He laughed quietly. "Thank you."

Farida waited a few more moments, then pulled herself away from the wall. After a cautious peek into the road, she motioned for them to follow as she crossed the street.

A small, run-down shack appeared to be their destination and Nettie pulled back in confusion. Granted, the emergency locations in London were hidden, but this structure appeared ready to fall over at any moment. And the mysterious foul order coming from it definitely didn't make her want to stand as close as she was, let alone go inside.

She put her arm over her nose as best she could. "Are you certain? Have you been inside?"

Even Darwish looked doubtful about the location. "This is odd even for the Society." Although no one was around, he continued to keep his voice low.

"It is. And no, I haven't been inside, but when I first started, they wanted all of their agents to know where these were. Something that changed quite quickly and not long after the six agents went missing."

Homer studied the small building, pulling on his beard as he took a few steps from side to side. "I need to figure out how to break in, without breaking it."

After a few tense moments of Homer scowling at the small structure, he nodded to himself and solidly pushed the middle of the door with one hand.

CHAPTER TWENTY-SIX

WITH HOMER, THAT WAS A lot of force applied and Nettie feared the entire hut would collapse. She agreed with the haste portion, however. The longer they stayed here, the greater the chance they would be seen.

The door and building were far more solid than they appeared and the door simply popped open a few inches.

Farida stared at Homer. "How did you do that? Could I have done it?"

"It's an old trick of the Society, an exact amount of pressure on a specific spot. They haven't used these types of doors for years in London. If you knew exactly where the spot was and could hit it hard enough, yes. But finding that location the first time is tricky and leaves you exposed while you're searching." He bowed. "I would say ladies first, however, that odor is definitely coming from inside."

Farida held out her hand for him to enter. "By all means, you did open it."

Homer took out his pistol and pushed open the door.

Nettie stayed right behind him. That smell was vile and if any creatures were hiding here, she might be better equipped to deal with them.

The room was larger than it appeared from the outside but was extremely bare. Aside from a table with a pair of

Mudgers and other small bits of technology across against the far wall and a battered stool in the corner.

Nettie turned and viewed everything in the room. "I don't see what's causing that smell though." It was getting worse, but there was so little in the room, she doubted that there was a dead body hiding there.

"Neither do I." Farida stalked along the empty walls with one hand out. She stopped at the footstool in the corner. "But there is a spell here." With the toe of her shoe, she nudged the stool away. Revealing a pile of familiar creatures.

"Scarabs? Kill them!" Darwish didn't shout, but he did raise his voice.

Homer had been fussing with the equipment on the table but spun with his gun pointing toward the pile.

"Easy there, they are already dead." Farida found a pencil and poked at the pile. "They were experimented on, dissected, and then a spell of extended putrescence was placed upon them."

Nettie came closer as Farida moved the dead bugs around. "Thusly, they not only hid the scarabs but kept anyone from wanting to come in here—even other agents, unless they already knew about them."

"But why keep them at all? Couldn't the stink spell work without them?" Caden didn't look as upset as Homer, but he also hadn't had one of those things crawling inside him.

Homer hadn't shot the dead bugs, yet. But he also hadn't lowered his gun.

"Magic works best with something to work off of, especially when casting a long-running, unattended spell." Farida got to her feet. "I could break the spell, but I think it might be best if whoever set this up is unaware that they've been discovered."

Homer scowled at the dead scarabs, shuddered, put

away his gun, and then went back to working on the nearest Mudger. "I'll try contacting London from here. My airship contact first, then Gaston. I'd like to take one of these with us."

Farida nodded. "Judging by the amount of dust that was dislodged when you opened the door, no one has probably been inside for a while. I want to leave the stink spell running, but we might as well take one of the devices. Anyone who comes inside would know we'd been here regardless." She pointed down at their footsteps in the dust on the ground. "I have a feeling someone is watching this place, but not entering."

Homer smiled as the Mudger warmed up and a strange male voice responded.

"Pilo! How are you?"

"Homer? Where the hell are you? And why are you contacting me before nightfall? You know I'm not a day person."

"Why are you answering this early? It's good to hear your voice, however. I'm in Egypt and we've got some problems." He quickly told his friend what they needed—a lot of armed airships including his own—but left out any Society details.

Nettie knew that some of Homer's airship pirate friends were aware of him being a spy of some sort, but it wasn't common knowledge. Being as this Pilo was in possession of a Mudger, something that only agents should have, she believed that he was fully aware of what Homer did.

"Aye. We can get some ships up, but it might take a few days to get there. Even with *enhancements*." The last word was heavily emphasized and again, was keeping things hidden.

Homer smiled. "Understood and thank you. Homer out." He ended the call after his friend clicked off.

"Do we try for Gaston while we're here as well? Taking the Mudger is all well and good, but we have no idea how to get to our friends in the temple, nor if the Mudger will work in Zarius' location," Caden said.

"Try for Gaston." Nettie wanted to call Gaston and the others herself, but as she was the missing agent, it might be best if one of the others made the initial contact. Just in case Edinburgh had gotten pushier.

It took a few moments longer than before, but eventually a very cranky, out-of-breath, and annoyed, Gaston answered. "What?!"

"Did we disturb you?"

"Homer? Thank the gods. We were worried about you. Did you rescue Nettie?"

Homer smiled and handed the Mudger control to Nettie. "I rescued myself but had assistance from a local agent. We're in a potentially compromised location right now. Is everyone all right there?" Hearing Gaston's voice hit her harder than she expected.

"Yes, child. We are fine. Holding off Edinburgh so they don't realize you're gone, but most of the outside interest in the mansion vanished when you did."

"I thought that might be the case. Please tell Rebecca that I am fine." She looked to her ring finger. "And we will have much to speak of over tea when I return." Somehow telling them about her sudden marriage over a Mudger seemed wrong. Caden took her hand and nodded.

"I shall. Now, if I were tracking activity on that Mudger of yours, I would be closing in on you."

"Aye. We're on the run. Will contact later." Nettie ended the contact and handed the control back to Homer. "I'd forgotten they can be traced. I've never been a semi-fugitive before." The Mudgers were mostly extremely secret and usually didn't usually travel. However, they could be traced if not shielded properly; it was one of the reasons that Gaston kept his in the dungeon—the specially-made bricks blocked tracking. Most likely

Homer's friend Pilo had his on an airship for that reason.

If they couldn't get Zarius to bring them into the temple, and shield the Mudger, using it was going to be extremely limited.

"I think we should go. Quickly." Darwish had stayed near the closed door and clearly heard something he didn't like.

Homer grabbed the Mudger and nodded.

Darwish opened the door slowly, and he and Farida paused at the doorway. Something was coming down the road and it was more aggressive sounding than King James and his litter.

"Whatever it is, it's heading this way but is distant enough not to be an immediate threat. Follow me closely," Farida said as she passed Darwish and darted out the door.

Darwish had appeared ready to take the lead, but smiled as she ran off. "Such a woman." Then he ran after her.

Homer, Caden, and Nettie all crossed the street and followed the other two.

"It sounds like a battle." Nettie's hearing wasn't as heightened as her eyesight, but still better than that of most people.

"It could be, I have heard strange sounds in the passageways before. Come this way." Farida was leading them back to her hidden location, but in a different way than they'd come before.

Nettie felt a chill again. That might not be the best location if her instincts were picking up on something dangerous. She tried reaching Zarius as the chill around her grew. It felt as if it were coming from her ankh tattoo.

"*I am here. I can barely feel you. Something is blocking me.*"

Nettie almost stumbled when the voice came to her. It was Zarius. "*We're in trouble and have an extra person. Can you bring us to you?*"

"*You need to get closer. Get to where Darwish got the camels. Hurry. There is something bad coming for you all.*"

"Darwish, we need to go back to where you got the camels before we left. We have help." She kept her voice as low as possible, but they were running. She didn't think shouting Zarius' name would be prudent.

Darwish glanced back and at her nod, he tapped Farida and pointed to a crossroad up ahead.

Nettie couldn't hear what they said, but Farida ran faster and she and Darwish turned down the new road.

"Our friend, I take it?" Caden kept pace with her. She could run faster, but while these skirts were handy for becoming a mermaid, they weren't conducive to running.

"Yes. But he sounded weak."

The sound of fighting seemed to change course. It was heading in the same direction they were.

Darwish heard it and he and Farida increased speed.

Nettie grabbed handfuls of her skirt and held them up as much as she could. And Homer kept pace with them.

They reached the spot where Darwish had waited for them with the camels just hours before, but the sounds of fighting were coming closer as well.

"*Zarius? We're here.*" Nettie called out in her mind.

Caden pulled out his gun and Homer did too, but unless he set down the Mudger he'd have difficulty using it.

Farida readied a spell of some sort and Darwish drew his short sword. Nettie called out to Zarius again and lowered her fangs.

Nothing from Zarius. And the raging mob was almost upon them.

The crowd came in sight, heavily fighting with each other and half of the forces looked like the guards who had been with King James-Seti. Only more authentic.

Nettie stepped in front of her friends, her fangs bared, and raised her arm showing the ankh. "Begone from this land! You do not belong here!" She felt an odd electrical charge race down her arm and slam into the fighters, just as they passed through her and her friends. They vanished.

She was pulled away to find herself, and the others, in the underground temple.

At which she nodded in approval and then collapsed.

"Nettie?" Lisselle's soothing voice was almost as comforting as the cool, wet cloth being rubbed over her forehead. Nettie's brain felt like it was on fire and she wasn't ready to open her eyes just yet.

"Is she okay?" That was Caden and he was holding her hand.

"I'm not sure what happened to you all up top, so I can't say," Lisselle's voice was tense.

"We were attacked by ghosts," Farida said calmly.

Nettie nodded and squinted open her eyes. The cool cloth was keeping her mind from bursting into flame, but it still hurt. "That's what I believe. I think I chased them off."

"You should probably stay down. You don't look well." Caden's brow was furrowed in concern, but he refrained from trying to force her to stay lying down.

Lisselle laughed and replaced the cloth on Nettie's head. "I know you're new to this, Caden, but never tell your wife, or any other woman whom you are fond of, that they don't look well. Ever."

Nettie laughed but stayed prone. "I would be surprised if I didn't look bad. I'm feeling better, but whatever happened up there hit me with great force. We were accosted by ghosts. And somehow myself and my new companion made them go away." She pulled up her sleeve to show the ankh. It felt warm to the touch but was cooling rapidly.

Lisselle put her hand over the ankh for a moment, then jumped back as if shocked. "There is something there, a presence..." She stared at it for a bit, then shook her head. "I do wish we had access to the dungeon lab back in London. I dearly would like to find out more about that mark. But there's nothing to be done about it for the moment." She got to her feet, smiled at Farida, and extended her hand. "Hello, I'm Lisselle. I'm a witch."

Farida's grin was open as she shook Lisselle's hand. "I am Farida, and I am also a witch."

"She was one of the agents from our headquarters. She escaped the attack." Darwish looked around the room. "Where are the other agents?"

"And where is Zarius? I need to see if his temple will block people from tracking our borrowed Mudger." Homer set it down on the table but wasn't moving far from it.

Torlian had been staying back but came forward. "The agents are still partially numb. They breathe, blink, and swallow, but just look mindlessly ahead. Zarius has been in a back room with them since we brought them in. Kicked us out as he tried to find out if they were still inside their minds. We didn't even know you were coming until you all appeared." He bowed to Farida. "I am Torlian, a former agent of the Society, and also a witch."

"Very nice to meet you." She paused, "*Former* agent?"

"Why does everyone think there are no former agents? It's not like they lock us up, you know."

"I've never seen nor heard of one, for one thing." Farida didn't seem upset about his former agent status, just curious.

Lisselle checked Nettie's eyes, then removed the cloth from her forehead and helped her sit up. "Slowly, whatever that mark of yours did up there, it was a doozy." She turned to Farida. "Don't worry, Torlian is the only former agent I have ever heard of, so you're not alone in your confusion. He's an oddity to many of us."

"At least I came back to help my agency friends in their time of need." Torlian pulled himself up.

"Because you're fascinated by Egypt and Egyptian history." Homer laughed. "Not saying that it hasn't been handy having you around, but it wasn't purely altruism that motivated you."

Before Torlian could defend himself, horrific screams came from the chamber where the Egyptian agents were.

CHAPTER TWENTY-SEVEN

CADEN HELPED NETTIE SCRAMBLE TO her feet. The persistently difficult skirt had twisted around her legs making it far more difficult than it should be. Everyone ran into the hallway and the large room at the end.

Zarius winced as he tried to calm down the agents in the large chamber, but they all continued to scream.

They weren't moving and their eyes were open but not focusing on anything. Yet the screaming continued.

Lisselle spoke some rapid words and all of them stopped. Eyes and mouths still open, but no more noise. "Something is trying to find them and was using magic to make them scream. From what I felt, they are still aware, but they are buried under a few spells." She turned to Zarius. "Can you reinforce this place against magic? The people behind this could be working with Horus and Sekhmet."

Zarius looked rattled for the first time that Nettie had seen. But he nodded and closed his eyes. Then opened them with a flash of anger. "It seems that I will need human witches to help me—our enemies have used human witches as well. Or at least their magic."

Lisselle and Torlian went to stand closer to him, but Farida hesitated.

"Do you need all of us? I'm Farida, by the way." She

hadn't shown to be worried about a mob of ghosts charging through them, but her dark eyes were wide with fear as she watched Zarius.

"I am Zarius." He did a soothing hand gesture and gave a small smile. "I believe two witches will be enough."

He touched Lisselle and Torlian and they all closed their eyes.

A gray mist came from the foreheads of all of the rescued agents and swirled around the ceiling—then vanished.

The agents stopped screaming, then sighed almost as one, and collapsed. Fortunately, they were all seated against the walls so didn't have far to fall.

Everyone raced to an agent, checking their pulse.

"They seem to be simply asleep," Nettie confirmed that with two of them and then checked two more. "Deeply asleep, it appears." Where their faces had appeared tense while they had been yelling, all of the ones she could see were relaxed.

If in awkward positions.

"That's good to know. Please move them to these bedrolls." Zarius waved his hand and fifteen bed rolls and pillows appeared in the center of the room.

Everyone helped relocate the sleeping people. None of whom even twitched as they were relocated.

Farida smiled and gently touched a few of the sleeping faces. "I recognize almost all of them and a few were good friends." There were tears in her eyes as she looked up. "Thank you all for saving them and giving me hope. I will stay beside you in this fight as long as we need to continue."

Darwish moved closer to her but didn't touch her. "We will get more of them back. I feel it."

"I believe it. Now, might we sit and rest? It's been a long day."

Nettie laughed. "That is an extremely accurate

assessment. Zarius? Will they be okay in here alone? Rest might be the best thing for them. They are exhausted." Nettie usually examined dead bodies, but she had gone through medical school. All of the agents who she briefly examined were showing classic signs of extreme fatigue.

"Yes. I am attuned to everything connected down here. If there is any sort of issue, I will be made aware." He held out his arm toward the hallway and the main chamber. "I have increased our seating and provided food. Please join me."

They went out to find a feast and a gaily decorated one at that.

Zarius clapped his hands together. "Now, I know we're in a dire situation, but today is Nettie and Caden's wedding day. I won't go into the celebrations of old, but I wanted to make sure we celebrated them and this union." He bowed to both of them and said some words in ancient Egyptian. "A blessing upon you. Now, let us feast and celebrate while we are able."

His last words were a bit of reality thrust upon them, but Nettie doubted that anyone in this room forgot what they were facing. They'd freed fifteen agents, but there were far too many still out there being held against their will. Freeing these and destroying the apparatus that had been stealing their ka might have slowed the enemy down—but not for long.

The food was wonderful and exotic and Nettie again wished that Rebecca was here. However, considering the danger they were all facing, it might be better that she wasn't.

Caden leaned into her. "You appear concerned. Not having second thoughts, I hope?"

"You're not getting out of this that easy, sir. You are my husband, and as such you shall stay. It is just missing friends. And if truth be told, dreary old England. I find I am not fond of sand. Or the desert." It was a bit disappointing.

In theory, she'd believed that she would enjoy the wide-open spaces, the sun, and the mysterious sand.

Sadly, she was already no longer enamored of any of it. The grandeur of the pyramids and the Sphinx were amazing, but after the events of their excursion, that interest waned as well.

"Agreed. I'm extremely happy that you're my wife, but this isn't the best situation."

Homer was on the other side of Caden and leaned forward. "No business talking right now. Give us an hour at least to celebrate you both, then we'll get back to the job at hand." He raised a glass of wine and nodded to them.

"He's right. I fear we will have plenty to keep us busy. But congratulations." Farida raised her glass as well. "Hopefully tomorrow I can recover some of my things. I'd figured on returning to my hideaway after we retrieved the Mudger."

"Never fear, we will make sure you are comfortable, and I see no reason why we can't go by there when we leave tomorrow." Darwish smiled.

"Aye." Homer set down his wine glass. "I do want to know if it's safe down here to use the Mudger."

Zarius pushed aside his now empty plate—although Nettie wondered if he really needed to eat. "I need to examine it, but I believe this temple should block tracking and still let your messages go through."

Soon everyone was discussing their situation, with updates from Farida about what had occurred when the Society's headquarters had been attacked.

Nettie and Caden were fully engaged in the conversations, although Farida didn't have much more information. Yes, this was the eve of their wedding, but they were also trying to save the world.

It was decided that the next morning they would go out in smaller groups to study the compound of King

James, with Zarius staying in the temple. King James had been a person of interest prior to meeting Farida, he was doubly so now.

Nettie and Caden would be the most hidden, as there was a good chance that King James was still looking for her. He might not be able to use his modified Runners to track them anymore, but he would recall what Nettie looked like. Wearing simple disguises, they would take a winding stroll around the far side of the compound, the one that wove through the crowded village market stalls. With a map, they'd found landmarks that would indicate where the extent of any proposed underground facility would be.

Lisselle and Homer would be investigating the open side of the compound, the one that faced the desert. Like Nettie and Caden, they would be looking for weaknesses and possible signs of underground hidden areas.

Darwish, Farida, and Torlian would take a sneakier approach—they were going into the tunnel that Nettie had escaped through. They were not to go too far past where Nettie had climbed into the tunnel from the compound, but enough to see if they could tell anything from under the compound. There had been a brief debate as to where Torlian should go, but this way there was a witch with two of the groups, and while neither Nettie nor Caden were witches, he was extremely well trained and Nettie had her vampire side and whatever the ankh was doing.

Homer had debated trying to reach his air pirate friends with the Mudger again—just to check in, but he didn't want to slow them down.

"How are the agents?" Darwish asked Zarius as they finished their plans and he stood to go to bed.

"I will stay with them, but I believe they will make a full recovery. If they are awake in the morning, it would be good to have you and Farida speak to them before you leave. It will be crucial that they stay down here until we know more of what was done to them."

Farida nodded. "They would be helpful in the field, but only if they are fully recovered and if we know how to protect them from those who took them. Too many people slinking around in disguises would be noticeable here."

"Quite true." Zarius pointed toward one of the room corridors. "There are new empty rooms for you to choose from and I have provided a simple garment for sleeping. Hopefully tomorrow you can get your items."

Farida nodded and followed Lisselle and the rest down the left corridor.

Zarius smiled at Nettie and Caden. "It's not a true wedding celebration, but I provided a few more comforts to your room. Good evening." He bowed and went back to the agents.

Nettie was by no means a prude, but she really hadn't thought of this aspect of being man and wife. She was extremely curious, however.

"Are you okay? We don't have to—"

Nettie placed her index finger over Caden's mouth to cut him off. "I am honored to be your wife. In all senses of the word." She gave him a kiss that was responded to and expanded upon. When they broke free it was Caden who seemed stunned.

She took his hand and they went to the right corridor. There was currently only one room, but it had wide double doors.

Caden opened one of the doors. Zarius had really outdone himself. This room was now larger than the main area and had exotic fabrics on the walls and floor. As well as the extremely large bed. Torches and candles filled the room with a magical soft glow, yet the lack of smoke pointed out it was truly magical.

"Well, Mrs. Jones-Smith. I find myself transfixed by you

today as always." He took her hands and sighed. "Thank you for agreeing to be my wife."

Nettie moved closer to him. "And you, Mr. Smith, thank you for being my husband. Now, I do have some questions about certain activities." She made a pointed look at the bed.

"I think I can help with that." He tilted his head and kissed her soundly.

CHAPTER TWENTY-EIGHT

NETTIE WOKE THE NEXT MORNING next to a very warm, and only partially clad, body. It was breathing and very male, but it took her a moment to catch up with who it was. Caden had made her forget about all of their troubles for a while last night. Then they'd fallen into an exhausted sleep.

Rebecca and Nettie had speculated about what being with a man would be like. Nettie would have to tell her that it exceeded all expectations. Although, if Rebecca and Damon had gone ahead with their wedding, Rebecca most likely already knew.

"Good morning, husband," Nettie said softly as she traced Caden's jawline with her finger. He was even more handsome than the day she met him, and dearer to her than she could have imagined on that fateful day. Overcome by emotion, she grabbed him in a fierce hug.

Luckily, he hadn't been completely asleep and quickly recalled who he was in bed with. He pulled back a bit to better see her face.

"What's wrong?"

"Nothing." She poked his chest. "However, you do bring out strong emotions in me. And it's…well, frightening to be honest."

"Nettie, emotions and loving someone aren't bad. Honestly." His brown eyes were soft. "But startling your husband, an overtrained agent of the Society, isn't a good idea." He lifted his pillow to show her the small knife he kept there.

She laughed. "Probably a very good idea. I would say the same, but I am a very light sleeper."

Caden kissed her but was cut off by a knock. "Who is it?" He hopped out of bed and wrapped a robe around himself. He had on sleeping trousers, but his chest was bare. He also closed the sheer curtains around the bed. It wouldn't hide Nettie but would give her a feeling of a bit more privacy. She did have sleeping clothes on, but still nice to have a little decorum.

"It's Homer. Wondering if you two were planning on coming out soon? We've got some news from London." He didn't open the door.

"Give us a few minutes, we'll be there."

Homer grunted in agreement and then left.

Nettie got out of bed and also donned a robe. "It couldn't be too dire, or he wouldn't have gone away that quickly."

Caden rubbed her arms and looked down at her with a small smile. "It could be the end of the world and he would give us time. For all his bluster, Homer is an incurable romantic. He feels horrible that this was our wedding."

Nettie hugged him. "We'll make it up to him when we're back in London, give him the wedding he wants." She wrinkled her nose. "As long as it's small."

He kissed her nose. "Deal. Small is wonderful. I'll be gallant and let you bathe first."

Nettie kissed him back, gathered fresh clothes, and went to the small bathroom for her washing.

The rest of their crew were quietly discussing matters over breakfast and tea when they came out. Farida kept looking toward the chamber the other agents were in and Zarius was nowhere in sight.

Food and tea were passed to Caden and Nettie.

"And, what's happened?" She finally asked when no one brought anything up.

"London has been attacked," Homer's voice was calmer than his words. "Specifically, the mansion and a few buildings closer to the Thames that might or might not have been related have been blown up. As far as I can tell, everyone is okay, but the building itself took heavy damage. Agents are coming over from Cardiff and Bath to help sort things out, plus some of the new crew stationed in Llandudno. Gaston couldn't talk long."

"What happened? That is one of the most secure buildings in England." Nettie was troubled—it *had* been. However, it had been compromised when the modified Runner Kilia infiltrated them. Not to mention that while she didn't believe that Edinburgh would go so far as to blow up the mansion, there did appear to be some problems there.

If the higher-up agents in Edinburgh continued to believe that Nettie was still in London, they might do whatever was needed to get her to come out.

Homer's beard jutted out in annoyance. "There was a package dropped off in the backyard, near where my airship docks, but my crew had already left to get supplies to come here. Because of the way it was left behind, one of the mansion staff believed it was something that had fallen off my airship and brought it into the kitchen. The alarms warned them to get out before it exploded." He shook his head. "It was a near thing."

"I didn't know we had alarms of that sort," Nettie said as she processed the information.

"We didn't. Gaston had agents working since you were captured to set up an alarm system for explosives or other dangerous elements. Didn't think it would be tested so soon."

Lisselle took over as he paused for some tea. "Chef is

probably furious at the destruction of his kitchen, but those internal alarms saved him and everyone else in the mansion. They were able to get out. Mostly."

Nettie froze. "You said there were no serious injuries?" She glanced down and saw she'd bent her fork almost in half. She set it down and shook out her fingers.

Lisselle gave her a comforting smile. "Easy there, there weren't. Just minor ones. However, Gaston, Rebecca, Damon, and Niles were down below when the alarm went off. You'll be glad to know the dungeon door is explosion-proof."

"That's something, I suppose." It was still distressing. The mansion was supposed to be safe, yet as of late, it was proving to be far less so than expected.

"We won't know more until Gaston has his people settled. He's sending the majority of the London agents to Bath and Cardiff. In case the attack was aimed at one of them."

Nettie let out a sigh of relief that everyone came out of it okay. But still, whoever planned this could have killed people. "But where will Gaston go?" If there was a chance that the attack was after someone who lived in the mansion, he certainly shouldn't stay there.

"He's coming here." Homer had gone back to eating but wiped his mouth with a napkin. "I had to order my crew to turn around my airship to go get him, Rebecca, and Damon. Niles will stay at the mansion overseeing the repairs. They'll all be here in a few days. Or less, possibly. My ships have all been recently augmented."

"I am sorry your people have been attacked. But part of me is grateful for more help coming here." Farida finally turned away from watching the other chamber door. "We will need far more allies to get our agents back."

"And we will get them." Darwish was more positive now that Farida was with them. But whether it was actual optimism or he was reacting to Farida, it was difficult to say.

"There was no other news?" At the shakes of the heads around her, Nettie buckled down and got ready to start eating. "Then we'd best get back out there as soon as possible. I don't believe there is a reason to change the original plans?" As much as she'd rather not face King James again, she had a disturbing feeling that he was essential in finding some answers. Even if she had to shake them out of him.

Homer and Lisselle shared a look, and then Lisselle smiled.

"I told him that even being wed would not rattle our Nettie." Lisselle smiled. "We are in as good of a position as could be expected right now. Our friends are safe and on their way here. Knowing Gaston, he would have packed Homer's airship with weapons—if there was any space with what was already onboard. Zarius is going to carefully check if any of the nicer deities who might have been accidentally awakened when Sekhmet and the others were called forth can be reached. We have a fighting chance if we can gather enough forces."

"But we still don't know who is behind it." Caden frowned. "Someone started this at least six years ago, possibly longer. That King James person wasn't here that long ago, correct?" At Darwish and Farida's nods, he continued. "The deities didn't wake themselves up, and they are most likely the ones giving him power."

"So, who woke them up?" Nettie finished for him. She didn't only love Caden for being brave, charming, and handsome—he was also quite smart.

"That is an extremely good question." Torlian had been working on something while they discussed the attack on the mansion. Something that involved a lot of paper. He had pieces scattered around his spot at the table, some looking like maps. Some old journals and books were also spread in front of him. "I believe there was a single someone behind getting this event started. Someone with a thirst for unimaginable power and a lot of planning. This is a translation of the walls in the entrance to the Khafre pyramid, that first large room we came across." He winced as everyone rose to see. "It's not translated well, nor in English. But I am making progress. It speaks of a way to raise the sleepers of time—the deities of Egypt."

"No offense, but if this master or mistress criminal had that, how did you get it?" Homer resumed his seat and more tea.

"I don't know that they had this. I doubt it. I found it in a charity shop outside of London a few years ago. When I heard about this adventure, I made certain to pack it. It makes more sense now that I have an idea of what it relates to."

Darwish stayed standing and peered down. "I might be able to help with some of it. It's Egyptian but extremely old. Whoever made the copy seems to have done an admirable job, however."

Zarius came out from the back room. "I believe they are all awake and aware. Perhaps send in Darwish and Farida first, since they would know them?"

Lisselle nodded. "Probably a good idea, we'll wait at the entrance to the hall. Once you feel they are comfortable with you, come get us. It's important we speak to them before we go out."

Darwish motioned for Farida to enter first.

Nettie found herself wanting to find out what they were saying. She trusted Darwish, and so far, Farida had shown to be trustworthy as well. But something was tugging at her.

She looked down. Literally tugging. The necklace she'd received from her mother was trying to float out of her shirt. She started patting it, which caused everyone to look at her. "Something is upsetting my mother's necklace. Or it's interested in something."

"Maybe take it out and see what it wants? Better than it ripping its way out of your shirt," Caden said.

Nettie looked down, this shirt had high buttons that would need privacy to undo. "Just one moment, please." She went down to their room, unbuttoned the shirt, fought to keep the necklace from strangling her in its haste to get back out to the front room, and then buttoned her shirt back up.

"Now, see here," she whispered to the necklace. "You need to not be so aggressive. I can have you locked up somewhere unpleasant if you cause too much trouble."

The necklace gave a twitch, then went still.

"Thank you. Once we get back out there, you may gently indicate what you are so excited about. Do you understand?" One should feel odd speaking to a piece of jewelry, but it did seem to understand her.

The necklace gave a slight vibration, which she interpreted as agreement, so she marched back into the front room.

"Who were you whispering to?" Caden asked.

"This. I told it to behave or else." Nettie didn't take the necklace off, but did raise the pendant so it could better indicate where it wanted her to go.

It led her to Torlian's papers. He was still waiting at the entrance to the back chamber, but glanced over. "You're welcome to move things about. I have them numbered."

Nettie nodded and held the necklace over all of them. "If you have something that you need us to know about, you should move toward it. We do have things to do."

The necklace shot out of her hand and dropped into the journal Torlian had been working on. Then flopped about. Luckily Nettie had exceptional balance so she wasn't knocked off her feet when it pulled free of her hand. However, it was extremely disconcerting. And not at all like something falling *out* of her hand—this pulled. "Do hold on, you don't have fingers to turn the pages." The necklace stopped its frantic movements long enough for her to turn a page, then another, then three more. Then it bounced on a seemingly blank page and went still.

What had originally appeared as a blank page slowly darkened, as a pencil and ink drawing appeared. At first, it looked like a rough sketch of some mountains, but then it became clearer. There were three pyramids in the distant background, and a hand holding a necklace in the foreground.

It was her mother's necklace, but it was a man's hand.

Chapter Twenty-Nine

"I DOUBT THIS IS A COINCIDENCE. But it is unexpected." Nettie gently lifted the pages before and after the drawing of the necklace. They were filled with scrawling text, but the necklace didn't appear to be interested in them.

Caden stayed next to her and looked between the necklace and the drawing. "And that image didn't appear until the necklace touched it? Am I the only one who thinks that's odd?"

Lisselle and the others came over. Zarius had been watching the corridor and stayed at the doorway, keeping an eye on both areas.

"That's definitely a man's hand holding it." Lisselle studied the drawing. "And I don't know if those are the Pyramids of Giza. They're too distant to be very detailed. But that's what it looks like."

"True, but what's that? It looks like they're building something in the distance?" Caden leaned closer.

"I have a magnifying glass under this mess over here." Torlian rustled through his papers. "That is very interesting." He pointedly looked between the necklace in Nettie's hand and the drawing. Then handed a magnifying glass to Caden.

"They're building a sphinx?"

"No, it's already…you said 'a' sphinx?" Nettie looked

closer at the drawing and Caden handed her the magnifying glass. The real Sphinx off to the side on the drawing—appeared to be completely intact. "They are building a smaller one? How have we never heard of it?"

Torlian held out his hand and she gave him the glass. "There's only one Sphinx out there. But that is what they appear to be doing. They are too far away even with this magnifying glass to be certain. But this angle looks like the other side, not the one we entered Khafre from. There are no reports of destroyed sphinxes in that area."

Zarius finally came over. "I wanted to make certain that our friends didn't have any relapses. But they seem to be recovering. I agree, they and their missing companions will be vital to stopping whatever is happening. We must protect them." He looked at the drawing. "Oh. Oh, my."

"Do you recognize that picture?" Nettie finally asked when he continued to stare at it.

"I do. That's *my* hand." He held his hand up at the same angle as the one in the drawing. Nettie took back the magnifying glass and looked at the drawing. There was an incredibly small tattoo on the inner bend of the man's wrist in the drawing. And a duplicate on his actual hand.

"That's you holding my mother's necklace? Or the necklace of whoever owned it before she did?"

He still looked stunned but slowly shook his head. "I don't recall ever seeing it before you came back with it. Nor posing for someone to draw my hand holding it. I don't understand—"

Screams from the back room cut him off and everyone crowded toward the door.

Darwish was sitting on Farida, a bloody knife near them on the ground. Farida fought and thrashed to get away from him and at first, Nettie feared that Darwish had snapped and attacked her.

Then she saw him kick the knife further away and

Lisselle ran to where one of the rescued agents had collapsed.

"He's still alive. Is anyone else injured?" She shouted to the rest of the agents, but they all slowly shook their heads.

Darwish looked heartbroken as he continued to try and keep Farida pinned down. Considering that she was not a large woman, the amount of effort he was having to expend was impressive.

Homer and Caden went to help him, and Torlian and Nettie ran to help Lisselle. Zarius started chanting and Farida froze.

"There is a possession in that one." His eyes flashed gold. "It's not safe for any of you to be near her. Take everyone except her out of here. I must secure her myself."

Homer and Caden helped escort the rest of the agents out. They appeared stunned and exceptionally confused, but they moved quickly. Lisselle and Nettie helped the injured man. Fortunately, the knife had hit his shoulder, not his chest.

Zarius nodded to Darwish to get up and take the bloody knife with him when he left.

He did but then stood over the frozen Farida. "That's not her. Farida wouldn't do that." Darwish looked ready to cry or find out who did this and destroy them. There were a lot of emotions on his face.

"I know child, go with the others." Zarius was only focusing on Farida but kept his voice gentle. "I will make sure the being inside her can't hurt anyone else."

Darwish followed Nettie and Lisselle out and the door shut and locked behind them.

"She was speaking to the agents, acting normal. Then she got to Saad, one of the senior agents, she yelled and jumped for him. I tried to stop her, but she got one strike in. She was far stronger than she should have been. But that's not Farida." Darwish was adamant.

The man who'd been stabbed winced as Lisselle started treating him, then focused on Darwish. "Darwish? What's happened? Where are we?" The man rubbed his head with the hand on his uninjured side. "I've had strange dreams."

"Hello. I'm Agent Lisselle Wilding from London. Things are extremely complicated right now, but you need to hold still so this doesn't become worse. I promise, once things are settled, we'll explain everything to all of you."

Saad nodded and relaxed. "You're all from the Society in London? Thank you for coming. Something is attacking our headquarters. We have to stop it."

Darwish started to respond, but Lisselle shook her head at him. "We'll explain everything after I stop the bleeding." She looked around at the other agents. "And all of you rest a bit more."

Nettie studied the other agents at her comment. They were conscious and appeared to be aware of their surroundings, but they also looked as if they'd been awake for a few weeks and were unable to focus on anything. There was no way to know what the machine that was stealing their kas had done, but they were in desperate need of rest.

"There are more beds for them." Zarius' voice came into the room, although he stayed with Farida in the other chamber.

Saad nodded as Lisselle finished wrapping his shoulder and making a sling. "I agree we need rest." He turned to the other agents. "Go to the rooms, I will join you shortly."

Maybe it was the pain, but his eyes were more focused than before.

Torlian and Homer led the rest of the group to the corridor in search of the new empty rooms.

The injured man nodded to Lisselle but waited until

they were all gone. "I'm Agent Saad. I would like to know what has happened. I have odd memories of an attack on the headquarters, then nothing until moments ago." His eyes were extremely clear as he looked around the group. "How long have we been unconscious, what's happened to the headquarters, and why did Farida attack me?"

Nettie smiled. He reminded her of a much taller, and far less French, Gaston. The two of them together would be interesting to see. "It's a complicated story. I'm Agent Nettie Jones-Smith."

The rest introduced themselves, then Homer and Lisselle—as the senior agents—explained what had occurred.

Agent Saad looked stunned and turned to Darwish. "Thank you for stopping Farida. I agree, that is not the agent I've known these six years. How many of our agents remain free?"

"You're welcome. I've run into no more than ten since the rest of you were taken. We acknowledge each other when we see each other, but keep our communication and contact to a minimum."

Saad ran his hand through his hair and shook his head. "Over a hundred agents are missing then. And the gods and goddess of old Egypt are the cause?" He looked toward the chamber door where Zarius was still working on Farida—or rather, what had taken her over. "And he is one?"

Nettie shook her head. "Zarius is the attendant to Anubis. The two of them were most likely awakened by accident as they don't have the agenda of Sekhmet and Horus. But Zarius was followed last time he went out from here. He has abilities, but can't leave at this time."

"And the agents you freed are going to take a while to recover. I believe Farida, or whatever has taken her over, helped me to recover—pain is a great focus. But I don't think stabbing everyone is the best option." Saad slumped forward. "And I believe I am becoming fatigued again. My people will be safe here?"

"Yes. Although as we rescue more, I will have to do some remodeling. I can only expand this place so far." Zarius came into the room so silently that his words were startling. "I have secured the creature that is residing inside your agent. Do not fear, your agent is still there as well but is being suppressed. I can't determine for how long, but I fear we haven't been dealing with the real Farida since you found her."

Darwish shook his head. "She knew things only the real one would know; what magic is this?"

"It's a gkolin spirit. They were destroyed before Anubis and I went to sleep long ago. Which means that they too have been recreated." He frowned. "Most likely by the people we are fighting against. Gkolins can tap into basic information from the host."

Torlian scowled at the name. "I've never heard of them. How did they take her over?"

"And how do we keep it from happening to more of us?" Homer added.

Zarius nodded to Homer and Torlian. "Excellent points. As for why you've never heard of them, when they were destroyed all records of them were stricken in order to make it more difficult for them to be brought back. These creatures were never populous and are easier to defend against than remove. But fear not, I will remove this one from Farida. Prevention is as simple as a touch." He gave a sideways smile. "It's a bit trickier than that for me, but for you, it will be just a touch. It will also let me know if anyone else has already been compromised."

Lisselle stepped forward. "I will be first. I don't suppose you can pass this ability of yours to others?"

"I don't believe so, at least not at this point. But as magic users, I might be able to give you and Torlian at least a way to determine if someone is not themselves. Let's check all of you first."

Saad had been listing to the side, fatigue was hitting now that Lisselle had numbed the pain of the injury, but he sat up at attention now.

Zarius muttered a few exotic-sounding words under his breath and touched Lisselle, and then Torlian on the middle of the forehead.

Nettie kept a close watch and where he'd pressed his thumb on them glowed a soft green, which quickly faded away. He went to Saad next, then Homer, Caden, and Darwish. All had the same glowing green reaction.

He paused in front of Nettie with a slight frown. "I believe you are going to be the most difficult due to your complicated nature. The daughter of pharaohs appears to be real, and you are it. Plus, the mermaid element as well as a vampire, makes for a unique combination."

Saad's eyes went wide at Zarius' words and stared at Nettie with a look equally of interest and concern.

"Half-vampire," Nettie corrected. "But do what you can. I would hope that any invading spirit would be overwhelmed by confusion if they tried to take me over."

Saad appeared ready to ask questions, but simply watched her instead. He might have heard of Agent Jones as a vampire, but the rest was new.

Zarius spoke his words, but even this close, Nettie couldn't retain what they were. Then he scowled and repeated them.

Nettie became nervous after the fourth time, but finally he put his thumb on her forehead. She felt a soft warmth, but he smiled and stepped back. The relief on Caden's face was almost palpable.

"You are clear. But due to your abilities, I would like to add a layer of additional protection to you. It wouldn't make a difference for the others, but it could keep you hidden from the people we are against." He waited for her response.

"What do you need to do?" Thanks to being around Lisselle and other witches, magic wasn't the unheard-of thing it had been a few years ago. But Zarius wasn't a witch.

"Nothing too noticeable. But I'd like to add a mark of empowerment and strength around your ankh tattoo. I believe the mark has appeared at this time for a purpose."

"Hopefully not a bad one, right?" Caden was so close to her that he was almost stepping on her feet. "*Right*?" He took Nettie's hand when Zarius paused before answering.

"No, I don't believe it is a bad reason, I believe Nettie is coming into her full heritage. However, I believe we need to work with it and anything or anyone who may be on our side. I don't need to remind you all how uneven this match is right now."

"I'm fine with whatever you need to do. But will this tattoo ever go away? I normally do wear long sleeves, but there are times that short sleeves would be preferred." Nettie normally didn't worry about her appearance. In fact, prior to meeting Caden, she hadn't concerned herself about it at all. But there were some rules of decorum to follow upon occasion. Not to mention that she was sort of a spy and going undercover with such a distinctive mark would be extremely problematic.

"I'm still determining exactly what it is, but I believe once it has completed its task, it will vanish." He peered closer at it. "Or at least fade. You'll need to hold still as I add to it. This will stay as long as the ankh does, but it would be best if I can make it seem to be part of the original design."

Nettie nodded and held her arm out to him. There was an odd tingling sensation as he bent his head over the ankh. Then the reaction was gone and he stepped back.

Nettie pulled her arm closer to see what he'd done. "I don't see anything different. Wait, is there a line around the ankh?" It now looked like there was an extremely slender and delicate chain drawn in gold and silver around the entire ankh. It was so thin that it was difficult to notice, even if you were aware that it hadn't been there before.

"That is my mark. Well, my mark as made into a line." Zarius held up his hand to show her the tattoo that had been shown in the drawing. It was a delicate and twisted chain pulled into an elaborate knot. "Which I still need to sort out that drawing of it, as neither my hand nor I actually participated in. That I can recall."

Saad perked up during the testing process, but was fading fast. "I was hoping that I could hear more of what has been happening recently, but I find myself unable to keep my eyes open."

Lisselle came and checked his injury. "Whatever was being done to all of you, and no this isn't the time to speak of it in detail, drained your energy. It will probably take a few days to recover. For all of you." She gave him a stern look on the last sentence.

His eyes flew open at that, but his image of alertness was hindered by a huge yawn. "I do apologize, but we can't afford a few more days. The rest of our people are out there somewhere."

"And we will find them. But surely you realize that impaired agents will do more harm than good." Homer held out his arm to help Saad up. "You and your people can't join the fight until you're recovered. We'll find a way to delay things until more help has arrived."

"Help? Beyond my agents?"

"Yes. Armed airships are heading this way with agents and others from Mother England." Homer smiled and patted Saad's arm as he led him down the hall. "Don't fear, we have more help coming our way."

But his smile dropped when he came back to the main room. "I hope I wasn't just lying to Agent Saad. These body-stealing creatures are extremely disturbing and we're still short on people on our side. How are you going to get Farida free of that thing?"

"Your friends will be here soon enough. And I still have hope that you'll come back with information on more of the missing agents when you go out today." Zarius sat and for a moment, looked exhausted. "As for Farida, it will take a bit of effort to draw the gkolin free of her. As I said, they are easier to prevent than expel." He turned to Darwish. "Do not fret so. I will free your friend. I am concerned at how long it might have been in her, however. And everyone you bring in will have to be tested."

"You believe that she escaped when their headquarters was attacked because she was already carrying that thing," Caden said it first but by the faces around them, he wasn't the only one who thought it.

CHAPTER THIRTY

ZARIUS' FACE WAS GRIM. "I do. It would make sense. She could have been stricken by it long before the attack, but not have realized it. They can stay dormant once they have infested someone—but I will notice them even when they are inactive. The gkolin would have taken over once it was told to do so by whoever is commanding it. I do hope that it hadn't found other agents through her who were hiding and turned them in. But that might have happened."

The silence lingered for a few moments. The implications weren't good. Darwish's level of concern was growing. He'd known of a few surviving agents, but from the look on his face, he was now wondering if staying separate from each other had been the best idea.

"Do we proceed with the plan? Minus Farida of course." Torlian looked around the room. "Darwish and I can still investigate the tunnel."

"I don't see why not, unless Darwish has a reason?" Homer asked.

Darwish had been staring at the corridor that led to the room Farida was being held in, but startled when he heard his name. "Sorry. I was listening. Yes, I believe Torlian and I can successfully carry the assignment out."

"Are you certain that you're okay?" Lisselle kept her voice low but she had a good point. He and Torlian would be in the most precarious situation if they were found.

"I'll be fine." His smile barely lifted the corners of his mouth.

An eerie feeling hit Nettie as she watched him. And the ankh tattoo began itching. "Perhaps Caden and I should take the tunnel route." The itching and odd feeling vanished. "Even in disguise, I still might be too noticeable prowling around the village near the compound. They won't expect me to be down there." That was partially true, but more importantly, some extra sense had told her that Darwish shouldn't go down there.

Torlian started to shake his head, but then saw Nettie's face and shrugged. "That might be a good idea. We can cover more ground on the surface without worry of being seen. Darwish has avoided being spotted for a while."

"I'm fine with going below, but if you feel safe doing so instead?" Darwish almost appeared relieved at her nod, even though leading the group in the tunnels had been his idea. However, that had been before Farida showed what she really was. "I'll go find robes for Torlian and myself." With a nod, he went down the hall.

Lisselle waited until he left, then she and Torlian quickly went to Nettie's side. "Something magical just happened. I felt it. But you aren't a witch." The look on her face was one of waiting for confirmation.

Nettie pushed her sleeve away from the tattoo. "No, I haven't added witch to my collection of exotic attributes. But I felt a sharp and sudden danger about Darwish going into those tunnels. This tattoo seemed to be the focus of the feeling. As soon as I spoke of changing the plan, the feeling vanished."

Zarius got up from his chair and walked over to scowl at the ankh. "Precognition shouldn't be one of its attributes, but these were really more theory than reality. Unless what it seems to suggest goes against something you feel is horrifically wrong, I'd say listen to it."

Lisselle held her hand over the tattoo for a few moments but finally shrugged. "I feel an energy to it, but nothing malevolent. Perhaps Zarius' accent mark is assisting it?"

Zarius shrugged. "It could be. It's difficult to fully understand some mystical items."

Nettie started to button her sleeve back, then stopped. She'd worn a plain dark dress in order to facilitate going around the town in disguise. However, it wouldn't be conducive to the tunnels. She had one pair of lady's trousers with her, and they would be far more useful.

As long as whatever triggered her mermaid change in the pyramid didn't strike her again.

"You're thinking." Caden's tone indicated that he knew it wasn't her normal constant thinking.

Nettie explained her clothing dilemma.

"Could you bundle a thin skirt into your small pack? Just in case?"

Nettie grabbed him and kissed him. "Thank you husband. I was overthinking things." She turned to Zarius. "Is there any way for you to find out who or what forced my change before? Being a water-needing creature in the desert could be far more problematic than just the wrong clothing."

"You are such an extremely unique person that I'm not sure what I can find. Aside from the thilia, we never had mermaids during my time. Not here, anyway. But I will see what can be done. I'll also continue to reach out subtly to see if there were other deities on our side awoken by accident."

"I'll go change then." Nettie darted into their room and quickly switched clothing. She did so love trousers; the freedom of movement was liberating. She buckled on her utility belt, added the goggles—a bit odd for going underground, but very handy for what they really did, and her bracers.

Looking herself over in the small mirror in the room, she was pleased with the result. Then scowled. She didn't usually carry a gun, but in this case, it might be prudent. She dug out her small holster and lady's gun out of her pack. It was handy that Caden had thought to bring them.

There were some adjustments required—the utility belt had to come off to layer the gun belt underneath it. The gun holster was sadly more noticeable than she would have liked. That was one advantage of voluminous skirts, it was easier to hide things in them. But there was no comparison for comfort against the trousers. She put on her light cloak which covered the gun a bit more, then folded a thin skirt into her pack.

"I'm ready," she announced, as she went back into the room. At first she thought she hadn't spoken loudly enough, as no one turned toward her. Then she realized that no one had even moved.

She ran to Caden first. He had been in conversation with Homer, an animated one from the looks on both their faces, but even shaking him received no response.

Zarius was the only one missing. And there was an odd keening in the chamber Farida had been held in.

Nettie dropped her fangs in place and marched toward the room. Lisselle and Torlian were both powerful witches, they wouldn't have fallen to a spell easily.

Neither should Zarius.

The door was locked, but vampire strength helped break it down.

Farida was rocking back and forth, eyes closed, a high-pitched noise coming from her mouth. Zarius was moving toward her with increasing slowness, his hands held tightly over his eyes and his face contorted in pain.

Whatever Farida, or the thing inside her, was doing was not impacting Nettie. However, the ankh flared brightly through her shirt sleeve.

Nettie charged Farida, knocking her over. Then she punched her soundly in the jaw. It was a solid hit and Farida's eyes briefly flickered open, then she collapsed and the horrific noise stopped.

Zarius stumbled forward but caught himself before hitting the ground. "Thank you. How did you stop her? I doubt I would have been able to."

"I struck her. Not very gently, but I couldn't think of any other options." She shook out her hand. She'd mostly done it correctly, but still felt a sting in her fingers. "Is she what made everyone out there freeze?"

Before he could respond, Caden and the rest came charging into the room with weapons drawn.

"Easy everyone, Nettie took care of the problem." Zarius moved to Farida, but stopped in front of Nettie first. "Although you should have been frozen as well."

Caden grabbed her and held her tight. "I saw you come out and felt you shake me, but I couldn't respond or move."

Nettie hugged him back, then looked over his shoulder to Zarius. "I didn't feel it at all. But, if Farida was spewing some sort of Egyptian spell, maybe the ankh assisted again? We really do need to find out more about this thing. It is proving to be more powerful than previously believed." Right now, that power was on their side, but that could change with disastrous results. She was only slightly successful in shoving aside the possibility of the daughter of pharaohs situation helping. It could be the case, and she wasn't dismissing it. However, it wasn't something she had time to really look into at the moment. Nor did she want to count on it.

"It might have. There was a delayed spell hidden inside Farida. Once everyone was frozen, she would have exploded. Not only destroying this place, but possibly the entire village."

Lisselle and Torlian went to Farida.

Lisselle grimaced. "I can feel a spell fading away, but not what it was. Is this standard for gkolin? And while I'm glad it didn't happen, why freeze us, couldn't she simply have blown up?"

"It is not standard for those creatures," Zarius muttered some ugly-sounding words, and a dim shadow encased Farida. "I believe that Nettie's physical action was so unexpected that whatever was added to the gkolin was thrown off. The encasement I've now put on her will keep it from happening again. As for simply exploding, I had spells around her for anything grand like that. And you and Torlian might have been aware of it before it happened as well."

Darwish stayed silently near the back but finally spoke. "Which means you can't work on saving her at the moment." It wasn't a question.

"No, I can't. I believe that my trying to free her triggered this response, but I've never seen anything so strong. We will need to take this recovery slower than I'd hoped. But the thing inside her can't hurt anyone while in that casing. Including Farida herself." He nodded to Nettie. "There's an excellent chance that I also would have frozen before I could touch her if Nettie's intervention hadn't been so swift."

Caden grinned. "That's my Nettie, always a fighter."

"I'm just glad it worked." Nettie continued to stretch her fingers. She'd had basics in fist fighting while during her agent training, but she might need more if this was to become a habit. "I was at a loss for what else to do. It was instinct really."

Torlian laughed and bowed to Nettie. "You'd best be careful with this one, Caden. She hits hard."

"Indeed." Caden smiled and rubbed her shoulders.

Lisselle investigated the shadowed case surrounding Farida, then did a quick check to make sure everyone else was okay. Including Zarius. "Of course, I have no real idea what's normal for a being like you, but you seem fine."

Zarius shrugged. "Honestly, I never expected to be up and about again once we went to our slumber thousands of years ago. But I do feel as normal as I have felt since I was awakened."

They all went out into the main room. Zarius said a few words and a shadow appeared to cover the door to the chamber that Farida was in. "Just an extra layer of protection. Once your friends get here and those agents recover, there will be many people passing through. We can't take a chance of someone accidentally letting that free."

Everyone quickly gathered their gear; all wore the goggles and extra equipment.

"Don't forget that I don't know that I will be able to reach you. Any of you." Zarius appeared worried. "I will try to keep the new agents asleep and recovering—they truly need it. But if any of them wake up completely, I will let them. Stay safe, be swift, and gather as much information as you can. I'll send you all up together to reduce exposure, but I'd advise you to separate quickly."

Caden took Nettie's hand. "We're ready." He not only had his pack, but he had weapons and digging equipment tucked around him. Just in case.

Nettie squeezed his hand.

The next moment they were all in the village. Not exactly where they'd appeared before—probably a good idea just in case anyone had seen them—but still nearby.

Homer and Lisselle were dressed as rich English tourists and they both nodded then strolled arm and arm down a side road.

Torlian and Darwish were heavily cloaked and went

down to circle the compound from a good distance away.

"That leaves us, my dear." Caden nodded for her to lead their way. Both of them weren't really disguised, but appeared to be archeologists on the prowl. Helpful and quite accurate if anyone knew the truth of what they were doing.

Nettie put her arm through his and led them to the field where she'd come out of the tunnel. Darwish had reminded her of his shed nearby if they needed anything—or to hide.

They did a meandering approach after quietly discussing the benefits of going slowly or quickly. Slow left more chances for being seen, but they might not be noticed as they wouldn't be that unusual. Quickly moving would be highly suspect even it would get them into the tunnels faster.

"Two farmers are watching us in the next field."

Nettie glanced over at Caden's words and observed them to confirm they were in fact, farmers. There hadn't been any signs of guards out here when she'd escaped, but that might have changed if they figured out how she did so.

However, even after watching them carefully, they appeared to be simply curious farmers. They went back to work when Nettie and Caden stopped to admire a pile of old bricks.

She took a deep breath, squared her shoulders, and headed toward the tunnel. It appeared as she and Darwish had left it. He'd not refilled the hole and she was grateful. Both for making it easier to access, but also an indication that the people working with King James might not have discovered it.

"There's a lot of debris down there," Caden commented as he helped her climb down and then followed her once she'd cleared the area.

"There was far more when I had to get out. It appears

to be rubble from a dig location." Nettie wasn't happy about being back here, but there was a job to do.

"I have a feeling there may be many stashes around this village. If we weren't fighting for our lives, it could prove interesting to go through them." He stooped down and picked something up.

"A relic?"

He held it up with a grin. "Just a nice throwing stone. Guns are convenient, but loud. A good rock can be quite handy."

She picked up one of similar size. Yes, she had fangs and vampiric strength, but taking out an opponent from a distance silently could be better. Especially when stealth was required.

The tunnel appeared both larger and smaller than what she recalled, but the trip was completely different from her escape. At the time, she'd had no idea if she could find help or get out.

Let alone that Zarius would find a way to bring her companions to her.

They paused at the split tunnel that she'd passed before. A careful examination indicated the correct route.

Caden looked back to the other tunnel. "How do you know this is the right way?"

"I made a false trail down the way I didn't go. I think we're getting closer." Nettie was surprised when a strange feeling hit her stomach—she was actually afraid. That was not only uncommon for her, it was annoying. She couldn't spend time worrying about what might happen. Or what did happen.

"Is anything wrong? You're slowing down." Caden kept his voice low and touched her elbow gently.

She had to fight not to jump. "I have realized that I was far more upset about the events here, most importantly being captured and held, then I previously believed. I might prove to be a hinderance on this task."

Caden pulled her to a stop, turned her toward him, and kissed her. Not just any kiss, but a soul-reaching, powerful kiss that almost knocked her off her feet.

When they finally broke apart he rubbed her arms. "You are the strongest, most amazing person I know. Not to mention that you take my breath away every time I look at you. You couldn't be a hindrance if you tried. You've realized that even with all of your exotic additions, you are still human. What happened to you would have been upsetting for anyone. Yet, you didn't have time to process it." He kept watching her closely. "We can turn back."

Nettie took a breath, then a second deeper one. His kiss and words had brought her back to her senses. "Thank you. Apparently, I married you for more than just your charm and good looks. I feel better. And I promise to work out my reaction to the events when we are back in London and this little adventure is behind us." She leaned in for another kiss when the sounds of heavy feet and clinking of weapons came down the tunnel.

CHAPTER THIRTY-ONE

NETTIE AND CADEN FROZE. IF whoever that was came this way, they didn't have many options.

Listening closely, it sounded as if they were coming down the other tunnel. However, they were heading this direction. It would remain to be seen if they took this split or went to the entrance.

Nettie and Caden had tried to be careful on their way in to not show their passage, but there were always clues. Not to mention that if the guards knew the exit had been blocked, the fact that it wasn't might be a tipoff.

They might be given away not by today's actions but by her escape days ago.

"I don't think we can take the time to go back to the main tunnel." Caden picked up a second small rock. "Is there anything farther down that might give us a way to hide?"

Nettie tried to recall her escape. Sadly, strong emotions weren't helpful for memory details sometimes. "Not from where I joined the tunnel that I recall. We might have to go past where I escaped." They'd said that they wouldn't do so, but so far this trip had given no further information as to what King James was up to, or whether the missing agents were down here.

Plus, there appeared to be armed guards behind them.

"Agreed. Let's go." He nodded for her to lead and they moved as quickly as they quietly could.

Her plan had been to go back to where she escaped, assess the condition and possible access, then go back and see if the side tunnel had any information. That, apparently, wasn't going to occur.

The distance to the section of wall that she escaped through felt significantly shorter than it had on her way out. They'd turned off their flashlights when they heard the people behind them, but her vision was still strong and she peered closely at the battered wood.

"As far as I can tell, no one has come through this way since I did." She wanted to remove the slats of wood to confirm, but there was the risk that someone could be in that room. She did push lightly on the piece that she'd replaced the sliding lock on, but it didn't move.

The sounds of heavy footsteps were still behind them, but weren't getting louder.

Caden warned her to shield her eyes, then did a quick flash of his flashlight aimed at the ground in the direction they had been heading. "I think we have to go on. They're somewhere behind us, whoever they are. And the path that direction looks well used. If we want answers, that might be the way to go."

Nettie examined the path as well once he'd shut off his flashlight—he was right. "Which is good and bad. They might have some of the prisoners down there, but that means they are using this regularly and we could get caught." She squinted at the tunnel floor. "Actually, here it's not disturbed. But down further it is." She slowly walked forward, watching for the change in the dirt and rubble on the tunnel floor. "Here. And this does appear to be a door."

It was about fifteen feet from where she'd come out but would have been at the same level as the room she'd been held in.

Caden studied the door. "It has a lock, but it's a simple one. I can get us in if we need to do so. But I say we keep going."

The footsteps behind them were growing louder again. She nodded and continued on.

The tunnel here had many turns and felt like it was descending. Subtly at first, then steeper.

"Are those unlit torches in the walls?" Caden paused.

"Yes, and I missed those before." Nettie nudged herself to stay on task and they kept going.

The marching footfalls behind them increased in volume. They were definitely coming this direction. Could they be going to the locked door they passed? Or were they following them?

The air around them grew colder and the torch sconces became more frequent. There seemed to be a pause in the sound of the footsteps.

Then they grew louder.

"Whoever they are I'd say they're running. We need a detour." Caden stayed behind her but picked up the pace.

Nettie agreed, but even with her advanced eyesight she couldn't see any other tunnels or passageways breaking into this one. The people following them had the advantage of not caring if they were heard. She and Caden didn't have that luxury.

The ankh tattoo flared brightly, clearly showing through her shirtsleeve. At the same time her fangs dropped down without her wanting them too. She froze, grabbing Caden as he almost ran into her. "Something's affecting me." She didn't feel fishy, but it had come on suddenly before. If someone was controlling aspects of her, they might make her turn mermaid again.

Caden nodded and turned to face the ones after them. They had no place to escape to.

No mermaid change yet, so Nettie pulled out her gun as she saw Caden pocket one of his rocks and do the same. Sound wasn't going to be as important as survival at this point and those people running for them might be blocking the only way out.

There was no light proceeding the ones who were after them, which was more than a little odd. Nettie was able to see down here somewhat, but her eyesight was enhanced. Standard humans would have a rough time of it.

Without warning, the torches around them burst into flame. And they could see those coming after them.

The ones in front appeared to be almost modern Egyptian police, but behind them were another twenty or so warriors who didn't look at all modern.

"Are they like that mob?" Caden steadied his gun and took a few deep breaths.

"They appear to be more solid than they were," Nettie answered as the ones running toward them slowed down. On a hunch, she raised the arm with the ankh tattoo. Unlike the prior time, she didn't feel compelled to shout certain words, but it continued to glow.

Instead of vanishing as the mob had, these men all stopped, dropped to their knees, and bowed toward her.

"That was not expected." Nettie was now able to retract her fangs, but the tattoo was still bright. "Rise." She tried to make it sound as if she commanded people all the time.

They sat up from their bowing, but remained seated on the heels of their feet.

"Who are you?" She kept her voice fairly low in volume; they'd gone a distance from the doorway and signs of the compound, but it wasn't a good idea to tempt fate. Hopefully they would understand her.

"We support the pharaoh." They bowed again. The words were in perfect English.

Nettie also caught that while they were focusing on her, they said pharaoh, not daughter of pharaohs.

"Which pharaoh do you support?" Neither she nor Caden had lowered their weapons, but none of the men before them seemed to notice.

The closest man, an Egyptian of middle age and dressed as if he was only fifty years from the past, raised his head. "We do not know what name you have chosen. But we follow you."

Caden shared a look of surprise with Nettie. There had been female pharaohs recorded in history, Hatshepsut and Nefertiti were two that she thought of immediately. But they were hardly common.

"How do you know I am the pharaoh?"

"The pharaoh tests us," one of the ones in the back, wearing clothes of an ancient Egyptian soldier, said softly.

"We were told of your coming. You bear the mark on your arm and in your blood. And you banished the wild ones. You are our pharaoh. What is your wish?" This again came from the one in the front—one wearing an outfit of an old-style constable.

"I would know who you are." She lowered her gun but didn't put it away. However, there was an extremely good chance that it wouldn't hurt these beings at all.

That made all of them speak at once, which wasn't at all helpful. "Wait." She pointed to the one who had first spoken. "*You* will speak for the group. I ask again, followers of the Pharaoh Nettie the First, who are you?"

She hadn't really meant to call herself that but it was as good as anything. And if these men would follow her, and help against whatever Horus, Sekhmet, and the rest were doing—she'd be whatever they wanted. Besides, sticking with her own name made it easier to recall.

"We are the watchful dead. In life, we defended others, protected the weak, and followed the just gods. We waited in death for our time to serve once again. Your arrival called us forth."

"More ghosts." Caden put away his gun. "How can

you help the pharaoh and her cause if you have no solid form? I am Caden, husband of the pharaoh." He gave a regal tilt of his head.

"We acknowledge the husband of the pharaoh." They all nodded.

"You were chased by the wild ones. They should not be waking, but I fear the arrival of our pharaoh called them as well. They are evil spirits and although have no solid form could have severely injured all of you had Pharaoh Nettie not disbursed them. We are granted more substance than them." He picked up a rock and tossed it into the air a few times, catching it with a small smile. "We are more magic than human as we are now, but we will be able to fight when the time comes."

Nettie smiled. "You ignited the torches. And somehow we speak the same language."

"We did. We follow you, therefore we speak your tongue. It is how it should be. And there will be more of us, but something is holding back their awakening. What would you have us do now?"

"We need to see if some of our people are down here. I need five of you to go with us, including...what may I call you?"

He smiled. "I am Amr."

"Thank you, Amr. Select four others to travel with us. Then leave pairs of guards to watch our way as we go down the tunnel."

"Very well, Pharaoh Nettie." He started to turn to the rest but paused. "Do you follow Anubis? There is a strong feeling of him around you."

Hopefully, none of these beings disliked Anubis. "He and I have the same goals." She almost brought up Zarius, but better to hold off on that. The feeling of Anubis they were getting was most likely due to Zarius' protection around the ankh. But it would be complicated to explain and this wasn't the time for it.

They all nodded as they got to their feet and Amr sorted them out. He selected another more recently alive man to come with them, then three of the older ones. It was interesting as she studied them more that they all did appear to have been police or guards of some type. Their dedication continued into the afterlife.

"Pharaoh Nettie, shall I lead?" Caden managed to keep his smile from twitching completely free. The torches meant that being able to see wasn't a problem for him as it had been before.

"I would greatly appreciate that, husband." She turned to Amr. "Could you have the torches extinguished behind us? There may be those we don't want to see following us."

"It shall be done." He bowed.

She would ask him to stop doing that, it was a bit distracting and she wasn't someone to bow to. However, it was part of what he wanted to do. All of the faces around her looked pleased to be back in the good fight. With a nod more to herself than them, she turned and motioned for Caden to lead the way.

Amr and the other four were silent, aside from the sounds of their boots. Odd for partial ghosts. A pair had stayed where they'd started and the rest followed a distance behind. They would split off as they went and guard the way out.

Nettie turned to Amr. "Is there a way in which you and your people can travel silently?"

Amr looked surprised. "But how will the innocent know we come to save them? How will the evil ones know we bring their demise?"

"Both are true. And there will be times when making sure people know you are coming will be important. However, in this case, we need to be stealthy."

Confusion crossed his face, but he turned to the one behind him and all of them became silent.

The torches continued to light ahead of them and extinguish after they'd passed. And the slope became steeper. Eventually, the rest of the guards stationed themselves behind them.

"Amr, do you know this place? Where we are walking toward?"

"I do not. However, Bassem can travel fast and swift." He motioned to one of the ancient-looking garbed guards. One who had been struck down far too early in life and still had a youthful, happy countenance. "Bassem, travel forward as far as the tunnel goes and report back to our pharaoh what you find. Be quick."

Bassem gave a small bow to Amr and a deeper one to Nettie, then raced off.

Nettie wanted to ask questions about how they all became what they were. But it might be rude to ask people how they died. She was completely at a loss in terms of decorum for such a situation.

The loud sound that echoed up from the bottom of the tunnel they were in brought her thoughts back to the current situation.

The slow, deep reverberation of the drums did not bode well.

CHAPTER THIRTY-TWO

"AMR? DO YOU KNOW WHAT that sound is?" She didn't believe that he and his people were waiting in these tunnels just in case she happened by, but he could have more knowledge than she did.

"I do not. And until Bassem returns I would not recommend sending more of us down. Those drums could be a distraction to lure us, your protectors, away from your side." He looked back up the way they'd come. "I now wish we had brought more of my people with us. I could call them if you would like." The tone in his voice said he thought that would be an excellent idea.

Nettie shook her head. "Thank you, but our way out must remain clear. If we find out there is another way out safely, we can call them to us. Until then, we cannot lose access to our exit."

Amr gave a small bow.

"Shall we continue slowly as a group?" Caden was being extremely solicitous, a good position for the husband of the pharaoh. But it was still odd. He normally wasn't pushy in his opinions, but he did usually make them more well-known.

"I believe we shall. Everyone be on the lookout for anything odd."

Amr stayed closest behind Nettie and his three remaining men spread out the width of the tunnel.

The drumming began to soften as they went further and the air grew even colder. Nettie began to wonder about those snow beasts from under the Khafre pyramid. It was easily three or four miles between the village and the pyramid. But there was no way to know where exactly the tunnels under the pyramid had led them. Nor where this one was now going. At the very least, she believed that they were now under the desert itself.

Caden had taken his gun back out after the drums began. Clearly, she wasn't the only one concerned.

Bassem came running up to them. He'd remained silent and the torches hadn't triggered at his passing. Which made sense if he was basically a ghost.

"Pharaoh Nettie. There are foul and vile deeds taking place at the end of this tunnel. We need to escort you back." How a ghost could be out of breath was a tricky question, but he was.

"Thank you for your report and your concern. But we have missing people and I fear they may be the victims down there. Is there anything of detail you can tell us?"

He gave a slow nod. "There are representatives of the god Horus and the goddess Sekhmet. Even in my time those two were no longer among the people—nor were their servants. But that is who I saw. They were preparing a group of six people in dress not unlike that of you and your husband to be sacrificed. We need to make sure you are safe."

"I will not leave my people to be killed or tortured. We must save them." Nettie was starting to enjoy this pharaoh business. She just wished that lives weren't hanging in the balance. Not to mention, while interesting right now, it would probably become tiresome quite quickly.

Bassem sent a pleading look to Amr. Then even one to Caden.

Amr shook his head. "We will protect our pharaoh and do what she requests."

Bassem nodded and took his place with the other three.

Caden motioned for her to come forward a bit. "Should we continue? We need more people. Or even more ghost people. Two of us with guns and whatever those five can do might not be enough."

"I know. But could you leave the kidnapped agents behind? If they were simply being held, that would be one thing, but we know that's not the case. We have to try and save them. There might not be time for us to come back."

Caden had put away both throwing rocks and ran his free hand through his hair, something he did when trying to not appear concerned. If he tugged on his hair, she'd know he was extremely concerned. "Agreed. We can't leave them to die. And if their ka is being removed then more evil beings will appear to fight against us. We're already outmatched."

Nettie nodded then turned back to Amr. "Amr, could you send for half of your men to come join us? Leave the rest to guard our way back out." She wasn't happy about it, but Caden had an excellent point. Saving the agents would only work if they could win whatever fight they faced at the bottom of this tunnel.

Amr smiled. "Yes, Pharaoh Nettie. One from each pairing will join us."

Nettie wasn't certain how he communicated with his people, but within a few moments, another ten fighters came silently running down the tunnel. She waited until they were together before outlining her plan—such as it was. Fifteen modified ghost-like beings, a half-vampire semi-pharaoh, and a well-train human secret agent weren't a lot to work with, depending on what they were facing. But it was what they had.

"We will continue down. Bassem, stay out front to give a warning when we are almost to them. And stop lighting the torches where they could be seen by those we hunt.

We know from past interactions that our enemies are stealing the ka of the people they have taken. It goes without saying, *that* must be stopped."

Of course, it had taken a lot of magic that neither she nor Caden had to break the agents free of the machines removing part of their souls when they rescued the others. She'd helped but had only been a conduit for Lisselle's magic. "Amr, you mentioned that your people are magical? How much so? If the evil ones have started the process to steal their kas, we will need magic to break it. I was not gifted with magic." She wondered if he would question his pharaoh admitting a shortcoming, but better he know upfront.

"Not all pharaohs have the same gifts. It takes a strong one to admit that." He gave a small bow. "I have never seen a machine that can remove one's ka, but I believe we can stop it if magic is what is needed."

Nettie turned to Caden and at his nod, they continued down the path. "Oh, I should warn you, I do have some unique gifts. Do not be alarmed if you see anything odd during the fighting." She didn't want Amr or his men to panic when her fangs appeared. Or even worse, if something triggered her mermaid form.

"We understand. Pharaohs, like the gods and goddesses themselves, move in their own ways." He sounded confident, but Nettie was still concerned about the first time they saw her fangs. However, there was nothing to be done about it. Time was of the essence.

They picked up speed as they all jogged down the tunnel. The soft footfalls from her and Caden were the only sound as the fifteen men remained completely silent.

After about ten minutes, Bassem held up his hand and all of the torches remained off. The drumming had vanished during their way down, but it was coming back now. Slowly, and at a low volume.

Nettie's soul felt like it had been stabbed and her ankh flared to extreme brightness, then died down.

"We go now?" Amr looked to confirm with Nettie.

"Yes, destroy the evil ones." Her fangs hadn't dropped yet, but she was getting a red film across her eyes—when they realized what was being done to the other agents they'd rescued, Nettie had been angry but had not felt the full impact of what was being done.

This time she felt the atrocity in her soul and wanted to rip apart the ones doing it. She had a feeling this reaction was due to the ankh, not her mother's vampiric blood.

Amr led his men charging forward, with Nettie in their midst. Caden was fast and kept up while he could, but he was drifting behind as they entered the chamber. A fast human was one thing, but Nettie was far more than that. And even she would have been hard-pressed to keep up with Amr and his men for much longer.

The scene was similar to the one they'd come across before. There were only six agents in cages this time, but all had the odd glowing ball connected to them. However, now six people were working on them. Three wore clothing with the head of Horus crudely drawn on, and three with the likeness of Sekhmet. All six came forward at their arrival.

"Amr, send some of your people to stop those machines. Destroy them." The agents being drained this time appeared to be in a slightly better state than the original group, but they needed to break them free of the machines immediately.

Six of Amr's men ran forward with each one going to a cage and immediately doing something to the balls at the victims' heads. Mostly it looked like they simply walked through the machines.

The Horus and Sekhmet followers were torn on which direction to go, but Nettie, Caden, Amr, and his remaining men, charged forward and took away any choice they had. Caden fired his gun at one coming for him with a long knife, the Horus supporter gave a surprised look, clutched his chest, and collapsed.

"They are human. Do you want them to all die?" Amr's voice indicated up until that moment he hadn't been certain if they were human on not. Nettie hadn't been sure either.

"If they won't stand down, yes." She stepped forward in front of the remaining five humans. "Surrender or die." She wasn't a violent person, even as she was half-vampire. But her soul ached with what was being done to those six agents. She felt it rattle through her bones.

"Never! You will fall to us! Your ka will be fodder for our—" The Sekhmet follower choked and collapsed. A tall, ancient-appearing watchful dead warrior had gotten behind him and run him through with his curved blade.

"As I said, we can kill them all if the pharaoh wishes," Amr said.

"Or I can just shoot them. But it will be less likely to make anyone who finds them look toward us if they don't see any more bullets." Caden watched the remaining four humans carefully.

"Agreed. Amr, since they will not surrender, destroy them if you would. Caden and I will check on the agents."

Whoever these followers of Horus and Sekhmet were, they weren't bright. Even seeing two more quickly die at the hands of the ghost men, the final two wouldn't surrender and ran to hide behind a sarcophagus.

"There are trying to stall us." Nettie and Caden ran to the cages. The balls were destroyed but the agents were still unconscious. Even though these appeared to be in better shape, they wouldn't wake up. "Kill those last two, then help us carry these people out." As she spoke she reached into the nearest cage and picked up the man lying there. He was breathing, but wouldn't open his eyes.

Caden started to grab one as well, but she called him

off. "Have our friends carry them. We might need your gun after all." The hairs on the back of her neck were rising as a feeling struck her. More people were coming this way—they simply hadn't heard them yet.

The last two Horus followers were quickly dispatched by the ancient swordsman. The five remaining agents were picked up as if they were children.

"Pharaoh, let me help you." Amr smiled gently and held out his arms for the agent she carried.

Under normal circumstances, she would have said she could carry the man. And she could. But image was important right now, not to mention as strong as she was these ghosts were stronger.

She handed the man over. Then they heard the sound of people fighting down the tunnel they'd come down. Someone was fighting the watchful dead guards they'd left behind.

Bassem took off and at first, she thought he was scouting for more lurking enemies. But he returned a moment later. "We can get out this way, I smell fresh air down the tunnel. But we must hurry."

Nettie motioned for everyone to follow Bassem. There was no way to know where this tunnel ended, but the fact that the sounds of fighting continued from behind them, even with the ten watchful dead guards, didn't bode well for their chances. Especially not if they wanted to get out with the unconscious agents.

This tunnel was far narrower and almost not visible unless someone stood at the right angle. The ancient swordsman guard waited for Nettie at the entrance. "I will protect you, my pharaoh."

Nettie nodded; she'd made sure everyone went out first. "What is your name?"

"I am called Farouk, Pharaoh Nettie."

"Farouk, with the magic you carry, can you bring down this rock?" She pointed to a large stone at the entrance of the tunnel. It could mean trapping them all somewhere unpleasant, but the ones following them were almost to the chamber.

They'd dispatched the ghost guards which meant, she, Caden, and the rest had little chance if they wanted to save the agents.

He tilted his head back and studied the rock for a moment, then looked to the entrance of the tunnel. "My pharaoh is wise. I can, and they will not follow. Please stand back." Farouk was tall and touched the rock overhead. Then he softly said a few words and stepped closer to Nettie. "We should move back."

The rock collapsed, taking the ceiling and sides of the tunnel down with it.

Caden came jogging back to them. "What happened?"

"I asked Farouk to bring down the passage. We have to hope that there is another way out at the end." She shook her head as the dust settled. The way was well and truly blocked. "The option to go back the way we came was lost when they defeated those ghost warriors we left behind. Thank you, Farouk. Now, let's continue."

There weren't any torches down this narrow passageway but Nettie and Caden both turned on their flashlights. The watchful dead waited a short way down and none of the ones carrying the agents appeared at all fatigued.

"Amr, I am sorry for the loss of your people."

He angled his head as if hearing something, seemingly not noticing the agent he carried over his shoulder. Then he smiled. "Thank you, but they will recover and join us. Their tasks are not yet finished." He sounded extremely confident, and given that she wasn't even completely certain what these watchful dead really were, Nettie accepted his statement as fact.

"Then let's carry on." She marched to the head of the line, not surprised to find Bassem in the lead.

"Pharaoh Nettie, I feel the air. I will lead us out to safety."

He had probably died over a thousand years ago, but he was still so young and enthusiastic that it tugged at her heart. "Thank you, Bassem. Continue, please."

Caden stayed with her and the ghost guards carrying agents directly behind him.

The path continued the downward slope from the prior tunnel and the chill crept through the rocks. The passageway narrowed severely at one point, causing some juggling of the unconscious agents to pass them through.

"Hold a moment." Nettie paused as the light from her flashlight hit some carvings on the tunnel wall. It was similar, if not the same, as that which they had seen under the Khafre pyramid. "Do any of you understand what this says?"

Amr and the other more recent ghosts shook their heads, but Farouk nodded slowly. "It is of an ancient mystical tongue. One only fully known by the priests. However, I did love learning when I was alive." He ran his hand reverently over the carvings. "This was a sacred passage. Built long before the three pyramids above were created. We need to proceed with care, as there are many traps."

"We're under the pyramids of Giza?" Caden kept his light, like Nettie's, on the carvings. Even though it was doubtful that Farouk needed it.

Farouk looked up as if studying the ceiling, then nodded. "Almost. We have crossed a distance and these tunnels are deceiving. But in a short while, we will be under the Great Pyramids."

CHAPTER THIRTY-THREE

CADEN SWORE. "HOPEFULLY WE CAN find another way out that doesn't involve the snow beasts."

"That would be preferred." Nettie turned to Farouk, who continued reading the carvings. "We came through the under part of the pyramid Khafre yesterday. There were complications. Is there a way to find out if that is where we will come out again?"

"I do not know, Pharaoh Nettie. This speaks of a massive underground realm. If my understanding of the carvings is correct, it was larger than all three of the great pyramids."

"Were they built atop this area on purpose?" Nettie wasn't certain it would make a difference, but it did seem odd that the structures were placed directly above this warren of caverns and tunnels. Especially when they had an entire desert to put them in.

"That is more difficult to determine, but I believe they might have been. However, it is not Khafre that is where this path appears to be leading us. If I am reading it correctly, this will lead us under the pyramid of Khufu."

"The Great Pyramid itself, and where that team of archeologists is currently working." Caden looked around at their group. "This is going to be extremely difficult to explain."

"True. But we don't have much of a choice and can't take the time to try and find another tunnel—not to mention that I'd rather not run into those snow beasts again. Nor become a mermaid."

Farouk looked down at her with a questioning glance at the last word but said nothing.

"Then we go onward," Caden said.

"I am truly lucky to have such an agreeable husband." Nettie smiled. "Bassem, lead on. We will deal with the archeologists when we come to them."

Amr came next to her. "These beings we need to avoid, they are human?"

"Yes. And we don't have time to explain who we are, or why we're bringing out six unconscious people from a pyramid that no one saw us going into. And that doesn't even deal with trying to explain all of you."

"My people who are not currently carrying your injured could scare the humans. Make them stay out of the way long enough for all of you to escape." Amr looked like it was something he would like to do as well. But he wouldn't give up his duty of carrying the agent to do so.

"Then we still have to figure out how to get back to town. We would be quite noticeable walking across the desert with these injured," Caden said. "And far too easy to capture, or worse, if the ones following us know where we went."

"I think we shall have to deal with that once we get out of the Great Pyramid unseen." Nettie pondered. "Perhaps if we get far enough away from the pyramids when we escape, we can return to them as if we'd befallen an accident in the desert."

"There are a lot of ifs involved with that, but I don't see that we have other options." Caden shrugged.

"I shall continue?" Bassem looked ready to race back and forth to the pyramid a few times.

Nettie briefly wondered if he had that energy when alive. "Yes. And Amr, your idea of scaring the archeologists away when we are closer is a sound one. Make sure that all who go with you know they just need to get them out of sight of the entrance. We will escape, change direction, and say we fell to bandits." She looked around. Some of the more recent ghosts could pass as modern day—but the older ones like Farouk couldn't. They had no time or resources to find alternative clothing either.

Amr followed where she was frowning. "Ah yes, they would have stood out in my time also. Perhaps a traveling show? Do they have them in your modern times?"

Nettie smiled. "We do. I'm not sure about here in Egypt, but if questioned we can claim it is an English tradition. Very good thinking, Amr, that should work well. Those who are not carrying an agent, move to the front. Only scare the archeologists, do not injure them."

There was a shifting around as Amr and the other five agent-laden ghosts dropped back to her and Caden.

"Do you think this will work? Two English, six obviously injured Egyptians, and fifteen performers? What kind of event were we having?" Caden looked around their group.

Nettie slipped her arm through his. "Our wedding celebration, of course."

Farouk and Bassem both held up their fists to indicate stopping. They were close enough to the dig location that Nettie could hear the soft mutters of people working and the sifting sound as dust and dirt were searched for important, but tiny, pieces.

She felt a twinge—hopefully, nothing crucial would be lost with what they were about to do. But there simply wasn't a choice. As it was, this plan was extremely weak.

On cue, Farouk, Bassem, and the rest of the empty-handed ghosts began wailing and shouting as they ran forward. They also managed to lift off the ground, hovering a foot or so above the floor—just high enough to be noticed.

"That is quite handy," she said to Amr.

"Yes, we don't do it often as it is tiring. Not to mention disturbing to others. Although as that is the need right now, it works well." He watched his men as they found all of the archeologists and chased them toward the passageway. "Be ready."

Nettie smiled and rubbed some dirt on herself and Caden. "We should at least appear to be stranded."

When the last of the ghosts ran out, Amr led the rest of them out the same way.

The passageway here was short and clean, and obviously well-used. There was no one else in sight so they made their way to the tunnel of blue sky at the far end.

Nettie and Caden were the last out and didn't see that the rest of their people were off to the side until they'd come completely out of the pyramid.

To find an airship loaded with weapons bearing down on them.

An unfamiliar voice boomed out. "Stay where you are. We're here under the authority of the English government, and you—"

"Nettie! Caden! Over here!" The prior speaker was cut off by Rebecca as she jumped up and down on the deck of the airship.

Gaston and Damon ran up behind her.

"Set this monstrosity down immediately! Those are my people down there!" Gaston bellowed.

"All of them?" This new speaker was one of the archeologists—judging by his attitude, the one funding the current dig site.

Gaston looked down to Amr and the rest, then to Nettie and she nodded. "Yes! Of course, they are. My people have been working with the Egyptians. Look, they rescued the injured people we were searching for."

He turned to the man behind the wheel of the airship. "Land us, NOW!"

The dark-haired man looked vaguely familiar, many of Homer's pirate buddies would drop by the mansion from time to time. He was about twice the size of Gaston and looked strong enough to toss Gaston over the side with one hand.

But he nodded to the crew and they worked on lowering the airship.

Nettie was impressed. It was difficult for an airship to land without a stand of some sort, but she had heard Homer bragging about modifications he'd made to his airship and the others in his unofficial fleet.

The airship didn't make a graceful landing, but it did land.

The archeologist who'd questioned them about all being together came forward before Gaston could get off the airship. Rebecca and Damon were on his heels and the rope ladder wasn't a quick way down.

"Now see here, how did all of you get into my pyramid? There are valuable finds in there and if you're really a band of tomb robbers, even England can't help you." The archeologist avoided looking at Gaston and the airship but spun on Caden and Nettie.

Nettie started to respond, but then nodded to Caden. She didn't feel up to a battle of the genders right now and the way this man was barely looking at her indicated that would be the case.

Caden stepped up and got into the man's face. Rather, since Caden was a good three inches taller than the man, he forced him to look up to him. "Are you that clueless that you missed seeing our injured? We risked our lives to save these people. The ones helping us are a traveling troop who delayed their performance to help us. And you fear that we are stealing relics?"

Gaston fought his way free of the rope ladder from the airship and stomped over.

Rebecca looked ready to run to Nettie but stayed behind Gaston.

Probably a good idea. At least until these men sorted things out.

"You will stand down until all of my people have been recovered." Gaston looked at the injured, to the airship, and then back to the archeologist. "And you will provide us with horses and carriage to transport the injured. Do not fret, I can pay." He gave his best condescending glare, managing to look down his nose at the taller man. "The sooner this is taken care of, the quicker your people can get back to working."

The archeologist looked torn. He didn't want to help them, he most likely believed they'd managed to ransack his dig. But his people couldn't go inside until Nettie's group moved. While Gaston had been getting down from the airship, Amr had moved their people to the entrance of the pyramid. They even went so far as to lower the injured to the ground.

"It would be more than you–"

"I can afford it. Trust me. But time is of the essence."

"Fine. Keep your people here, I will bring the carriage to you." The archeologist nodded and left.

Which caused Rebecca to run forward and grab Nettie in a fierce hug. "You have had some adventures." Her eyes went huge as she ran her hand down to Nettie's. "What's this?" She held up Nettie's ring finger.

"It's exceptionally complicated, but Caden and I are married. Needed to do so. But we will be having a formal wedding back in London."

Rebecca watched Nettie's face, then hugged her again. "I will wait to hear your story. Damon and I postponed our wedding until you returned. Maybe we can do them at the same time."

Nettie smiled. There was still no way she was going to have a big wedding. But right now, she was so glad to see Rebecca and the others that she didn't care. They'd work things out later.

Gaston and Damon joined them once Gaston was satisfied that the archeologist was doing what he said he would.

Gaston grabbed Nettie in a fierce hug. "I'm very glad no ill harm came to you when you were taken. You are like the daughter I never had." There were tears in his eyes as he stepped back to look at her. "Now, who are these men in truth? I assume the injured are more of the missing Egyptian agents?"

"It's a very long story, but these men saved Caden and myself. As well as the agents." Nettie would prefer to get everyone on the airship and leave immediately, but that rope ladder wouldn't work for getting the unconscious agents up to the deck.

"He's coming back." Caden and Damon had been talking quietly but Caden looked up at the approaching pair of horses and carriage.

The carriage wasn't fancy, but it would hold the six injured as well as a few others.

The money he demanded from Gaston was an amount equal to five full rigs with a dozen horses.

Gaston took great pleasure in shrugging the amount off and handing the man his money as if he should have asked for more.

"Can the airship stay close to the carriage? Not too close, obviously, but I feel we might need coverage." Nettie figured that she and Caden could ride with the carriage, but the narrow-eyed look Gaston gave them meant he didn't see it that way.

"I'd ask Captain Pilo, he's in charge since Homer isn't here. I assume the rest of our people aren't in that pyramid?" He nodded when Nettie shook her head. "*Tres bien*. However, I want you and Caden on that airship. The captain has some far fiercer people to ride with the carriage."

"But...fine." Nettie gave in. She wasn't terribly fierce looking unless she released her fangs. And that only worked when people were close to her and could actually see them. A sudden icy feeling shook her and she looked around for the source but saw nothing. "We need to leave. Now." The ones who'd been after them might not have been able to follow them through the tunnel, but they would have known where they went.

The chill up her back indicated they were coming.

CHAPTER THIRTY-FOUR

"I THINK THAT'S A GOOD IDEA." Rebecca had an odd tone to her voice as she stared at nothing. Rather, the side of the pyramid that had nothing of note to stare at.

"Are you having a vision?" Nettie kept her voice low.

"I believe so. More of a general feeling of evil coming near us." Her eyes went wide as she turned to Nettie. "It will swallow us all if we don't leave immediately. You shouldn't be here." She even went so far as to begin pulling on Nettie's arm.

"See here, what's wrong?" Gaston had been watching the loading of the unconscious agents into the carriage, along with three heavily armed, and quite burly, airship pirate guards, but picked up on the concerned whispering between Nettie and Rebecca.

"Both Rebecca and I sense something evil coming this way. There had been beings of some sort hunting us in the tunnels. We lost them underground, but they would have known where we'd have to come out."

Gaston watched both of them, then nodded. "We'll leave now. Please have your friends travel in the airship." He had a curious look on his face as he watched Amr, Bassem, and the rest of the ghosts. Gaston might not have supernatural abilities but he'd been in the Society long enough to pick up on oddities.

Amr waited, but Nettie nodded to him. He and his men quickly went up the rope ladder to the deck of the airship.

"Hmm, he waited for your command," Gaston said. "I will enjoy hearing the details when we are safe."

Rebecca hadn't noticed but now looked ready for questions as they walked to the rope ladder. "I'll be good, but I must hear it all."

Caden and Damon joined them going up the rope ladder. Nettie was most grateful for her trousers and noted that Rebecca was wearing a pair of split-skirt trousers. They made traveling so much easier.

The carriage waited until the airship lumbered into the sky—again, some of Homer's tricky modifications at work. It wasn't graceful, but it was up. And managing to hover at a close distance to the carriage. Not enough to spook the horses, but enough to provide coverage if needed.

"However, this airship will also make it easier to spot us and them," Damon said from the railing. He carried a long rifle that Nettie had never seen before. He grinned and patted it. "I'm an expert marksman, and Rebecca's becoming a crack shot herself. An airship's cannons aren't always the best deterrent."

Nettie turned to her friend. "I didn't know you were taking up riflery."

"Yes, it's quite relaxing really. Even more so than needlework." Rebecca grinned. "And more productive. But, I am playing a different part right now." She pulled out a long glass. "We had been searching for you everywhere. The Mudger isn't connecting to the one Homer used before, so we set out to find you. We came by the pyramids and went to aid that person back there when your friends came out and appeared to be attacking the archeologists." She hugged Nettie then stepped away and began scanning the desert as they flew.

Hopefully, anyone trying to attack the carriage would raise more than enough dust to be seen quickly, but Nettie still felt helpless up in the sky.

Caden had also taken a rifle from the stores onboard the airship and came next to her. "You look even more worried than before we lifted off."

"I wish I was down there to protect them. They are so exposed in that carriage." Ignoring the fact that the three pirates with them were armed well enough for a small army.

Amr silently came to her other side and kept his voice low. "My people and I can travel without being seen. We don't need to travel on this floating barge. Although, many of them are extremely fascinated by it. However, until your people know who and what we are, I don't think it would be good for us to vanish from here and appear down below in sight of your people here—at least not until it became desperate. But, Pharaoh Nettie, if those people in the wagon fall under attack, they will not be alone." His smile was warm as he gave a bow and then drifted to the other side of the ship.

"*Pharaoh* Nettie?" Rebecca had moved away with her glass as she watched the desert, but still not far enough to fail to hear Amr's words. "I think there has been *a lot* going on that needs to be discussed." She stepped closer and dropped her voice to a whisper. "This is an odd question, but are your new friends...not really alive?"

Nettie watched Amr gather his people. She felt better knowing that they would be able to help the carriage if needed. It would be exposing what they were, but anyone on this airship would be trustworthy or they wouldn't be part of Homer's crew.

"It's complicated." That was the best Nettie could give Rebecca at this point. "Do you sense something?"

Rebecca's clairvoyance was growing and changing. She

originally had only seen random snippets of the future. She'd started being able to tell other things about the worlds beyond now.

"Yes. As if they are there but not there. As odd as that sounds." She watched the ghost men for a few moments.

Nettie took her arm and smiled. "They are on the side of good, that I can tell you."

"That is good enough for me. For now." Rebecca watched the ghosts a moment more, then nodded to both Nettie and Caden and returned to watching the desert.

"They are most likely after you, as well as getting those agents back. Having you down there would increase the risk to everyone," Caden said softly.

"Logically, I know that. But emotionally?" Nettie took a deep breath. "I'm still working on that part."

The horses below were going at a good clip. The man had grossly over-charged Gaston, but at least the horses and carriage were sound.

"Dust off the port bow!" A woman shouted from the front of the airship where she was on lookout.

The trail spiraling into the air indicated that the people causing it were coming from the village. And that they were moving fast.

"Rifles to the bow!" Captain Pilo yelled.

Amr and his men watched Nettie for orders but she subtly shook her head. Having them go down now would negate the effectiveness of their sudden appearance if an attack came. The people riding in their direction could be nothing more than locals out for a race.

But she had a feeling they weren't that lucky.

"Dust off the stern too!" This was a man, also a pirate by appearance.

"Split the long guns to both sides! And drop our height." Captain Pilo stayed at the wheel.

"They're trying to trap us in the middle." Caden squinted toward the back of the airship. "But the ones coming from that direction don't appear to be coming from the pyramids."

Rebecca came over and pointed her glass behind them. "They aren't. I wish I could see them better to have an idea who they are." She held the glass out to Nettie.

"Thank you." She might see the cloud of dust clearer now with the glass, but she couldn't tell anything else. "Sadly, I can't tell either. Nor where they were coming from. We shall have to make a note of where they are in relation to the Great Pyramids of Giza and the Sphinx so we can look it up later on a map." She handed the glass back to Rebecca.

Bassem came over this time, but it appeared to be at Amr's urging. He motioned for Nettie to leave Rebecca. "Amr would like to know if you would like us to go down to the wagon yet?"

"Not yet. When you go down you would all have to run alongside the carriage. I am sure that wouldn't be a hardship for any of you, being what you are. But it would be difficult to explain. We still might just be in an unfortunate circumstance and neither group is actually pursuing us."

Even Bassem didn't appear to believe her, but he gave a short bow and went back to the rest of the ghost men.

"You don't believe that." Caden ran a thorough check of his borrowed rifle.

"No, I don't. But hope always springs eternal. I was thinking of trying to reach Zarius." She knew he couldn't bring them into the temple, not at this distance and not with so many, but if they could reach him perhaps he could help. And maybe send Lisselle and the rest out to meet them. If they were back from their own adventures.

"It can't hurt. Well, as long as some evil deity isn't haunting him." Caden shrugged.

"Good point, but with the airship's Mudger not reaching ours I'd say we need to do something." She sighed as her brain caught up. "Or both Mudgers could be working fine, but there are none of our people in the temple to answer the calls. I should have trained Zarius before we left."

"We all should have thought of it but I didn't think the airship would arrive quite this early."

"That's a good point. We can't use it to chase off one group as it would leave the carriage open for the other. But there could be a way to deal with both sides. If they are both aggressors." She nodded to Caden and went to Gaston.

He was watching the group of riders coming from the village through a long glass.

"How did this airship get here so quickly?"

"Always with the questions." He pulled away from the glass. "It's something that Homer had Lisselle help him with during the last few weeks. Unfortunately, it's far beyond my complete understanding as they pulled some witchcraft into it somehow. The rest of his airships are still crossing the ocean."

"Does he have anything onboard that will help us beat both of these two groups at the same time?" She narrowed her eyes as she looked ahead. The group coming from the village was easier to see. "Are those riders on camels?"

Gaston nodded and handed her his glass. "We should have gotten you one of these. I can only just make out what they're riding."

Nettie took the glass. "Yes, camels. And I believe that is Darwish. And Torlian. And seven men I have never seen before. Or the seven men could be chasing Darwish and Torlian. It's difficult for even me to tell." They appeared quite clumped together but the sand and dust made it difficult to tell.

"Who is Darwish?"

"He's the one who found me. He's an agent of the local Society branch who escaped being taken with the others." She watched for a few moments more, but they weren't any clearer. Either Darwish and Torlian were outrunning a group of bad people, or they found allies.

She handed Gaston back his glass. "I'm going to try and reach Zarius. If Homer and Lisselle are still out there's none of our people left in the temple." Gaston's eyes widened at the final word, but she waved him off. "It's where we're hiding, something Zarius controls." When Gaston nodded, she curled her fingers where the odd bead of Zarius' had vanished into the skin of her palm, and mentally called him. Even if he couldn't rescue them, or come join the fight, he might still be able to help.

She called his name in her head five times before she heard a faint response.

"*Nettie? I can barely hear you. Darwish and Torlian are looking for you.*"

"*Yes, it's me. Do you know if Darwish and Torlian found new friends?*"

There was a pause on the other end. "*Not that I had heard, but they did reach out to say they were going into the desert as there was a flying ship out there. I believe your friends are using those?*"

"*Yes, we found them. But Darwish and Torlian have people behind them and I can't tell from this distance if they are friend or foe. And there's another group coming at us from the opposite direction. We found more unconscious agents so we couldn't bring them onboard the airship.*" This wasn't the time to explain about Amr and his men.

"*I am limited in what I can see, sense, and do. Something is battering the temple.*"

"*How can something attack underground?*"

"*It's not a physical attack, but Horus appears to be trying to find me. Rather, us. Your agents are still asleep, but I believe he wants to finish the job. I'll do what I can, but be wary, he will be after the ones you just found as well.*"

Nettie watched Darwish and Torlian. Even without

the long glass, they appeared to be gaining distance from the other seven riders, but the desert could be deceiving. "*Should we find somewhere else to go*?" She had no idea where but if Horus was attacking the temple, that wasn't safe anymore.

"*Not yet. I have a plan that will block them all. It will just take a while to implement. I will do what I can to help you now, but contact me when you are closer.*"

"*I will. Stay safe.*"

"*You as well.*" The connection vanished.

"Well? Can he help?" Gaston asked as he continued to watch Darwish and Torlian.

"Not sure. He's facing an attack from Horus right now. But he will try." She wasn't sure how far Zarius could expand his hideout. Possibly enough to accommodate the airship crew and the newly rescued agents, but if they found the bulk of the missing agents, it could become problematic.

The camel riders following Darwish and Torlian seemed to be slowing down. That could be good if they were actually the enemy, perhaps Zarius was doing that. Then they sped up—far too quickly. *That* wasn't Zarius.

She marched over to Amr and his people. "I need one of you to appear directly after the two men in the front of that group. Perhaps two of you. I need you to attack those riders, make them stop running after my friends." She still wasn't certain which side they were on, but sometimes an educated guess was best. If something was giving that group after Darwish and Torlian speed, and not her two friends, the odds were good they were on the other side.

Amr grinned. "That is something we can do. Farouk and I will go down." He motioned to the rest of them and they closed ranks around him and Farouk.

Nettie saw both men vanish, but she doubted that anyone else did.

She turned to the front and was about ready to ask Gaston to borrow the long glass when the ground around the racing camels exploded in a wall of sand.

CHAPTER THIRTY-FIVE

NETTIE YELLED BUT KNEW THERE was nothing they could do to help Torlian and Darwish. Rifles had a long range, but not long enough to shoot that far with complete accuracy. And right now, their two friends were as well hidden as their possible attackers.

"Can this thing go faster?" Gaston yelled to the airship captain.

"Not if you want us to protect that carriage."

"He's right, and that could be why they did that." Caden came closer. "Moving us out of the way and leaving them exposed."

His words stopped Nettie in her tracks. She'd just been ready to send Bassem and the rest of the ghost men down to the whirlwind. Which would also remove defenders from the carriage.

But she could send one man to find out what happened. "Bassem, can you jump over to the whirlwind and see what's happened?"

He tilted his head. "I could, Pharaoh Nettie. But you can reach Amr. As our leader, he will always hear his pharaoh. Until our task is finished and we have our final rest."

That was unexpected. "I just think of him?" This talking to other beings in her head was more than a bit odd. But handy.

"Yes."

Nettie closed her eyes and thought of Amr. Then almost jumped as he immediately appeared between her and Bassem.

"What do you need, Pharaoh Nettie?"

"What's happening down there?" She ignored the questioning looks from two of the pirates, they'd seen Amr appear this time.

"Farouk is calling a windstorm. We are having a difficult time convincing your two friends to ride through it, however. And the ones behind them are confusing. They are both good and evil at the same time." His scowl showed his opinion of such unacceptable behavior.

"Tell Torlian that I sent you and going through the sand is just like riding his broomstick." That didn't make much sense; however, it would hopefully let Torlian know that Amr and Farouk were with her.

Judging by the way Amr deepened his scowl, it didn't make sense to him either. But he nodded. "As you wish." Then he vanished.

Gaston had been watching them and saw Amr disappear. He called her to him.

"Your new friends are…?"

"Unique. I'll explain later."

He paused, then nodded. But the look on his face indicated there would be a lot of explaining.

"The riders off the stern are gaining!" The pirate watching behind them yelled and more people armed with rifles ran to him.

The whirlwind in front of them parted, or at least thinned, and Torlian and Darwish raced out on their camels. The other seven, along with Amr and Farouk, remained hidden behind the wall of sand.

"That's convenient, a specifically focused windstorm." Gaston wasn't going to badger her for answers yet, but he clearly knew there was oddness happening.

"New tricks for a new way of fighting." Nettie gave him an odd smile. That didn't make much sense either, but she was focusing on many fronts at this point.

Darwish and Torlian were making good time on their camels and would soon reach the carriage.

"Oh no. Bassem?"

He was next to her immediately. "Yes?"

"I need you to tell the…that won't work." She shook her head. She'd planned on having him tell the pirates in the carriage that Torlian and Darwish were friends. But they didn't have the time to explain it to three strangers. "Change of plan. If you carry me, can you safely get us to the ground between the carriage and our friends?"

"Yes, Pharaoh Nettie. We cannot move others, but all of us can carry our pharaoh."

"Okay, Gaston, I'm sorry I don't have time to clear this with you. Those pirates don't know Darwish and Torlian are with us. We have to warn them not to shoot." Then she nodded to Bassem.

He swept her up almost faster than even she could see and they vanished.

Which was an extremely odd few seconds.

Then he was standing, with her still in his arms, between the riders and the horses. He quickly set her on her feet and stepped back.

She knew he felt most uncomfortable about what had just happened, no doubt handling one's pharaoh as such was simply not done in ancient Egypt, but she had no other way to resolve this. She dropped her goggles over her eyes and held up both hands—one facing the carriage and the other Darwish and Torlian. "Halt!" She yelled as loud as she could without screaming and the horses and camels came to an abrupt stop.

Barely ten feet away from each other.

"It's too long to explain, but these men are with us." She looked to the pirates but waved to Torlian and Darwish.

"However, I believe the ones still in that sandstorm are not?"

Torlian recovered first. "We thought they were, but they attacked us as we started riding out here to rescue you."

"We need to go around that sandstorm then." She walked over to the carriage. "Move a bit over, Bassem and I will ride. Do you have an extra rifle?"

The pirate driver looked stunned, they all did actually. But they first needed to get to safety. Explanations could come later.

They did, however, make room for her and Bassem.

"I can run—"

Nettie cut Bassem off. No reason to add to the mystery they had just exposed. "You will be fine up here. I'd feel better guarding our friends up close." Once she and Bassem were seated, she waved Torlian and Darwish over. "These gentlemen are with Homer's airship. I need all of us to ride back to the village as quickly as possible. And if you see anything peculiar, simply store it away for later. We need clear heads right now."

Once she got their agreement, she nodded to the driver. "With great haste if you please." Farouk's windstorm was still going and so far the other seven camel riders hadn't come out, but she had no idea how long that would last.

She glanced back as they started. The group behind them was picking up speed as well. "Bassem, I have changed my mind. Do you or any of your fellows on the airship have the ability to do what Farouk is doing?"

"I do not. But another one of the very old ones does."

"Very good. Please go to him on the airship, and the two of you stop the ones behind us. Or at least slow them down."

Bassem nodded. "If they are evil may we fight them?" The excitement in his large dark eyes was possibly what got him killed at such a young age.

"Yes, but only if they are evil." Bassem vanished before she could say anything more. Amr seemed to have the ability to sense good versus evil in the hearts of men, hopefully that held true for all of the ghosts.

The pirate driving the carriage gave only a small jump when Bassem vanished and the other two pirates remained stoically still. Homer had trained his people well.

Darwish looked a bit white around the eyes, but said nothing. Torlian simply grinned and nudged his camel to pick up speed to match the carriage.

The airship adjusted course to stay with them and Nettie could almost feel more than a few pairs of irritated eyes watching her from above. The only one who might not chastise her, aside from the ones who didn't know her, would be possibly Damon.

They rode past Farouk's sandstorm but were far enough away that she couldn't make out the shapes inside. It did appear to be slowing down a bit. She wasn't certain at what point to call them back, but they needed to get this carriage well past them first.

There was a muffled explosion behind them. A sandstorm had begun to engulf the riders following them, but then it crumbled. And an explosive was flung at the airship. It missed but only by about ten feet.

She focused on Amr as she couldn't call the other ghosts this way. This time none of the pirates, nor Darwish, even startled when Amr appeared in the seat next to her. "I sent Bassem and another old one to slow down those riders behind us, but I fear something has gone wrong."

Amr nodded and vanished again. He reappeared holding a badly injured Bassem. "Ramose is gone, they destroyed him. I do not believe he can come back to us—he has gone to the final resting. They have Sekhmet and someone else of power riding with them."

Nettie glanced back. The other ghosts who had fallen

while fighting in the tunnel were supposed to return, but from the anger in Amr's voice, that wouldn't be the case this time. "Will Bassem recover?"

"I will, Pharaoh Nettie, but I cannot fight right now," Bassem's voice was weak and he didn't move.

She patted Bassem's arm soothingly, and a rage flowed over her. Similar to her vampire rage, but far stronger and more encompassing. Her ankh tattoo flared the brightest it had been, almost feeling like it was burning through the fabric of her sleeve.

"This will not stand." She knew what she had to do, and a vague feeling of how to do it, but mostly her mind was swirling with emotions. Anger being the strongest. Sekhmet had destroyed one of *her* people. Yes, he had actually died long ago—but he was fulfilling his destiny. "Keep going. Amr, please return to the airship with Bassem and inform my husband that they must not come after me. The people in this carriage need to be escorted to safety. Then come back here and stay unless Farouk needs you." Without waiting for a response from pirate or ghost, she jumped off the carriage.

Which should have been fatal or at least extremely painful, as the horses were racing at top speed now. But her ankh tattoo flared and she floated to the ground. Darwish started to turn back to get her.

"No! I'm fine, keep going!" She burst into a faster speed to leave them behind. They needed to protect those agents now.

More people to be upset at her reckless behavior. But it would be dealt with when things settled. None of the deities had appeared when they'd rescued the fifteen agents and destroyed the underground area.

So why now? What was so important about these six? Nettie knew she was the only one able to take care of this and that her ability to do so would wane quickly.

The ankh tattoo was giving her a temporary gift, not permanent powers.

She gave a primal yell and raced toward the cloud of dust indicating where the newest danger came from. If she had more than fury in her mind, she would have marveled at her speed, as it was she tucked the feeling aside for later review. Nettie was not one for furious outbursts, but it felt as if she was carrying the anger of a hundred people. Sekhmet had irritated her before, but now Nettie wanted to see if she could destroy her. Real goddess or not.

After a quick glance back to verify that the airship and carriage were continuing toward the village, Nettie ignored the fading yelling coming from behind her.

There was going to be far more than simply a lot of explaining to do once they settled this.

Maybe the ankh was helping her eyesight as well, for she could now make out the figures racing toward her. Or she simply had run that quickly.

Sekhmet was in the lead on a sleek, all black camel. There were no other deities that she could see at first, but the last rider was cloaked and looked odd. Seven total besides Sekhmet.

They shifted direction at once, to move away from her direct path, but Nettie grinned and shifted as well. Honestly, she had never felt so alive in her life. As if her prior existence had been nothing but shadow.

She also had no clear plan of attack. Aside from taking out Sekhmet and removing those who were threatening her people.

"Nettie! Have you come to join us?" If Sekhmet was surprised to realize that Nettie was the form racing across the desert, she didn't sound it.

"I have come to destroy you!" Her fangs dropped down, her eyes went red, and she raised her arm. The ankh tattoo blazed across the distance between them.

Sekhmet yelled and turned her camel away from the light. Three of the ones riding with her weren't so lucky and the riders screamed, then vanished.

Their confused camels continued running but veered away from Nettie and the rest.

"What are you?" Sekhmet slowed down but continued coming forward.

Nettie noticed that half of her face, where the light had struck her, was red and burnt in appearance.

"I am the one who will stop you!" Then she shouted some words that she had no idea the meaning of, but they, more than the words in English, brought Sekhmet to a halt.

"You do not exist!" The remaining riders with the goddess came to a stop behind her. The oddly cloaked one pushed back her hood and snarled. Her head was that of a crocodile.

"Ammit, I presume?" Nettie continued moving forward, but some force was trying to keep her back. Like an unseen sandstorm.

"You are a worthy foe." Ammit's voice was low and her cloak flew back to reveal her lion forefront. Clearly, that was no normal camel she rode. "We will meet again." Then she nodded and vanished along with her camel.

"You cannot leave me!" Sekhmet screamed at the sky. The three remaining riders with her appeared human and were seriously reconsidering the wisdom of staying by Sekhmet's side.

Nettie grinned and the fear on Sekhmet's face grew.

She felt her mother's pendant glow and held it in her hand. "You have no right to destroy people to rule this world. We have forgotten you. This is not your world!" Another bolt of light from the ankh struck Sekhmet and she tumbled off her camel.

The remaining three riders, and Sekhmet's camel, raced off.

"You are ruining everything!" Sekhmet rolled to her feet and leaped at Nettie.

CHAPTER THIRTY-SIX

THE STRENGTH OF THE FURIOUS goddess was strong, but Nettie was furious as well. And while she might not be a goddess, she had some impressive abilities at the moment.

The two tumbled onto the sand, both clawing, kicking, and in Nettie's case, biting. She didn't think that attacking a goddess with her fangs was a particularly wise idea, but the anger and fury raging through her disagreed.

It took a few tries, but her fangs reached Sekhmet's neck.

Sekhmet's eyes flew open and she gave a primal scream.... then vanished.

Leaving Nettie spitting out a mouthful of sand and feeling as if a dozen chariots had run over her.

The glow from the ankh, along with the energy and power she'd had before, vanished, and left her alone in the desert with no ride and no strength of her own. Her only hope was that Caden would forgive her at some point when she never returned.

And that when Sekhmet vanished, it was for good.

She rolled over to see if perhaps she'd missed some nearby shelter, or lingering camel, but the sand was everywhere. The abandoned camels had wisely taken off on their own. The rage of before trickled out of her mind, leaving behind a most disturbing feeling—it reminded her of the one time she had tried to get inebriated in her youth. Her vampire metabolism made that almost impossible, although at the time she hadn't known what she was.

Currently, she felt ill, dizzy, and her mind was full of cotton balls. An exceptionally unglamorous way for a member of the Society to expire.

But, she did what she could to save her people. It was fitting she die out here.

"Pharaoh Nettie?"

Nettie had her eyes closed against the sun when she heard the faint voice. The fog in her head cleared a moment later and she opened her eyes. "Amr?"

"Behind you, Pharaoh Nettie," he said, gently.

She turned and saw ten of the ghosts, including Farouk but not Bassem, standing there.

"I thought only Amr could hear me?" At least she now recalled that. It would have been helpful to remember fifteen minutes ago.

"I am the only one who can hear you, but we have all pledged to you. All of us can find you. Your friends have reached the village and the attendant Zarius was bringing them to his temple. The flying barge has turned and is heading this way. But they were damaged by the explosion of before and are moving slowly." He pointed past here and she saw Homer's airship heading toward them.

Nettie started laughing.

"Pharaoh? Are you all right?" Farouk dropped in front of her with so much concern on his ancient face that she almost hugged him. But that would not be fitting for a pharaoh.

"I am fine. I was having some foolishness earlier, and you saved me from it. As well as saving my life. Your pharaoh gives you all many thanks."

Farouk, Amr, and the rest bowed low. Granted, if the

airship had made it back to her, and managed to find her, they could have rescued her. But, her ghost warriors were there to make certain it happened.

The airship slowed even further as it came closer to her. Then, as done at the pyramids, it slowly began its lowering procedure. She could have had her ghosts carry her up to the deck, but the airship was almost completely lowered by the time that thought burbled to the surface.

Nettie was almost afraid to look up at the faces peering down at her. But when she finally did, all she saw were looks of relief.

The anger would come later, but she'd stand by her actions. Sekhmet might not have been destroyed, or returned to her slumber, but she was injured at the very least. And they'd saved those six agents.

Caden almost didn't wait for the rope ladder to drop completely before sliding down it to run to her. Rebecca was right behind him, her split skirts kicking up barrels of sand, and Gaston, moving a bit slower, was after her.

Amr and his men stood aside as Caden got to her, dropped down, and engulfed her in the tightest hug she'd ever experienced.

"Are you okay? Your face is red. Are you injured? Can you stand?"

"I know you're her husband, but I get to hug her too." Rebecca didn't hug her as tightly, but there were a lot of tears involved.

Gaston caught up at that point. "I won't drop down to hug you, or I won't be able to get back on my feet. But I am glad to see you alive." There was an unspoken chastisement there, but he held it back. There would be time for that later.

"Thank you for coming back for me, after you got the others to safety." She let Caden and Rebecca help her to her feet, as her legs were still uncooperative. "I will explain more when we are back in the temple, but Amr and his men aren't…" she'd been calling them ghosts, but they really were more than that.

Amr smiled and bowed to Gaston. "I am Amr, I lead these men. We are the watchful dead. We serve Pharaoh Nettie the First."

Gaston's eyes widened, but he'd been in the Society too long to let most things ruffle him. He gave a nod to Amr and his men. "I am Gaston and I lead these people. I am grateful for your assistance."

Caden and Rebecca walked Nettie to the rope ladder.

"Are you going to be able to climb that?" Caden asked with one hand on the rope. "I will carry you back to the village myself, if need be."

She gave him a quick kiss. "I know you would, husband. And then we'd die heroically in each other's arms in the sand." She took a deep breath and looked up the rope ladder. It seemed three times as long as just a short time ago. "I might need help, but I can do this." Her arms were shaking by the time she reached the top even with Caden's help.

Amr and his men came up the ladder after Rebecca and Gaston. Better not to have everyone know everything. The airship crew was curious about the watchful dead, but kept their thoughts to themselves.

"We'll be a bit slower than before, and Homer isn't going to like what the shrapnel from that explosion did to his airship, but we'll get you back." Captain Pilo nodded as they lifted up.

"Where will you stay?" Nettie asked.

"Since there's no way to hide this airship—and there are five more at least on their way—I suggested they stay right outside the village but remain in the air. At least until Homer gets them sorted." Gaston nodded. "They are his purview, after all."

They'd seated Nettie in a chair made mostly of sail fabric. But it was comfortable and much better than standing at the moment.

Rebecca dropped next to her as Caden stopped to discuss something with Amr.

"They're truly ancient Egyptians, come back to life?" She kept her voice low and leaned close to Nettie, but continued watching Farouk and the others. "And you're their pharaoh? I didn't think I could be more surprised about anything than you getting married out here. However, I was wrong."

She turned back to Nettie before she could answer about Amr and his people. "And I don't like thinking I've lost you. The others haven't said it yet, but I will. You're my sister, just as much as if we'd been born to the same parents. I know you would have only done what you did with an extremely good reason, and we'll hear it later, but if you do something so reckless again—without help—I'll have Lisselle bring you back from the dead as a ghost."

Nettie took Rebecca's hand. "There was an excellent reason, and I wasn't quite myself. But I will promise to try." She turned to the ghost men. "In answer to your first question, it's complicated. But it appears they were warriors for the side of good when they lived. Now they have been called to serve one more pharaoh and save Egypt. There were ten more who should be coming back soon, and Amr said there were a hundred more than that trying to get through the afterlife to join us."

"And you're their pharaoh." Not a question and for the first time since they'd gotten onboard the airship, Rebecca laughed and shook her head at it all.

"I am. This appeared on me while inside the pyramid tunnels the first time." She unbuttoned and pushed back her sleeve. It was nice to not see it glowing, although that had been a fierce weapon against Sekhmet. "Apparently, among other things, it called Amr and his people to me to lead them."

Rebecca pulled Nettie's arm closer and peered at the ankh. "Did it hurt? It looks almost like it's painted on though."

"Not at all, but Lisselle confirmed that it is a tattoo. I do hope it decides to leave once we take care of all of this. Homer and his crews are fond of these things, and that's well and good. I just don't know if it is proper for me."

"I think it's a mark of distinction." Caden left Amr and dropped to the other side of Nettie. "And I so pledge, that if it doesn't leave, I will get something to match it on my own arm. Let people of London talk all they want." He was smiling but he also had a look like he was torn between hugging the breath out of her again and yelling at her. She had scared him badly.

Aside from their adversarial start when they first met, he'd never yelled at her. She felt it might be warranted this time. The more she recovered and took stock of her actions, the more she felt it had been someone else doing them.

And that someone was extremely reckless.

The airship came to a stop at the edge of the village. Nettie let Caden and Rebecca help her to her feet, as she wasn't sure she could have risen on her own just yet. Hopefully, Lisselle would have something to help her. She could have asked Torlian, but he was busy talking to one of Amr's men. And not all witches were healers.

She looked over the railing as the airship made its slow descent and was not terribly surprised to see a few dozen villagers watching the spectacle closely. Clearly, they'd never seen an airship until today. Which was another issue to discuss with the leaders of this branch of the Society—once they retrieved them all, at any rate. Airships could be handy out here in the desert. While Homer's small fleet was defiantly not officially part of the Society, the Society did have a few airships and war zeppelins within their arsenal. Egypt could have requested some as well. At least the basic airships, Queen Victoria was quite stingy with who was allowed to use the war zeppelins. With good reason in Nettie's opinion. All the airships she'd seen carried weapons. At least a cannon or two. But the war zeppelins were armored things that flew through the sky with more weapons than people. They were also far faster and more deadly than an airship.

And she'd seen up close the brutal results of a collision between the two. When she was still working as a coroner, a regular passenger airship and a war zeppelin collided, killing all on board.

The airship lowered and she saw two shapes waving at them from the ground. Homer and Lisselle. Lisselle appeared to be relieved, Homer was already scowling at the damage to his airship that he could see from a distance.

Nettie still needed some help down the rope ladder, but she and the rest all came off the airship intact. Five of the airship crew stayed on board, but the remaining four, including the captain, went to Homer. Coming up behind him were the three pirates who had safeguarded the carriage.

"You look horrible." Lisselle wasn't going to mince words as she looked Nettie up and down. "Can you walk?"

"Good, I'd hate to think I felt this bad and didn't show it." Nettie judged the distance. "To the stables? With assistance from my husband, I believe so."

Lisselle smiled, then her eyes widened as she looked past Nettie to Amr and his companions. "I don't want to frighten anyone, but there are ghosts following you again."

Torlian came up and laughed. "They are the watchful dead, and follow Pharaoh Nettie the First." He gave Nettie a bow. "Chatted with a few on the way back, amazing fellows."

Lisselle relaxed. "That's at least good. But first, we need to recover before we have to go back into fighting. If everyone who's heading back will follow me, please." She raised her voice on the last line and started for the stables.

"I'm staying here for a bit." Homer waved her on, as he spoke to his captain. The look on their faces were grim, even though from what Nettie could see the airship wasn't that damaged.

Gaston looked torn but finally waved as well. "I'll come back with Homer; I want to see about getting some of the larger things off the airship."

Caden and Rebecca, with Damon on the other side of Rebecca, kept a close watch on Nettie as they followed Lisselle.

"I will be fine, I promise. I refuse to fall over here in the streets." She did her best to look haughty, but a coughing fit ended her posturing.

She diligently ignored the looks of concern of those around her.

They made good time to the, now very familiar, stables. As had happened before, there was no one around. "Does Zarius have a deal with this man?" Nettie barely finished her sentence when she vanished and she found herself inside the main room of the temple. At first no one else was there, then Caden, Rebecca, and Damon appeared. Quickly followed by the rest of their people in groups.

Caden led her to the table and all but forced her into a chair. The six new injured agents had already been given cots in the front room.

Rebecca slowly spun in a circle as she took in the design. "This is amazing. Where exactly are we?"

Nettie looked around. "I hadn't asked. I assume under the village? But now I am wondering if we're somewhere else entirely."

Caden nodded. "Good point. We all made that assumption. Zarius?"

Zarius stuck his head out from what looked to be a new corridor. "Yes? Oh, very good, you found everyone. And who have we here?" He came over to Amr and his group. "You are of the watchful dead, are you not? Farouk? Is that you?" Zarius gave a wide smile and nodded to Farouk.

"It is I." Farouk gave a low bow. "We are indeed the watchful dead. It is good to see you, old friend."

Zarius came forward and hugged Farouk. "He was one of Anubis' most faithful. Anubis will be gladdened to know you are completing your journey."

"There will be more of us, with hope soon. I am Amr and honored to meet you." Amr gave a deep bow. Then introduced the rest of his people.

Zarius' smile was broad when he finished. "I didn't even hope that you would be called to aid us. I am most grateful." He turned and bowed to Nettie. "And honored to welcome Pharaoh Nettie the First. May your reign be short and triumphant." His face grew serious. "I fear you will all be tried greatly in the coming days. Egypt thanks you for your effort."

CHAPTER THIRTY-SEVEN

"WE WILL NOT FAIL." NETTIE'S cough swallowed whatever else she was going to say.

"Now, *that*, I can take care of." Lisselle came to Nettie's side. "I took over a room as a small ward of healing. You, young lady need to come with me, that cough doesn't sound good."

Nettie got to her feet gingerly. She knew better than to argue with Lisselle about healing. Not to mention that she did feel truly awful. "I understand that I might have burned through a lot of energy while I was doing what I was doing. I'm not sure where these coughs are coming from, however."

Lisselle held out her arm and Nettie begrudgingly took it. She was used to being stronger than those around her. And not the type who needed to be escorted around like a little old lady.

It was simply unacceptable.

"That is worrying. But we've no idea what exactly you have become, or what you did. I know Gaston wants to hear it all as well, but you'll simply have to repeat your tale when everyone is back here. I can't fix you without knowing what happened." Lisselle stepped into a small room with three cots in it and steeply sloping beige walls; a mass of small lights kept it from being dreary.

"Those look like candles, but I don't believe they are?"

There were dozens in various holders around the room. But they didn't feel like they had fire.

"They are not. Zarius created them, like everything in here, but he can't fully explain their existence to human minds." She shrugged. "His words. Now get on that cot and unbutton your blouse. I want to listen to your heart and your lungs, then you can explain all that happened."

Nettie did so and held still while Lisselle listened, scowled, then listened and scowled again.

On the third round, Nettie stopped her. "Can you tell me what you *believe* is wrong?"

Lisselle stepped back. "I would love to, alas right now I'm not sure. Your heart appears a bit stressed but the beat is strong. However, your lungs seem to be filled with something unnatural and that is causing the coughing and possibly impacting your fatigue. But it doesn't sound like anything I've heard before." She held out the earpieces of the stethoscope to Nettie. "See what you think?"

Nettie took it. She'd listened to her own heart and lungs enough in medical school to know what they should sound like. And to know that this was not it. Her heart sounded a little strained, but still doing its job. Her lungs however, sounded like a murky swamp.

"That can't be good. I've never heard anything like it."

"That was why I was scowling." Lisselle left the room and came back with a large glass of water and pulled up a chair. "We will sort it out, I assure you. But drink some water and tell me the entire tale. Start from when you and Caden went into that tunnel. There could be things that will assist our prognosis."

It took two more refills of the water glass for Nettie to tell the entire story. Her last actions of going after Sekhmet, and their hand-to-hand fight, brought a look of surprise and concern to Lisselle's face.

"You had quite an adventure, but that last bit…that's not like you, Nettie."

"I know. And the more I look back at it, the less it feels like it was me. Yet, emotionally, it felt right. Through this ankh tattoo, I am connected to Amr and his men just as I am to all of you. The destruction of one of them by someone we continue to have problems with, infuriated me. I had no choice but to avenge him. And stop her from taking more of my people."

Lisselle smiled. "A very pharaoh-like thing to say. However, I'm not certain that what happened to you caused this health issue. You are exhausted, but I believe that was due to expending more energy than even you are normally are capable of. You are one of the strongest people I have ever examined, yet in going after Sekhmet as you did, you exhausted even that vigor."

She frowned. "You are also an increasingly complicated being. Half-vampire, mermaid, and now whatever abilities your blood and that ankh have given you." Lisselle narrowed her eyes as if through her fierce look alone she could find the solution. Then she shrugged. "I might have an idea. You *are* complicated and something inside the pyramid transformed you before, against your will. What if your lungs transformed this time alone? Or at least partially?" She paused. "This is a sensitive question and we don't need to speak of it to others, but did you ingest any of Sekhmet's blood when you bit her?"

"I ate some sand when she vanished, but I spit it back out." Nettie didn't normally ingest blood. Unlike full vampires she didn't need to, nor did she find it anything less than disgusting. Of course, she didn't ingest any of Sekhmet's blood.

Then a little part of her mind slowed down the lighting fast battle between she and Sekhmet and gave her pause. "I might have." She shook her head as she went through the fight a few more times in her mind. The more she recalled, the more she felt she could have.

"Now, I'm sure that's a disturbing admission, but there

could some component from Sekhmet that got into your body. I believe I can get your lungs back to normal, but it may only be temporary until we figure out more fully what's happening inside you. I do wish we were back in the mansion with the labs."

"Agreed. Do we know if Gaston brought any equipment with him?" Nettie knew he said he was going to have Homer coordinate getting some of the larger items off the airship, but they could be other things.

"I believe so, but it might take them a while to move anything large through the village. We will have to resolve the issue witch-style for now. This won't remove the problem permanently, but will help you recover your strength." Lisselle took Nettie's chin and looked her directly in the eyes. "Do not do anything extreme until we actually fix you, is that understood?"

"Yes ma'am." Nettie smiled.

"Okay then. Lie down and close your eyes. This will feel odd, I'm going to have to call forth your mermaid essence in order to balance your lungs. Don't worry, you're going to be fine." She squeezed Nettie's arm.

"I'm ready." Nettie closed her eyes and took a deep calming breath. As long as she was expecting the transformation, she should be okay. That thought lasted about thirty seconds before her entire body felt scaly and itchy. And as if the air around her was trying to crush her.

"Don't move. And keep your eyes closed. Almost done." The odd feeling continued to flow over her, but instead of trying to fight it or even open her eyes, she focused on not moving. Which was far more difficult than she would have expected.

"You're doing great, I think this is working."

Slowly the itchiness and the crushing sensation eased up, then vanished. She took a deep breath. No more unnatural pressure and she didn't cough.

"Done. You can open your eyes and sit up. How do you feel?"

Nettie opened her eyes and took another deep breath. "I feel wonderful. Still a bit tired, but my lungs are clear and my energy is mostly back. Thank you."

Lisselle stepped back, but then frowned. "You're *temporarily* recovered, don't forget that. I'm not an expert in mermaids, but it did seem as if the lung issue was due to a partial internal transformation. Whether it was from whatever forced your transmogrification in the Khafre pyramid previously, or from your fight with Sekhmet, I doubt we'll ever know for certain. But you are not healed. I have no idea how long this will hold."

Nettie buttoned up her blouse, again grateful for the agency-supplied clothing that made it quick and simple. "I understand. And I will make certain that Caden and the ghost warriors know to watch out for me possibly collapsing or turning into a mermaid." The idea that she would remain here while the rest fought to resolve this battle was so far from acceptable that she didn't even bring it up.

"Never fear, I was going to tell everyone when we had our council. Providing Gaston did bring some equipment, I will be needing some of your blood." Lisselle started for the door, then looked back. "And do report if you suddenly begin feeling goddess-like. We have no idea what Sekhmet's blood might have done to you."

"That's a cheery thought." Nettie got off the cot. "But yes, I will report back anything that seems in that direction." She still was hopeful that Sekhmet had been sent back to her eternal slumber after their fight.

A lot had changed in the rest of the underground compound when they came out. The six agents they'd just rescued and their cots were gone, most likely Zarius had created another room. Gaston and Homer were arguing over the location of two large and very welcome machines, with Damon trying to help in their placement as well, but finally he stood back to let them argue. The Spectra Graph Analytic Computator, which would break down anything to its smallest components and the Sanguine Rotor would come in extremely handy both in tracking down a permanent solution for Nettie and finding out more about what had been done to the Egyptian agents.

Caden and Torlian were back at the table where Torlian's collection of journals, maps, and scrolls were piled and seemed to be engrossed in, and debating, a single book.

Caden looked up before she went to him and came to her side. "You look better. No more coughing? Fatigue?"

Nettie laughed. "I feel much better. But Lisselle will tell everyone of my current situation when we gather." She looked around. "Where are Amr and his men? Bassem can't travel." It was still odd that ghost men could be severely injured or killed, but nothing about this trip had been what anyone would refer to as normal.

"Bassem is resting with the new agents, who are all still unconscious at this point," Zarius said as he came out of the room that Farida had been locked up in. "The rest of the watchful dead have gone on patrol and to search for their missing people. Amr said that if you have need, simply call him forth and they shall return."

"Are those going to work down here?" Lisselle walked over to deal with Homer, Gaston, and the equipment. Nettie started to follow, but Rebecca came out of a new side tunnel and ran toward she and Caden.

"This place is wondrous. And we've all had our trackers removed." She rubbed her arm. "You do look better, are you recovered? Don't think to lie to me, by the way." She folded her arms and gave Nettie a stern stare.

"I am temporarily in recovery." Nettie saw the looks of concern on both their faces. "It will be fine and something we will discuss soon enough, I warrant." She looked around. "Where is Darwish?" She noticed that the airship crew who had come down with them were also gone, but that wasn't surprising. Most likely, given their chosen profession, underground would be the last place they'd want to remain.

"He is in with the original fifteen recovered agents," Lisselle answered as she walked away from Homer, Gaston, and Damon. "They are recovering slowly, but still need to rest. However, Saad insisted on speaking to Darwish as soon as you and I left the room. I overheard it when I came out for your water."

Nettie turned to Zarius. "How is Farida?"

He frowned. "That is part of what we must discuss. If we are all together, we should talk." He waved his hand and a massive, round table, with just enough seats to accommodate everyone there, appeared. "I recall that you English have a fondness for round tables. They are also the best manner to have a discussion." He nodded for everyone to sit.

Gaston and Homer were the last as they continued to debate the placement of the machines.

Nettie wanted to hear about Farida first, but Zarius nodded to Gaston to first explain the attack on London.

"The explosion was well-timed and had it not been for our new, and now destroyed, alarm system, we could have lost many lives. We will rebuild and make even better alarm and defenses."

"What did Edinburgh say about it?" Homer asked, but there were nods from all of the London agents at his question.

Gaston frowned. "Nothing at first. Then they claimed that they hadn't received my initial messages. I called in the agents from Bath, Cardiff, and Llandudno myself. When Scotland did respond they expressed concern and stated that our agents should retreat to Bath. For their safety." He shook his head. "By then I was already planning on coming here. Something I did not share with them. The rest of our agents who did go to Bath will try to confuse the issue of where we are when the Edinburgh agents arrive there, but that won't hold long."

"Your agency is lost then?" Zarius asked.

"I don't believe so. I fear that something has taken over part of the main headquarters, but I now don't think it is all of them." Gaston looked to Lisselle and Homer. "I received this in the post yesterday before the explosion." He handed a folded letter to them. "In brief, it is from Agent Ramsey. Agent Zero went missing two weeks ago, and Ramsey and a handful of people he trusted went underground to find him. It might have saved them from whatever has happened within headquarters."

"Or his disappearance had been a lure to get them out of the way." Homer looked up as he and Lisselle shared reading the letter.

"That crossed my mind and when you get further down, you'll see that it crossed his as well. But the options weren't good."

"He took the Runners with him?" Lisselle asked as she continued reading.

"Most of them. He couldn't call back five. But the remaining ones are in hiding with him and the other agents."

"The attack on my people was part of a larger plan, wasn't it?" Darwish asked.

Gaston nodded. "It appears so. And there may be others, we won't know until we resolve this crisis and get back to London—and then go to Edinburgh if need be. Now, I want to hear all that has happened while you've been here—I fear Egypt, and what happens here, will be the linchpin for the world."

CHAPTER THIRTY-EIGHT

THE SILENCE THAT SETTLED IN the room was almost more disturbing than the statement. And this was not a quiet bunch.

Zarius looked around the room. "This is my chamber, but you have come to save my land. I will give whatever help I can to save your country as well."

Darwish nodded but from the concern on his face, he'd been counting on stronger support from Scotland and England.

They quickly got Gaston, Rebecca, and Damon caught up on the events before that day.

Gaston asked only a few questions about the attack under the Khafre pyramid, but would most likely be picking out individuals for further details.

Lisselle and Homer briefly went over what they'd found on their exploration, but aside from noting where King James' guards were stationed on the desert side of the compound, and that some were extremely well hidden, they didn't get much intel and had been the first group to return.

Torlian and Darwish reported more of the same. The compound was extremely secure on the surface.

Then Nettie and Caden told them of the underground.

"There's no way that man isn't connected to the missing agents and what's being stolen from them."

Darwish looked ready to jump to his feet and go beat up King James himself.

"Agreed." Gaston nodded, with a pointed look at Nettie and Caden. "You two were extremely fortunate that you weren't captured. You were far too close to the enemy."

"We did have the watchful dead on our side," Caden said. "We're not certain of how many people King James, or whatever he calls himself, has working with him, but if Amr can gather more of his ghost warriors, that will be a major asset."

Lisselle and Homer finished reading the letter from Agent Ramsey and Homer handed the letter to Torlian. "There are five more airships coming and should be here by tomorrow morning. But there will be limits to what the airships can accomplish. We will still need to recover more agents."

"Saving more people is vital, but they won't be able to help if we can't restore them." Lisselle sighed and ran her hand through her short gray hair. "I'm still trying to sort out what has happened to them on a level that I can help with. It's not like anything I've ever seen."

Zarius nodded. "I believe their continued condition could be tied, at least in part, to Farida. That thing inside her is a magical entity and I believe it is being used against all of the captured agents. Whoever put the gkolin in Farida had multiple reasons to do so. The amount of their ka that had been removed in both groups so far shouldn't be enough to keep them so unresponsive. The first group is maintaining conscious, but simply has no energy nor cognitive abilities to do more than take care of basic needs. They appear to be recovering far more slowly than I would have expected."

"Which leads us back to, how is Farida?" Nettie asked. That question was even more important if the lives of over a hundred agents were tied to it.

"She is complicated. There is something at work inside her that goes beyond the gkolin infestation." Zarius looked around the room. "And yes, everyone here has been checked and given the protection against being invaded by the gkolin, the ones onboard the flying ship as well. But Farida's energy is being drawn out in such a way that I feel I can almost follow it." He turned to Nettie. "There was a break that I believe coincided with your attack on Sekhmet. The link is back now, but weaker."

"That's a good thing, right? If we can break the connection, we can release Farida?" Darwish looked around, flushed, and then added. "It will help the captured agents." That he was smitten with Farida was clear, probably even to the people who had just joined them.

But he was also right.

"Hopefully. I am still concerned about Ammit being awake. She could be unpredictable," Zarius said.

"Does she really have the head of a crocodile, the forebody of a lion, and the back legs of a hippo?" Torlian was too excited about a goddess whose presence was upsetting someone like Zarius.

"I couldn't answer to anything beyond the head of a crocodile. She was wearing a long flowing cloak that covered her far too well." Nettie shook her head at his enthusiasm. "Her appearance that I saw was terrifying. I wouldn't be too excited to see her in person if I were you."

"Most likely true." He sounded like he still didn't believe it, but that was his concern.

"Then we're still not certain which deities have been awakened? Could there be some more on our side as well? And you mentioned that Anubis had to go into hiding, can he come out?" Gaston spoke to Zarius but looked around the table. "Even with Homer's airship crews, and the ghost men, we don't have near enough to take on a bunch of gods and goddesses and whoever else that madman who kidnapped Nettie has with him—including rogue Runners. We need more information and more beings on our side."

"Agreed," Zarius responded. "But without seeing them, I'm not sure how we can confirm which deities have been awakened and which ones might be on our side. As for Anubis, the last time we spoke he told me he was working on a solution that would allow him to come out of hiding safely. But as of this morning, he has not sensed any other deities who might be on our side."

Caden looked around the table. "What is our plan? We just wait here, hiding? We charge forth with the airships and do what? Bomb that compound from the sky?"

"I think the first thing is to sort out how to bring the Egyptian agents into full recovery quickly. The original ones we rescued are still recovering, as we said. We just need to increase the speed in which they do so," Lisselle said. "We not only need to find and rescue the remaining agents, but we need to get them up and ready to fight. This King James/Seti the First person, is obviously involved with the kidnapping of the agents, and possibly stealing their ka. But is he working for Horus and Sekhmet? Someone else? Why did they only have six of the agents in that area near his compound that Nettie and Caden found when there are still almost a hundred missing?"

"I would guess that they are having trouble removing the ka of their prisoners," Zarius said. "That larger group you found first was still only fifteen. I've never heard of the removal of the ka as you described it. This is something completely new and they might be having to go slowly. The drumming Nettie and Caden described sounds ritualistic and not familiar."

"Shock." Nettie looked up as she spoke out loud unintentionally. "I apologize, I was thinking about the other issue, how to get the agents to recover faster. How is Saad?"

Lisselle nodded. "Almost completely recovered. He has been helping with the others and wanted to be in this meeting, but I told him he needed to wait until he was stronger."

"When Farida stabbed him, he focused very quickly, and was the first to recover. While we can't stab them all, might a slight shock bring them out of their semi-stupor? Just enough to startle, not injure." Nettie wasn't sure it would work, but something had to be done. And soon.

Lisselle frowned as she clearly weighed the options. Finally, she nodded. "It might work. I'm normally not a fan of injuring my patients, but being trapped in that stupor can't be good for them either. And I think we can all agree that having more local agents rescued, up, and functioning can only help us."

Darwish had been in his own thoughts again, but looked up. "Even the ones we have already will help once they regain full consciousness. Saad is the highest ranking with us, but there are at least four more high ranking agents within both groups. And there could be more that I simply don't know. The higher levels stick to themselves unless they have something specific they need lower agents for."

"That could be crucial," Homer said. "Part of why we're so good is that we know London. Even in Llandudno, we were in semi-familiar territory. None of us know Egypt well, aside from Darwish, Zarius, and the ghosts. We need more knowledge."

There was a series of soft pings from the machines brought up from London.

"And speaking of knowledge." Homer grinned to Gaston. "I told you they would be fine there. I believe Lisselle wanted to run Nettie's blood first?"

Lisselle was already moving for the machines. "Indeed. And I should be able to look for elements that need to be corrected in our rescued agents. Endeavor to withdraw the problem components. But we might still need to lightly shock them."

Nettie rose, she wanted to get whatever was going on in her blood sorted out quickly. She was muddled up enough as it was.

Zarius also got up. "I would be fascinated to observe. This time you live in is remarkable in many ways."

Gaston looked around. "I believe we should prepare for further explorations above ground and well as work on the scientific aspect. The rest of you are with me."

Rebecca smiled. "I would like to assist Lisselle if I could."

He nodded then went to gather his smaller group, including Darwish, into a planning meeting.

Nettie unbuttoned her sleeve as she joined Lisselle, Rebecca, and Zarius at the Spectra Graph Analytic Computator and Sanguine Rotor. "Just how are they running? They require an electrical current." Which she would have asked earlier, but she had truly been exhausted when Lisselle brought her in for treatment. The impact that basic physical issues could have on one's cognition was frustrating.

Extremely annoying, to be honest.

"That was me." Zarius didn't look over from his close examination of the machines. "Once I understood what was required, I was able to create the power needed. These are extremely interesting."

"Just you wait until you see what they can do." Lisselle readied the Spectra Graph Analytic Computator, then motioned for Nettie to come closer. "Rebecca? Could you bring a chair over? I'm not planning on drawing a lot of blood, but Nettie has been through a lot recently."

Nettie started to shake her head; she was not going to

collapse from a simple blood draw. The determined look on both of her friends' faces made her remain quiet. It was easier.

"Thank you." Nettie rolled up her sleeve as she took the offered chair. "Take what you need."

Rebecca and Zarius kept an eye on the machine as the sample of blood that Lisselle drew ran through it.

"This will tell you how to remove components from her blood? Without a full exsanguination? Truly fascinating." If Zarius moved any closer he would be inside the machine.

Lisselle looked up. "Your people could do that without killing the patient? A full one?" She glanced to Nettie. They'd sort of done that when they used Nettie's vampiric blood to purge Queen Victoria of her vampiric influence. But it hadn't been precisely the same.

Zarius looked up from his close examination of the Spectra Graph Analytic Computator. "My people and the deities we served could. We gifted some of our followers with it, but it was misused."

"There are more like you? Could they be awakened without their gods and goddesses?" Rebecca stayed near Nettie, presumably to catch her in case she collapsed.

Nettie had no intention of doing so, but she appreciated the sentiment.

"There are, most of the deities had us. Which is another item we may be concerned about. We've now seen Horus, Sekhmet, and Ammit, but none of them had their attendants with them. Horus used thilia during his attack on London, something no god or goddess would use."

Lisselle was watching as the Spectra Graph Analytic Computator ran through the sample of Nettie's blood, but turned partially toward them. "Could that mean these are not the true gods and goddesses? Some sort of usurpers?"

Nettie frowned. "Sekhmet felt incredibly goddess-like

when we fought. I was enhanced, but had I not bitten her, I don't know who would have won the fight."

"And Horus vanished without a trace in the mansion," Rebecca added. "That can't be easy."

Now it was Zarius' turn to frown. "No, it wouldn't have been. But I could have done it, and I did when I brought the others here to rescue Nettie. Not to mention, while I would never challenge any of you to a fight, I do believe I could hold my own. Even against our enhanced pharaoh."

"Could the ones we've seen so far have been attendants pretending to be the deities they served?" Nettie almost felt better if they'd faced actual gods and goddesses and lived to tell the tale. But what if the Horus and Sekhmet they fought weren't actually them? Zarius was powerful enough that if he dressed like Anubis, and claimed to be him, he could probably convince people he *was* Anubis.

"That is something I hadn't thought of, to be honest," Zarius said. "It seemed natural that if Anubis and I both woke at the same time, then the ones representing the deities would be actually them. It would explain why we haven't seen any other attendants, however."

Lisselle turned away from the clicking and whirling machine to focus on Zarius. "You said Sekhmet followed you to Anubis' hiding place. Could her attendant have done that?"

"If she'd tapped into the powers of Sekhmet in slumber, she might be able to. That could also explain why those other deities are able to roam the land. Even before the attack on him, Anubis wasn't able to do so easily."

The machine pinged, causing all of them to turn their attention to it. Lisselle frowned as she read the small printout that was extruded from a slot on the side.

"It identifies a dangerous element in Nettie's blood. But it isn't providing me enough information to remove it. We will have to run more tests." She looked to Zarius.

"Could you create some food? I'm going to need more of Nettie's blood to sort this out. No matter what she says, she is still human and this much of a blood draw could cause issues."

He nodded and food appeared on the table—far more than Nettie needed, no matter how much blood was taken. "Please, everyone help themselves." He watched Lisselle glare at the paper in her hand before holding out his hand for it.

She shrugged and handed it over to him.

Nettie held out her arm, but Lisselle shook her head. "Not before you drink more tea and eat more food. There is something familiar in the results, but I can't sort where I've seen it before."

Rebecca came back from the table with a mountain of food and another chair. "We might be here a while."

"Good idea." Lisselle brought a chair and plate over for herself.

"If I gather it, could you analyze Farida's blood as well?" Zarius continued to study the slip of paper and he appeared concerned.

"Definitely. I can give you the blood drawing equipment." Lisselle sighed as she piled some meat into a flatbread. "I didn't realize how hungry I was."

Zarius gave her back the printed paper and took the blood drawing equipment with a fresh needle and collecting vial. "I'll be back quickly."

The three of them ate in silence for a few moments, then the other group broke up to get food and Caden and Damon joined them.

Caden rubbed Nettie's shoulders. "Anything yet?"

Lisselle frowned. "Just that I need more of Nettie's blood. Hence, the food."

Nettie finished her food. Clearly, she'd been far hungrier than expected. "My blood is apparently being difficult."

"Is Zarius going to get blood from Farida?" Caden

brought Nettie a second plate of food, then looked to where Zarius had gone.

"Yes, we're wondering if we can find anything that will help her recover. I'd also like to compare it to Nettie's blood."

"You think that I might have one of those gkolin things in me?" That was a disturbing concept that she'd missed. "But Zarius checked me along with the rest of you."

"And it took him three times to get a clear result. There could be elements in both of you. Or it could be the blood of pharaohs and what it's doing to you."

Nettie sighed. She still wasn't certain how she felt about the daughter of pharaohs issue turning her into a pharaoh. But perhaps it was what was needed at this point.

She just hoped that everything went back to normal once they resolved this. She still hadn't completely come to terms with the mermaid situation. Although to be fair, until they came here, she hadn't had much of a problem with it.

CHAPTER THIRTY-NINE

THEY FINISHED THEIR FOOD IN silence. Zarius came out of Farida's room with the collected blood vial, but also with a confused look.

"Farida seems to be in a stupor. At first, I believed the gkolin in her was doing it to make me drop my guard, but there was no response when I drew her blood. That is not normal gkolin behavior."

"Is she all right otherwise?" Nettie put aside her second empty plate. She normally had a healthy appetite but this was above and beyond normal.

"She appears so, just locked into a very deep sleep. Hopefully, Lisselle's machine will tell us more." He handed over the vial of blood and Lisselle put it in the Spectra Graph Analytic Computator.

"We'll see what we can find." Lisselle motioned for Nettie's arm. "We'll need some more from you as well. Rebecca, I have enough blood draw kits ready for five of the Egyptian agents. Could you draw some blood? One from Saad, two from agents who came in with him. Then two from our newest rescues." She nodded to Nettie as Rebecca gathered the equipment and left. "You've had an exciting day, I'm afraid the rest of it will be doing science."

"I do enjoy that, you know." Nettie could spend days

simply doing research if there was enough mystery involved with what was there.

Caden kissed her cheek, then he and Damon went back to Gaston and the others.

The machine made an odd grumbling noise as Farida's blood sample circulated through it.

"That's not normal." Lisselle frowned and she and Zarius stepped closer to the equipment.

Suddenly a violent chill slammed into Nettie's stomach. "Step back! There's something wrong!"

Zarius pushed Lisselle out of the way as a sharp piece of the Spectra Graph Analytic Computator broke off and flew into the air.

It missed Lisselle but struck Zarius. He growled, then removed the barb and waved his hand at the machine—since he had created the power to run it, removing that power wasn't difficult. It came to a halt and fell silent.

"What was that?" Homer and the rest came running over.

"The Spectra Graph Analytic Computator decided to attack." Lisselle looked at the barb in Zarius' hand. "Thank you for saving me. That could have done some serious damage."

Homer took the barb from Zarius. "That could have killed you. Where did it come from?"

"Deep inside the Spectra Graph Analytic Computator, if I could make a guess." Gaston plucked it from Homer's hand and glared at the barb and the machine in equal measure. "Yes. This is an internal staff to keep the moving parts, moving. Not only was it coming out of the machine highly improbable, and possibly fatal, the removal has now rendered the machine useless. At least until we can take it apart and repair it."

"This couldn't have been an accident," Caden said.

Gaston shook his head. "It wasn't. I'd say something doesn't want you looking at Farida's blood."

Nettie stepped back as the Spectra Graph Analytic Computator gave one last rattle and collapsed. "We're going to have to repair the entire thing. I'd suggest that we get Farida's blood out of it first, however."

Zarius tilted his head as he slowly walked around the damaged machine. "I believe we're being tricked." He held out his hand and after a few moments, Gaston gave him the barb. Zarius closed his fist around it and said a few odd sounding words that even Darwish didn't appear to recognize. Then the barb vanished in a puff of thin smoke. He spoke again, this time sounding like he was growling, and the Spectra Graph Analytic Computator rebuilt itself before their eyes.

"How did you do that? You can't have ever seen one of these before." Gaston stalked forward and patted the machine on each side to confirm it was, in fact, intact.

"I did nothing but remove the illusion. I've tested my shields and whoever did that was not attacking from outside the temple." He looked back at the door where Farida was. "I fear there might be more in our agent than simply a gkolin. Her blood cast the illusion of the attack, then the collapse of your machine. Those are not normal gkolin abilities."

"I held that barb." Gaston folded his arms. "It was solid. Are you saying that if it had hit Lisselle it wouldn't have done any damage?"

"Precisely. The way these spells work is something would have blocked it, or moved her over, or something else to keep us from realizing it was all a lie." He stepped back from the machine. "Run it again. I will make sure that nothing else happens."

He folded his arms and stood between the machine and the door to Farida's room.

Lisselle shrugged but started the machine again. Everyone else moved a few feet away. The Spectra Graph

Analytic Computator started to cough, but a growl from Zarius made it stop.

Torlian watched the action between Zarius and the machine with wide eyes. "Are you and the machine communicating?"

"Not really. More that I'm simply dealing with the entity that is making its presence known in Farida's blood. I believe that was the reason behind Farida being so still. It was controlling what blood I removed."

"Hopefully it continues to behave." Lisselle stepped to the side a bit but stayed near the machine. She did keep hold of something in her left hand. As Nettie couldn't see anything physical, she presumed it was a witchy spell of some sort.

The machine whirled through its processing, then stopped.

"Is it broken or finished?" Nettie asked. Lisselle hadn't added Nettie's blood for comparison yet, but the way it stopped seemed abrupt.

Lisselle stepped to the printout area. "I believe it is finished but still showing willfulness. See here, blood of whatever you are. We will get our answers and you shall lose in the end." She paused, grinned, and muttered a few odd words that vanished from memory as they were uttered.

The machine rocked and spit out a slip of paper.

"What was that you said?" Zarius stayed between the machine and the door but leaned closer to Lisselle.

"It was a witch language." Lisselle smiled. "I had a feeling that Farida was still part of her body, therefore would respond as she is a witch. I told her to fight back." She waved the printout. "She did."

"Will she still be herself when she recovers?" Darwish had remained on the edge of the group but held a trace of hope on his face.

"I am optimistic that she will be. The fact that her core

self responded to my command speaks volumes. She is still there." With a nod to Darwish, Lisselle read the printout.

She read it again, scowling, then gave a soft smile. "We definitely want to compare Nettie's blood with this blood. The markers in Farida's blood are unique, but there are a few which appear to be similar to Nettie's." She handed the paper to Nettie first, motioned for her to pass it around when done, then took the new vial of Nettie's blood and added it to the extractor.

Nettie read the coding twice. While she could use the Spectra Graph Analytic Computator, she didn't often have call for it. The results were interesting, however. There were the standard human blood markers, then a few odd ones. And one that looked possibly familiar.

"Is Farida a vampire? Or rather, was she before? That marker on the third line is a vampiric strain. Weaker than my own, but that's what it appears to be."

Lisselle stepped back as the machine started its analysis. "That was my thought when I saw it. There could be other things that leave a similar mark, but my guess is it will become clearer once we compare it to your blood. She might not even be aware of it."

"May I?" Zarius didn't move far from his spot but reached out his hand for the printout.

Since he might be blocking Farida's guest, or guests, from interfering, Nettie went to him to give him the sheet.

He nodded. "That *is* a vampiric strain. A weaker one. Nettie is half-vampire by birth, correct? Highly uncommon in my day, but it did happen. The vampire lines can reproduce, but it is extremely rare. It's difficult to carry life when you're undead. However, this does appear that someone down Farida's line was one of those rare vampires also. I don't believe it was given to her when the gkolin and whatever else was added."

He handed the paper to Gaston who gave it a narrowed eye read over, before passing it to the rest.

Rebecca came out with a tray of vials. "Saad and his agents appear to be recovering much better and are requesting more food. Actually, Saad wanted to come out here, but I thought it best to let one of you decide. Even the newest retrieved agents are beginning to stir." She looked over to Farida's door. "Has the connection been broken?"

"Not completely, but I believe it has been weakened." Zarius nodded but remained where he stood. "I will send them refreshments."

Gaston nodded. "I will go speak with Agent Saad, but until we have a better handle on these things, I want them to stay clear." He started down the hall. "Get me if there are any drastic changes."

Torlian and Lisselle nodded, then returned to muttering together at the side of the machine. From what Nettie gathered, they were discussing the witch aspect. The machine pinged, normally this time, drawing all of them closer.

Lisselle read it twice, looked to Nettie, then read it again and handed it to Torlian. He repeated the same, then handed it to Zarius.

"If one of you don't tell me what you are looking so confused about, I will have to take that paper by force." Aside from her fairly recent bout of fierceness concerning her ghost warriors, Nettie was not a demanding sort. But she had a feeling this was something that she needed to know.

Zarius looked to Torlian, who looked to Lisselle, who finally nodded.

"It appears that you and Farida share another marker." She took a deep breath. "The one that we identified as belonging to the daughter of pharaohs. I could be wrong;

we need to study more. But it appears that Farida might be related to you through your mother."

Nettie backed into her chair and sat heavily. Once her father had died, she really had no family. She was passed around to different families growing up, but none of them seemed to be closely related to her.

"My vampire mother gave birth twice? How? Shouldn't once have been rare enough?"

Lisselle shrugged. "It is a mystery, that is for sure. But the unique pharaoh's blood that you carry, would have been carried by her. And whoever Farida's parent was. The blood of both vampire and pharaoh is diluted in her as compared to you. I'd say your mother was either the parent of one of her parents, grandparents, or great-grandparents."

The silence that followed indicated that Nettie wasn't the only one having difficulty processing this new information. She might have a cousin? Or whatever their relationship was. That was almost as surprising as everything else that had taken place here so far.

"Another member of our family!" Rebecca hugged Nettie.

Since Nettie had no family, and Rebecca had more than enough up in Northern Wales, Rebecca had simply adopted Nettie a few months ago. Any relation of Nettie's was now part of the family group.

"We must save her." Rebecca looked around the room. "I do mean we were going to save her anyway, it's what we do. But, now it is even more crucial that we get whatever is taking her over, out."

"Indeed. I do wish my mother had told me that there were others when we met." Nettie had stopped missing her mother when she was still a child. But now she missed her for new reasons. She did seem to be in the middle of some of this mess.

"Oh! You met her? We need a far longer conversation

for that." Rebecca narrowed her eyes at the door to Farida's room. "Could her blood, and the connection to the powers that Nettie is experiencing, be why Farida was taken and infected?"

"That's an excellent point, Rebecca." Homer also looked to Farida's door, then back to Nettie. "Strategically, someone with your gifts would be a major boon to the other side. I do hope your mother didn't have any other children. No offense."

She nodded. "None taken, and I agree. But even if she didn't…Darwish? Do you know anything about Farida's family?"

Darwish had been locked in his own thoughts again but came out when Nettie said his name. "Not really. Just a few mentions. Her parents are both gone I believe, but she did have siblings."

Nettie shared a look of concern with Lisselle and Homer. "Do you know how many?"

He looked up at the ceiling as if trying to capture a fleeting memory. "I think five? Maybe six? Her father was half-English and they were well-off. I don't know how many she kept in contact with, however. Ah, but she did mention her family was from Cairo."

"There's a chance that the genetic components weren't passed to all of the children. And they would be diluted like Farida's even if they were." Lisselle still appeared concerned.

"But if Rebecca is correct and the reason Farida was compromised was because of this blood, then anyone else with it could be in danger and not know it," Homer said.

"I agree. But if they don't live in this village, they might not have been noticed yet," Zarius said. "That does also bring up the question of why this village. Yes, most of the deities, their attendants, and higher followers went to sleep deep beneath the Great Pyramids. But there are other places not far from here with larger populations. Including Cairo."

"Did you and Anubis notice anything odd when you first awoke here?" Caden stood next to Nettie.

"Not much, aside from confusion. It was only when I went out and felt the wrongness in the village and surrounding areas, that we realized something drastic took place."

"But wouldn't the time difference have appeared as wrongness?" Damon asked.

"That was what I believed at first. It caused physical pain for Anubis to leave his chamber, so I went out and reported to him. Even with the time difference, there is a disturbance to the air. And magic has vanished from the places it flowed for thousands of years. Someone, or something, recently removed it. It used to spread freely across the land. The disturbance is slowly crossing the land, but the focus of it was in this village."

"Then Farida's family might be safe at this point. And, once we get this being out of her, we will have two pharaohs on our side." Darwish's smile was broad. His hope was returning.

"Her abilities won't be the same as Nettie's." Lisselle took the remaining vial of Nettie's blood and set up the Spectra Graph Analytic Computator machine as she spoke. "Even though Nettie's mother gave birth to Nettie long after her exposure to the pharaoh's blood, the connection between them was more direct. Farida's family has had several generations to dilute it."

"That is good to know," Saad's voice came from behind them. "And something that my people will be glad to hear. They did know of Farida's ancestry, you were correct in that was why she was changed, but not that there were more. Or about Nettie. No one move quickly, please. I don't want to kill her."

Saad stood at the edge of the room; a gun aimed at Nettie's head.

CHAPTER FORTY

"SAAD? YOU WERE OUR LEADER." Darwish looked shocked, almost more so than when Farida turned on him.

"Yes, I was. And do you know how much pay I received? Almost nothing. The people above me got promotions and more money for doing less work. I contacted Edinburgh about it once and was told it wasn't their concern. So, I cut off our communications with them. Horus has been speaking to me for almost a year now." He started pacing but didn't lower his gun nor drop his gaze from Nettie's head. "He told me his time would come to rule this world—with me at his side."

Nettie judged the distance between them and estimated that she could get to Saad before he shot her. But the impact could send the bullet into one of her friends. She presumed that was the same reason that Zarius hadn't acted.

"You can't get out of here. Not without help." Homer didn't move but Nettie saw him out of the corner of her eye. He was tense and ready to leap.

There must be another way… "*Amr? I need you and your men to come to the temple. Saad is holding us at gunpoint.*"

No one moved and Saad shifted on his feet. "I will be saved. I have found not only the puppet of Anubis but the One Who Will Destroy All." He gave Nettie a bow.

Nettie hadn't heard that term and wasn't pleased to have it applied to her. She was also back to debating tackling the man when a disturbance in the air around him occurred and Amr, Farouk, and ten more of the ghost warriors surrounded Saad.

Saad screamed and fired his gun, but Zarius flew forward at that moment and the bullet and gun vanished.

Nettie held both Caden and Rebecca back as the ghost men overpowered and restrained Saad. Both were ready to wade in with fists flying.

Zarius came next to Nettie. "I believe we have more problems than we thought." He grimaced and held one hand over his ribs. He removed it and a trickle of blood flowed through.

"I thought you couldn't be killed or injured?" She glanced back at Amr and his men, but it appeared that Saad was rendered unconscious and was restrained should he wake up.

"I can be killed, but injury is another thing. This shouldn't have happened. And like the times that I've died, it hurts."

Lisselle rushed forward and looked at his side. "Not life-threatening, but that is disturbing if you previously couldn't be injured and are now able to."

Homer went to Amr and the men. "Lock this one up in an empty room, keep someone watching him inside the room and outside." He didn't look upset or surprised when Amr turned to Nettie for confirmation.

"Yes, please. And he said someone was going to rescue him; we need to block against that." Later she would explain to Amr that along with Caden, he and his men should obey Homer and Lisselle. And… "Where's Gaston?" He'd gone to speak to Saad.

Homer raced down the corridor with Nettie, Torlian, Caden, and Damon on his heels. Rebecca stayed to assist

Lisselle in treating Zarius' wound. He'd still been fine enough to create a sturdy cot for himself to rest on.

Nettie didn't pass Homer but entered the room on his heels. The door was intact, but the lock was broken from the inside. Gaston was unconscious, as were the rest of the agents. Considering that Rebecca commented on their being in full recovery not fifteen minutes earlier, their status must be due to something Saad had done to them.

Nettie and Homer ran to Gaston. Unlike the agents, who appeared untouched, Gaston had a slight bump on the back of his head. Given his position, he'd been coming into the room when he was attacked.

Homer saw the bump as well and stopped from grabbing Gaston. "Is he okay? What's wrong with them?" Caden, Torlian, and Damon all ran to separate agents checking their pulses and lifting their eyelids.

"They seem to be simply sleeping." Caden turned to another one when he snored. "Yes, sleeping. There's something on their faces." He pulled a cloth out of his trouser pocket and wiped the first agent's chin. He took a cautious sniff, then shook his head. "Standard sleeping powder. Our agents are immune to it, I'd say that exposure training didn't make it to Egypt."

"Explains why Saad needed to hit Gaston." Homer looked to Nettie. "How's his head?"

She'd been looking but there was no blood. The blow was planned to knock him out, luckily nothing more. "I think it will be fine."

"I would be if you weren't both chattering so loudly," Gaston spoke but didn't open his eyes. "What large vehicle hit me?"

Damon held up a rock. "I think this. Sorry, you were rendered unconscious by a simple rock."

"Saad. Damn him. He's a double agent. Caught him using sleeping powder on the others. Need smelling salts for the agents." He squinted. "And something for my head."

Homer and Nettie helped him slowly sit up. Nettie would have preferred that he rested a bit more, head injuries could be tricky. But she knew he would completely refuse.

"I'll get some salts, Lisselle and Rebecca have full kits." Damon flashed a smile to Gaston and ran out.

"I presume you have taken care of Saad?" Gaston allowed them to lead him to an empty cot and sit him down.

Homer nodded."He had a gun. He aimed it at Nettie's head, but she called her ghost friends and they took care of him."

"However, an errant shot hit Zarius. I have a feeling that it might not have been as much of a mistake as we believed, however." Nettie looked around at the quizzical looks. "Think about it, Zarius will return from the dead—our enemies might know that. But what if he could be injured, and kept incapacitated? That could cause us some issues."

"I thought he couldn't be hurt?" The color was returning to Gaston's face but he made no move to get off the cot.

"We all did, including him." Caden poured some water from a nearby table into a clean glass. "He was going to explain but we needed to rescue you."

"And I'm certain that Lisselle and Rebecca won't let him explain anything until his wound is addressed." Nettie peered closer at Gaston's bump. "And you need the same attention."

"I'm fine." He glared around at them all. "He just snuck up on me is all. However, this raises a potential problem with these agents as we rescue them. There could be more spies in their ranks."

"We have to find a way to sort them out, otherwise, even

if we retrieve and treat all of them, we can't let them free to help us." Homer looked around at the sleeping agents as Damon returned with a handful of small smelling salt vials and handed them out.

All agents carried single-use paper packets of smelling salts, but these held more. Soon all of the remaining fourteen agents in this group were jolting awake and peering around in confusion.

Gaston nodded to them all. "I am Agent Gaston Bessette of London. I have taken over this agency under orders from Edinburgh." He kept his face solemn and stern, not showing the slightest hints of the lie as he spoke.

Nettie felt he was safe in making that statement. Clearly, Edinburgh was ignoring the Egyptian agents. And that was before it was taken over by hostiles.

Which was another concerning issue that there was no way to resolve at this time.

"Is something else wrong? You're scowling." Caden asked her.

"What? No. Just annoyed that we have too many fronts to fight on." She tilted her head and contemplated the agents. First and foremost was sorting out any other traitors. "I'll be right back; I want to check something." She was halfway out the door before Gaston nodded.

She could call Amr to her, but that might ruin the element of surprise.

He and his men were assisting, or it appeared, just watching, with Lisselle and Rebecca's work on Zarius. Saad and two of the ghost men were out of sight.

"Amr? Could I speak to you?"

He was at her side immediately and they walked back to the corridor leading to the room with the agents. "What do you need, Pharaoh Nettie?"

She was going to say for him to simply call her Nettie, but the title seemed to mean a lot to he and his men. "I need a way to tell if the hearts of our prisoners are true. The man you and your people subdued, was a high-ranking person in the Society here. Yet he betrayed his people. We have more rescued agents and are hoping to recover additional ones soon—but we need to know if they are true or not." That seemed the best way to say it and as she spoke the words, she knew it was right.

Amr nodded solemnly. "We can see into their hearts for Pharaoh Nettie."

"How will you know what is truly there?" Yes, she knew the watchful dead had abilities far beyond normal beings, but this was still a tricky business. And lives would depend on their accuracy.

"Most of us can see into the hearts of beings, to feel what and who they truly are. If they are lying about either, it will be made clear to us." He gave a bow.

Nettie nodded in return, then motioned for Amr to follow her into the room. As their options were limited, and that Amr and his men had shown to be trustworthy and wishing to serve their new pharaoh, she would need to trust them. "Gaston? Do you object to my men verifying these agents and the ones we just rescued?"

Gaston had been muttering to Homer, most likely complaining about Homer not letting him get off the cot. But he looked up. "I would welcome it, thank you for assisting us." His voice was cranky while speaking to Homer, but was extremely solicitous as he spoke to Amr.

Amr gave him a slightly less deep bow than he gave Nettie. "I will begin with these." He walked to one of the recovering agents and stood before him. "I call upon you." There were more words, but they were in that ancient Egyptian language.

The agent's eyes went wide and locked open. Then he stumbled to his feet and spoke some words that Nettie was fairly certain even he didn't know.

Amr patted the agent's shoulder and smiled to Nettie. "He is true."

The rest of the agents in this group all came back clear, which was a relief to Nettie. She knew having one high ranking traitor was going to cause problems, they didn't need more.

Lisselle came in to check on Gaston and the agents. She gave his head a thorough examination—as well as could be under the circumstances and given his current disposition, and pronounced him fit for duty.

The agents were well enough to ask numerous questions about what had happened and where they were.

Nettie and the rest left Gaston, Lisselle, Rebecca, and Damon to it. As the ranking Society agent, Gaston's words would have the most weight, and the other three were good medical support.

Amr walked out alongside Nettie. "Shall I check upon the people we just rescued? Had we known of their possible duplicity, we could have looked into them before we brought them here."

"Yes. And if you find any who are false, please remove them. They might not be completely conscious at this point, so this would be a good time."

"That will make it easier to find. The one who tried to kill you was not like the gkolin you have locked up. She was taken against her will and fights against the spirit invading her. He did all of his actions willfully against his own people." He gave a terse nod. "I do hope there aren't many like him."

"I do as well, thank you Amr."

He nodded and went down the hall to the room the recently retrieved agents were in.

Zarius was up and pacing when she came into the main room. Torlian had come out as well and while not pacing, was having a serious conversation with Zarius.

As she got closer she realized it was actually a debate between them concerning the attributes of cricket and something called seker-hemat.

"I assume you are feeling better?" She asked Zarius.

Zarius looked up. "I am. But the wound is still there, which is most disturbing. Almost as much as this one's assertion that seker-hemat, you would call it batting the ball, is inferior to cricket. I fail to see his points."

It was nice to have something under discussion other than gloom and disaster, although Nettie knew it would not last for long.

CHAPTER FORTY-ONE

NETTIE STUDIED BOTH MEN AND shrugged. "I am not a fan of sports, so I'll remain out of it. I am concerned about your injury, however. Was the reason the barb from the Spectra Graph Analytic Computator didn't hurt you earlier because the change in you hadn't happened yet, or because it wasn't real?" The illusion of both the barb and the Spectra Graph Analytic Computator collapsing had appeared real enough, but there was still some confusion in her head as to whether it could have hurt anyone.

"That is an excellent question." Zarius continued his pacing even though the topic had changed. He looked like a caged animal, perhaps being trapped in here was wearing on him. "I believe that the barb, had it struck anyone else, would have caused a brief discomfort. My lack of injury at that time indicates that my transformation was more recent."

"Which doesn't give us much to look for," Torlian said. "If it were a spell, which I believe it had to be, it could have been set to delay its reaction. And therefore, could have been placed on you, or attached to one of us to bring to you, at any time."

Zarius stopped pacing long enough to glare around the room. "True, and few beings would have the power to cast such a spell against someone like me. We did not have witches in my time, but we did have magicians even among the human population."

"That's one new issue, but the second one could help us. Saad said he'd been hearing Horus, in his head I presume, for the prior year. Yet, his ka was almost taken before we rescued him

which would have destroyed him. Why?" Nettie was certain there was more beyond what they were seeing. She didn't know if they would have time to sort it out before things became aggressively worse.

"My guess would be that Horus and Sekhmet aren't completely working together in spite of what we saw." Caden had returned to the table spread with scrolls and books but looked up. "Nettie and I faced fighters wearing crude shirts of both Sekhmet and Horus, but what if they betrayed each other? It says in this book that she helped protect him when he was young—what if she's not on his side anymore?"

"Then Sekhmet is in charge of taking the kas, and Horus might be the one in charge of preparing the troops to be gathered." Zarius nodded. "Honestly, even if both are just the attendants of the god and goddess, they might not care if their own people were sacrificed. Not if they had already used them for what they needed."

Gaston came out with Lisselle, Rebecca, Damon, and fourteen agents. The agents were upright and seemed to be recovered but still appeared confused. They all stopped when they saw Amr and his men gathered in one corner.

"It's okay, they are on our side." Gaston's voice was gentle but it might have been as much to not rattle his own head as to keep the newly recovered agents calm. If, like Saad, they thought their building was currently under attack, finding out that they'd lost time was probably coming as a shock.

A woman in the lead nodded. She was older than Nettie, possibly a similar age to Lisselle. Unlike the others, she appeared to be more curious than fearful about the ghost men. She turned to the rest of the agents. "It's okay, we're safe now."

"I would like to present my people." Gaston introduced everyone aside from Amr and his men. Then he gave a nod to Nettie.

"These are my men. They are the watchful dead and serve me. Do not fear them or what they can do. They have helped us bring in another group of agents. And will help us rescue more of your people."

"I am pleased to meet you, Agent Jones, and your watchful dead. I am Neith, and I was the second in command to Saad. He had been acting odd the past few months, and I now wish that I had investigated further at the time." She gave a deep bow to Amr and his men. "I am honored to meet some of the watchful dead warriors. We shall fight side by side."

Amr returned the bow. "I too am honored that the new line of warriors has joined us." He turned to Nettie. "The recently gathered ones are all clear, but they might need food. They are still quite groggy. And I believe that we can find more of the remaining lost agents. There was a uniqueness to the places they were kept."

"Please be careful. We know they can strike you down and I fear we will need all of you for the battle. Has there been any indication of where your missing men are?" Bassem hadn't rejoined his people yet, which indicated that he was still recovering. Nettie didn't know how long it would take a ghost to recover.

He frowned. "Yes and no. The hundred have still been blocked in descending to this plane and we can't determine why. Our missing ten from our original encounter are back but I've kept them in the village to watch people."

"Travel in safety, my friend." Zarius looked like he would say more, but simply nodded.

Amr and his men bowed to Nettie and then vanished.

Nettie watched Neith and her people as the ghost men vanished, but they didn't seem too concerned.

Zarius came toward them. "I believe the other agents were hungry and you might be also." He waved his hand and a new table, as the other one was covered in books, scrolls, and a few artifacts, appeared laden with food.

Neith smiled and nodded. "We thank you for your bounty, attendant of Anubis."

He smiled; he'd only been introduced by name. "You're welcome and it is good to be remembered."

Neith led the agents to the table and Damon went to retrieve the newer ones.

Zarius watched them. "I'm grateful for Amr and his men being able to search them. But I believe we probably want another area—separate from us here—to examine them in."

"Or if they could check them before we freed them," Homer said. "That would save us trouble. The space issue brings up another point, there have been times that you couldn't be reached. I know we're risking more exposure by being above ground, but I don't know how safe it is here if we might not be able to get in. Or get out."

"Excellent point. I will increase access for Lisselle and Torlian in entering and leaving this place before you next leave." Zarius winced as his wound pulled and shook his head. "This might not be a fatal wound, but it is working to distract me. I will still need to search the new agents as they arrive for more gkolin infestations, but I can do that as they are resting. And I will need to create new spaces to keep them in." He lifted an eyebrow toward Lisselle. "Unless by the time the next group is brought back, we are able to speed up their recovery?"

Lisselle nodded. "Hopefully, I can sort out more of what is impacting the agents and develop a countermeasure. I believed it had been part of the taking of their ka, but I now wonder if their sleepiness is something they were given to keep them complacent. We'll use the current agents' blood to sort it out."

Rebecca brought out the newly freed six agents and set them up at the table with the original fourteen. Darwish made the rounds of both groups, then came back to Gaston and Lisselle.

"I'd like to see if I can find some of the agents who I know escaped the original attack. But I'd want them searched for being spies first."

Gaston turned away from the Sanguine Rotor, as he was running tests of a slightly different kind there. Neither machine was exciting to watch while they went through their calculations, however. "I don't want anyone to go alone." He looked to the retrieved and recovering agents.

"I can go with him. It's less likely most people have seen my face; the Egyptian agents might be recognized." Damon was usually quiet—an oddity in this group—but he was also stealthy and well-trained.

Darwish nodded. "And I can make both of us even less memorable. But we'd need one of the watchful dead to review what's in their hearts."

Nettie waited for Gaston to nod in agreement, then mentally called to Amr.

He appeared immediately.

"We need for one of your men to go with these two and search the hearts of the ones they find." Asking didn't seem to be a thing for pharaoh commands, but it was getting easier.

Amr nodded and one of the more recently deceased ghost warriors, at least to judge by the clothing, appeared next to him.

"This is Raki, he will help you search their hearts." Amr bowed to Nettie. "We believe we have found a larger holding area and possibly how to free the rest of my warriors." Then he vanished.

"Well, that's hopeful," Caden said. "I assume we're doing research until we know where to go?"

"I'm returning to my airship." Homer looked to Gaston, but didn't seem to be asking permission. "I want to do a few sweeps over the village and surrounding areas. We can't hide, but we can make sure everyone is aware that we're armed, in place, and watching them."

Homer and Gaston quietly made a few plans, then Zarius sent Homer to the surface.

Zarius pulled Lisselle and Torlian away into a corner and the three worked on magic to allow Lisselle and Torlian to move people in and out of the temple.

Darwish and Damon added hoods and cloaks to their ensembles, then Lisselle, with some pointers from Zarius, sent them to the surface.

Caden went back to the table with the books and scrolls, and Nettie was about to join him, when the Mudger crackled to life.

Gaston normally didn't move quickly, but he did now as he ran to the machine. "Gaston here, who is this?"

"Thank the gods, man!" That robust Scottish accent could only be Agent Ramsey. "I hope you and your crew are in Egypt, because we might need some help."

CHAPTER FORTY-TWO

"RAMSEY? DAMN MAN, YOU'VE BEEN hard to get a hold of. How can we help?"

All of the London agents came closer to the table with the Mudger and even the Egyptian agents moved in a bit. Agent Ramsey was the second-in-command for the entire Society.

"We've been captured, long story, but we tracked Agent Zero to Egypt. We got as far as Cairo, then we were grabbed by some illegal Runners and brought to a small village. Broke out with some help from our own Runners who managed to find us, but we're now being followed."

"Where are you now?" Gaston's voice now had a wariness to it. Ramsey had been grabbed in front of the Edinburgh Runners? That was more than a little suspicious.

Nettie agreed with his caution.

"We're hiding in a storage closet—or something. It's quite small for all of us. Our Runners are staying out of sight outside. This location was the only information I could retrieve on the Egyptian group before we left Edinburgh. Did you know their headquarters is nothing but a hole? Oh, and, 'To the winter winner goes the spring loss'."

Gaston grinned. "And the summer loser wins the fall gambit. Thank you."

Nettie relaxed. The code phrases helped reduce her concerns. With all that was going on this could still be a trap, but the odds were lessening.

"Where is this shack?" Gaston grabbed a piece of paper and pen.

Nettie responded before Agent Ramsey could. "Ask him if there is anything dead in the room he's in," Darwish said there had been three safe spots with Mudgers in the village, and this could be one of the other two—or the one they'd found earlier.

Gaston barely finished asking Ramsey that when he was cut off and an only partially understandable tirade about stinky, boggin', dead scarabs followed.

"We know where they are," Nettie said. "Caden and I can bring one of Amr's men and have the agents searched. But I have no idea how to check the Runners." The Runners wouldn't have the same hearts to check for duplicity. They might have to take a risk with the Edinburgh Runners, or lose the support they could give. And they needed support to win this.

She called Amr and this time he brought Farouk to join them before leaving again.

Gaston finished his call with Ramsey, telling him to hold tight.

"I will have Lisselle and Torlian practice bringing them down here once you've checked them. Actually, we can have them placed directly in my new secure room." Zarius pointed where another door appeared. "I should be able to sense if the metal men are intact. If they haven't been modified, then we will have to assume they are on our side." A look of concern, one shared by everyone, crossed his face.

The Runners could be extremely helpful, if they were on the right side. Deadly if they weren't.

Zarius closed his eyes for a moment, then opened them with a nod. "The room I have created should contain them if there is a problem. But my knowledge of their inner workings is minimal."

Gaston nodded. "We might be able to create something to help, but these were the only two machines we brought. We need Agent Zero. He knows more about the Runners than anyone."

Caden, Nettie, and Farouk gathered for Torlian to send them to the surface. Even though they knew where Agent Ramsey and his people were, appearing there out of nothing could lead to too much exposure.

As usual, they were near the stables.

Caden led the way, with Nettie and Farouk staying behind and watching people as they moved out into busier lanes. It was interesting that no one looked twice at Farouk, even with his ancient dress and weapons.

Nettie believed they simply thought him to be another one of King James' eccentricities.

There weren't many people near the shack they'd found the Mudger in, but Caden approached it cautiously.

Farouk froze. "I can smell the metal men. There are quite a few all around us." He was calm and didn't look around as he spoke. "They are well hidden."

Caden came back to them. "Farouk? Can you remove Nettie if need be?"

Nettie opened her mouth to protest but Farouk spoke first. "Yes, I can. I would not be able to remove you, however. But I agree, the pharaoh must be protected."

"I *can* fight, you know." Nettie pushed down her initial response which was to tell Farouk absolutely not. Then she looked at the larger picture—she was needed to resolve this and stop whatever was going on. "Fine. Agreed. But, I will say *when* you take me." She wasn't leaving Caden.

They both nodded.

"Shall we approach the shack? If the Runners watching this area wanted to stop us, they could have already." Without waiting for either to respond, Nettie marched to the small building and knocked.

Caden and Farouk stayed behind her and appeared dangerous.

The door opened and all that could be seen was a blue eye. Then the door flung open and Agent Ramsey picked up Nettie in a massive bear hug.

"Good to see you! And Caden!" Agent Ramsey was a classic Scot: large, fierce, and with a huge heart. His red beard was longer than the last time she saw him, and he looked a bit unkempt as he studied Farouk.

Once Ramsey put her back on her feet, Nettie introduced Farouk, then all three crowded inside.

"This is half of the agents I brought when we fled Edinburgh. I can take you to the rest. Where are you hiding? We couldn't pick up on any trackers."

Nettie felt this was the Ramsey she knew and trusted, but this wasn't the time to go on simply instinct. "My friend Farouk can sense things about people. We've had issues recently and would like him to check you and your people." There were nine other agents squished into the room and they all watched Ramsey at Nettie's words.

"Aye, lass, please have him do what needs to be done." Ramsey held his arms out from his sides.

At Nettie's nod, Farouk stepped closer to Ramsey and briefly closed his eyes. "He is on the side of good."

Farouk then checked the rest as Nettie found herself holding her breath. "They are all on the side of good."

Ramsey watched Farouk carefully. "Aye, that's good to know. Let's go find and check the rest, then join Gaston. I have much information to share. The Runners will follow us. But we need to obtain a safer location before we are found again." He removed the second Mudger and handed it to a nearby agent. "It was handy that this was here, but better not to leave it behind."

"Good idea. And they're using your tracking devices to follow you. I'd say take them out now, but there's a feeling..." Nettie paused. It felt like a heavy storm was coming their way, even though the sky outside was still clear. "I believe we need to get the rest of your people and seek shelter immediately."

Farouk scowled but nodded at Nettie's words.

Ramsey narrowed his eyes, but motioned for everyone to leave the building. "The rest are in a warehouse, just this way."

The pressure of incoming danger continued to build even though it only took a few minutes to get to the battered building.

Ramsey knocked, gave a code word, and the door opened wide. The building was much larger than the shack, but was also full of fabric so there wasn't that much more room for the agents.

Ramsey motioned to Nettie and Farouk. "Obey them."

Farouk stepped forward and searched the first eight. There were three who Nettie noticed continued to slowly move away from him.

"I wouldn't keep moving if I were you. I am far faster than you can imagine." Nettie rarely flashed her fangs to fellow agents, but these three were upsetting and needed to know who they faced.

Farouk moved toward them. Two men and one woman stepped back and the closest man swung out with a hidden knife at Farouk. Had Farouk not been one of the watchful dead, he could have been killed. However, like Nettie, he was far faster than they thought and quickly stayed out of reach.

Ramsey and Caden grabbed the other two questionable agents and the already cleared agents blocked the door. Nettie held onto the one with the knife. She squeezed his hand tight enough that the blade fell from his fingers.

Farouk checked him, then snarled, and stepped back. "He is false. Shall I kill him now?" He didn't say pharaoh, but it was implied by his tone.

"Not yet. Please check the other two."

If Agent Ramsey had any concerns about Nettie's odd friend and what he was doing, he didn't show them.

"Both of them are tainted. Their thoughts are mostly hidden, but they do wish to destroy that one." He pointed to Ramsey. "And you." Then to Nettie.

The rest of this group had checked out clear, at least for not being traitors. Zarius still needed to verify a lack of gkolin infestation for all of them. But this was cautiously optimistic. Twenty well-trained agents to add to their fight. Plus the Runners hopefully.

Ramsey turned to the two "tainted" agents. "Tie them up. And gag them." He added when all three protested their innocence—even the one who had tried to stab Farouk.

Farouk approached Nettie and dropped his voice. "I can also render them unconscious with a planned strike to the head."

"That might be an excellent idea." Ramsey had still been close enough to hear Farouk.

Nettie nodded and soon all three agents were unconscious. "Our mode of transportation will be odd, and I'd like to try it from here. But you all need to remove or disable your tracking devices first." Hopefully, the protections Zarius had in the temple would block the tiny machines from sending their location, but better not to find out.

"Then our own Runners can't find us." Ramsey frowned. He and his people had been on the run for a few weeks, they'd counted on their Runners.

"I know, but the enemy is using them against us," Caden said.

"Let me get our primary Runner here first." Ramsey waited until both Nettie and Caden responded, then closed his eyes.

A Runner appeared almost immediately. Nettie was impressed but this wasn't the time for it.

Ramsey quickly explained the situation and the Runner nodded. "We can follow her." It turned to Nettie. "She has different blood."

"That's not good. What if the others can do that too?" Nettie was ready to take off on her own if needed.

"Compromised Runners would not be able to. You remain safe." The Runner's voice was a bit less stilted then before, and there was an attempt at conversation.

"Good enough for me." Ramsey and his people removed their trackers.

"Let's try this then." Nettie closed her fingers over her palm and thought of Zarius. It took four times and she was about to suggest they move closer to the stable when Ramsey, the three prisoners, and five other agents vanished. Then the rest of the agents, including the Runner who'd come inside, disappeared. Finally, Nettie, Caden, and Farouk were pulled out.

They ended up in the new room, or at least Nettie believed that was where they were. Aside from Gaston and Zarius none of their friends were in it. And it didn't have any doors.

CHAPTER FORTY-THREE

"I TAKE IT THEY ARE ALL clear?" Gaston raised the gun he'd kept hidden as he focused on Ramsey and his companions. "You understand, things have been extremely trying lately."

Ramsey raised his hands and nodded for the rest to do them same. "Another test? The three in the center were found to be wanting by your ghost friend, by the way."

Nettie was impressed. She hadn't mentioned what Farouk was.

"Yes, sadly one more." Gaston smiled but didn't lower his gun. "This is Zarius. He also needs to check you all."

Ramsey gave a bow to Zarius. "By all means."

Zarius quickly went through the group searching for any gkolin infestation. One of the unconscious agents did appear to have been taken over, but no one else was. "I will lock these up in separate rooms." Zarius touched all three, then vanished.

"So, he is what was reported. An attendant to a god." Ramsey didn't sound as surprised as the words implied. He'd been in the Society for over thirty years—it would take more than dead deities and their attendants to concern him.

"As far as we know." Caden turned to the lone Runner with them. "Can your people stop the ones who were modified?"

The Runner gave a short nod. "Yes. But they have been changed too much to come back to us and they will be difficult to find. The rest of our people will remain above ground to watch for them."

If the Runner had been an emotional being, Nettie would have said there was sorrow in its voice.

Farouk looked around, then bowed to Nettie. "If I am no longer needed, I would like to rejoin Amr. I believe we will be freeing more of our people, and your people, soon."

Nettie smiled. "Thank you for helping us. By all means, please get more of your people—and ours."

"We shall, Pharaoh Nettie," his voice faded at the end as he vanished, but Agent Ramsey caught the final words.

"Pharaoh now?" Ramsey laughed. "This fight is looking more hopeful, but I believe there is much to discuss."

Gaston said a single word, one that vanished immediately, and a doorway appeared. "Zarius assured me that would work, so glad it did. Follow me, we can get you all rooms to leave your things, then as you said, we have much to discuss and do."

Gaston lead the agents out with the Runner trailing behind.

Nettie caught up to the Runner. "Is there a way that we can tell your people from the modified ones?"

It stopped and tilted its head. Then nodded. "Yes. There would be. But we will have to develop it. I will communicate with the others now. We have never lost our people in this fashion. It is as if one of your people died, and then came back from the dead."

Aside from beings like the watchful dead, that was a chilling thought. "Thank you, and I'm sorry this happened to them."

The Runner nodded. "Thank you. I will appear dormant while we converse."

Nettie left the still Runner to check on Lisselle and Rachael and the machines. "Any luck?"

Lisselle handed her a printout. "Yes, and while it would be best to compare against agents who still had their ka intact, I believe they have been drugged with an oddly modified opium derivative."

Nettie read the printout, but it was fairly straight forward. Opium diluted with a few obscure, yet mostly harmless, components.

"And, yes, with a magical boost, we can break it down and dissolve it completely." Rebecca grinned and raised a vial with a light green fluid in it. "We give them a shot of this with Lisselle or Torlian standing by to give them a magical kick, and it will clear out the fatigue in moments." Her smiled dropped. "Or so we believe. We need people to test it on."

"I can see how Amr is doing in finding more of the kidnapped agents. Not to mention, I had an odd foreboding up on the surface. I'd like to know if he's sensed anything." The feeling still lingered although not as intense as it had been. However, that she was feeling the odd pressure even with all of Zarius' protections down here was disturbing.

Lisselle took the printout back. "Both are good ideas. I'm hoping Darwish and Damon will return soon with some agents as well."

"*Amr?*" She called in her head, but there was no response. Worse than that, it felt as if something was blocking her from reaching him. After five tries, she shook her head. "I'm not getting through to him."

Lisselle and Torlian shared a frown, then she checked Nettie's eyes and pulse. "It doesn't appear to be on your end, although we're not completely certain how you and he communicate."

"I'm worried about them and the others up above."

"I am as well," Ramsey said as he and Gaston joined

them. "There was something happening up there, my more sensitive agents felt it."

"Can you put a few of us on the surface? Just long enough to see what is happening?" Caden asked Lisselle as he put his pack back on.

Rebecca nodded. "Me as well. My abilities don't always behave as I'd like, but I might sense something." The lines on her face pointed out that she was also concerned about Damon, but she wasn't going to mention it.

"I believe I can do it, especially since Zarius appears occupied. Stand close together, however." Lisselle made a motion to start the spell, but the Runner cut her off.

"I am needed up top as well. Something is wrong."

Everyone waited for more information, it was more than a little disturbing to have something vague be wrong with Runners. But it did not provide more information.

Gaston had been still updating Agent Ramsey and from the deepening frown on his face, the news wasn't good. But he looked up. "I'd like to go as well, but I fear Ramsey and I have far more to discuss. Don't remain out there long if there is a problem—that includes the Runners."

Caden nodded and Nettie adjusted her utility belt. If this was a short trip she didn't need her full pack, but her gun and belt should suffice.

Rebecca squeaked, then ran off. She came back a moment later with a pair of goggles. "I almost forgot these, Thank you for them, Torlian."

A moment later, Nettie, Caden, Rebecca, and the Runner were in the village. Darkened skies now hung low overhead and cracks of lightning were in the distance. The wind felt strong enough to pick people up.

"I must find the others." The Runner gave a small head nod and vanished.

Nettie turned to Rebecca. "Do you feel anything?" The winds were getting worse and although they lowered their goggles, it was difficult to see through the flying sand.

"I don't...wait. Yes. There." Her eyes were wide under the lenses of the goggles and she pointed out toward the pyramids. "It's bad. We have to stop it." Then she started running toward the way out of the village.

Fortunately, Nettie and Caden were both faster and caught her before she got far.

"Easy there." Caden held Rebecca's arm. "There's a lot of bad people around here."

Rebecca blushed. "Sorry, but this feeling was just so clear. They're building something that will focus power of some sort, then take over the world."

Nettie looked around but the storm was pushing most people inside. "What are they building?"

"It was more of a feeling than actual seeing, but I think it was another sphinx." Rebecca sounded confused, but adamant.

"A smaller one, maybe?" Had she been asked, that drawing of Zarius' hand holding her mother's necklace had come from thousands of years ago. Yet, the workers in the distance of the sketch were building what appeared to be a smaller sphinx.

"Yes! That's it! But it's powerful, they're dragging something deadly up from the heart of the desert and using the sphinx to do it." She pulled her arm free. "We need to get there and stop them. Maybe Homer can take us."

Nettie gave her friend a close stare. "I don't believe even he would go up in weather like this." Rebecca was by no means stupid, but the panic of whatever was going to happen was causing issues.

Rebecca grinned. "On the way out here, Captain Pilo was bragging about some of the secret adjustments made to Homer's airship. One of them was creating a storm chaser." She shrugged. "Or something like that. They can move storms and are prepared to handle them. We can at least ask. This storm is bad and I don't think natural. I can feel it, but what's taking place out there will be worse."

Nettie looked to Caden and shrugged.

"We won't have much time out here if this storm gets worse. But might as well ask, I guess." Caden went back to watching the sky.

"You are my favorite brother-in-law." Rebecca gave him a side hug then they all ran for Homer's airship.

The fact it wasn't grounded yet supported Rebecca's claim.

The airship was clearly Homer's, but at the same time didn't look much like it did a few hours ago. It was now covered in an odd metallic net and had rods stuck all over it.

"Wouldn't that just make it a better target for lightning strikes?" Caden shook his head as he studied the additions.

"According to Captain Pilo, that's how it moves the storms, and protects the airship." Rebecca started jumping up and down to gain the attention of those onboard.

Homer leaned over the side. "What are you three doing out in this weather?"

"I'd ask you the same thing. But we might need a ride." Caden tightened the straps on his goggles as a stronger wind came up.

Nettie did as well. There was no way this was natural. "Is this storm energy going to the desert?" The wind was pushing through the village, but heading out toward the pyramids.

"It looks like." Rebecca held on to her goggles and watched the winds.

"Hold on, we're lowering back down."

At Homer's words, Nettie realized that the airship had been getting ready to leave when they arrived.

Homer might not completely answer to Gaston, or

even Agent Ramsey, but this wouldn't have made either man happy.

"Nettie? Caden? Rebecca? How did you know to come find us out here?" Darwish yelled as he came running toward them.

From the desert side.

Damon, Raki, and about nine more men and women— the missing agents who Darwish knew were around the village, she assumed— were struggling through the shifting sand toward them.

Rebecca ran to Damon and hugged him tightly, but aside from being wind tossed, he, like the others, looked fine.

"How and why were you out there?" Caden shook his head as they sought shelter behind a building on the edge of the village.

"We were deceived. We found these agents, Raki cleared them, then that storm came up and tried to trick us into the desert. Raki saved us," Damon said. He and Darwish had their goggles, but the rest of the agents had wrapped cloths around their eyes.

Raki was almost as tall as Farouk and bowed deeply. "To serve Pharaoh Nettie."

"Thank you, Raki. Can you reach any of your people? I can't reach Amr."

He shook his head. "I cannot. This storm has cut me off. There are foul deeds happening."

Nettie watched as Homer lowered his airship, it was as if the wind simply went around his airship. Tricky, and she could tell by the look in Caden's eyes, they would be hearing all of the specifics later.

There was a bit of a conflict as Darwish wanted to bring the new agents aboard. He was quickly outvoted. Yes, Raki had cleared them of having a good heart, but the gkolin influence could still be in one or more of them.

Farida might not have been the only one who had been released after being infested.

Caden closed his fingers over his palm, and a moment later Darwish and the agents vanished.

The rest quickly climbed up the rope ladder, and Homer was getting ready to lift off when Darwish reappeared.

"Gaston said I might be needed up here. He's not pleased with your airship changes, but he said that will wait." They lowered the ladder again and he climbed up.

Rebecca stayed alongside Homer and pointed the direction.

He shook his head, but bellowed out commands to do so. "Right in the center of things. Even I would say we should get more people, but there's no way to tell how long this will last."

Nettie lifted her goggles slowly. No sand nor excessive wind came through the deck of the airship. "This is quite wonderous. Just how are you doing this?"

"It's part of the storm chaser protocol." Captain Pilo's smile came out of his massive black beard. "This is the first ship of its kind to have this equipment, but hopefully all airships will have it. For a price." His grin went wider.

Caden laughed. "Found another angle, Homer?"

"Aye. This agent work is hard on the body. Might become an entrepreneur. One of those fancy businessmen of leisure."

Both Caden and Nettie laughed at that. He might say he wanted to be lazy, but Homer would die of old age doing what he loved.

Rebecca and Damon stayed near the bow, both kept their goggles on, even though there was no wind. The specialized goggles could help with long-range seeing as well.

Raki seemed as curious about the pirates running the airship as they were about him and he walked around watching what each did carefully.

Nettie tried to reach Amr again. There was a chance that the sand and wind had contributed to the lack of contact. However, he still didn't respond.

As they rose higher, it was easier to see the waves of sand flowing toward the pyramid. But Nettie felt there was more than sand.

"Raki? Do you know what is going on down there?"

He was at her side in an instant and closely peered down. "Magic. They are pulling the last of the residual magic to them. Even that of humans."

CHAPTER FORTY-FOUR

RAKI PAUSED. "IT IS GOOD that your magic users are being protected, they would be drained quickly if they came into this."

Nettie wasn't sure if he meant of their magic, their lives, or both. But they needed to keep Lisselle and Torlian safe.

"Clearing dead ahead!" The call came from a raised bucket stand where a woman with a huge looking glass stood.

Nettie would take her word for it at this point. Even with her goggles and already enhanced vision, all she could see was a line of sand around them.

A few minutes later the wall of sand broke.

"That's it! They can't be allowed to finish that!" Rebecca yelled as she pointed to a small shape not far from the pyramids.

With a borrowed looking glass, Nettie was able to see the shape was of a sphinx. It appeared to be only a tenth of the size of the real one, but there was no doubt what it was. And there were odd waves of color flowing toward it even as the workers scrambled around trying to finish it. The waves of color almost made her ill.

Caden turned to Homer. "Can you fire cannons at it? I know they work better against other airships, but maybe try to destroy it?"

"I must find Amr and the others. This cannot be allowed." Raki bowed to Nettie and then vanished.

"I wish he had stayed long enough to clarify what exactly *that* is." Homer scowled out across the desert at the small sphinx. "We might be able to destroy it with our cannons, but I'd feel better knowing what we're destroying. Blowing up a collection of explosives could have extremely negative results for many people, including this airship."

Rebecca leaned forward intensely for a few moments, but then shook her head. "I was hoping that I could sort it out, but all I can feel is that it must not be completed. I'm getting images of what will happen if we don't. First this village, then Egypt, then the world." Her voice dropped to a whisper.

"What will happen to them?" Nettie felt a chill go up her spine.

"They'll all fall." She tilted her head as if staring at something only she could see. "There are two forces in this against us. One wants power, nothing more than complete control over the entire world. The other wants revenge. They want to demolish this world for no other reason." She shook her shoulders and stepped away from the railing. "Destroying that thing will slow them down."

Nettie looked to Caden. Slowing down was one thing, but they needed to stop the ones behind both issues.

"Slowing down is better than nothing, and we don't have time to check with Gaston at this point—nor find out what it is we're blowing up." Homer kept looking through his glass and frowning. "Pilo, bring the airship around so our pass near them will end with us facing the village. We might have to get out of here quickly and I'd rather not go further into the desert."

The dark-haired pirate nodded and the airship changed direction. From the way the small forms below seemed to be jumping about, the airship had been spotted.

"I see you haven't given up." Sekhmet appeared next to Nettie. The pirates froze, but none of the agents did.

Nettie was disappointed at Sekhmet's continued survival after the fight in the desert, but not surprised. "We will stop you." She motioned for the others to stay back. Caden especially appeared extremely reckless.

Sekhmet turned to look behind her. "That? Pish. Ammit and a few others are doing that thing down there. Some rebels tried it before we went to slumber and it didn't work then either. Your friend Zarius stopped it then, but he probably doesn't remember." She stepped closer, forcing Nettie to look up to see her. "I want you to join us. Become a goddess, help rule this world. The blood in you calls to it."

"My blood is mine and it doesn't call to anything. Shall we jump to the desert and fight again? Or did you forget who was winning when you fled?"

"I was caught unaware. I misjudged you, but it will not happen again. Join us or die."

Nettie took a step closer. "Leave us or die." There was a calmness and surety in her voice that wasn't hers. Not completely, at any rate.

"You sound different." Sekhmet narrowed her feline eyes and sniffed her. "You feel different. What has happened to you?"

"I will protect my daughter." Those words came out of Nettie's mouth and were in her voice, but she didn't say them.

"*Mother*?" Nettie asked inside her head—it was less confusing to others.

"Yes, child. I could not become one of the watchful dead, as I wasn't always on the side of good. But I can do this." As she spoke, Nettie's hand flung up and a bolt of lightning shot out at Sekhmet. Nettie felt the lightning called to her and sent to Sekhmet in a fluid motion.

Sekhmet took the hit better than a human would, but

she still folded over briefly, then stood up but kept one hand over the location where she'd been struck. "You are constantly amazing me. I will be back."

She vanished.

"I think she was bleeding." Rebecca dropped to the deck where Sekhmet had stood, but didn't touch the drops. "I don't think anyone should come in contact with it, but this is blood."

Caden took Nettie's arm. "Are you okay? Who was speaking to you and Sekhmet?"

"Me, Nettie's mother. I did move on, but was able to come back. There are too many doors open between the planes of life and death. I can't stay long, take care of each other."

The pressure that she hadn't noticed until it left, vanished from Nettie's mind. "She's gone now. Trust me, that trick with the lightning wasn't me."

The moment Sekhmet vanished, the airship crew continued moving and speaking as if nothing had happened.

Homer came closer. "Given what just happened, do we still destroy that sphinx?"

"Yes," Rebecca responded before anyone else could. "The level of evilness around it has increased."

Nettie and Caden nodded, although Caden was still watching Nettie carefully.

"Okay, lets finish it before another deity shows up." Homer turned and barked more orders as Captain Pilo swung wide of the clearing to come from the other side.

"Are you certain you're all right?" Caden asked Nettie. "You look pale."

"I'm English, how can you tell?" Nettie gave a soft laugh at her attempt at a joke. "I do feel a bit drawn. But having one's dead, vampire mother take one over has to be a decent cause."

"That is unique. Do you think she'll come back? It was disturbing how quickly she moved in."

"I don't know. I am concerned about her comment of too many doors being open."

"Brace!" Homer yelled. "Fire at will! Aim for the ground in front of it, we'll give those workers time to flee."

The first cannonball arced away from the airship and hit the sand about fifteen feet from the workers.

Nettie couldn't hear the yells but judging from the running around on the ground, the workers were probably yelling. She just hoped they got clear in time. There was a chance they weren't aware of who they were helping.

"That was your warning shot, leave the area immediately." Homer was naturally loud, but he was also using a large horn to amplify his voice.

"They're firing at us with rifles." The woman in the lookout basket called over.

"Aim for the structure!" Homer yelled and the airship came around again and two cannons fired from that side.

A number of things happened at once. Both cannonballs smashed into the small sphinx crumbling the left side. Sekhmet suddenly reappeared on the deck, she grabbed Caden, then they both vanished.

"Caden!" Nettie screamed. He'd been taken while standing no more than a few inches away from her. Neither she nor he had time to react.

Rebecca grabbed her as Nettie moved toward the railing. "She wouldn't take him down there—she'll want you to follow her."

"But where did she go? Mother! I need you!" Nettie was hysterical and she knew it. The love of her life had been taken by an evil goddess.

"Do we fire another round?" Pilo called out to Homer.

Homer looked to Nettie. "Yes."

She fought to maintain her composure, Caden had been in life-threatening situations before—even one time against her. But there was a fire in her blood she'd never felt before. Pharaohs didn't deal with this type of loss well it seemed.

The airship fired another round of cannonballs.

Rebecca stayed next to Nettie with her arm around her. "We will get him back; you have to know that. You ha—" Her voice vanished as Horus this time appeared, grabbed Rebecca, and disappeared.

"NO!" That was echoed by Nettie and Damon.

Homer grabbed Damon before he could climb over the railing. "Killing yourself won't bring her back, lad. We will get them both back." Damon stopped struggling but Homer didn't release him.

"Amr! Your pharaoh needs you!" Nettie yelled aloud and in her mind with a force she didn't know she had. There had to be a way to reach them. She was their pharaoh.

It wasn't the watchful dead, but a wave of energy that came from the remains of the destroyed sphinx and slammed into the airship. The wood of the airship groaned as the power that hit it cracked the hull, and punctured the balloon. The balloon didn't explode, but it started leaking quickly and the airship spiraled down toward the sand.

"Brace!" Homer, still holding Damon, yelled moments before they crashed.

CHAPTER FORTY-FIVE

NETTIE HUNG ONTO THE RAILING and mentally yelled out to her mother, Amr, and Zarius. They needed help. SHE needed help. No one responded, but she held onto the hope that any or all of them would be coming soon as she jumped over the railing the moment the airship crashed into the sand.

She spun back to the airship. Its landing wasn't as bad as she would have expected. But it clearly wouldn't be flying for a while. "Is everyone okay?"

"Aye, but you shouldn't have done that." Homer released Damon, only to have him follow Nettie over the railing.

"We're going to have to fight, there's no choice." Nettie pointed to the mob of workers charging at them across the sand. All were heavily armed.

The pirates didn't need encouragement and soon everyone was in the sand and fully armed.

Darwish took Nettie's shoulder. "They are protected. I feel that."

At first she thought that he meant the ones running for them, but then his smile and nod pointed out that he meant Caden and Rebecca.

"Thank you. I will need to hear that again once we destroy these people." With a nod, Nettie raced forward, her gun in one hand and a borrowed short sword in the other. The enemies had rifles but so far hadn't demonstrated much skill with them and many threw them away as they ran and raised swords as well.

Nettie's little gun didn't have much range, but she quickly dispatched the forerunners charging them. However, it took all of her bullets, so she tucked the gun away and raised her sword as she ran.

"To me!" She wasn't sure why she yelled it, but it felt right. "TO ME!" All of her fear at losing Caden and Rebecca flowed into the words and it felt as if they echoed off the sky and sand itself.

Suddenly she was running in the midst of a mob of ghost men—the watchful dead, all of them—had heard her. Bassem gave her a bow as he took his place alongside her.

"Our pharaoh calls!" Amr shouted and the hundred warriors yelled back as they ran forward.

There were easily twice as many armed workers against them, but the enemy was outmatched regardless. They appeared in shock as the watchful dead ran through them. Finally, the few surviving workers ran out into the desert.

"Do we follow?" Amr had been with his men, but appeared at Nettie's side.

Part of her wanted to say yes, as if they were responsible for Caden and Rebecca being taken, but then she shook her head. "They are not worthy, the power they were trying to build needs to be destroyed, however."

She still couldn't tell exactly what the sphinx would have done when completed, but she now felt an evilness flowing from it. Homer's cannonballs had done damage to it, but not enough. It needed to be ground into sand.

Amr nodded and his men swarmed over it. Soon only a single boulder remained.

"My pharaoh, we cannot remove or destroy that." Amr was next to her again as his men continued to work on the stone. Nothing they did impacted it at all.

"I have a few explosives on the airship we could try." Homer was dusty and bloody but the blood on him wasn't his.

"No. Nettie needs to do it." Her mother took over her voice again. "Take my pendant, hold it in your left hand, and repeat the words I'll say in your mind. I can't say them even in your voice—it must be you."

Nettie quickly took the pendant off, held it as she'd seen in the journal, and repeated the words as a chill flowed over her. It was as if death was touching her soul. Then the ankh tattoo flared brightly.

She repeated the words three times, focusing on the boulder as a trio of whirlwinds approached them from the open desert.

The boulder finally exploded and collapsed into a pile of sand and the whirlwinds stopped. Ammit, Ra, and Tefnut appeared.

"You have only but slowed us. We will rebuild. You can't stop us. This world will pay." Ammit started to come forward, her face in a horrific snarl, when Ra touched her arm. She looked to him, then to the watchful dead, and gave a small nod.

All three of the deities vanished.

"Can you get back to the village?" Nettie asked Homer. The airship was clearly down for now. She doubted that even Homer's crew could do the needed repairs out here without help.

"If we can capture some of the camels, horses, and donkeys milling around here, then yes. Where are you going?"

"I have another mission and will travel in ways you cannot." She slipped her mother's pendant back over her head and the ankh dimmed. "Keep him and everyone else safe." She nodded to Damon, who now that there was no one to fight in front of him, appeared lost. She knew what he was feeling but they couldn't give into it now. At least she couldn't.

At Homer's nod, she called Amr to her side. "We must go."

Amr nodded and picked Nettie up. "Where?"

"The compound near where we found each other." With a small smile to the rest of her friends, she and the watchful dead vanished.

Amr took her at her word and they reappeared in the tunnel where they'd first met. She'd been thinking it would be more dramatic to invade James' place from the front doors, with a hundred watchful dead at her heels, but this would suffice.

"Were you successful in finding more of the missing agents?" They'd clearly found the rest of their own people.

Amr nodded. "They are in a large cavern almost to the bottom of Khafre. We didn't want to free them until we knew you could revive them. There are not only agents but common villagers, as well, and they number over two hundred. We couldn't get close enough to see their faces, but they all appear to remain in a stupor."

Nettie's heart gave a lurch as she almost asked Rebecca to go help them. The liquid they created would work best with a magic boost, but should still get the captured people mobile even alone. She shoved the fear for her friend and her husband aside.

"Is it safe for magic users now?" she asked Raki.

He tilted his head and slightly closed his eyes. Then opened them and nodded. "Yes, pharaoh."

"Can you send someone to speak to Gaston, Lisselle, and Zarius? Explain the situation, and tell them they need to bring supplies and weapons to the tunnel to rescue and treat the kidnapped people. Then send half of our men down to the captured people to guard them and help release them when my friends arrive."

Bassem bowed to her and Amr. "I can complete this

task." He waited for both Nettie and Amr to nod, then vanished.

Amr quickly selected half of the watchful dead and they silently jogged down the hall, placing pairs of guards every turn as they went. Then he faced Nettie with a small smile before she could say anything. "Yes, we can travel through the nothing, but I believe that was why we became stuck before and would like to limit the use. Your calling us in the desert, freed us."

"Were we in danger coming here as we did?"

"No, your energy empowered us, which is how we were able to join the glorious fight. It still remains in our hearts, but we should remain cautious about using that path of travel unless things become dire."

"Thank you. I believe that the man in this compound is a puppet of higher sources, but he needs to be stopped. And, if he has information as to where Sekhmet and Horus took Caden and Rebecca, we will get him to tell us." Torture was not something Nettie ever thought she would consider. But the loss of Caden and Rebecca, plus the fire in her blood, made her think of it as an unwelcome, yet viable, option.

"Easy there, child." Her mother's voice stayed inside her head this time. *"You have tapped into powers far beyond anything even I had. You could end up destroying yourself."*

"They took my husband and best friend, Mother. I will do whatever needs to be done to get them back." She'd never felt this fierce…or if she was honest, this violent. She didn't like it, but was grateful for it now.

"I understand and feel it in your heart. Just don't go so far that you cannot come back. I will help with what I can through the pendant. However, once the balance is returned and the doors to the realms of the dead are shut again, you will be on your own. I am proud of who you became, daughter."

"I understand, thank you." Nettie turned toward Amr. "I think it's time to break into this location and get some

answers." She patted the door she'd come out of, but Farouk waited in front of the other door that she and Caden had seen.

"The room beyond this door feels larger than that one. It could be a better place to enter." He gave a low bow.

"I am grateful to have such wise men with me. Let's get inside." Her fists clenched as they disassembled the wooden door. She'd thought they might just break through, but they quietly, and quickly, took it apart and piled the pieces next to it.

The room was dark inside, but like the tunnel, Nettie could see fine. She hadn't even noticed that she hadn't turned on her flashlight until now. She turned to Amr as he helped her up the large gap into the room. "Are my eyes red?" They felt different than when she went vampire, but still odd.

"Yes, Pharaoh Nettie, and glowing. They are most striking and will bring fear to our enemies."

"Good then. Let's continue."

Amr left four of the watchful dead to guard the open door. She had no intention of leaving through anything aside from the front door, but she agreed with his plan to protect them against incursion from this direction.

The room was far larger than it appeared at first, but aside from rows of rough benches, it contained nothing.

"They held people here, before they were moved recently." Raki nodded as he continued through with his head tilted as if listening to the benches themselves.

Nettie shook with anger. This James person had a lot to answer for.

Raki and two others cautiously went out a smaller door at the end of the room, and then came back. "There is no one down here. There is noise on the floors above us. Do we kill them?"

Nettie's bloodlust was fading. And the people working with James might not fully understand the stakes of what he was doing. "No, unless there is no other choice. Capture them, secure them, and render them unconscious if you need. But keep them alive. For now."

All of the watchful dead around her bowed then moved into the hall and toward a flight of stairs.

The noise became noticeable as they reached the bottom of the stairs. There was more activity than she'd expected, but they were too loud for her to believe that James knew she and her ghosts were down here.

Nettie tried to walk silently, but she knew that if anyone gave away where they were it would be her. She wanted to be in the first wave, to see James' face as they attacked. But there was too much of a chance that she would give them away.

Amr motioned for a group of ten watchful dead to move past her. Then he and the rest followed as she moved again.

They were only a few steps below the next floor when the yelling started.

"Let's go then." Even though her eyes had changed, her fangs didn't slide down until she allowed them to. And the ankh tattoo blazed through her sleeve.

The sight was an interesting one. James had more people than when she'd been here before, most dressed as pharaoh's guards who appeared to be fighting poorly against former *real* pharaoh's guards.

"Stop her! HER!" James had run into a corner, one with a small partially hidden door, and pointed at her as he screamed.

"Take care of the rest, this one is mine." Nettie didn't see any of the modified Runners as she raced to James, but they could appear at any moment.

James tried to fit under his massive throne when the door wouldn't open. It appeared that someone had painted over it and sealed it shut.

Nettie dragged him out and raised him in the air with one hand. "Who are you working for?"

"I...I am a ruler; I work for no one." He gave his feet a little kick, then at a glare from her stayed still.

Nettie shook him hard. "Who do you work for? If you can't help me, then there is no reason to keep you alive. Do you see my men who are destroying your own? They are called the watchful dead, warriors of the past to right your wrongs. Speak now."

"Horus. He brought me here. He and Sekhmet. They gave me power. I got them into the Society headquarters and kept the agents drugged. Then they told me to take you."

"Where did you get those metal men?"

"I found them. In Bath. I'm a scientist by trade, and not Egyptian."

Nettie would have laughed if things weren't so dire. James was paler than her. He'd kept his accent scattered so it wasn't clear where in England he was from, but there was no doubt he was British.

"You rebuilt them? Alone?"

"There was one still in better shape, I fixed it. Then it helped me build the rest. I sent it to London in disguise when Horus ordered me to gather information. He wanted someone else besides you—a leader of the metal men. But I couldn't find him."

Agent Zero. Few knew that the mysterious leader of the Society, Agent Zero, was also the leader of the Runners. He was even more advanced than the rest of them and built a reputation for being reclusive. That explained why he'd fled Edinburgh weeks ago.

If the returning deities could gain him for their side, they would easily take over the world.

"You failed. Where are Caden and Rebecca?"

He tried giving a wide-eyed look of innocence, but she shook him again. "Two English, a man and a woman.

Kidnapped by your god and goddess." She hadn't been certain they were here when they broke in, but she felt he knew something now.

"I…they were sent to the pyramid. To have their kas removed with the others—in a single massive ceremony."

Nettie picked up a large round polished stone from a desk and hit him in the head with it. Then dropped him to the floor.

"We have to go to Khafre!"

Amr was beside her in a moment. "Bassem said your friends are still on their way, they have just reached the tunnel."

"We can't wait, they are going to kill them all." She looked around, all of James' people were unconscious and tied with various fabrics.

"Come with me!" She knew without Lisselle's liquid and her and Torlian's magic, they couldn't wake them, but if something big was happening they needed to stop it.

They were racing to the stairs they'd come up, when the watchful dead all slowed down. And three modified Runners appeared in front of them.

CHAPTER FORTY-SIX

NETTIE WAS STILL MOVING, BUT the Runners were affecting the ghost warriors. Two of the watchful dead maintained enough speed to reach the Runners. A small bolt of light came from the foremost Runner's hand and both watchful dead vanished.

She felt a chill. "They are gone for good, aren't they?"

Amr nodded in slow motion.

"My watchful dead, stand down. This is now my battle, not yours. When these are removed, you will destroy the machines gathering the kas from everyone in that room under Khafre. You will obey your pharaoh." She kept her eyes on the Runners, but she saw Amr and his men stop trying to move. She wasn't certain if it was a result of her order, or whatever the Runners were doing.

She turned to the modified, and formerly dead, Runners. "You were destroyed in Bath. You sacrificed yourselves for your kind, yet you have now become this? Is there nothing of who you were left?" She wasn't certain, even in her altered state, just what she could do against a single Runner, let alone three. But even if it cost her life, she had to stop them and let Amr and his people free the others.

"Surrender." The foremost Runner raised its arm and fired a bolt. Nettie couldn't move fast enough but the energy hit her mother's pendant, then deflected into a nearby wall. Not as handy as if it had gone back at the Runner, but it was better than having struck her.

"Never." She prepared to go down fighting and started to approach the Runners when two new ones appeared in front of her.

They faced the other three, which gave her hope they were on the right side. She stopped moving forward.

"Abominations. Return to the great beyond where you belong." That was from one of the new Runners and the first time she'd heard mention of the Runners believing in an afterlife.

"Join us."

"They need to get out of our way." Nettie stepped closer to the new Runners.

"You served well, it was not your fault this happened to you. Move on." The Runner who spoke took a step closer to the other three and so did the one who arrived with it.

"No, we have a higher purpose now. We—"

The new Runner struck the one speaking in the middle of the chest. The modified Runner stopped speaking and froze in place.

"You two can shut yourselves off, or we will," the second new Runner said. When neither of the remaining two acted, both of the new Runners struck the changed ones and shut them down. They then gently moved all three bodies out of the way.

"Your companions are coming." The Runner nodded to Nettie.

"Thank you, but we can't wait. Tell Gaston to send people down the tunnel—including Lisselle and her supplies to wake the agents." She looked behind her. "If anyone here wakes up, subdue them but don't kill them. Gaston and Ramsey will want to speak to them." When the Runner nodded, she motioned for Amr and his men to join her as she ran down the stairs and into the tunnel.

"I will keep the guards placed here in the tunnel to assist your friends," Amr said as he ran alongside her.

"Thank you." Nettie increased her speed but tried to keep her breath steady. Fear for Caden and Rebecca terrified her, but panicking wouldn't help them.

Most were keeping pace with Nettie, but Bassem ran ahead of the rest, then waited where the tunnel flatted out. The rockslide that Nettie had Farouk create was still there.

"I know you can get through those, but I cannot."

"We will take care of it." Amr didn't slow down as he began removing the rocks. Like their work on the door, they finished quickly.

Nettie smiled and ran through. She understood that this was their final calling and that the watchful dead would watch no more after this. But she would miss them greatly.

Bassem led them to the left, a different direction than they'd gone when escaping the last time.

Nettie stopped in shock. This chamber was only a few minutes from where they'd run through to escape the first time, yet no one knew it had been there.

Amr paused in front of a deep indentation in the rock wall. "There are beings in here."

Nettie ran in, maybe Caden and Rebecca had escaped. She stumbled as she saw two bodies, a man and a woman. But it was Sekhmet and Horus. They were badly beaten.

Sekhmet struggled to sit up. "You. Had I been Sekhmet in truth, you wouldn't have won." She was clearly dying. "I am Xial, Sekhmet's attendant. We were all tricked into this. He is Wol, attendant to Horus. He has already left this plane. You must destroy Ammit and her companions."

"Is she an attendant too?" Nettie felt a twinge of sympathy, but not when she thought of all Xial/Sekhmet had done.

"No. Ammit was awake when all the others slept, but

trapped and couldn't move until the last decade. She is insane now and tricked us." Xial coughed. "I go back to my sleep, but I bid you good luck. You were a worthy opponent." She gave a deep sigh and went still.

Nettie turned to Amr and nodded to both bodies. "We will stop Ammit and free those people."

The pause had been long enough for Lisselle, Torlian, and Ramsey, along with a bunch of recovered local agents, to join them. Five Runners ran in perfect formation behind them all.

Lisselle ran to Nettie and hugged her. "We will free them, I promise. Is that Sekhmet?" She peered into the indentation.

"It was the being pretending to be her." Nettie quickly filled them in. By the time she was done, Ramsey was almost shaking in anger and appeared to need to bash someone. Some of the higher-up agents stayed behind a desk. Ramsey kept his work mostly in Scotland, but he was still very active.

"What's the plan, then, Agent Jones-Smith?" He controlled himself and motioned down toward the chamber.

"Amr and his men can destroy the machines that are draining the kas. So far no one has come out to stop us, but we have to believe that Ammit and whoever is still working for her, knows where we are."

"Which is why we are here." Zarius had approached as silently as the watchful dead. And so had the jackal-headed form of Anubis. Zarius held a slightly glowing square tucked in one arm. "This will allow us to return Ammit and any others she has awoken to sleep." He turned to Anubis with a smile. "Thank you for helping us, you did pretend to be my Anubis extremely well."

Lisselle's eyes narrowed as she studied Anubis, then looked back to Zarius. "But if you're Anubis' attendant, then who is this?"

Anubis had remained silent, then he bowed and the jackal head vanished. A being very much like a cross between a human and a Runner stood there.

"Agent Zero?" Ramsey clasped his friend's arm. "You've set us on a merry chase."

"And it isn't over, my friend. The tale is long, and can be shared when lives are saved." He sounded more human than any Runner Nettie had met, and most likely could pass as a full human, albeit an eccentric one. "I had to hide and assume the persona of Anubis to bring forth Zarius to stop Ammit. There were breaches in Edinburgh that will be addressed, but it was too dangerous for me to stay there. Other attendants were also awoken, but they fell to Ammit's words of power. We must end this."

The Egyptian agents looked surprised at having the two leaders of the entire Society with them, but they recovered quickly.

"What's that?" Nettie asked Zarius as he shifted the glowing box in his arm.

"It is our not-so-secret weapon. Those weren't normal gkolin infestations in Farida or the others we found. With Agent Zero's help, we were able to contain their energy as we removed it from the agents. As they were created by Ammit, they have some of her essence and will help send her back to where she belongs. Asleep this time."

Agent Zero smiled at Nettie. "I believe this is your case, please lead."

Nettie took a deep breath, then she, Amr, Bassem, and Farouk took the lead. The cavern was massive and there were easily two hundred people on the ground with glowing balls attached to them.

The cavern was still unattended, but that didn't last long. As the watchful dead ran to disrupt the removal of the kas from the fallen, a group of warriors came into the cavern at the far side.

"We need Ammit." Agent Zero glared around the room and disbursed the Runners he had with him to face the new fighters along with the recovered Egyptian agents.

Nettie ran between the rows of people on the ground, finally finding Caden and Rebecca. She dropped down between them but they were both unconscious and twitching. "Amr! I need help!"

Amr and Bassem ran to her, and then immediately destroyed the connections between Caden and Rebecca to the machines. Then they worked their way out from them, destroying machines as they walked through them.

The watchful dead held enough magic in their being that simply walking through the balls disconnected them. They all looked up as the warriors began fighting.

"Keep working on freeing the people! You are the only ones who can do that!" Nettie yelled as she waved over to Lisselle. "We have to get them all out of here."

Lisselle gave Caden and Rebecca each a shot, then softly spoke a spell. Both began to wake up, so Lisselle followed Amr and Bassem, waking agents as they freed them.

Both Caden and Rebecca were groggy and appeared to have put up a fight when brought here, but Nettie kept hugging them both. Once Caden appeared a bit more aware, she kissed him soundly.

"I know you both want to fight, but you're too weak. Can you lead some of the others out of the tunnel? There are some of Amr's men stationed in the way and they can help if you are attacked." She fought not to cry, that could come later.

Both of them tried to speak at once, clearly in protest, but Nettie raised both hands. "No. I almost lost you both and that is simply unacceptable. You must help the others back. Their recovery is slower than hoped."

Caden gave her a solid kiss and then got to his feet without help, with Rebecca right behind him. "I do want the chance to address Sekhmet and Horus, however. I owe them."

"Too late, Ammit killed them," Torlian said while he followed two of the watchful dead as they walked through the machines. "Best if you two focus on getting these people out of here." He nodded and gave out another shot and spell.

Nettie hugged them both once more. "Go. Oh, Agent Zero is here too—long story." There was fighting in the chamber still, but mostly toward the far end.

Caden and Rebecca started pulling up freshly awakened agents, who in turn pulled up more. Eventually over half of the people in the room were heading out the doorway.

A pair of watchful dead joined them and escorted them out.

"You keep slowing me down. I knew I needed to stop you, but Xial insisted you would help our side because of your blood." Ammit appeared behind Nettie and hit her hard with the back of her hand. Considering it was more like a lion's claw, the positioning had been deliberate. Ammit still wasn't certain that she wanted Nettie dead.

"And I'm not going to let you finish your job." Zarius appeared next to Nettie.

"Anubis' attendant. You think you can stop me? Even without those kas, I will have my revenge." Ammit snapped her long toothy jaws at him.

"You weren't like this long ago. I'd forgotten many things when I was awakened, but I know who you were. You helped me stop the usurpers who built the false sphinx thousands of years ago. You need to sleep and return to who you were." Zarius had the glowing box hidden under his cloak but was stalling. "Nettie, might I borrow your necklace?"

She quickly took it off and handed it to him.

"Now!" Zarius yelled and the room filled with Runners and they began grabbing agents and vanishing then returning for more. The ones who were still fighting Ammit's people continued but the number of enemies dwindled.

The last of the agents and villagers who had been being drained were gone, and the ones fighting were drawing back toward the tunnel.

Agent Zero, Ramsey, and all the rest were on their way out at a good clip.

Zarius and Ammit were locked in a staring and snarling match.

"Ra and Tefnut said the same thing. They have joined Xial, Hol, and the rest in peaceful slumber now. I wonder if that peace will continue when I've destroyed everything?" Ammit flexed her claws.

"*Go. Now.*" Zarius spoke in Nettie's head and it sounded like it was echoed by the voice of her mother. The cavern was clear and Ammit seemed to be bristling with power.

Nettie ran. She'd just gotten to the first set of watchful dead guards when the earth shook and a blinding light came from the cavern.

"Run!" She raced up the tunnel, gathering watchful dead as she went.

Amr was at the top with the rest. "Thank you, Pharaoh Nettie, but Zarius is not winning this fight. He needs us." He bowed low, which was echoed by all of his men. "We go to save this world and find our peace." He leaned forward and kissed her cheek. "We will never forget you."

Without waiting, all of the watchful dead vanished.

A moment later the tunnel shook and a cloud of sand and debris came shooting up from the bottom.

CHAPTER FORTY-SEVEN

AGENT ZERO WAITED AT THE open doorway into James' compound and reached out a hand to help her up into the room. "Get down quickly." He dropped down after pushing her away from the doorway.

Even with him blocking the majority of the sand and debris, there was still almost a foot of it inside the door.

Nettie was just getting to her feet when an explosion hit. Rather, it was the result of an explosion far down the tunnel.

"Nettie!" Caden and Darwish came running into the chamber. "They destroyed Khafre!"

All four ran up the stairs, through James' front room, and out the wide-open front door.

Even from this distance, it was clear that Khafre was folding in on itself. The sound from the tunnels compacting radiated out from the compound and villagers were either running into their homes or frozen in shock.

In the distance, she saw five airships heading their way. Two of them split off and changed course toward the collapsing pyramid. The foremost one slowed down and began to lower. Homer waved to all of them.

"Very glad you're all alive, but you're losing a pyramid. We can bring you all up if need be."

Agent Zero had noticeably stayed inside the compound

and Ramsey responded. "We'll stay. We might need to help the locals."

Homer nodded and the airship he rode rose. Soon it and the remaining two were flying over the village in an apparent search pattern. Nothing had collapsed in the village, yet. But that could change very quickly.

There was one final crash and the pyramid was gone.

"Did we stop Ammit? But at what cost?" Lisselle looked out over the rising dust and sand.

"Wait…is it moving back?" Darwish made sure to stand as far from Agent Ramsey as possible, but he stepped forward now. "The pyramid is coming back? How is it coming back?" The note of panic in his voice was understandable.

As Nettie stood between Caden and Rebecca, she had to agree that was a bit odd.

A whisper flew through the room and out to where most of them stood, but there was nothing to see. Then Nettie's mother's pendant dropped out of the air and she caught it.

"Zarius?" The pendant was warm.

"Yes. I'm saying goodbye to all of you. The locals will speak of the mass hallucination of the fall of Khafre for a few days, then they will forget. I'm leaving now, thank you for saving Egypt, all of you." The wind blew strong enough to ruffle hair, then departed.

"He did it." Gaston grinned as the dust cleared away from the pyramid. "It's intact."

Nettie hugged Caden and Rebecca, with Damon hugging Rebecca on the other side. "We did it. Now, should I ask Agent Zero for a honeymoon?"

EPILOGUE

A month later.

NETTIE FUSSED WITH HER GOWN once more, she wasn't used to dressing up, or having her hair down as it currently was, but this was her wedding after all. She found that having a second, more recognized wedding, suited her, but she would always treasure her wedding in Zarius' temple. After Zarius vanished, Lisselle was able to let them back inside to gather their belongings, free Farida, and turn the traitors over to the rebuilding Society—which had claimed James' compound for the time being.

Sadly, once Agent Zero, Agent Ramsey, and a few more upstanding agents were added to the guest list, they couldn't hold the wedding on Homer's new airship. It was larger than his old one, but not enough for the increased number who would be attending.

Not to mention the addition of Darwish and Farida. It turned out that she had been falling for him before the gkolin took over and they were now going to be wed in a year.

Rebecca came bustling into the room in her full Matron of Honor garb. She and Damon had wed a few days after everyone returned. She'd noticed the look of terror in Nettie's eyes at the mere mention of a large, joint wedding. "Now, stop fussing! You look stunning. And, I sneaked a peek, Caden looks amazing."

Nettie wiggled her fingers to stop grabbing things to twist. "I just wish the group was smaller. But, Agent Zero did promise us a honeymoon in a secret Scottish location, so I should accept it."

Rebecca put her hands on her hips. "It's the large meeting room here in the mansion. Fifty people at most." She reached over and adjusted the necklace Nettie wore. "You twisted the chain." She smiled when she released it. "Are you sure there are no more powers in it? I felt…"

Nettie smiled. "A warmth? Like a hug? I feel it too. I don't think it can do anything more. But I like to think it's my mother watching out for me." She threw back her shoulders. "Now, one shouldn't keep a handsome man waiting."

Rebecca laughed and lowered the veil over Nettie's face.

DEAR READER,

Thank you for joining me on the final adventure (for now :)) of Nettie, Caden, and their crew.

If you want to keep up on the further adventures of any of my characters, make sure to visit my website and sign up for my mailing list. http://marieandreas.com/index.html

You can also sign up on Amazon to follow me and they will keep you updated. Marie Andreas Amazon

If you enjoyed this book, please spread the word! Positive reviews are like emotional gold to any writer. And mean more than you know.

Thank you again—and keep reading!

About the Author

MARIE IS A MULTI-AWARD-WINNING FANTASY and science fiction author with a serious reading addiction. If she wasn't writing about all the people in her head, she'd be lurking about coffee shops annoying total strangers with her stories. So really, writing is a way of saving the masses. She lives in Southern California and is owned by two very faery-minded cats. She is also a member of SFWA (Science Fiction and Fantasy Writers Association).

When not saving the masses from coffee shop shenanigans, Marie likes to visit the UK and keeps hoping someone will give her a nice summer home in the Forest of Dean or Conwy, Wales.

Made in the USA
Las Vegas, NV
31 October 2023

79956152R00256